O. HENRY STORIES

O. Henry STORIES

The American Scene
as Depicted by the Master of Short Stories

Each Story Complete

Special Introduction by Harry Golden

PLATT & MUNK, *Publishers*   NEW YORK

O. HENRY

An Introduction by
HARRY GOLDEN

EVERY WELL-KNOWN WRITER HAS HIS CRITICS, and William Sidney Porter—O. Henry to all of us—is no exception. He is one of the most widely popular writers ever to come from the American scene. Yet some of his stories have been dubbed "superficial" or lacking in real characterization. In other stories, some critics say, the hero or heroine overcomes trouble, conflict or pain and finds happiness, not by struggling and learning, but by a fortuitous combination of circumstances. In still others, the language may seem needlessly elaborate.

In the more than 30 stories here selected from the many hundreds of stories that poured from O. Henry's prolific pen, you will sample fully the broad range of his talents, as well as his faults. But, what is far more important, you will be moved and delighted and warmed by O. Henry's wonderful skill as a storyteller and by the wonderful people and paradoxical situations he created—the tramp who tried to be arrested, the boy who tormented his kidnappers, and many others.

O. Henry's gift to American literature was that he invented "the situation" and found that resolving it was enough to occupy the reader's attention, like trying to wriggle your way out of discovered check in chess.

O. Henry also is an artist whose situations lend themselves to a geometric formula. The situation resolves itself by making an "X"; or, in technical terms, it is a "chiastic resolution." In *The Gift of the Magi* Della Young has beautiful hair which she sells so that she may buy her husband Jim a watch chain. Jim has a wonderful watch which he sells so that he may buy his wife some beautiful combs for her crowning glory. In an O. Henry story, people work at cross-purposes but with the same motive.

It is this geometric quality which makes O. Henry's writing like a beautiful crystal that elicits gasps, not alone because of its radiance but because it is the only one of its kind. Again, technically, they are *sui generis*. His stories, like the crystal, have their worth not in their weight but in their singularity.

But like a fine jeweler, O. Henry reveals the crystal, full view, only at the end of his story. The last paragraph, or last sentence, reflects back and emblazons the whole. This surprise ending, this unexpected twist, that singles out the master storyteller as well as the showman, is O. Henry's hallmark.

He was one of the first writers to fall in love with New York City. It was an exotic capital to him. The city may no longer resemble the "Baghdad-on-Hudson" O. Henry described. Yet despite the intervening generations, where the city has taken the worst of it from other writers, hundreds of young men and women every year still make their pilgrimage to it, thereby sustaining O. Henry's greater truth: that the city is still, to the young, the fabulous American dream of endless possibility. (And this, I suspect, is one of the reasons why O. Henry remains perennially popular.)

Like O. Henry himself, I shall take no longer. O. Henry has a value that each generation discovers for itself. May you be entertained, amused and moved by the yarns of America's favorite storyteller.

CONTENTS

✦

O. HENRY: AN INTRODUCTION *by Harry Golden*

✢

O. HENRY STORIES

THE RANSOM OF

RED CHIEF

IT LOOKED LIKE A GOOD THING: BUT
wait till I tell you. We were down South, in Alabama—
Bill Driscoll and myself—when this kidnapping idea
struck us. It was, as Bill afterward expressed it, "during
a moment of temporary mental apparition"; but we
didn't find that out till later.

There was a town down there, as flat as a flannel
cake, and called Summit, of course. It contained inhabitants of as undeleterious and self-satisfied a class of
peasantry as ever clustered around a Maypole.

Bill and me had a joint capital of about six hundred
dollars, and we needed just two thousand dollars more

to pull off a fraudulent town-lot scheme in Western Illinois with. We talked it over on the front steps of the hotel. Philoprogenitiveness, says we, is strong in semi-rural communities; therefore, and for other reasons, a kidnapping project ought to do better there than in the radius of newspapers that send reporters out in plain clothes to stir up talk about such things. We knew that Summit couldn't get after us with anything stronger than constables and, maybe, some lackadaisical bloodhounds and a diatribe or two in the *Weekly Farmers' Budget*. So it looked good.

We selected for our victim the only child of a prominent citizen named Ebenezer Dorset. The father was respectable and tight, a mortgage fancier and a stern, upright collection-plate passer and forecloser. The kid was a boy of ten, with bas-relief freckles, and hair the color of the cover of the magazine you buy at the newsstand when you want to catch a train. Bill and me figured that Ebenezer would melt down for a ransom of two thousand dollars to a cent. But wait till I tell you.

About two miles from Summit was a little mountain, covered with a dense cedar brake. On the rear elevation of this mountain was a cave. There we stored provisions.

One evening after sundown, we drove in a buggy past old Dorset's house. The kid was in the street, throwing rocks at a kitten on the opposite fence.

"Hey, little boy!" says Bill, "would you like to have a bag of candy and a nice ride?"

The boy catches Bill neatly in the eye with a piece of brick.

"That will cost the old man an extra five hundred dollars," says Bill, climbing over the wheel.

That boy put up a fight like a welterweight cinnamon bear; but at last we got him down in the bottom of the buggy and drove away. We took him up to the cave, and I hitched the horse in the cedar brake. After dark I drove the buggy to the little village, three miles away, where we had hired it, and walked back to the mountain.

Bill was pasting court plaster over the scratches and bruises on his features. There was a fire burning behind the big rock at the entrance of the cave, and the boy was watching a pot of boiling coffee, with two buzzard tail feathers stuck in his red hair. He points a stick at me when I come up, and says:

"Ha! cursed paleface, do you dare to enter the camp of Red Chief, the terror of the plains?"

"He's all right now," says Bill, rolling up his trousers and examining some bruises on his shins. "We're playing Indian. We're making Buffalo Bill's show look like magic-lantern views of Palestine in the town hall. I'm Old Hank, the Trapper, Red Chief's captive, and I'm to be scalped at daybreak. By Geronimo! that kid can kick hard."

Yes, sir, that boy seemed to be having the time of his life. The fun of camping out in a cave had made him forget that he was a captive himself. He immediately christened me Snake-eye, the Spy, and announced that, when his braves returned from the warpath, I was to be broiled at the stake at the rising of the sun.

Then we had supper; and he filled his mouth full of bacon and bread and gravy, and began to talk. He made a during-dinner speech something like this:

"I like this fine. I never camped out before; but I had a pet 'possum once, and I was nine last birthday. I hate to go to school. Rats ate up sixteen of Jimmy Talbot's aunt's speckled hen's eggs. Are there any real Indians in these woods? I want some more gravy. Does the trees moving make the wind blow? We had five puppies. What makes your nose so red, Hank? My father has lots of money. Are the stars hot? I whipped Ed Walker twice, Saturday. I don't like girls. You dassent catch toads unless with a string. Do oxen make any noise? Why are oranges round? Have you got beds to sleep on in this cave? Amos Murray has got six toes. A parrot can talk, but a monkey or a fish can't. How many does it take to make twelve?"

Every few minutes he would remember that he was a pesky redskin, and pick up his stick rifle and tiptoe to the mouth of the cave to rubber for the scouts of the hated paleface. Now and then he would let out a war whoop that made Old Hank the Trapper shiver. That boy had Bill terrorized from the start.

"Red Chief," says I to the kid, "would you like to go home?"

"Aw, what for?" says he. "I don't have any fun at

home. I hate to go to school. I like to camp out. You won't take me back home again, Snake-eye, will you?"

"Not right away," says I. "We'll stay here in the cave awhile."

"All right!" says he. "That'll be fine. I never had such fun in all my life."

We went to bed about eleven o'clock. We spread down some wide blankets and quilts and put Red Chief between us. We weren't afraid he'd run away. He kept us awake for three hours, jumping up and reaching for his rifle and screeching: "Hist! pard," in mine and Bill's ears, as the fancied crackle of a twig or the rustle of a leaf revealed to his young imagination the stealthy approach of the outlaw band. At last, I fell into a troubled sleep, and dreamed that I had been kidnapped and chained to a tree by a ferocious pirate with red hair.

Just at daybreak, I was awakened by a series of awful screams from Bill. They weren't yells, or howls, or shouts, or whoops, or yawps, such as you'd expect from a manly set of vocal organs—they were simply indecent, terrifying, humiliating screams, such as women emit when they see ghosts or caterpillars. It's an awful thing to hear a strong, desperate, fat man scream incontinently in a cave at daybreak.

I jumped up to see what the matter was. Red Chief was sitting on Bill's chest, with one hand twined in Bill's hair. In the other he had the sharp case knife we used for slicing bacon; and he was industriously and

realistically trying to take Bill's scalp, according to the
sentence that had been pronounced upon him the evening before.

I got the knife away from the kid and made him lie
down again. But, from that moment, Bill's spirit was
broken. He lay down on his side of the bed, but he
never closed an eye again in sleep as long as that boy
was with us. I dozed off for a while, but along toward
sunup I remembered that Red Chief had said I was to
be burned at the stake at the rising of the sun. I wasn't
nervous or afraid; but I sat up and lit my pipe and
leaned against a rock.

"What you getting up so soon for, Sam?" asked Bill.

"Me?" says I. "Oh, I got a kind of pain in my shoulder.
I thought sitting up would rest it."

"You're a liar!" says Bill. "You're afraid. You was to
be burned at sunrise, and you was afraid he'd do it.
And he would, too, if he could find a match. Ain't it
awful, Sam? Do you think anybody will pay out money
to get a little imp like that back home?"

"Sure," said I. "A rowdy kid like that is just the kind
that parents dote on. Now, you and the Chief get up
and cook breakfast, while I go up on the top of this
mountain and reconnoitre."

I went up on the peak of the little mountain and
ran my eye over the contiguous vicinity. Over towards
Summit I expected to see the sturdy yeomanry of the
village armed with scythes and pitchforks beating the

countryside for the dastardly kidnappers. But what I saw was a peaceful landscape dotted with one man ploughing with a dun mule. Nobody was dragging the creek; no couriers dashed hither and yon, bringing tidings of no news to the distracted parents. There was a sylvan attitude of somnolent sleepiness pervading that section of the external outward surface of Alabama that lay exposed to my view. "Perhaps," says I to myself, "it has not yet been discovered that the wolves have borne away the tender lambkin from the fold. Heaven help the wolves!" says I, and I went down the mountain to breakfast.

When I got to the cave I found Bill backed up against the side of it, breathing hard, and the boy threatening to smash him with a rock half as big as a cocoanut.

"He put a red-hot boiled potato down my back," explained Bill, "and then mashed it with his foot; and I boxed his ears. Have you got a gun about you, Sam?"

I took the rock away from the boy and kind of patched up the argument. "I'll fix you," says the kid to Bill. "No man ever yet struck the Red Chief but he got paid for it. You better beware!"

After breakfast the kid takes a piece of leather with strings wrapped around it out of his pocket and goes outside the cave unwinding it.

"What's he up to now?" says Bill, anxiously. "You don't think he'll run away, do you, Sam?"

"No fear of it," says I. "He don't seem to be much

of a home body. But we've got to fix up some plan about the ransom. There don't seem to be much excitement around Summit on account of his disappearance; but maybe they haven't realized yet that he's gone. His folks may think he's spending the night with Aunt Jane or one of the neighbors. Anyhow, he'll be missed today. Tonight we must get a message to his father demanding the two thousand dollars for his return."

Just then we heard a kind of war whoop, such as David might have emitted when he knocked out the champion Goliath. It was a sling that Red Chief had pulled out of his pocket, and he was whirling it around his head.

I dodged, and heard a heavy thud and a kind of a sigh from Bill, like a horse gives out when you take his saddle off. A jagged rock, of the size of an egg, had caught Bill just behind his left ear. He loosened himself all over and fell in the fire across the frying pan of hot water for washing the dishes. I dragged him out and poured cold water on his head for half an hour.

By and by, Bill sits up and feels behind his ear and says: "Sam, do you know who my favorite Biblical character is?"

"Take it easy," says I. "You'll come to your senses presently."

"King Herod," says he. "You won't go away and leave me here alone, will you, Sam?"

I went out and caught that boy and shook him until his freckles rattled.

"If you don't behave," says I, "I'll take you straight home. Now, are you going to be good, or not?"

"I was only funning," says he, sullenly. "I didn't mean to hurt Old Hank. But what did he hit me for? I'll behave, Snake-eye, if you won't send me home, and if you'll let me play the Black Scout today."

"I don't know the game," says I. "That's for you and Mr. Bill to decide. He's your playmate for the day. I'm going away for a while, on business. Now, you come in and make friends with him and say you are sorry for hurting him, or home you go, at once."

I made him and Bill shake hands, and then I took Bill aside and told him I was going to Poplar Grove, a little village three miles from the cave, and find out what I could about how the kidnapping had been regarded in Summit. Also, I thought it best to send a peremptory letter to old man Dorset that day, demanding the ransom and dictating how it should be paid.

"You know, Sam," says Bill, "I've stood by you without batting an eye in earthquakes, fire and flood—in poker games, dynamite outrages, police raids, train robberies, and cyclones. I never lost my nerve yet till we kidnapped that two-legged skyrocket of a kid. He's got me going. You won't leave me long with him, will you, Sam?"

"I will be back sometime this afternoon," says I. "You must keep the boy amused and quiet till I return. And now we'll write the letter to old Dorset."

Bill and I got paper and pencil and worked on the

letter while Red Chief, with a blanket wrapped around
him, strutted up and down, guarding the mouth of the
cave. Bill begged me tearfully to make the ransom fifteen
hundred dollars instead of two thousand. "I ain't attempting," says he, "to decry the celebrated moral aspect of
parental affection, but we're dealing with humans, and
it ain't human for anybody to give up two thousand dollars for that forty-pound chunk of freckled wildcat. I'm
willing to take a chance at fifteen hundred dollars. You
can charge the difference up to me."

So, to relieve Bill, I acceded, and we collaborated a
letter that ran this way:

Ebenezer Dorset, Esq.:
We have your boy concealed in a place far from
Summit. It is useless for you or the most skilful detec-
tives to attempt to find him. Absolutely, the only terms
on which you can have him restored to you are these:
We demand fifteen hundred dollars in large bills for
his return; the money to be left at midnight tonight
at the same spot and in the same box as your reply—
as hereinafter described. If you agree to these terms,
send your answer in writing by a solitary messenger
tonight at half-past eight o'clock. After crossing Owl
Creek on the road to Poplar Grove, there are three
large trees about a hundred yards apart, close to the
fence of the wheat field on the right-hand side. At
the bottom of the fence post, opposite the third tree,
will be found a small pasteboard box.
The messenger will place the answer in this box
and return immediately to Summit.

If you attempt any treachery or fail to comply with our demand as stated, you will never see your boy again.

If you pay the money as demanded, he will be returned to you safe and well within three hours. These terms are final, and if you do not accede to them no further communication will be attempted.

Two Desperate Men

I addressed this letter to Dorset, and put it in my pocket. As I was about to start, the kid comes up to me and says:

"Aw, Snake-eye, you said I could play the Black Scout while you was gone."

"Play it, of course," says I. "Mr. Bill will play with you. What kind of a game is it?"

"I'm the Black Scout," says Red Chief, "and I have to ride to the stockade to warn the settlers that the Indians are coming. I'm tired of playing Indian myself. I want to be the Black Scout."

"All right," says I. "It sound harmless to me. I guess Mr. Bill will help you foil the pesky savages."

"What am I to do?" asks Bill, looking at the kid suspiciously.

"You are the hoss," says Black Scout. "Get down on your hands and knees. How can I ride to the stockade without a hoss?"

"You'd better keep him interested," said I, "till we get the scheme going. Loosen up."

Bill gets down on his all fours, and a look comes in his

eye like a rabbit's when you catch it in a trap.

"How far is it to the stockade, kid?" he asks, in a husky manner of voice.

"Ninety miles," says the Black Scout. "And you have to hump yourself to get there on time. Whoa, now!"

The Black Scout jumps on Bill's back and digs his heels in his side.

"For Heaven's sake," says Bill, "hurry back, Sam, as soon as you can. I wish we hadn't made the ransom more than a thousand. Say, you quit kicking me or I'll get up and warm you good."

I walked over to Poplar Grove and sat around the post office and store, talking with the chaw-bacons that came in to trade. One whiskerando says that he hears Summit is all upset on account of Elder Ebenezer Dorset's boy having been lost or stolen. That was all I wanted to know. I bought some smoking tobacco, referred casually to the price of black-eyed peas, posted my letter surreptitiously, and came away. The postmaster said the mail carrier would come by in an hour to take the mail to Summit.

When I got back to the cave Bill and the boy were not to be found. I explored the vicinity of the cave, and risked a yodel or two, but there was no response.

So I lighted my pipe and sat down on a mossy bank to await developments.

In about half an hour I heard the bushes rustle, and Bill wabbled out into the little glade in front of the cave. Behind him was the kid, stepping softly like a scout, with a broad grin on his face. Bill stopped, took off his hat, and wiped his face with a red handkerchief. The kid stopped about eight feet behind him.

"Sam," says Bill, "I suppose you'll think I'm a renegade, but I couldn't help it. I'm a grown person with masculine proclivities and habits of self-defense, but there is a time when all systems of egotism and predominance fail. The boy is gone. I sent him home. All is off. There was martyrs in old times," goes on Bill, "that suffered death rather than give up the particular graft they enjoyed. None of 'em ever was subjugated to such supernatural tortures as I have been. I tried to be faithful to our articles of depredation; but there came a limit."

"What's the trouble, Bill?" I asks him.

"I was rode," says Bill, "the ninety miles to the stockade, not barring an inch. Then, when the settlers was rescued, I was given oats. Sand ain't a palatable substitute. And then, for an hour I had to try to explain to him why there was nothin' in holes, how a road can run both ways, and what makes the grass green. I tell you, Sam, a human can only stand so much. I takes him by the neck of his clothes and drags him down the mountain. On the way he kicks my legs black and blue from the knees down; and I've got to have two or three bites on my thumb and hand cauterized.

"But he's gone" — continues Bill — "gone home. I showed him the road to Summit and kicked him about eight feet nearer there at one kick. I'm sorry we lose the ransom; but it was either that or Bill Driscoll to the madhouse."

Bill is puffing and blowing, but there is a look of ineffable peace and growing content on his rose-pink features.

"Bill," says I, "there isn't any heart disease in your family, is there?"

"No," says Bill, "nothing chronic except malaria and accidents. Why?"

"Then you might turn around," says I, "and have a look behind you."

Bill turns and sees the boy, and loses his complexion and sits down plump on the ground and begins to pluck aimlessly at grass and little sticks. For an hour I was afraid for his mind. And then I told him that my scheme was to put the whole job through immediately and that we would get the ransom and be off with it by midnight if old Dorset fell in with our proposition. So Bill braced up enough to give the kid a weak sort of a smile and a promise to play the Russian in a Japanese war with him as soon as he felt a little better.

I had a scheme for collecting that ransom without danger of being caught by counterplots that ought to commend itself to professional kidnappers. The tree under which the answer was to be left—and the money later on—was close to the road fence with big, bare fields on all sides. If a gang of constables should be watching for anyone to come for the note, they could see him a long

way off crossing the fields or in the road. But no, sirree!
At half-past eight I was up in that tree as well hidden as
a tree toad, waiting for the messenger to arrive.

Exactly on time, a half-grown boy rides up the road
on a bicycle, locates the pasteboard box at the foot of the
fence-post, slips a folded piece of paper into it, and
pedals away again back toward Summit.

I waited an hour and then concluded the thing was
square. I slid down the tree, got the note, slipped along
the fence till I struck the woods, and was back at the
cave in another half an hour. I opened the note, got near
the lantern, and read it to Bill. It was written with a pen
in a crabbed hand, and the sum and substance of it was
this:

Two Desperate Men.

Gentlemen: I received your letter today by post,
in regard to the ransom you ask for the return of my
son. I think you are a little high in your demands, and
I hereby make you a counter-proposition, which I am
inclined to believe you will accept. You bring Johnny
home and pay me two hundred and fifty dollars in
cash, and I agree to take him off your hands. You had
better come at night, for the neighbors believe he is
lost, and I couldn't be responsible for what they would
do to anybody they saw bringing him back. Very respectfully,

Ebenezer Dorset

"Great pirates of Penzance," says I. "Of all the impudent——"

But I glanced at Bill, and hesitated. He had the most appealing look in his eyes I ever saw on the face of a dumb or a talking brute.

"Sam," says he, "what's two hundred and fifty dollars, after all? We've got the money. One more night of this kid will send me to a bed in Bedlam. Besides being a thorough gentleman, I think Mr. Dorset is a spendthrift for making us such a liberal offer. You ain't going to let the chance go, are you?"

"Tell you the truth, Bill," says I, "this little he ewe lamb has somewhat got on my nerves too. We'll take him home, pay the ransom, and make our getaway."

We took him home that night. We got him to go by telling him that his father had bought a silver-mounted rifle and a pair of moccasins for him, and we were to hunt bears the next day.

It was just twelve o'clock when we knocked at Ebenezer's front door. Just at the moment when I should have been abstracting the fifteen hundred dollars from the box under the tree, according to the original proposition, Bill was counting out two hundred and fifty dollars into Dorset's hand.

When the kid found out we were going to leave him at home he started up a howl like a calliope and fastened himself as tight as a leech to Bill's leg. His father peeled him away gradually, like a porous plaster.

"How long can you hold him?" asks Bill.

"I'm not as strong as I used to be," says old Dorset,

"but I think I can promise you ten minutes."

"Enough," says Bill. "In ten minutes I shall cross the central, southern, and middle western states, and be legging it trippingly for the Canadian border."

And, as dark as it was, and as fat as Bill was, and as good a runner as I am, he was a good mile and a half out of Summit before I could catch up with him.

✦
✦

THE COP AND
THE ANTHEM

O<small>N HIS BENCH IN MADISON SQUARE</small>
Soapy moved uneasily. When wild geese honk high of
nights, and when women without sealskin coats grow
kind to their husbands, and when Soapy moves uneasily
on his bench in the park, you may know that winter is
near at hand.

A dead leaf fell in Soapy's lap. That was Jack Frost's
card. Jack is kind to the regular denizens of Madison
Square, and gives fair warning of his annual call. At the
corners of four streets he hands his pasteboard to the
North Wind, footman of the mansion of All Outdoors, so
that the inhabitants thereof may make ready.

Soapy's mind became cognizant of the fact that the
time had come for him to resolve himself into a singular

Committee of Ways and Means to provide against the coming rigor. And therefore he moved uneasily on his bench.

The hibernatorial ambitions of Soapy were not of the highest. In them were no considerations of Mediterranean cruises, of soporific Southern skies or drifting in the Vesuvian Bay. Three months on the Island was what his soul craved. Three months of assured board and bed and congenial company, safe from Boreas and bluecoats, seemed to Soapy the essence of things desirable.

For years the hospitable Blackwell's had been his winter quarters. Just as his more fortunate fellow New Yorkers had bought their tickets to Palm Beach and the Riviera each winter, so Soapy had made his humble arrangements for his annual hegira to the Island. And now the time was come. On the previous night three Sabbath newspapers, distributed beneath his coat, about his ankles and over his lap, had failed to repulse the cold as he slept on his bench near the spurting fountain in the ancient square. So the Island loomed big and timely in Soapy's mind. He scorned the provisions made in the name of charity for the city's dependents. In Soapy's opinion the Law was more benign than Philanthropy. There was an endless round of institutions, municipal and eleemosynary, on which he might set out and receive lodging and food accordant with the simple life. But to one of Soapy's proud spirit the gifts of charity are encumbered. If not in coin you must pay in humiliation of spirit for every benefit received at the hands of philanthropy. As Cæsar had his Brutus, every bed of charity must have its toll of a bath, every loaf of bread its compensation of a private and personal inquisition. Wherefore it is better to be a guest of the law, which, though conducted by rules, does not meddle unduly with a gentleman's private affairs.

Soapy, having decided to go to the Island, at once set about accomplishing his desire. There were many easy ways of doing this. The pleasantest was to dine luxuriously at some expensive restaurant; and then, after declaring insolvency, be handed over quietly and without uproar to a policeman. An accommodating magistrate would do the rest.

Soapy left his bench and strolled out of the square and across the level sea of asphalt, where Broadway and Fifth Avenue flow together. Up Broadway he turned, and halted at a glittering café, where are gathered together nightly the choicest products of the grape, the silkworm, and the protoplasm.

Soapy had confidence in himself from the lowest button of his vest upward. He was shaven, and his coat was decent and his neat black, ready-tied four-in-hand had been presented to him by a lady missionary on Thanksgiving Day. If he could reach a table in the restaurant unsuspected success would be his. The portion of him that would show above the table would raise no doubt in the waiter's mind. A roasted mallard duck, thought

Soapy, would be about the thing—with a bottle of Chablis, and then Camembert, a demitasse and a cigar. One dollar for the cigar would be enough. The total would not be so high as to call forth any supreme manifestation of revenge from the café management; and yet the meat would leave him filled and happy for the journey to his winter refuge.

But as Soapy set foot inside the restaurant door the head waiter's eye fell upon his frayed trousers and decadent shoes. Strong and ready hands turned him about and conveyed him in silence and haste to the sidewalk and averted the ignoble fate of the menaced mallard.

Soapy turned off Broadway. It seemed that his route to the coveted Island was not to be an epicurean one. Some other way of entering limbo must be thought of.

At a corner of Sixth Avenue electric lights and cunningly displayed wares behind plate glass made a shop window conspicuous. Soapy took a cobblestone and dashed it through the glass. People came running around the corner, a policeman in the lead. Soapy stood still, with his hands in his pockets, and smiled at the sight of brass buttons.

"Where's the man that done that?" inquired the officer, excitedly.

"Don't you figure out that I might have had something to do with it?" said Soapy, not without sarcasm, but friendly, as one greets good fortune.

The policeman's mind refused to accept Soapy even as

a clue. Men who smash windows do not remain to parley with the law's minions. They take to their heels. The policeman saw a man halfway down the block running to catch a car. With drawn club he joined in the pursuit. Soapy, with disgust in his heart, loafed along, twice unsuccessful.

On the opposite side of the street was a restaurant of no great pretensions. It catered to large appetites and modest purses. Its crockery and atmosphere were thick; its soup and napery thin. Into this place Soapy took his accusive shoes and telltale trousers without challenge. At a table he sat and consumed beefsteak, flapjacks, doughnuts and pie. And then to the waiter he betrayed the fact that the minutest coin and himself were strangers.

"Now, get busy and call a cop," said Soapy. "And don't keep a gentleman waiting."

"No cop for youse," said the waiter, with a voice like butter cakes and an eye like the cherry in a Manhattan cocktail. "Hey, Con!"

Neatly upon his left ear on the callous pavement two waiters pitched Soapy. He arose joint by joint, as a carpenter's rule opens, and beat the dust from his clothes. Arrest seemed but a rosy dream. The Island seemed very far away. A policeman who stood before a drugstore two doors away laughed and walked down the street.

Five blocks Soapy travelled before his courage permitted him to woo capture again. This time the opportunity presented what he fatuously termed to himself a "cinch." A young woman of a modest and pleasing guise was standing before a show window gazing with sprightly interest at its display of shaving mugs and inkstands, and two yards from the window a large policeman of severe demeanor leaned against a water plug.

It was Soapy's design to assume the role of the despicable and execrated "masher." The refined and elegant appearance of his victim and the contiguity of the conscientious cop encouraged him to believe that he would soon feel the pleasant official clutch upon his arm that would insure his winter quarters on the right little, tight little isle.

Soapy straightened the lady missionary's readymade tie, dragged his shrinking cuffs into the open, set his hat at a killing cant and sidled toward the young woman. He made eyes at her, was taken with sudden coughs and "hems," smiled, smirked and went brazenly through the impudent and contemptible litany of the "masher." With half an eye Soapy saw that the policeman was watching him fixedly. The young woman moved away a few steps, and again bestowed her absorbed attention upon the shaving mugs. Soapy followed, boldly stepping to her side, raised his hat and said:

"Ah there, Bedelia! Don't you want to come and play in my yard?"

The policeman was still looking. The persecuted young woman had but to beckon a finger and Soapy would be practically en route for his insular haven. Already he imagined he could feel the cozy warmth of the station house. The young woman faced him and, stretching out a hand, caught Soapy's coat sleeve.

"Sure, Mike," she said, joyfully, "if you'll blow me to a pail of suds. I'd have spoke to you sooner, but the cop was watching."

With the young woman playing the clinging ivy to his oak Soapy walked past the policeman, overcome with gloom. He seemed doomed to liberty.

At the next corner he shook off his companion and ran. He halted in the district where by night are found the lightest streets, hearts, vows and librettos. Women in furs and men in greatcoats moved gaily in the wintry air. A sudden fear seized Soapy that some dreadful enchantment had rendered him immune to arrest. The thought brought a little of panic upon him, and when he came upon another policeman lounging grandly in front of a transplendent theatre he caught at the immediate straw of "disorderly conduct."

On the sidewalk Soapy began to yell drunken gibberish at the top of his harsh voice. He danced, howled, raved, and otherwise disturbed the welkin.

The policeman twirled his club, turned his back to Soapy and remarked to a citizen.

" 'Tis one of them Yale lads celebratin' the goose egg they give to the Hartford College. Noisy, but no harm. We've instructions to lave them be."

Disconsolate, Soapy ceased his unavailing racket.

Would never a policeman lay hands on him? In his fancy the Island seemed an unattainable Arcadia. He buttoned his thin coat against the chilling wind.

In a cigar store he saw a well-dressed man lighting a cigar at a swinging light. His silk umbrella he had set by the door on entering. Soapy stepped inside, secured the umbrella and sauntered off with it slowly. The man at the cigar light followed hastily.

"My umbrella," he said, sternly.

"Oh, is it?" sneered Soapy, adding insult to petit larceny. "Well, why don't you call a policeman? I took it. Your umbrella! Why don't you call a cop? There stands one on the corner."

The umbrella owner slowed his steps. Soapy did likewise, with a presentiment that luck would again run against him. The policeman looked at the two curiously.

"Of course," said the umbrella man—"that is—well, you know how these mistakes occur—I—if it's your umbrella I hope you'll excuse me—I picked it up this morning in a restaurant—— If you recognize it as yours, why—I hope you'll——"

"Of course it's mine," said Soapy, viciously.

The ex-umbrella man retreated. The policeman hurried to assist a tall blonde in an opera cloak across the street in front of a streetcar that was approaching two blocks away.

Soapy walked eastward through a street damaged by improvements. He hurled the umbrella wrathfully into an excavation. He muttered against the men who wear helmets and carry clubs. Because he wanted to fall into their clutches, they seemed to regard him as a king who could do no wrong.

At length Soapy reached one of the avenues to the east where the glitter and turmoil was but faint. He set his face down this toward Madison Square, for the homing instinct survives even when the home is a park bench.

But on an unusually quiet corner Soapy came to a standstill. Here was an old church, quaint and rambling and gabled. Through one violet-stained window a soft light glowed, where, no doubt, the organist loitered over the keys, making sure of his mastery of the coming Sabbath anthem. For there drifted out to Soapy's ears sweet music that caught and held him transfixed against the convolutions of the iron fence.

The moon was above, lustrous and serene; vehicles and pedestrians were few; sparrows twittered sleepily in the eaves—for a little while the scene might have been a country churchyard. And the anthem that the organist played cemented Soapy to the iron fence, for he had known it well in the days when his life contained such things as mothers and roses and ambitions and friends and immaculate thoughts and collars.

The conjunction of Soapy's receptive state of mind and the influences about the old church wrought a sudden and wonderful change in his soul. He viewed with swift horror the pit into which he had tumbled, the degraded days, unworthy desires, dead hopes, wrecked faculties and base motives that made up his existence.

And also in a moment his heart responded thrillingly to this novel mood. An instantaneous and strong impulse moved him to battle with his desperate fate. He would pull himself out of the mire; he would make a man of himself again; he would conquer the evil that had taken possession of him. There was time; he was comparatively young yet: he would resurrect his old eager ambitions and pursue them without faltering. Those solemn but sweet organ notes had set up a revolution in him. Tomorrow he would go into the roaring downtown district and find work. A fur importer had once offered him a place as driver. He would find him tomorrow and ask for the position. He would be somebody in the world. He would——

Soapy felt a hand laid on his arm. He looked quickly around into the broad face of a policeman.

"What are you doin' here?" asked the officer.

"Nothin'," said Soapy.

"Then come along," said the policeman.

"Three months on the Island," said the Magistrate in the Police Court the next morning.

THE GIFT OF
THE MAGI

ONE DOLLAR AND EIGHTY-SEVEN CENTS. That was all. And sixty cents of it was in pennies. Pennies saved one and two at a time by bulldozing the grocer and the vegetable man and the butcher until one's cheeks burned with the silent imputation of parsimony that such close dealing implied. Three times Della counted it. One dollar and eighty-seven cents. And the next day would be Christmas.

There was clearly nothing to do but flop down on the shabby little couch and howl. So Della did it. Which instigates the moral reflection that life is made up of sobs, sniffles, and smiles, with sniffles predominating.

While the mistress of the home is gradually subsiding from the first stage to the second, take a look at the home.

A furnished flat at $8 per week. It did not exactly beggar description, but it certainly had that word on the lookout for the mendicancy squad.

In the vestibule below was a letter box into which no letter would go, and an electric button from which no mortal finger could coax a ring. Also appertaining thereunto was a card bearing the name "Mr. James Dillingham Young."

The "Dillingham" had been flung to the breeze during a former period of prosperity when its possessor was being paid $30 per week. Now, when the income was shrunk to $20, the letters of "Dillingham" looked blurred, as though they were thinking seriously of contracting to a modest and unassuming D. But whenever Mr. James Dillingham Young came home and reached his flat above he was called "Jim" and greatly hugged by Mrs. James Dillingham Young, already introduced to you as Della. Which is all very good.

Della finished her cry and attended to her cheeks with the powder rag. She stood by the window and looked out dully at a gray cat walking a gray fence in a gray backyard. Tomorrow would be Christmas Day, and she had only $1.87 with which to buy Jim a present. She had been saving every penny she could for months, with this result. Twenty dollars a week doesn't go far. Expenses had been greater than she had calculated. They always are. Only $1.87 to buy a present for Jim. Her Jim. Many a happy hour she had spent planning for something nice for him. Something fine and rare and sterling—something just a little bit near to being worthy of the honor of being owned by Jim.

There was a pier glass between the windows of the room. Perhaps you have seen a pier glass in an $8 flat. A very thin and very agile person may, by observing his reflection in a rapid sequence of longitudinal strips, obtain a fairly accurate conception of his looks. Della, being slender, had mastered the art.

Suddenly she whirled from the window and stood before the glass. Her eyes were shining brilliantly, but her face had lost its color within twenty seconds. Rapidly she pulled down her hair and let it fall to its full length.

Now, there were two possessions of the James Dillingham Youngs in which they both took a mighty pride. One was Jim's gold watch that had been his father's and his grandfather's. The other was Della's hair. Had the Queen of Sheba lived in the flat across the airshaft, Della would have let her hair hang out the window some day to dry just to depreciate Her Majesty's jewels and gifts. Had King Solomon been the janitor, with all his treasures piled up in the basement, Jim would have pulled out his watch every time he passed, just to see him pluck at his beard from envy.

So now Della's beautiful hair fell about her rippling and shining like a cascade of brown waters. It reached below her knee and made itself almost a garment for her. And then she did it up again nervously and quickly.

Once she faltered for a minute and stood still while a tear or two splashed on the worn red carpet.

On went her old brown jacket; on went her old brown hat. With a whirl of skirts and with the brilliant sparkle still in her eyes, she fluttered out the door and down the stairs to the street.

Where she stopped the sign read: "Mme. Sofronie. Hair Goods of All Kinds." One flight up Della ran, and collected herself, panting. Madame, large, too white, chilly, hardly looked the "Sofronie."

"Will you buy my hair?" asked Della.

"I buy hair," said Madame. "Take yer hat off and let's have a sight at the looks of it."

Down rippled the brown cascade.

"Twenty dollars," said Madame, lifting the mass with a practised hand.

"Give it to me quick," said Della.

Oh, and the next two hours tripped by on rosy wings. Forget the hashed metaphor. She was ransacking the stores for Jim's present.

She found it at last. It surely had been made for Jim and no one else. There was no other like it in any of the stores, and she had turned all of them inside out. It was a platinum fob chain simple and chaste in design, properly proclaiming its value by substance alone and not by meretricious ornamentation—as all good things should do. It was even worthy of The Watch. As soon as she saw it she knew that it must be Jim's. It was like him.

Quietness and value—the description applied to both. Twenty-one dollars they took from her for it, and she hurried home with the 87 cents. With that chain on his watch Jim might be properly anxious about the time in any company. Grand as the watch was, he sometimes looked at it on the sly on account of the old leather strap that he used in place of a chain.

When Della reached home her intoxication gave way a little to prudence and reason. She got out her curling irons and lighted the gas and went to work repairing the ravages made by generosity added to love. Which is always a tremendous task, dear friends—a mammoth task.

Within forty minutes her head was covered with tiny, close-lying curls that made her look wonderfully like a truant schoolboy. She looked at her reflection in the mirror long, carefully, and critically.

"If Jim doesn't kill me," she said to herself, "before he takes a second look at me, he'll say I look like a Coney Island chorus girl. But what could I do—on! what could I do with a dollar and eighty-seven cents?"

At 7 o'clock the coffee was made and the frying pan was on the back of the stove hot and ready to cook the chops.

Jim was never late. Della doubled the fob chain in her hand and sat on the corner of the table near the door that he always entered. Then she heard his step on the stair away down on the first flight, and she turned white for just a moment. She had a habit of saying little silent prayers about the simplest everyday things, and now she whispered: "Please God, make him think I am still pretty."

The door opened and Jim stepped in and closed it. He looked thin and very serious. Poor fellow, he was only twenty-two—and to be burdened with a family! He needed a new overcoat and he was without gloves.

Jim stopped inside the door, as immovable as a setter at the scent of quail. His eyes were fixed upon Della, and there was an expression in them that she could not read, and it terrified her. It was not anger, nor surprise, nor disapproval, nor horror, nor any of the sentiments that she had been prepared for. He simply stared at her fixedly with that peculiar expression on his face.

Della wriggled off the table and went for him.

"Jim, darling," she cried, "don't look at me that way. I had my hair cut off and sold it because I couldn't have lived through Christmas without giving you a present. It'll grow out again—you won't mind, will you? I just had to do it. My hair grows awfully fast. Say 'Merry Christmas,' Jim, and let's be happy. You don't know what a nice—what a beautiful, nice gift I've got for you."

"You've cut off your hair?" asked Jim, laboriously, as if he had not arrived at that patent fact yet even after the hardest mental labor.

"Cut it off and sold it," said Della. "Don't you like me just as well, anyhow? I'm me without my hair, ain't I?"

Jim looked about the room curiously.

"You say your hair is gone?" he said, with an air almost of idiocy.

"You needn't look for it," said Della. "It's sold, I tell you—sold and gone, too. It's Christmas Eve, boy. Be good to me, for it went for you. Maybe the hairs of my head were numbered," she went on with a sudden serious sweetness, "but nobody could ever count my love for you. Shall I put the chops on, Jim?"

Out of his trance Jim seemed quickly to wake. He enfolded his Della. For ten seconds let us regard with discreet scrutiny some inconsequential object in the other direction. Eight dollars a week or a million a year—what is the difference? A mathematician or a wit would give you the wrong answer. The magi brought valuable gifts, but that was not among them. This dark assertion will be illuminated later on.

Jim drew a package from his overcoat pocket and threw it upon the table.

"Don't make any mistake, Dell," he said, "about me. I don't think there's anything in the way of a haircut or a shave or a shampoo that could make me like my girl any less. But if you'll unwrap that package you may see why you had me going a while at first."

White fingers and nimble tore at the string and paper. And then an ecstatic scream of joy; and then, alas! a quick feminine change to hysterical tears and wails, necessitating the immediate employment of all the comforting powers of the lord of the flat.

For there lay The Combs—the set of combs, side and back, that Della had worshipped for long in a Broadway window. Beautiful combs, pure tortoise shell, with jewelled rims—just the shade to wear in the beautiful vanished hair. They were expensive combs, she knew, and her heart had simply craved and yearned over them without the least hope of possession. And now, they were hers, but the tresses that should have adorned the coveted adornments were gone.

But she hugged them to her bosom, and at length she was able to look up with dim eyes and a smile and say: "My hair grows so fast, Jim!"

And then Della leaped up like a little singed cat and cried, "Oh, oh!"

Jim had not yet seen his beautiful present. She held it out to him eagerly upon her open palm. The dull precious metal seemed to flash with a reflection of her bright and ardent spirit.

"Isn't it a dandy, Jim? I hunted all over town to find it. You'll have to look at the time a hundred times a day now. Give me your watch. I want to see how it looks on it."

Instead of obeying, Jim tumbled down on the couch and put his hands under the back of his head and smiled.

"Dell," said he, "let's put our Christmas presents away and keep 'em a while. They're too nice to use just at present. I sold the watch to get the money to buy your combs. And now suppose you put the chops on."

The magi, as you know, were wise men—wonderfully wise men—who brought gifts to the Babe in the manger. They invented the art of giving Christmas presents. Being wise, their gifts were no doubt wise ones, possibly bearing the privilege of exchange in case of duplication. And here I have lamely related to you the uneventful chronicle of two foolish children in a flat who most unwisely sacrificed for each other the greatest treasures of their house. But in a last word to the wise of these days let it be said that of all who give gifts these two were the wisest. Of all who give and receive gifts, such as they are wisest. Everywhere they are wisest. They are the magi.

AFTER TWENTY

YEARS

THE POLICEMAN ON THE BEAT MOVED
up the avenue impressively. The impressiveness was
habitual and not for show, for spectators were few. The
time was barely 10 o'clock at night, but chilly gusts of
wind with a taste of rain in them had well nigh de-
peopled the streets.

Trying doors as he went, twirling his club with many
intricate and artful movements, turning now and then
to cast his watchful eye adown the pacific thoroughfare,
the officer, with his stalwart form and slight swagger,
made a fine picture of a guardian of the peace. The vicinity was one that kept early hours. Now and then you
might see the lights of a cigar store or of an all-night
lunch counter; but the majority of the doors belonged to

business places that had long since been closed.

When about midway in a certain block, the policeman suddenly slowed his walk. In the doorway of a darkened hardware store a man leaned, with an unlighted cigar in his mouth. As the policeman walked up to him the man spoke up quickly.

"It's all right, officer," he said, reassuringly. "I'm just waiting for a friend. It's an appointment made twenty years ago. Sounds a little funny to you, doesn't it? Well, I'll explain if you'd like to make certain it's all straight. About that long ago there used to be a restaurant where this store stands—'Big Joe' Brady's restaurant."

"Until five years ago," said the policeman. "It was torn down then."

The man in the doorway struck a match and lit his cigar. The light showed a pale, square-jawed face with keen eyes, and a little white scar near his right eyebrow. His scarfpin was a large diamond, oddly set.

"Twenty years ago tonight," said the man, "I dined here at 'Big Joe' Brady's with Jimmy Wells, my best chum, and the finest chap in the world. He and I were raised here in New York, just like two brothers, together. I was eighteen and Jimmy was twenty. The next morning I was to start for the West to make my fortune. You couldn't have dragged Jimmy out of New York; he thought it was the only place on earth. Well, we agreed that night that we would meet here again exactly twenty years from that date and time, no matter what our conditions might be or from what distance we might have to come. We figured that in twenty years each of us ought to have our destiny worked out and our fortunes made, whatever they were going to be."

"It sounds pretty interesting," said the policeman. "Rather a long time between meets, though, it seems to me. Haven't you heard from your friend since you left?"

"Well, yes, for a time we corresponded," said the other. "But after a year or two we lost track of each other. You see, the West is a pretty big proposition, and I kept hustling around over it pretty lively. But I know Jimmy will meet me here if he's alive, for he always was the truest, stanchest old chap in the world. He'll never forget. I came a thousand miles to stand in this door tonight, and it's worth it if my old partner turns up."

The waiting man pulled out a handsome watch, the lids of it set with small diamonds.

"Three minutes to ten," he announced. "It was exactly ten o'clock when we parted here at the restaurant door."

"Did pretty well out West, didn't you?" asked the policeman.

"You bet! I hope Jimmy has done half as well. He was a kind of plodder, though, good fellow as he was. I've had to compete with some of the sharpest wits going to get my pile. A man gets in a groove in New York. It takes the West to put a razor-edge on him."

The policeman twirled his club and took a step or two.

"I'll be on my way. Hope your friend comes around all

right. Going to call time on him sharp?"

"I should say not!" said the other. "I'll give him half
an hour at least. If Jimmy is alive on earth he'll be here
by that time. So long, officer."

"Goodnight, sir," said the policeman, passing on along
his beat, trying doors as he went.

There was now a fine, cold drizzle falling, and the
wind had risen from its uncertain puffs into a steady
blow. The few foot passengers astir in that quarter hurried dismally and silently along with coat collars turned
high and pocketed hands. And in the door of the hardware store the man who had come a thousand miles to
fill an appointment, uncertain almost to absurdity, with
the friend of his youth, smoked his cigar and waited.

About twenty minutes he waited, and then a tall man
in a long overcoat, with collar turned up to his ears, hurried across from the opposite side of the street. He went
directly to the waiting man.

"Is that you, Bob?" he asked, doubtfully.

"Is that you, Jimmy Wells?" cried the man in the door.

"Bless my heart!" exclaimed the new arrival, grasping
both the other's hands with his own. "It's Bob, sure as
fate. I was certain I'd find you here if you were still in
existence. Well, well, well!—twenty years is a long time.
The old restaurant's gone, Bob; I wish it had lasted, so
we could have had another dinner there. How has the
West treated you, old man?"

"Bully; it has given me everything I asked it for. You've

changed lots, Jimmy. I never thought you were so tall by two or three inches."

"Oh, I grew a bit after I was twenty."

"Doing well in New York, Jimmy?"

"Moderately. I have a position in one of the city departments. Come on, Bob; we'll go around to a place I know of, and have a good long talk about old times."

The two men started up the street, arm in arm. The man from the West, his egotism enlarged by success, was beginning to outline the history of his career. The other, submerged in his overcoat, listened with interest.

At the corner stood a drugstore, brilliant with electric lights. When they came into this glare each of them turned simultaneously to gaze upon the other's face.

The man from the West stopped suddenly and released his arm.

"You're not Jimmy Wells," he snapped. "Twenty years is a long time, but not long enough to change a man's nose from a Roman to a pug."

"It sometimes changes a good man into a bad one," said the tall man. "You've been under arrest for ten minutes, 'Silky' Bob. Chicago thinks you may have dropped over our way and wired us she wants to have a chat with you. Going quietly, are you? That's sensible. Now, before we go to the station here's a note I was asked to hand to you. You may read it here at the window. It's from Patrolman Wells."

The man from the West unfolded the little piece of

paper handed him. His hand was steady when he began to read, but it trembled a little by the time he had finished. The note was rather short.

Bob: I was at the appointed place on time. When you struck the match to light your cigar I saw it was the face of the man wanted in Chicago. Somehow I couldn't do it myself, so I went around and got a plain-clothes man to do the job.

Jimmy

A RETRIEVED
REFORMATION

A GUARD CAME TO THE PRISON SHOE shop, where Jimmy Valentine was assiduously stitching uppers, and escorted him to the front office. There the warden handed Jimmy his pardon, which had been signed that morning by the governor. Jimmy took it in a tired kind of way. He had served nearly ten months of a four-year sentence. He had expected to stay only about three months, at the longest. When a man with as many friends on the outside as Jimmy Valentine had is received in the "stir" it is hardly worth while to cut his hair.

"Now, Valentine," said the warden, "you'll go out in the morning. Brace up, and make a man of yourself. You're not a bad fellow at heart. Stop cracking safes, and live straight."

"Me?" said Jimmy, in surprise. "Why, I never cracked a safe in my life."

"Oh, no," laughed the warden. "Of course not. Let's see, now. How was it you happened to get sent up on that Springfield job? Was it because you wouldn't prove an alibi for fear of compromising somebody in extremely high-toned society? Or was it simply a case of a mean old jury that had it in for you? It's always one or the other with you innocent victims."

"Me?" said Jimmy, still blankly virtuous. "Why, warden, I never was in Springfield in my life!"

"Take him back, Cronin," smiled the warden, "and fix him up with outgoing clothes. Unlock him at seven in the morning, and let him come to the bull pen. Better think over my advice, Valentine."

At a quarter past seven on the next morning Jimmy stood in the warden's outer office. He had on a suit of the villainously fitting, readymade clothes and a pair of the stiff, squeaky shoes that the state furnishes to its discharged compulsory guests.

The clerk handed him a railroad ticket and the five-dollar bill with which the law expected him to rehabilitate himself into good citizenship and prosperity. The warden gave him a cigar, and shook hands. Valentine, 9762, was chronicled on the books "Pardoned by Governor," and Mr. James Valentine walked out into the sunshine.

Disregarding the song of the birds, the waving green trees, and the smell of the flowers, Jimmy headed straight for a restaurant. There he tasted the first sweet joys of liberty in the shape of a broiled chicken and a bottle of white wine—followed by a cigar a grade better than the one the warden had given him. From there he proceeded leisurely to the depot. He tossed a quarter into the hat of a blind man sitting by the door, and boarded his train. Three hours set him down in a little town near the state line. He went to the café of one Mike Dolan and shook hands with Mike, who was alone behind the bar.

"Sorry we couldn't make it sooner, Jimmy, me boy," said Mike. "But we had that protest from Springfield to buck against, and the governor nearly balked. Feeling all right?"

"Fine," said Jimmy. "Got my key?"

He got his key and went upstairs, unlocking the door of a room at the rear. Everything was just as he had left it. There on the floor was still Ben Price's collar button that had been torn from that eminent detective's shirtband when they had overpowered Jimmy to arrest him.

Pulling out from the wall a folding bed, Jimmy slid back a panel in the wall and dragged out a dust-covered suitcase. He opened this and gazed fondly at the finest set of burglar's tools in the East. It was a complete set, made of specially tempered steel, the latest designs in drills, punches, braces and bits, jimmies, clamps, and augers, with two or three novelties invented by Jimmy himself, in which he took pride. Over nine hundred dollars they had cost him to have made at——, a place where they make such things for the profession.

In half an hour Jimmy went downstairs and through the café. He was now dressed in tasteful and well-fitting clothes, and carried his dusted and cleaned suitcase in his hand.

"Got anything on?" asked Mike Dolan, genially.

"Me?" said Jimmy, in a puzzled tone. "I don't understand. I'm representing the New York Amalgamated Short Snap Biscuit Cracker and Frazzled Wheat Company."

This statement delighted Mike to such an extent that Jimmy had to take a seltzer-and-milk on the spot. He never touched "hard" drinks.

A week after the release of Valentine, 9762, there was a neat job of safe-burglary done in Richmond, Indiana, with no clue to the author. A scant eight hundred dollars was all that was secured. Two weeks after that a patented, improved, burglarproof safe in Logansport was opened like a cheese to the tune of fifteen hundred dollars, currency; securities and silver untouched. That began to interest the rogue-catchers. Then an old-fashioned bank-safe in Jefferson City became active and threw out of its crater an eruption of bank notes amounting to five thousand dollars. The losses were now high enough to bring the matter up into Ben Price's class of work. By comparing notes, a remarkable similarity in the methods of the burglaries was noticed. Ben Price investigated the scenes of the robberies, and was heard to remark:

"That's Dandy Jim Valentine's autograph. He has

resumed business. Look at that combination knob—jerked out as easy as pulling up a radish in wet weather. He's got the only clamps that can do it. And look how clean those tumblers were punched out! Jimmy never has to drill but one hole. Yes, I guess I want Mr. Valentine. He'll do his bit next time without any short-time or clemency foolishness."

Ben Price knew Jimmy's habits. He had learned them while working up the Springfield case. Long jumps, quick getaways, no confederates, and a taste for good society— these ways had helped Mr. Valentine to become noted as a successful dodger of retribution. It was given out that Ben Price had taken up the trail of the elusive cracksman, and other people with burglarproof safes felt more at ease.

One afternoon Jimmy Valentine and his suitcase climbed out of the mail-hack in Elmore, a little town five miles off the railroad down in the blackjack country of Arkansas. Jimmy, looking like an athletic young senior just home from college, went down the board sidewalk toward the hotel.

A young lady crossed the street, passed him at the corner and entered a door over which was the sign "The Elmore Bank." Jimmy Valentine looked into her eyes, forgot what he was, and became another man. She lowered her eyes and colored slightly. Young men of Jimmy's style and looks were scarce in Elmore.

Jimmy collared a boy that was loafing on the steps of

the bank as if he were one of the stockholders, and began
to ask him questions about the town, feeding him dimes
at intervals. By and by the young lady came out, looking
royally unconscious of the young man with the suitcase,
and went her way.

"Isn't that young lady Miss Polly Simpson?" asked
Jimmy, with specious guile.

"Naw," said the boy. "She's Annabel Adams. Her pa
owns this bank. What'd you come to Elmore for? Is that
a gold watch chain? I'm going to get a bulldog. Got any
more dimes?"

Jimmy went to the Planters' Hotel, registered as Ralph
D. Spencer, and engaged a room. He leaned on the desk
and declared his platform to the clerk. He said he had
come to Elmore to look for a location to go into business.
How was the shoe business, now, in the town? He had
thought of the shoe business. Was there an opening?

The clerk was impressed by the clothes and manner of
Jimmy. He, himself, was something of a pattern of
fashion to the thinly gilded youth of Elmore, but he now
perceived his shortcomings. While trying to figure out
Jimmy's manner of tying his four-in-hand he cordially
gave information.

Yes, there ought to be a good opening in the shoe line.
There wasn't an exclusive shoe store in the place. The dry
goods and general stores handled them. Business in all
lines was fairly good. Hoped Mr. Spencer would decide
to locate in Elmore. He would find it a pleasant town to

live in, and the people very sociable.

Mr. Spencer thought he would stop over in the town a few days and look over the situation. No, the clerk needn't call the boy. He would carry up his suitcase, himself; it was rather heavy.

Mr. Ralph Spencer, the phœnix that arose from Jimmy Valentine's ashes—ashes left by the flame of a sudden and alternative attack of love—remained in Elmore, and prospered. He opened a shoe store and secured a good run of trade.

Socially he was also a success, and made many friends. And he accomplished the wish of his heart. He met Miss Annabel Adams, and became more and more captivated by her charms.

At the end of a year the situation of Mr. Ralph Spencer was this: he had won the respect of the community, his shoe store was flourishing, and he and Annabel were engaged to be married in two weeks. Mr. Adams, the typical, plodding, country banker, approved of Spencer. Annabel's pride in him almost equalled her affection. He was as much at home in the family of Mr. Adams and that of Annabel's married sister as if he were already a member.

One day Jimmy sat down in his room and wrote this letter, which he mailed to the safe address of one of his old friends in St. Louis:

Dear Old Pal:

I want you to be at Sullivan's place, in Little Rock,

next Wednesday night at nine o'clock. I want you to
wind up some little matters for me. And, also, I want
to make you a present of my kit of tools. I know you'll
be glad to get them—you couldn't duplicate the lot for
a thousand dollars. Say, Billy, I've quit the old business—a year ago. I've got a nice store. I'm making an
honest living, and I'm going to marry the finest girl
on earth two weeks from now. It's the only life, Billy
—the straight one. I wouldn't touch a dollar of another man's money now for a million. After I get married I'm going to sell out and go West, where there
won't be so much danger of having old scores brought
up against me. I tell you, Billy, she's an angel. She
believes in me; and I wouldn't do another crooked
thing for the whole world. Be sure to be at Sully's,
for I must see you. I'll bring along the tools with me.

> Your old friend,
> Jimmy

On the Monday night after Jimmy wrote this letter,
Ben Price jogged unobtrusively into Elmore in a livery
buggy. He lounged about town in his quiet way until he
found out what he wanted to know. From the drugstore
across the street from Spencer's shoe store he got a good
look at Ralph D. Spencer.

"Going to marry the banker's daughter are you,
Jimmy?" said Ben to himself, softly. "Well, I don't know!"

The next morning Jimmy took breakfast at the Adamses.
He was going to Little Rock that day to order his
wedding-suit and buy something nice for Annabel. That
would be the first time he had left town since he came

to Elmore. It had been more than a year now since those last professional "jobs," and he thought he could safely venture out.

After breakfast quite a family party went downtown together—Mr. Adams, Annabel, Jimmy, and Annabel's married sister with her two little girls, aged five and nine. They came by the hotel where Jimmy still boarded, and he ran up to his room and brought along his suitcase. Then they went on to the bank. There stood Jimmy's horse and buggy and Dolph Gibson, who was going to drive him over to the railroad station.

All went inside the high, carved oak railings into the banking-room—Jimmy included, for Mr. Adams's future son-in-law was welcome anywhere. The clerks were pleased to be greeted by the good-looking, agreeable young man who was going to marry Miss Annabel. Jimmy set his suitcase down. Annabel, whose heart was bubbling with happiness and lively youth, put on Jimmy's hat and picked up the suitcase. "Wouldn't I make a nice drummer?" said Annabel. "My! Ralph, how heavy it is. Feels like it was full of gold bricks."

"Lot of nickel-plated shoehorns in there," said Jimmy, coolly, "that I'm going to return. Thought I'd save express charges by taking them up. I'm getting awfully economical."

The Elmore Bank had just put in a new safe and vault. Mr. Adams was very proud of it, and insisted on an inspection by everyone. The vault was a small one, but it had a new patented door. It fastened with three solid steel bolts thrown simultaneously with a single handle, and had a time lock. Mr. Adams beamingly explained its workings to Mr. Spencer, who showed a courteous but not too intelligent interest. The two children, May and Agatha, were delighted by the shining metal and funny clock and knobs.

While they were thus engaged Ben Price sauntered in and leaned on his elbow, looking casually inside between the railings. He told the teller that he didn't want anything; he was just waiting for a man he knew.

Suddenly there was a scream or two from the women, and a commotion. Unperceived by the elders, May, the nine-year-old girl, in a spirit of play, had shut Agatha in the vault. She had then shot the bolts and turned the knob of the combination as she had seen Mr. Adams do.

The old banker sprang to the handle and tugged at it for a moment. "The door can't be opened," he groaned. "The clock hasn't been wound nor the combination set."

Agatha's mother screamed again, hysterically.

"Hush!" said Mr. Adams, raising his trembling hand. "All be quiet for a moment. Agatha!" he called as loudly as he could: "Listen to me." During the following silence they could just hear the faint sound of the child wildly shrieking in the dark vault in a panic of terror.

"My precious darling!" wailed the mother. "She will die of fright! Open the door! Oh, break it open! Can't you men do something?"

"There isn't a man nearer than Little Rock who can open that door," said Mr. Adams, in a shaky voice. "My God! Spencer, what shall we do? That child—she can't stand it long in there. There isn't enough air, and, besides, she'll go into convulsions from fright."

Agatha's mother, frantic now, beat the door of the vault with her hands. Somebody wildly suggested dynamite. Annabel turned to Jimmy, her large eyes full of anguish, but not yet despairing. To a woman nothing seems quite impossible to the powers of the man she worships.

"Can't you do something, Ralph—*try*, won't you?"

He looked at her with a queer, soft smile on his lips and in his keen eyes.

"Annabel," he said, "give me that rose you are wearing, will you?"

Hardly believing that she heard him aright, she unpinned the bud from the bosom of her dress, and placed it in his hand. Jimmy stuffed it into his vest-pocket, threw off his coat and pulled up his shirt-sleeves. With that act Ralph D. Spencer passed away and Jimmy Valentine took his place.

"Get away from the door, all of you," he commanded, shortly.

He set his suitcase on the table, and opened it out flat. From that time on he seemed to be unconscious of the presence of anyone else. He laid out the shining, queer implements swiftly and orderly, whistling softly to himself as he always did when at work. In a deep silence and immovable, the others watched him as if under a spell.

In a minute Jimmy's pet drill was biting smoothly into the steel door. In ten minutes—breaking his own burglarious record—he threw back the bolts and opened the door.

Agatha, almost collapsed, but safe, was gathered into her mother's arms.

Jimmy Valentine put on his coat, and walked outside the railings toward the front door. As he went he thought he heard a faraway voice that he once knew call "Ralph!" But he never hesitated.

At the door a big man stood somewhat in his way.

"Hello, Ben!" said Jimmy, still with his strange smile. "Got around at last, have you? Well, let's go. I don't know that it makes much difference, now."

And then Ben Price acted rather strangely.

"Guess you're mistaken, Mr. Spencer," he said. "Don't believe I recognize you. Your buggy's waiting for you, ain't it?"

And Ben Price turned and strolled down the street.

ONE DOLLAR'S
WORTH

THE JUDGE OF THE UNITED STATES
court of the district lying along the Rio Grande border
found the following letter one morning in his mail:

Judge:
When you sent me up for four years you made a
talk. Among other hard things, you called me a rattlesnake. Maybe I am one—anyhow, you hear me rattling
now. One year after I got to the pen, my daughter
died of—well, they said it was poverty and the dis-
grace together. You've got a daughter, Judge, and I'm
going to make you know how it feels to lose one. And
I'm going to bite that district attorney that spoke
against me. I'm free now, and I guess I've turned to

rattlesnake all right. I feel like one. I don't say much,
but this is my rattle. Look out what I strike.

Yours respectfully,

Rattlesnake

Judge Derwent threw the letter carelessly aside. It was
nothing new to receive such epistles from desperate men
whom he had been called up to judge. He felt no alarm.
Later on he showed the letter to Littlefield, the young
district attorney, for Littlefield's name was included in
the threat, and the judge was punctilious in matters between himself and his fellow men.

Littlefield honored the rattle of the writer, as far as it
concerned himself, with a smile of contempt; but he
frowned a little over the reference to the Judge's daughter, for he and Nancy Derwent were to be married in
the fall.

Littlefield went to the clerk of the court and looked
over the records with him. They decided that the letter
might have been sent by one Mexico Sam, the border
desperado who had been imprisoned for manslaughter
some four years before. Then official duties crowded the
matter from his mind, and the rattle of the revengeful
serpent was forgotten.

Court was in session at Brownsville. Most of the cases
to be tried were charges of smuggling, counterfeiting,
post-office robberies, and violations of Federal laws along
the border. One case was that of a young Mexican, Rafael
Ortiz, who had been rounded up by a clever deputy

marshal in the act of passing a counterfeit silver dollar. He had been suspected of many such deviations from rectitude, but this was the first time that anything provable had been fixed upon him. Ortiz languished cozily in jail, smoking brown cigarettes and waiting for trial. Kilpatrick, the deputy, brought the counterfeit dollar and handed it to the district attorney in his office in the courthouse. The deputy and a reputable druggist were prepared to swear that Ortiz paid for a bottle of medicine with it. The coin was a poor counterfeit, soft, dull-looking, and made principally of lead. It was the day before the morning on which the docket would reach the case of Ortiz, and the district attorney was preparing himself for the trial.

"Not much need of having in high-priced experts to prove the coin's queer, is there, Kil?" smiled Littlefield, as he thumped the dollar down upon the table, where it fell with no more ring than would have come from a lump of putty.

"I guess Ortiz is as good as behind the bars," said the deputy, easing up his holsters. "You've got him dead. If it had been just one time, these Mexicans can't tell good money from bad; but this rascal belongs to a gang of counterfeiters, I know. This is the first time I've been able to catch him doing the trick. He's got a girl down there in them Mexican jacals on the river bank. I seen her one day when I was watching him. She's as pretty as a red heifer in a flower bed."

Littlefield shoved the counterfeit dollar into his pocket, and slipped his memoranda of the case into an envelope. Just then a bright, winsome face, as frank and jolly as a boy's, appeared in the doorway, and in walked Nancy Derwent.

"Oh, Bob, didn't court adjourn at twelve today until tomorrow?" she asked of Littlefield.

"It did," said the district attorney, "and I'm very glad of it. I've got a lot of rulings to look up, and——"

"Now, that's just like you. I wonder you and Father don't turn into law books or rulings or something! I want you to take me out plover-shooting this afternoon. Long Prairie is just alive with them. Don't say no, please! I want to try my new twelve-bore hammerless. I've sent to the livery stable to engage Fly and Bess for the buckboard; they stand fire so nicely. I was sure you would go."

They were to be married in the fall. The glamour was at its height. The plovers won the day—or, rather the afternoon—over the calf-bound authorities. Littlefield began to put his papers away.

There was a knock at the door. Kilpatrick answered it. A beautiful, dark-eyed girl with a skin tinged with the faintest lemon color walked into the room. A black shawl was thrown over her head and wound once around her neck.

She began to talk in Spanish, a voluble, mournful stream of melancholy music. Littlefield did not understand Spanish. The deputy did, and he translated her talk by portions, at intervals holding up his hands to check the flow of her words.

"She came to see you, Mr. Littlefield. Her name's Joya Treviñas. She wants to see you about—well, she's mixed up with that Rafael Ortiz. She's his—she's his girl. She says he's innocent. She says she made the money and got him to pass it. Don't you believe her, Mr. Littlefield. That's the way with these Mexican girls; they'll lie, steal, or kill for a fellow when they get stuck on him. Never trust a woman that's in love!"

"Mr. Kilpatrick!"

Nancy Derwent's indignant exclamation caused the deputy to flounder for a moment in attempting to explain that he had misquoted his own sentiments, and then he went on with the translation:

"She says she's willing to take his place in the jail if you'll let him out. She says she was down with the fever, and the doctor said she'd die if she didn't have medicine. That's why he passed the lead dollar on the drugstore. She says it saved her life. This Rafael seems to be her honey, all right; there's a lot of stuff in her talk about love and such things that you don't want to hear."

It was an old story to the district attorney.

"Tell her," said he, "that I can do nothing. The case comes up in the morning, and he will have to make his fight before the court."

Nancy Derwent was not so hardened. She was looking with sympathetic interest at Joya Treviñas and at Littlefield alternately. The deputy repeated the district attorney's words to the girl. She spoke a sentence or two in a low voice, pulled her shawl closely about her face, and left the room.

"What did she say then?" asked the district attorney.

"Nothing special," said the deputy. "She said: 'If the life of the one'—let's see how it went—'*Si la vida de ella a quien tu amas*—if the life of the girl you love is ever in danger, remember Rafael Ortiz.' "

Kilpatrick strolled out through the corridor in the direction of the marshal's office.

"Can't you do anything for them, Bob?" asked Nancy. "It's such a little thing—just one counterfeit dollar—to ruin the happiness of two lives! She was in danger of death, and he did it to save her. Doesn't the law know the feeling of pity?"

"It hasn't a place in jurisprudence, Nan," said Littlefield, "especially *in re* the district attorney's duty. I'll promise you that the prosecution will not be vindictive; but the man is as good as convicted when the case is called. Witnesses will swear to his passing the bad dollar which I have in my pocket at this moment as 'Exhibit A.' There are no Mexicans on the jury, and it will vote Rafael Ortiz guilty without leaving the box."

The plover-shooting was fine that afternoon, and in the excitement of the sport the case of Rafael and the grief of Joya Treviñas were forgotten. The district attorney and Nancy Derwent drove out from the town three miles along a smooth, grassy road, and then struck across a rolling prairie toward a heavy line of timber on Piedra Creek. Beyond this creek lay Long Prairie, the favorite haunt of the plover. As they were nearing the creek they heard the galloping of a horse to their right, and saw a man with black hair and a swarthy face riding toward the woods at a tangent, as if he had come up behind them.

"I've seen that fellow somewhere," said Littlefield, who had a memory for faces, "but I can't exactly place him. Some ranchman, I suppose, taking a short cut home."

They spent an hour on Long Prairie, shooting from the buckboard. Nancy Derwent, an active, outdoor Western girl, was pleased with her twelve-bore. She had bagged within two brace of her companion's score.

They started homeward at a gentle trot. When within a hundred yards of Piedra Creek a man rode out of the timber directly toward them.

"It looks like the man we saw coming over," remarked Miss Derwent.

As the distance between them lessened, the district attorney suddenly pulled up his team sharply, with his eyes fixed upon the advancing horseman. That individual had drawn a Winchester from its scabbard on his saddle and thrown it over his arm.

"Now I know you, Mexico Sam!" muttered Littlefield

to himself. "It *was* you who shook your rattles in that gentle epistle."

Mexico Sam did not leave things long in doubt. He had a nice eye in all matters relating to firearms, so when he was within good rifle range, but outside of danger from No. 8 shot, he threw up his Winchester and opened fire upon the occupants of the buckboard.

The first shot cracked the back of the seat within the two-inch space between the shoulders of Littlefield and Miss Derwent. The next went through the dashboard and Littlefield's trouser leg.

The district attorney hustled Nancy out of the buckboard to the ground. She was a little pale, but asked no questions. She had the frontier instinct that accepts conditions in an emergency without superfluous argument. They kept their guns in hand, and Littlefield hastily gathered some handfuls of cartridges from the pasteboard box on the seat and crowded them into his pockets.

"Keep behind the horses, Nan," he commanded. "That fellow is a ruffian I sent to prison once. He's trying to get even. He knows our shot won't hurt him at that distance."

"All right, Bob," said Nancy, steadily. "I'm not afraid. But you come close, too. Whoa, Bess; stand still, now!"

She stroked Bess's mane. Littlefield stood with his gun ready, praying that the desperado would come within range.

But Mexican Sam was playing his vendetta along safe lines. He was a bird of different feather from the plover.

His accurate eye drew an imaginary line of circumference around the area of danger from bird shot, and upon this line he rode. His horse wheeled to the right, and as his victims rounded to the safe side of their equine breastwork he sent a ball through the district attorney's hat. Once he miscalculated in making a detour, and overstepped his margin. Littlefield's gun flashed, and Mexico Sam ducked his head to the harmless patter of the shot. A few of them stung his horse, which pranced promptly back to the safety line.

The desperado fired again. A little cry came from Nancy Derwent. Littlefield whirled, with blazing eyes, and saw the blood trickling down her cheek.

"I'm not hurt, Bob—only a splinter struck me. I think he hit one of the wheel-spokes."

"Lord!" groaned Littlefield. "If I only had a charge of buckshot!"

The ruffian got his horse still, and took careful aim. Fly gave a snort and fell in the harness, struck in the neck. Bess, now disabused of the idea that plover were being fired at, broke her traces and galloped wildly away. Mexican Sam sent a ball neatly through the fullness of Nancy Derwent's shooting jacket.

"Lie down—lie down!" snapped Littlefield. "Close to the horse—flat on the ground—so." He almost threw her upon the grass against the back of the recumbent Fly. Oddly, enough, at that moment the words of the Mexican girl returned to his mind:

"If the life of the girl you love is ever in danger, remember Rafael Ortiz."

Littlefield uttered an exclamation.

"Open fire on him, Nan, across the horse's back! Fire
as fast as you can! You can't hurt him, but keep him
dodging shot for one minute while I try to work a little
scheme."

Nancy gave a quick glance at Littlefield, and saw him
take out his pocketknife and open it. Then she turned
her face to obey orders, keeping up a rapid fire at the
enemy.

Mexico Sam waited patiently until this innocuous fu-
sillade ceased. He had plenty of time, and he did not
care to risk the chance of a bird shot in his eye if it could
be avoided by a little caution. He pulled his heavy Stetson low down over his face until the shots ceased. Then
he drew a little nearer, and fired with careful aim at what
he could see of his victims above the fallen horse.

Neither of them moved. He urged his horse a few steps
nearer. He saw the district attorney rise to one knee, and
deliberately level his shotgun. He pulled his hat down
and awaited the harmless rattle of the tiny pellets.

The shotgun blazed with a heavy report. Mexico Sam
sighed, turned limp all over, and slowly fell from his
horse—a dead rattlesnake.

At ten o'clock the next morning court opened, and the
case of the United States *versus* Rafael Ortiz was called.

The district attorney, with his arm in a sling, rose and addressed the court.

"May it please your honor," he said, "I desire to enter a *nolle pros.* in this case. Even though the defendant should be guilty, there is not sufficient evidence in the hands of the government to secure a conviction. The piece of counterfeit coin upon the identity of which the case was built is not now available as evidence. I ask, therefore, that the case be stricken off."

At the noon recess, Kilpatrick strolled into the district attorney's office.

"I've just been down to take a squint at old Mexico Sam," said the deputy. "They've got him laid out. Old Mexico was a tough outfit, I reckon. The boys was wonderin' down there what you shot him with. Some said it must have been nails. I never see a gun carry anything to make holes like he had."

"I shot him," said the district attorney, "with Exhibit A of your counterfeiting case. Lucky thing for me—and somebody else—that it was as bad money as it was! It sliced up into slugs very nicely. Say, Kil, can't you go down to the jacals and find where that Mexican girl lives? Miss Derwent wants to know."

THE SKYLIGHT ROOM

IRST MRS. PARKER WOULD SHOW YOU
the double parlors. You would not dare to interrupt her
description of their advantages and of the merits of the
gentleman who had occupied them for eight years. Then
you would manage to stammer forth the confession that
you were neither a doctor nor a dentist. Mrs. Parker's
manner of receiving the admission was such that you
could never afterward entertain the same feeling toward
your parents, who had neglected to train you up in one
of the professions that fitted Mrs. Parker's parlors.

Next you ascended one flight of stairs and looked at
the second-floor back at $8. Convinced by her second-
floor manner that it was worth the $12 that Mr. Toosen-
berry always paid for it until he left to take charge of

his brother's orange plantation in Florida near Palm Beach where Mrs. McIntyre always spent the winters—she had the double front room with private bath—you managed to babble that you wanted something still cheaper.

If you survived Mrs. Parker's scorn, you were taken to look at Mr. Skidder's large hall room on the third floor. Mr. Skidder's room was not vacant. He wrote plays and smoked cigarettes in it all day long. But every room-hunter was made to visit his room to admire the lambrequins. After each visit, Mr. Skidder, from the fright caused by possible eviction, would pay something on his rent.

Then—oh, then—if you still stood on one foot, with your hot hand clutching the three moist dollars in your pocket, and hoarsely proclaimed your hideous and culpable poverty, nevermore would Mrs. Parker be cicerone of yours. She would honk loudly the word "Clara," she would show you her back, and march downstairs. Then Clara, the colored maid, would escort you up the carpeted ladder that served for the fourth flight, and show you the Skylight Room. It occupied 7 x 8 feet of floor space in the middle of the hall. On each side of it was a dark lumber closet or storeroom.

In it were an iron cot, a washstand and a chair. A shelf was the dresser. Its four bare walls seemed to close in upon you like the sides of a coffin. Your hand crept to your throat, you gasped, you looked up as from a well—

and breathed once more. Through the glass of the little skylight you saw a square of blue infinity.

"Two dollars, suh," Clara would say in her half-contemptuous, half-Tuskegeenial tones.

One day Miss Leeson came hunting for a room. She carried a typewriter made to be lugged around by a much larger lady. She was a very little girl, with eyes and hair that had kept on growing after she had stopped and that always looked as if they were saying: "Goodness me! Why didn't you keep up with us?"

Mrs. Parker showed her the double parlors. "In this closet," she said, "one could keep a skeleton or anæsthetic or coal——"

"But I am neither a doctor nor a dentist," said Miss Leeson, with a shiver.

Mrs. Parker gave her the incredulous, pitying, sneering, icy stare that she kept for those who failed to qualify as doctors or dentists, and led the way to the second-floor back.

"Eight dollars?" said Miss Leeson. "Dear me! I'm not Hetty if I do look green. I'm just a poor little working girl. Show me something higher and lower."

Mr. Skidder jumped and strewed the floor with cigarette stubs at the rap on his door.

"Excuse me, Mr. Skidder," said Mrs. Parker, with her demon's smile at his pale looks. "I didn't know you were in. I asked the lady to have a look at your lambrequins."

"They're too lovely for anything," said Miss Leeson,

smiling in exactly the way the angels do.

After they had gone Mr. Skidder got very busy erasing the tall, black-haired heroine from his latest (unproduced) play and inserted a small, roguish one with heavy, bright hair and vivacious features.

"Anna Held'll jump at it," said Mr. Skidder to himself, putting his feet up against the lambrequins and disappearing in a cloud of smoke like an aërial cuttlefish.

Presently the tocsin call of "Clara!" sounded to the world the state of Miss Leeson's purse. A dark goblin seized her, mounted a Stygian stairway, thrust her into a vault with a glimmer of light in its top and muttered the menacing and cabalistic words "Two dollars!"

"I'll take it!" sighed Miss Leeson, sinking down upon the squeaky iron bed.

Every day Miss Leeson went out to work. At night she brought home papers with handwriting on them and made copies with her typewriter. Sometimes she had no work at night, and then she would sit on the steps of the high stoop with the other roomers. Miss Leeson was not intended for a skylight room when the plans were drawn for her creation. She was gay-hearted and full of tender, whimsical fancies. Once she let Mr. Skidder read to her three acts of his great (unpublished) comedy, "It's No Kid or The Heir of the Subway."

There was rejoicing among the gentlemen roomers whenever Miss Leeson had time to sit on the steps for an hour or two. But Miss Longnecker, the tall blonde

who taught in a public school and said, "Well, really!"
to everything you said, sat on the top step and sniffed.
And Miss Dorn, who shot at the moving ducks at Coney
every Sunday and worked in a department store, sat on
the bottom step and sniffed. Miss Leeson sat on the
middle step and the men would quickly group around
her.

Especially Mr. Skidder, who had cast her in his mind
for the star part in a private, romantic (unspoken) drama
in real life. And especially Mr. Hoover, who was forty-
five, fat, flush and foolish. And especially very young Mr.
Evans, who set up a hollow cough to induce her to ask
him to leave off cigarettes. The men voted her "the funniest and jolliest ever," but the sniffs on the top step and
the lower step were implacable.

I pray you to let the drama halt while Chorus stalks
to the footlights and drops an epicedian tear upon the
fatness of Mr. Hoover. Tune the pipes to the tragedy of
tallow, the bane of bulk, the calamity of corpulence.
Tried out, Falstaff might have rendered more romance to
the ton than would have Romeo's rickety ribs to the
ounce. A lover may sigh, but he must not puff. To the
train of Momus are the fat men remanded. In vain beats
the faithfullest heart above a 52-inch belt. Avaunt,
Hoover! Hoover, forty-five, flush and foolish, might carry
off Helen herself; Hoover, forty-five, flush, foolish and
fat is meat for perdition. There was never a chance for
you, Hoover.

As Mrs. Parker's roomers sat thus one summer's evening, Miss Leeson looked up into the firmament and cried with her little gay laugh:

"Why, there's Billy Jackson! I can see him from down here, too."

All looked up—some at the windows of skyscrapers, some casting about for an airship, Jackson-guided.

"It's that star," explained Miss Leeson, pointing with a tiny finger. "Not the big one that twinkles—the steady blue one near it. I can see it every night through my skylight. I named it Billy Jackson."

"Well, really!" said Miss Longnecker. "I didn't know you were an astronomer, Miss Leeson."

"Oh, yes," said the small star gazer, "I know as much as any of them about the style of sleeves they're going to wear next fall in Mars."

"Well, really!" said Miss Longnecker. "The star you refer to is Gamma, of the constellation Cassiopeia. It is nearly of the second magnitude, and its meridian passage is——"

"Oh," said the very young Mr. Evans, "I think Billy Jackson is a much better name for it."

"Same here," said Mr. Hoover, loudly breathing defiance to Miss Longnecker. "I think Miss Leeson has just as much right to name stars as any of those old astrologers had."

"Well, really!" said Miss Longnecker.

"I wonder whether it's a shooting star," remarked Miss

Dorn. "I hit nine ducks and a rabbit out of ten in the gallery at Coney Sunday."

"He doesn't show up very well from down here," said Miss Leeson. "You ought to see him from my room. You know you can see stars even in the daytime from the bottom of a well. At night my room is like the shaft of a coal mine, and it makes Billy Jackson look like the big diamond pin that Night fastens her kimono with."

There came a time after that when Miss Leeson brought no formidable papers home to copy. And when she went out in the morning, instead of working, she went from office to office and let her heart melt away in the drip of cold refusals transmitted through insolent office boys. This went on.

There came an evening when she wearily climbed Mrs. Parker's stoop at the hour when she always returned from her dinner at the restaurant. But she had had no dinner.

As she stepped into the hall Mr. Hoover met her and seized his chance. He asked her to marry him, and his fatness hovered above her like an avalanche. She dodged, and caught the balustrade. He tried for her hand, and she raised it and smote him weakly in the face. Step by step she went up, dragging herself by the railing. She passed Mr. Skidder's door as he was red-inking a stage direction for Myrtle Delorme (Miss Leeson) in his (unaccepted) comedy, to "pirouette across stage from L to the side of the Count." Up the carpeted ladder she crawled at last and opened the door of the skylight room.

She was too weak to light the lamp or to undress. She fell upon the iron cot, her fragile body scarcely hollowing the worn springs. And in that Erebus of a room she slowly raised her heavy eyelids, and smiled.

For Billy Jackson was shining down on her, calm and bright and constant through the skylight. There was no world about her. She was sunk in a pit of blackness, with but that small square of pallid light framing the star that she had so whimsically and oh, so ineffectually, named. Miss Longnecker must be right: it was Gamma, of the constellation Cassiopeia, and not Billy Jackson. And yet she could not let it be Gamma.

As she lay on her back, she tried twice to raise her arm. The third time she got two thin fingers to her lips and blew a kiss out of the black pit to Billy Jackson. Her arm fell back limply.

"Good-bye, Billy," she murmured, faintly. "You're millions of miles away and you won't even twinkle once. But you kept where I could see you most of the time up there when there wasn't anything else but darkness to look at, didn't you? . . . Millions of miles. . . . Good-bye, Billy Jackson."

Clara, the coloured maid, found the door locked at 10 the next day, and they forced it open. Vinegar, and the slapping of wrists and burnt feathers proving of no avail, someone ran to phone for an ambulance.

In due time it backed up to the door with much gong-clanging, and the capable young medico, in his white linen coat, ready, active, confident, with his smooth face half debonair, half grim, danced up the steps.

"Ambulance call to 49," he said briefly. "What's the trouble?"

"Oh, yes, doctor," sniffed Mrs. Parker, as though her trouble that there should be trouble in the house was the greater. "I can't think what can be the matter with her. Nothing we could do would bring her to. It's a young woman, a Miss Elsie—yes, a Miss Elsie Leeson. Never before in my house—"

"What room?" cried the doctor in a terrible voice, to which Mrs. Parker was a stranger.

"The skylight room. It—"

Evidently the ambulance doctor was familiar with the location of skylight rooms. He was gone up the stairs, four at a time. Mrs. Parker followed slowly, as her dignity demanded.

On the first landing she met him coming back bearing the astronomer in his arms. He stopped and let loose the practiced scalpel of his tongue, not loudly. Gradually Mrs. Parker crumpled as a stiff garment that slips down from a nail. Ever afterwards there remained crumples in her mind and body. Sometimes her curious roomers would ask her what the doctor said to her.

"Let that be," she would answer. "If I can get forgiveness for having heard it I will be satisfied."

The ambulance physician strode with his burden through the pack of hounds that follow the curiosity chase, and even they fell back along the sidewalk abashed, for his face was that of one who bears his own dead.

They noticed that he did not lay down, upon the bed prepared for it in the ambulance, the form that he carried, and all that he said was: "Drive like h—l, Wilson," to the driver.

That is all. Is it a story? In the next morning's paper I saw a little news item, and the last sentence of it may help you (as it helped me) to weld the incidents together.

It recounted the reception into Bellevue Hospital of a young woman who had been removed from No. 49 East —— Street, suffering from debility induced by starvation. It concluded with these words:

"Dr. William Jackson, the ambulance physician who attended the case, says the patient will recover."

FROM THE

CABBY'S SEAT

THE CABBY HAS HIS POINT OF VIEW.
It is more single-minded, perhaps, than that of a follower
of any other calling. From the high, swaying seat of his
hansom he looks upon his fellow men as nomadic particles, of no account except when possessed of migratory
desires. He is Jehu, and you are goods in transit. Be you
president or vagabond, to cabby you are only a fare. He
takes you up, cracks his whip, joggles your vertebræ and
sets you down.

When time for payment arrives, if you exhibit a familiarity with legal rates you come to know what contempt
is; if you find that you have left your pocketbook behind

you are made to realize the mildness of Dante's imagination.

It is not an extravagant theory that the cabby's singleness of purpose and concentrated view of life are the results of the hansom's peculiar construction. The cock-of-the-roost sits aloft like Jupiter on an unsharable seat, holding your fate between two thongs of inconstant leather. Helpless, ridiculous, confined, bobbing like a toy mandarin, you sit like a rat in a trap—you, before whom butlers cringe on solid land—and must squeak upward through a slit in your peripatetic sarcophagus to make your feeble wishes known.

Then, in a cab, you are not even an occupant; you are contents. You are a cargo at sea, and the "cherub that sits up aloft" has Davy Jones's street and number by heart.

One night there were sounds of revelry in the big brick tenement house next door but one to McGary's Family Café. The sounds seemed to emanate from the apartments of the Walsh family. The sidewalk was obstructed by an assortment of interested neighbors, who opened a lane from time to time for a hurrying messenger bearing from McGary's goods pertinent to festivity and diversion. The sidewalk contingent was engaged in comment and discussion from which it made no effort to eliminate the news that Norah Walsh was being married.

In the fullness of time there was an eruption of the merrymakers to the sidewalk. The uninvited guests enveloped and permeated them, and upon the night air rose joyous cries, congratulations, laughter, and unclassified noises born of McGary's oblations to the hymeneal scene.

Close to the curb stood Jerry O'Donovan's cab. Nighthawk was Jerry called; but no more lustrous or cleaner hansom than his ever closed its doors upon point lace and November violets. And Jerry's horse! I am within bounds when I tell you that he was stuffed with oats until one of those old ladies who leave their dishes unwashed at home and go about having expressmen arrested, would have smiled—yes, smiled—to have seen him.

Among the shifting, sonorous, pulsing crowd glimpses could be had of Jerry's high hat, battered by the winds and rains of many years; of his nose like a carrot, battered by the frolicsome, athletic progeny of millionaires and by contumacious fares; of his brass-buttoned green coat, admired in the vicinity of McGary's. It was plain that Jerry had usurped the functions of his cab, and was carrying a "load." Indeed, the figure may be extended and he be likened to a bread-wagon if we admit the testimony of a youthful spectator, who was heard to remark "Jerry has got a bun."

From somewhere among the throng in the street or else out of the thin stream of pedestrians a young woman tripped and stood by the cab. The professional hawk's eye of Jerry caught the movement. He made a lurch for the cab, overturning three or four onlookers and himself— no! he caught the cap of a water-plug and kept his feet. Like a sailor shining up the ratlins during a squall Jerry mounted to his professional seat. Once he was there McGary's liquids were baffled. He seesawed on the mizzenmast of his craft as safe as a Steeple Jack rigged to the flagpole of a skyscraper.

"Step in, lady," said Jerry, gathering his lines.

The young woman stepped into the cab; the doors shut with a bang; Jerry's whip cracked in the air; the crowd in the gutter scattered, and the fine hansom dashed away crosstown.

When the oat-spry horse had hedged a little his first spurt of speed Jerry broke the lid of his cab and called down through the aperture in the voice of a cracked megaphone, trying to please:

"Where, now, will ye be drivin' to?"

"Anywhere you please," came up the answer, musical and contented.

" 'Tis drivin' for pleasure she is," thought Jerry. And then he suggested as a matter of course:

"Take a thrip around in the park, lady. 'Twill be ilegant cool and fine."

"Just as you like," answered the fare, pleasantly.

The cab headed for Fifth Avenue and sped up that perfect street. Jerry bounced and swayed in his seat. The potent fluids of McGary were disquieted and they sent new fumes to his head. He sang an ancient song of Killis-nook and brandished his whip like a baton.

Inside the cab the fare sat up straight on the cushions, looking to right and left at the lights and houses. Even in the shadowed hansom her eyes shone like stars at twilight.

When they reached Fifty-ninth Street Jerry's head was bobbing and his reins were slack. But his horse turned in through the park gate and began the old familiar nocturnal round. And then the fare leaned back, entranced, and breathed deep the clean, wholesome odors of grass and leaf and bloom. And the wise beast in the shafts, knowing his ground, struck into his by-the-hour gait and kept to the right of the road.

Habit also struggled successfully against Jerry's increasing torpor. He raised the hatch of his storm-tossed vessel and made the inquiry that cabbies do make in the park.

"Like shtop at the Cas-sino, lady? Gezzer r'freshm's, 'n lish'n the music. Ev'body shtops."

"I think that would be nice," said the fare.

They reined up with a plunge at the Casino entrance. The cab doors flew open. The fare stepped directly upon the floor. At once she was caught in a web of ravishing music and dazzled by a panorama of lights and colors. Some one slipped a little square card into her hand on which was printed a number—34. She looked around and saw her cab twenty yards away already lining up in its place among the waiting mass of carriages, cabs, and motor cars. And then a man who seemed to be all shirt front danced backward before her; and next she was seated at a little table by a railing over which climbed a jessamine vine.

There seemed to be a wordless invitation to purchase; she consulted a collection of small coins in a thin purse, and received from them license to order a glass of beer. There she sat, inhaling and absorbing it all—the new-colored, new-shaped life in a fairy palace in an enchanted wood.

At fifty tables sat princes and queens clad in all the silks and gems of the world. And now and then one of them would look curiously at Jerry's fare. They saw a plain figure dressed in a pink silk of the kind that is tempered by the word "foulard," and a plain face that wore a look of love of life that the queens envied.

Twice the long hands of the clocks went round. Royalties thinned from their *al fresco* thrones, and buzzed or clattered away in their vehicles of state. The music retired into cases of wood and bags of leather and baize. Waiters removed cloths pointedly near the plain figure sitting almost alone.

Jerry's fare rose, and held out her numbered card simply:

"Is there anything coming on the ticket?" she asked.

A waiter told her it was her cab check, and that she should give it to the man at the entrance. This man took it, and called the number. Only three hansoms stood in line. The driver of one of them went and routed out Jerry asleep in his cab. He swore deeply, climbed to the captain's bridge and steered his craft to the pier. His fare entered, and the cab whirled into the cool fastnesses of the park along the shortest homeward cuts.

At the gate a glimmer of reason in the form of sudden suspicion seized upon Jerry's beclouded mind. One or two things occurred to him. He stopped his horse, raised the trap and dropped his phonographic voice, like a lead plummet, through the aperture:

"I want to see four dollars before goin' any further on th' thrip. Have ye got th' dough?"

"Four dollars!" laughed the fare, softly, "dear me, no. I've only got a few pennies and a dime or two."

Jerry shut down the trap and slashed his oat-fed horse. The clatter of hoofs strangled but could not drown the sound of his profanity. He shouted choking and gurgling curses at the starry heavens; he cut viciously with his whip at passing vehicles; he scattered fierce and ever-changing oaths and imprecations along the streets, so that a late truck driver, crawling homeward, heard and was abashed. But he knew his recourse, and made for it at a gallop.

At the house with the green lights beside the steps he pulled up. He flung wide the cab doors and tumbled heavily to the ground.

"Come on, you," he said, roughly.

His fare came forth with the Casino dreamy smile still on her plain face. Jerry took her by the arm and led her into the police station. A gray-moustached sergeant looked keenly across the desk. He and the cabby were no strangers.

"Sergeant," began Jerry in his old raucous, martyred, thunderous tones of complaint. "I've got a fare here that——"

Jerry paused. He drew a knotted, red hand across his brow. The fog set up by McGary was beginning to clear away.

"A fare, sergeant," he continued, with a grin, "that I want to introduce to ye. It's me wife that I married at ould man Walsh's this evening. And a divil of a time we had, 'tis thrue. Shake hands wit th' sargeant, Norah, and we'll be off to home."

Before stepping into the cab Norah sighed profoundly.

"I've had such a nice time, Jerry," said she.

THE THEORY AND
THE HOUND

Not many days ago my old friend
from the tropics, J. P. Bridger, United States consul on
the island of Ratona, was in the city. We had wassail
and jubilee and saw the Flatiron building, and missed
seeing the Bronxless menagerie by about a couple of
nights. And then, at the ebb tide, we were walking up
a street that parallels and parodies Broadway.

A woman with a comely and mundane countenance
passed us, holding in leash a wheezing, vicious, waddling
brute of a yellow pug. The dog entangled himself with
Bridger's legs and mumbled his ankles in a snarling,
peevish, sulky bite. Bridger, with a happy smile, kicked
the breath out of the brute; the woman showered us

with a quick rain of well-conceived adjectives that left us in no doubt as to our place in her opinion, and we passed on. Ten yards farther an old woman with disordered white hair and her bankbook tucked well hidden beneath her tattered shawl begged. Bridger stopped and disinterred for her a quarter from his holiday waistcoat.

On the next corner a quarter of a ton of well-clothed man with a rice-powdered, fat, white jowl, stood holding the chain of a devil-born bulldog whose forelegs were strangers by the length of a dachshund. A little woman in a last-season's hat confronted him and wept, which was plainly all she could do, while he cursed her in low, sweet, practised tones.

Bridger smiled again—strictly to himself—and this time he took out a little memorandum book and made a note of it. This he had no right to do without due explanation, and I said so.

"It's a new theory," said Bridger, "that I picked up down in Ratona. I've been gathering support for it as I knock about. The world isn't ripe for it yet, but—well, I'll tell you; and then you run your mind back along the people you've known and see what you make of it."

And so I cornered Bridger in a place where they have artificial palms and wine; and he told me the story which is here in my words and on his responsibility.

One afternoon at three o'clock on Ratona island, a boy raced along the beach screaming, "*Pájaro*, ahoy!"

Thus he made known the keenness of his hearing and

the justice of his discrimination in pitch.

He who first heard and made oral proclamation concerning the toot of an approaching steamer's whistle, and correctly named the steamer, was a small hero in Ratona —until the next steamer came. Wherefore, there was rivalry among the barefoot youth of Ratona, and many fell victims to the softly blown conch shells of sloops which, as they enter harbor, sound surprisingly like a distant steamer's signal. And some could name you the vessel when its call, in your duller ears, sounded no louder than the sigh of the wind through the branches of the cocoanut palms.

But today he who proclaimed the *Pájaro* gained his honors. Ratona bent its ear to listen; and soon the deep-tongued blast grew louder and nearer, and at length Ratona saw above the line of palms on the low "point" the two black funnels of the fruiter slowly creeping toward the mouth of the harbor.

You must know that Ratona is an island twenty miles off the south of a South American republic. It is a port of that republic; and it sleeps sweetly in a smiling sea, toiling not nor spinning, fed by the abundant tropics where all things "ripen, cease and fall toward the grave."

Eight hundred people dream life away in a green-embowered village that follows the horseshoe curve of its bijou harbor. They are mostly Spanish and Indian mestizos, with a shading of San Domingo Negroes, a lightening of pure-blood Spanish officials, and a slight leavening of the froth of three or four pioneering white races. No steamers touch at Ratona save the fruit steamers which take on their banana inspectors there on their way to the coast. They leave Sunday newspapers, ice, quinine, bacon, watermelons, and vaccine matter at the island and that is about all the touch Ratona gets with the world.

The *Pájaro* paused at the mouth of the harbor, rolling heavily in the swell that sent the whitecaps racing beyond the smooth water inside. Already two dories from village—one conveying fruit inspectors, the other going for what it could get—were halfway out to the steamer.

The inspector's dory was taken on board with them, and the *Pájaro* steamed away for the mainland for its load of fruit.

The other boat returned to Ratona bearing a contribution from the *Pájaro* store of ice, the usual roll of newspapers, and one passenger—Taylor Plunkett, sheriff of Chatham County, Kentucky.

Bridger, the United States consul at Ratona, was cleaning his rifle in the official shanty under a breadfruit tree twenty yards from the water of the harbor. The consul occupied a place somewhat near the tail of his political party's procession. The music of the band wagon sounded very faintly to him in the distance. The plums of office went to others. Bridger's share of the spoils—the consulship at Ratona—was little more than a prune—a dried prune from the boarding-house depart-

ment of the public crib. But $900 yearly was opulence in
Ratona. Besides, Bridger had contracted a passion for
shooting alligators in the lagoons near his consulate, and
he was not unhappy.

He looked up from a careful inspection of his rifle
lock and saw a broad man filling his doorway. A broad,
noiseless, slow-moving man sunburned almost to a Van-
dyke brown. A man of forty-five, neatly clothed in homespun, with scanty light hair, a close-clipped brown-and-
gray beard and pale blue eyes expressing mildness and
simplicity.

"You are Mr. Bridger, the consul," said the broad man.
"They directed me here. Can you tell me what those big
bunches of things like gourds are in those trees that look
like feather dusters along the edge of the water?"

"Take that chair," said the consul, reoiling his cleaning rag. "No, the other one—that bamboo thing won't
hold you. Why, they're cocoanuts—green cocoanuts.
The shell of 'em is always a light green before they're
ripe."

"Much obliged," said the other man, sitting down carefully. "I didn't quite like to tell the folks at home they
were olives unless I was sure about it. My name is Plunkett. I'm sheriff of Chatham County, Kentucky. I've got
extradition papers in my pocket authorizing the arrest of
a man on this island. They've been signed by the President of this country, and they're in correct shape. The
man's name is Wade Williams. He's in the cocoanut-

raising business. What he's wanted for is the murder of his wife two years ago. Where can I find him?"

The consul squinted an eye and looked through his rifle barrel.

"There's nobody on the island who calls himself 'Williams,' " he remarked.

"Didn't suppose there was," said Plunkett mildly. "He'll do by any other name."

"Besides myself," said Bridger, "there are only two Americans on Ratona—Bob Reeves and Henry Morgan."

"The man I want sells cocoanuts," suggested Plunkett.

"You see that cocoanut walk extending p to the point?" said the consul, waving his hand toward the open door. "That belongs to Bob Reeves. Henry Morgan owns half the trees to loo'ard on the island."

"One month ago," said the sheriff, "Wade Williams wrote a confidential letter to a man in Chatham County, telling him where he was and how he was getting along. The letter was lost; and the person that found it gave it away. They sent me after him, and I've got the papers. I reckon he's one of your cocoanut men for certain."

"You've got his picture, of course," said Bridger. "It might be Reeves or Morgan, but I'd hate to think it. They're both as fine fellows as you'd meet in an all-day auto ride."

"No," doubtfully answered Plunkett; "there wasn't any picture of Williams to be had. And I never saw him myself. I've been sheriff only a year. But I've got a pretty accurate description of him. About 5 feet 11; dark hair and eyes; nose inclined to be Roman; heavy about the shoulders; strong, white teeth, with none missing; laughs a good deal, talkative; drinks considerably but never to intoxication; looks you square in the eye when talking; age thirty-five. Which one of your men does that description fit?"

The consul grinned broadly.

"I'll tell you what you do," he said, laying down his rifle and slipping on his dingy black alpaca coat. "You come along, Mr. Plunkett, and I'll take you up to see the boys. If you can tell which one of 'em your description fits better than it does the other you have the advantage of me."

Bridger conducted the sheriff out and along the hard beach close to which the tiny houses of the village were distributed. Immediately back of the town rose sudden, small, thickly wooded hills. Up one of these, by means of steps cut in the hard clay, the consul led Plunkett. On the very verge of an eminence was perched a two-room wooden cottage with a thatched roof. A Carib woman was washing clothes outside. The consul ushered the sheriff to the door of the room that overlooked the harbor.

Two men were in the room, about to sit down, in their shirt-sleeves, to a table spread for dinner. They bore little resemblance one to the other in detail; but the general description given by Plunkett could have been justly applied to either. In height, color of hair, shape of nose, build, and manners each of them tallied with it. They were fair types of jovial, ready-witted, broadgauged Americans who had gravitated together for companionship in an alien land.

"Hello, Bridger!" they called in unison at sight of the consul. "Come and have dinner with us!" And then they noticed Plunkett at his heels, and came forward with hospitable curiosity.

"Gentlemen," said the consul, his voice taking an unaccustomed formality, "this is Mr. Plunkett—Mr. Reeves and Mr. Morgan."

The cocoanut barons greeted the newcomer joyously. Reeves seemed about an inch taller than Morgan, but his laugh was not quite as loud. Morgan's eyes were deep brown; Reeves's were black. Reeves was the host and busied himself with fetching other chairs and calling to the Carib woman for supplemental tableware. It was explained that Morgan lived in a bamboo shack to "loo'ard," but that every day the two friends dined together. Plunkett stood still during the preparations, looking about mildly with his pale blue eyes. Bridger looked apologetic and uneasy.

At length two other covers were laid and the company was assigned to places. Reeves and Morgan stood side by side across the table from the visitors. Reeves nodded genially as a signal for all to seat themselves. And then suddenly Plunkett raised his hand with a ges-

ture of authority. He was looking straight between
Reeves and Morgan.

"Wade Williams," he said quietly, "you are under
arrest for murder."

Reeves and Morgan instantly exchanged a quick,
bright glance, the quality of which was interrogation,
with a seasoning of surprise. Then, simultaneously they
turned to the speaker with a puzzled and frank depreca-
tion in their gaze.

"Can't say that we understand you, Mr. Plunkett," said
Morgan, cheerfully. "Did you say 'Williams'?"

"What's the joke, Bridgy?" asked Reeves, turning to
the consul with a smile.

Before Bridger could answer, Plunkett spoke again.

"I'll explain," he said, quietly. "One of you don't
need any explanation, but this is for the other one. One
of you is Wade Williams of Chatham County, Kentucky.
You murdered your wife on May 5, two years ago, after
ill-treating and abusing her continually for five years.
I have the proper papers in my pocket for taking you
back with me, and you are going. We will return on the
fruit steamer that comes back by this island tomorrow
to leave its inspectors. I acknowledge, gentlemen, that
I'm not quite sure which one of you is Williams. But
Wade Williams goes back to Chatham County tomorrow.
I want you to understand that."

A great sound of merry laughter from Morgan and
Reeves went out over the still harbor. Two or three

fishermen in the fleet of sloops anchored there looked up at the house of the *diablos Americanos* on the hill and wondered.

"My dear Mr. Plunkett," cried Morgan, conquering his mirth, "the dinner is getting cold. Let us sit down and eat. I am anxious to get my spoon into that shark-fin soup. Business afterward."

"Sit down, gentlemen, if you please," added Reeves, pleasantly. "I am sure Mr. Plunkett will not object. Perhaps a little time may be of advantage to him in identifying—the gentleman he wishes to arrest."

"No objections, I'm sure," said Plunkett, dropping into his chair heavily. "I'm hungry myself. I didn't want to accept the hospitality of you folks without giving you notice; that's all."

Reeves set bottles and glasses on the table.

"There's cognac," he said, "and anisada, and Scotch 'smoke,' and rye. Take your choice."

Bridger chose rye, Reeves poured three fingers of Scotch for himself, Morgan took the same. The sheriff, against much protestation, filled his glass from the water bottle.

"Here's to the appetite," said Reeves, raising his glass, "of Mr. Williams!" Morgan's laugh and his drink encountering sent him into a choking splutter. All began to pay attention to the dinner, which was well cooked and palatable.

"Williams!" called Plunkett, suddenly and sharply.

All looked up wonderingly. Reeves found the sheriff's mild eye resting upon him. He flushed a little.

"See here," he said, with some asperity, "my name's Reeves, and I don't want you to——" But the comedy of the thing came to his rescue and he ended with a laugh.

"I suppose, Mr. Plunkett," said Morgan, carefully seasoning an alligator pear, "that you are aware of the fact that you will import a good deal of trouble for yourself into Kentucky if you take back the wrong man—that is, of course, if you take anybody back?"

"Thank you for the salt," said the sheriff. "Oh, I'll take somebody back. It'll be one of you two gentlemen. Yes, I know I'll get stuck for damages if I make a mistake. But I'm going to try to get the right man."

"I'll tell you what you do," said Morgan, leaning forward with a jolly twinkle in his eyes. "You take me. I'll go without any trouble. The cocoanut business hasn't panned out well this year, and I'd like to make some extra money out of your bondsmen."

"That's not fair," chimed in Reeves. "I got only $16 a thousand for my last shipment. Take me, Mr. Plunkett."

"I'll take Wade Williams," said the sheriff, patiently, "or I'll come pretty close to it."

"It's like dining with a ghost," remarked Morgan, with a pretended shiver. "The ghost of a murderer, too! Will somebody pass the toothpicks to the shade of the naughty Mr. Williams?"

Plunkett seemed as unconcerned as if he were dining at his own table in Chatham County. He was a gallant trencherman, and the strange tropic viands tickled his palate. Heavy, commonplace, almost slothful in his movements, he appeared to be devoid of all the cunning and watchfulness of the sleuth. He even ceased to observe, with any sharpness or attempted discrimination, the two men, one of whom he had undertaken with surprising self-confidence to drag away upon the serious charge of wife-murder. Here, indeed, was a problem set before him that if wrongly solved would have amounted to his serious discomfiture, yet there he sat puzzling his soul (to all appearances) over the novel flavor of a broiled iguana cutlet.

The consul felt a decided discomfo   Reeves and Morgan were his friends and pals; yet the sheriff from Kentucky had a certain right to his official aid and moral support. So Bridger sat the silentest around the board and tried to estimate the peculiar situation. His conclusion was that both Reeves and Morgan, quickwitted, as he knew them to be, had conceived at the moment of Plunkett's disclosure of his mission—and in the brief space of a lightning flash—the idea that the other might be the guilty Williams; and that each of them had decided in that moment loyally to protect his comrade against the doom that threatened him. This was the consul's theory, and if he had been a bookmaker at a race of wits for life and liberty he would have offered heavy odds against the plodding sheriff from Chatham County, Kentucky.

When the meal was concluded the Carib woman came and removed the dishes and cloth. Reeves strewed the table with excellent cigars, and Plunkett, with the others, lighted one of these with evident gratification.

"I may be dull," said Morgan, with a grin and a wink at Bridger; "but I want to know if I am. Now, I say this is all a joke of Mr. Plunkett's concocted to frighten two babes-in-the-woods. Is this Williamson to be taken seriously or not?"

"'Williams,'" corrected Plunkett, gravely. "I never got off any jokes in my life. I know I wouldn't travel 2,000 miles to get off a poor one as this would be if I didn't take Wade Williams back with me. Gentlemen!" continued the sheriff, now letting his mild eyes travel impartially from one of the company to another, "see if you can find any joke in this case. Wade Williams is listening to the words I utter now; but out of politeness I will speak of him as a third person. For five years he made his wife lead the life of a dog—no; I'll take that back. No dog in Kentucky was ever treated as she was. He spent the money that she brought him—spent it at races, at the card table, and on horses and hunting. He was a good fellow to his friends, but a cold, sullen demon at home. He wound up the five years of neglect by striking her with his closed hand—a hand as hard as a stone—when she was ill and weak from suffering. She

died the next day; and he skipped. That's all there is to
it. It's enough. I never never saw Williams; but I knew
his wife. I'm not a man to tell half. She and I were
keeping company when she met him. She went to Louis-
ville on a visit and saw him there. I'll admit that he spoilt
my chances in no time. I lived then on the edge of the
Cumberland Mountains. I was elected sheriff of Chatham County a year after Wade Williams killed his wife.
My official duty sends me out here after him; but I'll
admit that there's personal feeling, too. And he's going
back with me. Mr.—er—Reeves, will you pass me a
match?"

"Awfully imprudent of Williams," said Morgan, putting his feet up against the wall, "to strike a Kentucky
lady. Seems to me I've heard they were scrappers."

"Bad, bad Williams," said Reeves, pouring out more
Scotch.

The two men spoke lightly, but the consul saw and
felt the tension and the carefulness in their actions and
words. "Good old fellows," he said to himself; "they're
both all right. Each of 'em is standing by the other like
a little brick church."

And then a dog walked into the room where they sat—
a black-and-tan hound, long-eared, lazy, confident of
welcome.

Plunkett turned his head and looked at the animal,
which halted, confidently, within a few feet of his chair.

Suddenly the sheriff, with a deep-mouthed oath, left

his seat and bestowed upon the dog a vicious and heavy kick, with his ponderous shoe.

The hound, heartbroken, astonished, with flapping ears and in-curved tail, uttered a piercing yelp of pain and surprise.

Reeves and the consul remained in their chairs, saying nothing, but astonished at the unexpected show of intolerance from the easy-going man from Chatham County.

But Morgan, with a suddenly purpling face, leaped to his feet and raised a threatening arm above the guest.

"You—brute!" he shouted, passionately; "why did you do that?"

Quickly the amenities returned, Plunkett muttered some indistinct apology and regained his seat. Morgan with a decided effort controlled his indignation and also returned to his chair.

And then Plunkett, with the spring of a tiger, leaped around the corner of the table and snapped handcuffs on the paralyzed Morgan's wrists.

"Hound-lover and woman-killer!" he cried; "get ready to meet your God."

When Bridger had finished I asked him:

"Did he get the right man?"

"He did," said the consul.

"And how did he know?" I inquired, being in a kind of bewilderment.

"When he put Morgan in the dory," answered Bridger,

"the next day, to take him aboard the *Pájaro,* this man Plunkett stopped to shake hands with me and I asked him the same question.

" 'Mr. Bridger,' said he, 'I'm a Kentuckian, and I've seen a great deal of both men and animals. And I never yet saw a man that was overfond of horses and dogs but what was cruel to women.' "

THE ATAVISM OF
JOHN TOM LITTLE BEAR

I SAW A LIGHT IN JEFF PETER'S ROOM over the Red Front Drugstore. I hastened toward it, for I had not known that Jeff was in town. He is a man of the Hadji breed, of a hundred occupations, with a story to tell (when he will) of each one.

I found Jeff repacking his grip for a run down to Florida to look at an orange grove for which he had traded, a month before, his mining claim on the Yukon. He kicked me a chair, with the same old humorous, profound smile on his seasoned countenance. It had been eight months since we had met, but his greeting was such as men pass from day to day. Time is Jeff's servant, and the continent is a big lot across which he cuts to his many roads.

For a while we skirmished along the edges of un-

profitable talk which culminated in that unquiet problem
of the Philippines.

"All them tropical races," said Jeff, "could be run out
better with their own jockeys up. The tropical man
knows what he wants. All he wants is a season ticket to
the cockfights and a pair of Western Union climbers to
go up the breadfruit tree. The Anglo-Saxon man wants
him to learn to conjugate and wear suspenders. He'll be
happiest in his own way."

I was shocked.

"Education, man," I said, "is the watchword. In time
they will adopt our standard of civilization. Look at
what education has done for the Indian."

"O-ho!" sang Jeff, lighting his pipe (which was a good
sign). "Yes, the Indian! I'm looking. I hasten to contem-
plate the red man as a standard bearer of progress. He's
the same as the tropical boys. You can't make an Anglo-
Saxon of him. Did I ever tell you about the time my
friend John Tom Little Bear bit off the right ear of the
arts of culture and education and spun the teetotum back
round to where it was when Columbus was a little boy?
I did not?

"John Tom Little Bear was an educated Cherokee
Indian and an old friend of mine when I was in the Terri-
tories. He was a graduate of one of them eastern football
colleges that have been so successful in teaching the
Indian to use the gridiron instead of burning his victims
at the stake. As an Anglo-Saxon, John Tom was copper-

colored in spots. As an Indian, he was one of the whitest
men I ever knew. As a Cherokee, he was a gentleman on
the first ballot. As a ward of the nation, he was mighty
hard to carry at the primaries.

"John Tom and me got together and began to make
medicine—how to get up some lawful, genteel swindle
which we might work in a quiet way so as not to excite
the stupidity of the police or the cupidity of the larger
corporations. We had close upon $500 between us, and
we pined to make it grow, as all respectable capitalists
do.

"So we figured out a proposition which seemed to be
as honorable as a gold mine prospectus and as profitable
as a church raffle. And inside of thirty days you find us
swarming into Kansas with a pair of fluent horses and
a red camping wagon on the European plan. John Tom
is Chief Wish-Heap-Dough, the famous Indian medicine
man and Samaritan Sachem of the Seven Tribes. Mr.
Peters is business manager and half owner. We needed a
third man, so we looked around and found J. Conyngham
Binkly leaning against the want column of a newspaper.
This Binkly has a disease for Shakespearian roles, and
an hallucination about a 200 nights' run on the New York
stage. But he confesses that he never could earn the
butter to spread on his William S. roles, so he is willing
to drop to the ordinary baker's kind, and be satisfied
with a 200-mile run behind the medicine ponies. Besides
Richard III, he played twenty-seven minstrel song-and-

banjo specialties, and was willing to cook, and curry the horses. We carried a fine line of excuses for taking money. One was a magic soap for removing grease spots and quarters from clothes. One was a Sum-wah-tah, the great Indian Remedy made from a prairie herb revealed by the Great Spirit in a dream to his favorite medicine men, the great chiefs McGarrity and Siberstein, bottlers, Chicago. And the other was a frivolous system of pick-pocketing the Kansasters that had the department stores reduced to a decimal fraction. Look ye! A pair of silk garters, a dream book, one dozen clothespins, a gold tooth, and 'When Knighthood Was in Flower' all wrapped up in a genuine Japanese silkarina handkerchief and handed to the handsome lady by Mr. Peters for the trivial sum of fifty cents, while Professor Binkly entertains us in a three-minute round with the banjo.

" 'Twas an eminent graft we had. We ravaged peacefully through the State, determined to remove all doubt as to why 'twas called bleeding Kansas. John Tom Little Bear, in full Indian chief's costume, drew crowds away from the parchesi sociables and government ownership conversaziones. While at the football college in the East he had acquired quantities of rhetoric and the art of calisthenics and sophistry in his classes, and when he stood up in the red wagon and explained to the farmers, eloquent, about chilblains and hyperæsthesia of the cranium, Jeff couldn't hand out the Indian Remedy fast enough for 'em.

"One night we was camped on the edge of a little town out west of Salina. We always camped near a stream, and put up a little tent. Sometimes we sold out of the Remedy unexpected, and then Chief Wish-Heap-Dough would have a dream in which the Manitou commanded him to fill up a few bottles of Sum-wah-tah at the most convenient place. 'Twas about ten o'clock, and we'd just got in from a street performance. I was in the tent with a lantern, figuring up the day's profits. John Tom hadn't taken off his Indian make-up, and was sitting by the campfire minding a fine sirloin steak in the pan for the Professor till he finished his hair-raising scene with the trained horses.

"All at once out of dark bushes comes a pop like a firecracker, and John Tom gives a grunt and digs out of his bosom a little bullet that has dented itself against his collarbone. John Tom makes a dive in the direction of the fireworks, and comes back dragging by the collar a kid about nine or ten years young, in a velveteen suit, with a little nickel-mounted rifle in his hand about as big as a fountain pen.

"'Here, you papoose,' says John Tom, 'what are you gunning for with that howitzer? You might hit somebody in the eye. Come out, Jeff, and mind the steak. Don't let it burn, while I investigate this demon with the pea shooter.'

"'Cowardly redskin,' says the kid like he was quoting from a favorite author. 'Dare to burn me at the stake and the paleface will sweep you from the prairies like—like everything. Now, you lemme go, or I'll tell mamma.'

"John Tom plants the kid on a campstool, and sits down by him. 'Now, tell the big chief,' he says, 'why you try to shoot pellets into your Uncle John's system. Didn't you know it was loaded?'

"'Are you a Indian?' asks the kid, looking up cute as you please at John Tom's buckskin and eagle feathers. 'I am,' says John Tom. 'Well, then, that's why,' answered the boy, swinging his feet. I nearly let the steak burn watching the nerve of the youngster.

"'O-ho!' says John Tom, 'I see. You're the Boy Avenger. And you've sworn to rid the continent of the savage redman. Is that about the way of it, son?'

"The kid halfway nodded his head. And then he looked glum. 'Twas indecent to wring his secret from his bosom before a single brave had fallen before his parlor rifle.

"'Now, tell us where your wigwam is, papoose,' says John Tom—'where you live? Your mamma will be worrying about your being out so late. Tell me, and I'll take you home.'

"The kid grins. 'I guess not,' he says. 'I live thousands and thousands of miles over there.' He gyrated his hand toward the horizon. 'I come on the train,' he says, 'by myself. I got off here because the conductor said my ticket had ex-pirated.' He looks at John Tom with sudden suspicion. 'I bet you ain't a Indian,' he says. 'You don't talk like a Indian. You look like one, but all a Indian

can say is "heap good" and "paleface die." Say, I bet you
are one of them make-believe Indians that sell medicine
on the streets. I saw one once in Quincy.'

" 'You never mind,' says John Tom, 'whether I'm a
cigar sign or a Tammany cartoon. The question before
the council is what's to be done with you. You've run
away from home. You've been reading Howells. You've
disgraced the profession of boy avengers by trying to
shoot a tame Indian, and never saying: "Die, dog of a
redskin! You have crossed the path of the Boy Avenger
nineteen times too often." What do you mean by it?'

"The kid thought for a minute. 'I guess I made a mistake,' he says. 'I ought to have gone farther west. They
find 'em wild out there in the cañons.' He holds out his
hand to John Tom, the little rascal. 'Please excuse me,
sir,' says he, 'for shooting at you. I hope it didn't hurt
you. But you ought to be more careful. When a scout
sees a Indian in his war dress, his rifle must speak.'

"Little Bear gave a big laugh with a whoop at the end
of it, and swings the kid ten feet high and sets him on
his shoulder, and the runaway fingers the fringe and the
eagle feathers and is full of joy. It is very plain that
Little Bear and that kid are chums from there on in.
The little renegade has already smoked the pipe of peace
with the savage; and you can see in his eye that he is
figuring on a tomahawk and a pair of moccasins, children's size.

"We have supper in the tent. The youngster looks upon

me and the Professor as ordinary braves, only intended
as a background to the camp scene. When he is seated
on a box of Sum-wha-tah, with the edge of the table
sawing his neck, and his mouth full of beefsteak, Little
Bear calls for his name.

"'Roy,' says the kid, with a sirloiny sound to it. But
when the rest of it and his post office address are referred
to, he shakes his head. 'I guess not,' he says. 'You'll send
me back. I want to stay with you. I like this camping out.
At home, we fellows had a camp in our back yard. They
called me Roy, the Red Wolf! I guess that'll do for a
name. Gimme another piece of beefsteak, please.'

"We had to keep that kid. We knew there was a
hullabaloo about him somewheres, and that Mamma,
and Uncle Harry, and Aunt Jane, and the Chief of Police
were hot after finding his trail, but not another word
would he tell us. In two days he was the mascot of the
Big Medicine outfit, and all of us had a sneaking hope
that his owners wouldn't turn up. When the red wagon
was doing business he was in it, and passed up the bottles
to Mr. Peters as proud and satisfied as a prince that's
abjured a two-hundred-dollar crown for a million-dollar
parvenuess. Once John Tom asked him something about
his papa.

"'I ain't got any papa,' he says. 'He runned away and
left us. He made my mamma cry. Aunt Lucy says he's a
shape.' 'A what?' somebody asks him. 'A shape,' says the
kid; 'some kind of a shape—lemme see—oh, yes, a

feendenuman shape. I don't know what it means.'

"John Tom was for putting our brand on him, and
dressing him up like a little chief, with wampum and
beads, but I vetoed it. 'Somebody's lost that kid, is my
view of it, and they may want him. You let me try him
with a few stratagems, and see if I can't get a look at his
visiting card.'

"So that night I goes up to Mr. Roy Blank by the
campfire, and looks at him contemptuous and scornful.
'Snickenwitzel!' says I, like the word made me sick;
'Snickenwitzel! Bah! Before I'd be named Snickenwitzel!'

" 'What's the matter with you, Jeff?' says the kid, opening his eyes wide.

" 'Snickenwitzel!' I repeats, and I spat the word out.
'I saw a man today from your town and he told me your
full name. I'm not surprised you was ashamed to tell it.
Snickenwitzel! Whew!'

" 'Ah, here, now,' says the boy, indignant and wriggling
all over. 'What's the matter with you? That ain't my
name. It's Conyers. What's the matter with you?'

" 'And that's not the worst of it,' I went on quick, keeping him hot and not giving him time to think. 'We
thought you was from a nice, well-to-do family. Here's
Mr. Little Bear, a chief of the Cherokee, entitled to wear
nine otter tails on his Sunday blanket, and Professor
Binkly, who plays Shakespeare and the banjo, and me,
that's got hundreds of dollars in that black tin box in
the wagon, and we've got to be careful about the com-

pany we keep. That man tells me your folks live 'way
down in little old Hencoop Alley, where there are no
sidewalks, and the goats eat off the table with you.'
"That kid was almost crying now. ' 'Tain't so,' he
splutters. 'He—he don't know what he's talking about.
We live on Poplar Av'noo. I don't 'sociate with goats.
What's the matter with you?'
" 'Poplar Avenue,' says I, sarcastic. 'Poplar Avenue!
That's a street to live on! It only runs two blocks and
then falls off a bluff. You can throw a keg of nails the
whole length of it. Don't talk to me about Poplar Avenue.'
" 'It's—it's miles long,' says the kid. 'Our number's
862 and there are lots of houses after that. What's the
matter with—aw, you make me tired, Jeff.'
"Well, well, now,' says I. 'I guess that man made a
mistake. Maybe it was some other boy he was talking
about. If I catch him I'll teach him to go around slander-
ing people.'
"After supper I goes up town and telegraphs to Mrs.
Conyers, 862 Poplar Avenue, Quincy, Ill., that the kid
is safe and sassy with us, and will be held for further
orders. In two hours an answer comes to hold him
tight, and she'll start for him by next train.
"The next train was due at 6 P.M. the next day, and
me and John Tom was at the depot with the kid. You
might scour the plains in vain for the big Chief Wish-
Heap-Dough. In his place is Mr. Little Bear, in the
human habiliments of the Anglo-Saxon sect; and the

leather of his shoes is patented and the loop of his necktie
is copyrighted. For these things John Tom had grafted
on him at college along with metaphysics and the
knockout guard for the low tackle. But for his complexion, which is some yellowish, and the black mop of
his straight hair, you might have thought here was an
ordinary man out of the city directory that subscribes
for magazines and pushes the lawn mower in his shirt-
sleeves of evenings.

"Then the train rolled in, and a little woman in a gray
dress, with sort of illuminating hair, slides off and looks
around quick. And the Boy Avenger sees her, and yells
'Mamma,' and she cries 'O!' and they meet in a clinch,
and now the pesky redskins can come forth from their
caves on the plains without fear any more of the rifle of
Roy, the Red Wolf. Mrs. Conyers comes up and thanks
me an' John Tom without the usual extremities you always look for in a woman. She says just enough, in a
way to convince, and there is no incidental music by the
orchestra. I made a few illiterate requisitions upon the art
of conversation, at which the lady smiles friendly, as if
she had known me a week. And then Mr. Little Bear
adorns the atmosphere with the various idioms into which
education can fracture the wind of speech. I could see
the kid's mother didn't quite place John Tom; but it
seemed she was apprised of his dialects, and she played
up to his lead in the science of making three words do the
work of one.

"That kid introduced us, with some footnotes and explanations that made things plainer than a week of rhetoric. He danced around, and punched us in the back, and tried to climb John Tom's leg. 'This is John Tom, mamma,' says he. 'He's an Indian. He sells medicine in a red wagon. I shot him, but he wasn't wild. The other one's Jeff. He's a fakir, too. Come on and see the camp where we live, won't you, mamma?'

"It is plain to see that the life of the woman is in that boy. She has got him again where her arms can gather him, and that's enough. She's ready to do anything to please him. She hesitates the eighth of a second and takes another look at these men. I imagine she says to herself about John Tom, 'Seems to be a gentleman, if his hair don't curl.' And Mr. Peters she disposes of as follows: 'No ladies' man, but a man who knows a lady.'

"So we all rambled down to the camp as neighborly as coming from a wake. And there she inspects the wagon and pats the place with her hand where the kid used to sleep, and dabs around her eyewinkers with her handkerchief. And Professor Binkly gives us 'Trovatore' on one string of the banjo, and is about to slide off into Hamlet's monologue when one of the horses gets tangled in his rope and he must go look after him, and says something about 'foiled again.'

"When it got dark me and John Tom walked back to the Corn Exchange Hotel, and the four of us had supper there. I think the trouble started at that supper, for then

was when Mr. Little Bear made an intellectual balloon
ascension. I held on to the tablecloth, and listened to him
soar. That redman, if I could judge, had the gift of information. He took languages, and did with it all a Roman
can do with macaroni. His vocal remarks was all embroidered over with the most scholarly verbs and prefixes.
And his syllables was smooth, and fitted nicely to the
joints of his idea. I thought I'd heard him talk before, but
I hadn't. And it wasn't the size of his words, but the way
they come; and 'twasn't his subjects, for he spoke of
common things like cathedrals and football and poems
and catarrh and souls and freight rates and sculpture.
Mrs. Conyers understood his accents, and the elegant
sounds went back and forth between 'em. And now and
then Jefferson D. Peters would intervene a few shopworn,
senseless words to have the butter passed or another leg
of the chicken.

"Yes, John Tom Little Bear appeared to be inveigled
some in his bosom about that Mrs. Conyers. She was of
the kind that pleases. She had the good looks and more,
I'll tell you. You take one of those cloak models in a big
store. They strike you as being on the impersonal system.
They are adapted for the eye. What they run to is inches
around and complexion, and the art of fanning the delu-
sion that the sealskin would look just as well on the lady
with the warts and the pocketbook. Now, if one of them
models was off duty, and you took it, and it would say
'Charlie' when you pressed it, and sit up at the table,

why, then you would have something similar to Mrs. Conyers. I could see how John Tom could resist any inclination to hate that white squaw.

"The lady and the kid stayed at the hotel. In the morning, they say, they will start for home. Me and Little Bear left at eight o'clock, and sold Indian Remedy on the courthouse square till nine. He leaves me and the Professor to drive down to camp, while he stays up town. I am not enamored with that plan, for it shows John Tom is uneasy in his composures, and that leads to firewater, and sometimes to the green-corn dance and costs. Not often does Chief Wish-Heap-Dough get busy with the firewater, but whenever he does there is heap much doing in the lodges of the palefaces who wear blue and carry the club.

"At half past nine Professor Binkly is rolled in his quilt snoring in blank verse, and I am sitting by the fire listening to the frogs. Mr. Little Bear slides into camp and sits down against a tree. There is no symptoms of firewater.

" 'Jeff,' says he, after a long time, 'a little boy came West to hunt Indians.'

" 'Well, then?' says I, for I wasn't thinking as he was.

" 'And he bagged one,' says John Tom, 'and 'twas not with a gun, and he never had on a velveteen suit of clothes in his life.' And then I began to catch his smoke.

" 'I know it,' says I. 'And I'll bet you his pictures are on valentines, and fool men are his game, red and white.'

" 'You win on the red,' says John Tom, calm. 'Jeff, for

how many ponies do you think I could buy Mrs. Conyers?'

" 'Scandalous talk!' I replies. ' 'Tis not a paleface custom.' John Tom laughs loud and bites into his cigar. 'No,'
he answers; ' 'tis the savage equivalent for the dollars of
the white man's marriage settlement. Oh, I know. There's
an eternal wall between the races. If I could do it, Jeff,
I'd put a torch to every white college that a redman has
ever set foot inside. Why don't you leave us alone,' he
says, 'to our own ghost dances and dog feasts and our
dingy squaws to cook our grasshopper soup and darn our
moccasins?'

" 'Now, you don't mean disrespect to the perennial
blossom entitled education?' says I, scandalized, 'because
I wear it in the bosom of my own intellectual shirtwaist.
I've had education,' says I, 'and never took any harm from
it.'

" 'You lasso us,' goes on Little Bear, not noticing my
prose insertions, 'and teach us what is beautiful in literature and life, and how to appreciate what is fine in men
and women. What have you done to me?' says he. 'You've
made me a Cherokee Moses. You've taught me to hate
the wigwams and love the white man's ways. I can look
over into the promised land and see Mrs. Conyers, but my
place is—on the reservation.'

"Little Bear stands up in his chief's dress, and laughs
again. 'But, white man Jeff,' he goes on, 'the paleface
provides a recourse. 'Tis a temporary one, but it gives a
respite and the name of it is whiskey.' And straight off he

walks up the path to town again. 'Now,' says I in my mind, 'may the Manitou move him to do only bailable things this night!' For I perceive that John Tom is about to avail himself of the white man's solace.

"Maybe it was 10:30, as I sat smoking, when I hear pit-a-pats on the path, and here comes Mrs. Conyers running, her hair twisted up any way, and a look on her face that says burglars and mice and the flour's-all-out rolled in one. 'Oh, Mr. Peters,' she calls out, as they will. 'Oh, oh!' I made a quick think, and I spoke the gist of it out loud. 'Now,' says I, 'we've been brothers, me and that Indian, but I'll make a good one of him in two minutes if——'

" 'No, no,' she says, wild and cracking her knuckles, 'I haven't seen Mr. Little Bear. 'Tis my—husband. He's stolen my boy. Oh,' she says, 'just when I had him back in my arms again! That heartless villain! Every bitterness life knows,' she says, 'he's made me drink. My poor little lamb, that ought to be warm in his bed, carried off by that fiend!'

" 'How did all this happen?' I ask. 'Let's have the facts.'

" 'I was fixing his bed,' she explains, 'and Roy was playing on the hotel porch and he drives up to the steps. I heard Roy scream, and ran out. My husband had him in the buggy then. I begged him for my child. This is what he gave me.' She turns her face to the light. There is a crimson streak running across her cheek and mouth. 'He did that with his whip,' she says.

" 'Come back to the hotel,' says I, 'and we'll see what can be done.'

"On the way she tells me some of the wherefores. When he slashed her with the whip he told her he found out she was coming for the kid, and he was on the same train. Mrs. Conyers had been living with her brother, and they'd watched the boy always, as her husband had tried to steal him before. I judge that man was worse than a street railway promoter. It seems he had spent her money and slugged her and killed her canary bird, and told it around that she had cold feet.

"At the hotel we found a mass meeting of five infuriated citizens chewing tobacco and denouncing the outrage. Most of the town was asleep by ten o'clock. I talks to the lady some, quiet, and tells her I will take the one o'clock train for the next town, forty miles east, for it is likely that the esteemed Mr. Conyers will drive there to take the cars. 'I don't know,' I tells her, 'but what he has legal rights; but if I find him I can give him an illegal left in the eye, and tie him up for a day or two, anyhow, on a disturbal of the peace proposition.'

"Mrs. Conyers goes inside and cries with the landlord's wife, who is fixing some catnip tea that will make everything all right for the poor dear. The landlord comes out on the porch, thumbing his one suspender, and says:

" 'Ain't had so much excitement in town since Bedford Steegall's wife swallowed a spring lizard. I seen him through the winder hit her with the buggy whip, and everything. What's that suit of clothes cost you you got on? 'Pears like we'd have some rain, don't it? Say, doc, that Indian of yorn's on a kind of a whizz tonight, ain't he? He comes along just before you did, and I told him about this here occurrence. He gives a cur'us kind of a hoot, and trotted off. I guess our constable'll have him in the lockup 'fore morning.'

"I thought I'd sit on the porch and wait for the one o'clock train. I wasn't feeling saturated with mirth. Here was John Tom on one of his sprees, and this kidnapping business losing sleep for me. But then, I'm always having trouble with other people's trouble. Every few minutes Mrs. Conyers would come out on the porch and look down the road the way the buggy went, like she expected to see that kid coming back on a white pony with a red apple in his hand. Now, wasn't that like a woman? And that brings up cats. 'I saw a mouse go in this hole,' says Mrs. Cat; 'you can go prize up a plank over there if you like; I'll watch this hole.'

"About a quarter to one o'clock the lady comes out again, restless, crying easy, as females do for their own amusement, and she looks down that road again and listens. 'Now, ma'am,' says I, 'there's no use watching cold wheel tracks. By this time they're halfway to——'

" 'Hush,' she says, holding up her hand. And I do hear something coming 'flip-flap' in the dark; and then there is the awfullest war whoop ever heard outside of Madison Square Garden at a Buffalo Bill matinée. And up the

steps and on to the porch jumps the disrespectable Indian. The lamp in the hall shines on him, and I fail to
recognize Mr. J. T. Little Bear, alumnus of the class of
'91. What I see is a Cherokee brave, and the warpath is
what he has been traveling. Firewater and other things
have got him going. His buckskin is hanging in strings,
and his feathers are mixed up like a frizzly hen's. The
dust of miles is on his moccasins, and the light in his eye
is the kind the aborigines wear. But in his arms he brings
that kid, his eyes half closed, with his little shoes dangling
and one hand fast around the Indian's collar.

"'Papoose!' says John Tom, and I notice that the
flowers of the white man's syntax have left his tongue. He
is the original proposition in bear's claws and copper
color. 'Me bring,' says he, and he lays the kid in his
mother's arms. 'Run fifteen mile,' says John Tom—'Ugh!
Catch white man. Bring papoose.'

"The little woman is in extremities of gladness. She
must wake up that stir-up trouble youngster and hug him
and make proclamation that he is his mamma's own
precious treasure. I was about to ask questions, but I
looked at Mr. Little Bear, and my eye caught the sight
of something in his belt. 'Now go to bed, ma'am,' says I,
'and this gadabout youngster likewise, for there's no more
danger, and the kidnapping business is not what it was
earlier in the night.'

"I inveigled John Tom down to camp quick, and when
he tumbled over asleep I got that thing out of his belt and

disposed of it where the eye of education can't see it. For even the football colleges disapprove of the art of scalp-taking in their curriculums.

"It is ten o'clock next day when John Tom wakes up and looks around. I am glad to see the nineteenth century in his eyes again.

" 'What was it, Jeff?' he asked.

" 'Heap firewater,' says I.

"John Tom frowns, and thinks a little. 'Combined,' says he directly, 'with the interesting little physiological shake-up known as reversion to type. I remember now. Have they gone yet?'

" 'On the 7:30 train,' I answers.

" 'Ugh!' says John Tom; 'better so. Paleface, bring big Chief Wish-Heap-Dough a little bromo-seltzer, and then he'll take up the red man's burden again.' "

✦

JIMMY HAYES
AND MURIEL

SUPPER WAS OVER, AND THERE HAD
fallen upon the camp the silence that accompanies the
rolling of corn-husk cigarettes. The water hole shone from
the dark earth like a patch of fallen sky. Coyotes yelped.
Dull thumps indicated the rocking-horse movements of
the hobbled ponies as they moved to fresh grass. A half-
troop of the Frontier Battalion of Texas Rangers were
distributed about the fire.

A well-known sound—the fluttering and scraping of
chaparral against wooden stirrups—came from the thick
brush above the camp. The rangers listened cautiously.
They heard a loud cheerful voice call out reassuringly:

"Brace up, Muriel, old girl, we're 'most there now! Been
a long ride for ye, ain't it, ye old antediluvian handful of
animated carpet tacks? Hey, now, quit a tryin' to kiss me!
Don't hold on to my neck so tight—this here paint hoss

ain't any too shore-footed, let me tell ye. He's liable to
dump us both off if we don't watch out."

Two minutes of waiting brought a tired "paint" pony
single-footing into camp. A gangling youth of twenty
lolled in the saddle. Of the "Muriel" whom he had been
addressing, nothing was to be seen.

"Hi, fellows!" shouted the rider, cheerfully. "This here's
a letter fer Lieutenant Manning."

He dismounted, unsaddled, dropped the coils of his
stake-rope, and got his hobbles from the saddle-horn.
While Lieutenant Manning, in command, was reading
the letter, the newcomer rubbed solicitously at some
dried mud in the loops of the hobbles, showing a con-
sideration for the forelegs of his mount.

"Boys," said the lieutenant, waving his hand to the
rangers, "this is Mr. James Hayes. He's a new member of
the company. Captain McLean sends him down from El
Paso. The boys will see that you have some supper,
Hayes, as soon as you get your pony hobbled."

The recruit was received cordially by the rangers. Still,
they observed him shrewdly and with suspended judgment. Picking a comrade on the border is done with ten
times the care and discretion with which a girl chooses a
sweetheart. On your "side-kicker's" nerve, loyalty, aim,
and coolness your own life may depend many times.

After a hearty supper Hayes joined the smokers about
the fire. His appearance did not settle all the questions in
the minds of his brother rangers. They saw simply a loose,

lank youth with tow-colored sunburned hair and a berry-brown, ingenuous face that wore a quizzical, good-natured smile.

"Fellows," said the new ranger, "I'm goin' to interduce to you a lady friend of mine. Ain't ever heard anybody call her a beauty, but you'll all admit she's got some fine points about her. Come along, Muriel!"

He held open the front of his blue flannel shirt. Out of it crawled a horned frog. A bright red ribbon was tied jauntily around its spiky neck. It crawled to its owner's knee and sat there motionless.

"This here Muriel," said Hayes, with an oratorical wave of his hand, "has got qualities. She never talks back, she always stays at home, and she's satisfied with one red dress for everyday and Sunday, too."

"Look at that blame insect!" said one of the rangers with a grin. "I've seen plenty of them horny frogs, but I never knew anybody to have one for a side-partner. Does the blame thing know you from anybody else?"

"Take it over there and see," said Hayes.

The stumpy little lizard known as the horned frog is harmless. He has the hideousness of the prehistoric monsters whose reduced descendant he is, but he is gentler than the dove.

The ranger took Muriel from Hayes's knee and went back to his seat on a roll of blankets. The captive twisted and clawed and struggled vigorously in his hand. After holding it for a moment or two, the ranger set it upon the ground. Awkwardly, but swiftly, the frog worked its four oddly moving legs until it stopped close by Hayes's foot.

"Well, dang my hide!" said the other ranger. "The little cuss knows you. Never thought them insects had that much sense!"

Jimmy Hayes became a favorite in the ranger camp. He had an endless store of good nature, and a mild, perennial quality of humor that is well adapted to camp life. He was never without his horned frog. In the bosom of his shirt during rides, on his knee or shoulder in camp, under his blankets at night, the ugly little beast never left him.

Jimmy was a humorist of a type that prevails in the rural South and West. Unskilled in originating methods of amusing or in witty conceptions, he had hit upon a comical idea and clung to it reverently. It had seemed to Jimmy a very funny thing to have about his person, with which to amuse his friends, a tame horned frog with a red ribbon around its neck. As it was a happy idea, why not perpetuate it?

The sentiments existing between Jimmy and the frog cannot be exactly determined. The capability of the horned frog for lasting affection is a subject upon which we have no symposiums. It is easier to guess Jimmy's feelings. Muriel was his *chef d'œuvre* of wit, and as such he cherished her. He caught flies for her, and shielded her from sudden northers. Yet his care was half selfish, and when the time came she repaid him a thousandfold. Other

Muriels have thus overbalanced the light attentions of other Jimmies.

Not at once did Jimmy attain full brotherhood with his comrades. They loved him for his simplicity and drollness, but there hung above him a great sword of suspended judgment. To make merry in camp is not all of a ranger's life. There are horse thieves to trail, desperate criminals to run down, bravos to battle with, bandits to rout out of the chaparral, peace and order to be compelled at the muzzle of a six-shooter. Jimmy had been "'most generally a cowpuncher," he said; he was inexperienced in ranger methods of warfare. Therefore the rangers speculated apart and solemnly as to how he would stand fire. For, let it be known, the honor and pride of each ranger company is the individual bravery of its members.

For two months the border was quiet. The rangers lolled, listless, in camp. And then—bringing joy to the rusting guardians of the frontier—Sebastiano Saldar, an eminent Mexican desperado and cattle thief, crossed the Rio Grande with his gang and began to lay waste the Texas side. There were indications that Jimmy Hayes would soon have the opportunity to show his mettle. The rangers patrolled with alacrity, but Saldar's men were mounted like Lochinvar, and were hard to catch.

One evening, about sundown, the rangers halted for supper after a long ride. Their horses stood panting, with their saddles on. The men were frying bacon and boiling

coffee. Suddenly, out of the brush, Sebastiano Saldar and
his gang dashed upon them with blazing six-shooters and
high-voiced yells. It was a neat surprise. The rangers
swore in annoyed tones, and got their Winchesters busy;
but the attack was only a spectacular dash of the purest
Mexican type. After the florid demonstration the raiders
galloped away, yelling, down the river. The rangers
mounted and pursued; but in less than two miles the
fagged ponies labored so that Lieutenant Manning gave
the word to abandon the chase and return to the camp.

Then it was discovered that Jimmy Hayes was missing.
Someone remembered having seen him run for his pony
when the attack began, but no one had set eyes on him
since. Morning came, but no Jimmy. They searched the
country around, on the theory that he had been killed or
wounded, but without success. Then they followed after
Saldar's gang, but it seemed to have disappeared. Manning concluded that the wily Mexican had recrossed the
river after his theatric farewell. And, indeed, no further
depredations from him were reported.

This gave the rangers time to nurse a soreness they
had. As has been said, the pride and honor of the company is the individual bravery of its members. And now
they believed that Jimmy Hayes had turned coward at
the whiz of Mexican bullets. There was no other deduction. Buck Davis pointed out that not a shot was fired by
Saldar's gang after Jimmy was seen running for his horse.
There was no way for him to have been shot. No, he had

fled from his first fight, and afterward he would not return, aware that the scorn of his comrades would be a worse thing to face than the muzzles of many rifles.

So Manning's detachment of McLean's company, Frontier Battalion, was gloomy. It was the first blot on its escutcheon. Never before in the history of the service had a ranger shown the white feather. All of them had liked Jimmy Hayes, and that made it worse.

Days, weeks, and months went by, and still that little cloud of unforgotten cowardice hung above the camp.

Nearly a year afterward—after many camping grounds and many hundreds of miles guarded and defended—Lieutenant Manning, with almost the same detachment of men, was sent to a point only a few miles below their old camp on the river to look after some smuggling there. One afternoon, while they were riding through a dense mesquite flat, they came upon a patch of open hog-wallow prairie. There they rode upon the scene of an unwritten tragedy.

In a big hog-wallow lay the skeletons of three Mexicans. Their clothing alone served to identify them. The largest of the figures had once been Sebastiano Saldar. His great, costly sombrero, heavy with gold ornamentation—a hat famous all along the Rio Grande—lay there pierced by three bullets. Along the ridge of the hog-wallow rested the rusting Winchesters of the Mexicans—all pointing in the same direction.

The rangers rode in that direction for fifty yards. There, in a little depression of the ground, with his rifle still bearing upon the three, lay another skeleton. It had been a battle of extermination. There was nothing to identify the solitary defender. His clothing—such as the elements had left distinguishable—seemed to be of the kind that any ranchman or cowboy might have worn.

"Some cowpuncher," said Manning, "that they caught out alone. Good boy! He put up a dandy scrap before they got him. So that's why we didn't hear from Don Sebastiano any more!"

And then, from beneath the weather-beaten rags of the dead man, there wriggled out a horned frog with a faded red ribbon around its neck, and sat upon the shoulder of its long quiet master. Mutely it told the story of the untried youth and the swift "paint" pony—how they had outstripped all their comrades that day in the pursuit of the Mexican raiders, and how the boy had gone down upholding the honor of the company.

The ranger troop herded close, and a simultaneous wild yell arose from their lips. The outburst was at once a dirge, an apology, an epitaph, and a pæan of triumph. A strange requiem, you may say, over the body of a fallen comrade; but if Jimmy Hayes could have heard it he would have understood.

HYGEIA AT THE
SOLITO

If you are knowing in the chroni-
cles of the ring you will recall to mind an event in the
early nineties when, for a minute and sundry odd seconds, a champion and a "would-be" faced each other
on the alien side of an international river. So brief a
conflict had rarely imposed upon the fair promise of
true sport. The reporters made what they could of it, but,
divested of padding, the action was sadly fugacious.
The champion merely smote his victim, turned his back
upon him, remarking, "I know what I done to dat stiff,"
and extended an arm like a ship's mast for his glove
to be removed.

Which accounts for a trainload of extremely disgusted
gentlemen in uproar of fancy vests and neckwear being

spilled from their Pullman in San Antonio in the early morning following the fight. Which also partly accounts for the unhappy predicament in which "Cricket" Mc-Guire found himself as he tumbled from his car and sat upon the depot platform, torn by a spasm of that hollow, racking cough so familiar to San Antonian ears. At that time, in the uncertain light of dawn, that way passed Curtis Raidler, the Nueces County cattleman—may his shadow never measure under six feet two.

The cattleman, out this early to catch the southbound for his ranch station, stopped at the side of the distressed patron of sport and spoke in the kindly drawl of his ilk and region, "Got it pretty bad, bud?"

"Cricket" McGuire, ex-featherweight prize fighter, and tout, jockey, follower of the "ponies," all-around sport, and manipulator of the gum balls and walnut shells, looked up pugnaciously at the imputation cast by "bud."

"G'wan," he rasped, "telegraph pole. I didn't ring for yer."

Another paroxysm wrung him, and he leaned limply against a convenient baggage truck. Raidler waited patiently, glancing around at the white hats, short overcoats, and big cigars thronging the platform. "You're from the No'th, ain't you, bud?" he asked when the other was partially recovered. "Come down to see the fight?"

"Fight!" snapped McGuire. "Puss-in-the-corner! 'Twas a hypodermic injection. Handed him just one like a squirt of dope, and he's asleep, and no tanbark needed in front of his residence. Fight!" He rattled a bit, coughed, and went on, hardly addressing the cattleman, but rather for the relief of voicing his troubles. "No more dead sure t'ings for me. But Rus Sage himself would have snatched at it. Five to one dat de boy from Cork wouldn't stay t'ree rounds is what I invested in. Put my last cent on, and could already smell the sawdust in dat all-night joint of Jimmy Delaney's on T'irty-seventh Street I was goin' to buy. And den—say, telegraph pole, what a gazaboo a guy is to put his whole roll on one turn of the gaboozlum!"

"You're plenty right," said the big cattleman; "more 'specially when you lose. Son, you get up and light out for a hotel. You got a mighty bad cough. Had it long?"

"Lungs," said McGuire comprehensively. "I got it. The croaker says I'll come to time for six months longer— maybe a year if I hold my gait. I wanted to settle down and take care of myself. Dat's why I speculated on dat five to one perhaps. I had a t'ousand iron dollars saved up. If I winned I was goin' to buy Delaney's café. Who'd a t'ought dat stiff would take a nap in de foist round— say?"

"It's a hard deal," commented Raidler, looking down at the diminutive form of McGuire crumpled against the truck. "But you go to a hotel and rest. There's the Menger and the Maverick, and——"

"And the Fi'th Av'noo, and the Waldorf-Astoria," mimicked McGuire. "Told you I went broke. I'm on de

bum proper. I've got one dime left. Maybe a trip to
Europe or a sail in me private yacht would fix me up—
paper!"

He flung his dime at a newsboy, got his *Express*,
propped his back against the truck, and was at once rapt
in the account of his Waterloo, as expanded by the ingenious press.

Curtis Raidler interrogated an enormous gold watch,
and laid his hand on McGuire's shoulder.

"Come on, bud," he said. "We got three minutes to
catch the train."

Sarcasm seemed to be McGuire's vein.

"You ain't seen me cash in any chips or call a turn
since I told you I was broke, a minute ago, have you?
Friend, chase yourself away."

"You're going down to my ranch," said the cattleman,
"and stay till you get well. Six months'll fix you good as
new." He lifted McGuire with one hand, and half-
dragged him in the direction of the train.

"What about the money?" said McGuire, struggling
weakly to escape.

"Money for what?" asked Raidler, puzzled. They eyed
each other, not understanding, for they touched only as
at the gear of bevelled cogwheels—at right angles, and
moving upon different axes.

Passengers on the southbound saw them seated together, and wondered at the conflux of two such anti-
podes. McGuire was five feet one, with a countenance

belonging to either Yokohama or Dublin. Bright-beady
of eye, bony of cheek and jaw, scarred, toughened,
broken and reknit, indestructible, grisly, gladiatorial as a
hornet, he was a type neither new nor unfamiliar. Raidler
was the product of a different soil. Six feet two in height,
miles broad, and no deeper than a crystal brook, he
represented the union of the West and South. Few accurate pictures of his kind have been made, for art galleries are so small and the mutoscope is as yet unknown
in Texas. After all, the only possible medium of portrayal
of Raidler's kind would be the fresco—something high
and simple and cool and unframed.

They were rolling southward on the International. The
timber was huddling into little, dense green motts at
rare distances before the inundation of the downright,
vert prairies. This was the land of the ranches, the domain
of the kings of the kine.

McGuire sat, collapsed into his corner of the seat,
receiving with acid suspicion the conversation of the
cattleman. What was the "game" of this big "geezer"
who was carrying him off? Altruism would have been
McGuire's last guess. "He ain't no farmer," thought the
captive, "and he ain't no con man, for sure. W'at's his
lay? You trail in, Cricket, and see how many cards he
draws. You're up against it, anyhow. You got a nickel
and gallopin' consumption, and you better lay low. Lay
low and see w'at's his game."

At Rincon, a hundred miles from San Antonio, they

left the train for a buckboard which was waiting there
for Raidler. In this they travelled the thirty miles between the station and their destination. If anything
could, this drive should have stirred the acrimonious
McGuire to a sense of his ransom. They sped upon velvet
wheels across an exhilarant savanna. The pair of Spanish
ponies struck a nimble, tireless trot, which gait they
occasionally relieved by a wild, untrammelled gallop.
The air was wine and seltzer, perfumed, as they absorbed it, with the delicate redolence of prairie flowers.
The road perished, and the buckboard swam the un-
charted billows of the grass itself, steered by the practised hand of Raidler, to whom each tiny distant mott
of trees was a signboard, each convolution of the low
hills a voucher of course and distance. But McGuire
reclined upon his spine, seeing nothing but a desert, and
receiving the cattleman's advances with sullen distrust.
"W'at's he up to?" was the burden of his thoughts; "w'at
kind of a gold brick has the big guy got to sell?" McGuire
was only applying the measure of the streets he had
walked to a range bounded by the horizon and the
fourth dimension.

A week before, while riding the prairies, Raidler had
come upon a sick and weakling calf deserted and bawl-
ing. Without dismounting he had reached and slung the
distressed bossy across his saddle, and dropped it at the
ranch for the boys to attend to. It was impossible for
McGuire to know or comprehend that, in the eyes of

the cattleman, his case and that of the calf were identical
in interest and demand upon his assistance. A creature
was ill and helpless; he had the power to render aid—
these were the only postulates required for the cattleman
to act. They formed his system of logic and the most of
his creed. McGuire was the seventh invalid whom Raidler
had picked up thus casually in San Antonio, where so
many thousand go for the ozone that is said to linger
about its contracted streets. Five of them had been
guests of Solito Ranch until they had been able to leave,
cured or better, and exhausting the vocabulary of tearful
gratitude. One came too late, but rested very comfortably, at last, under a ratama tree in the garden.

So, then, it was no surprise to the ranchhold when
the buckboard spun to the door, and Raidler took up
his debile *protégé* like a handful of rags and set him
down upon the gallery.

McGuire looked upon things strange to him. The ranch
house was the best in the country. It was built of brick
hauled one hundred miles by wagon, but it was of but
one story, and its four rooms were completely encircled
by a mud floor "gallery." The miscellaneous setting of
horses, dogs, saddles, wagons, guns, and cowpunchers'
paraphernalia oppressed the metropolitan eye of the
wrecked sportsman.

"Well, here we are at home," said Raidler, cheeringly.

"It's a h—l of a looking place," said McGuire promptly,
as he rolled upon the gallery floor, in a fit of coughing.

"We'll try to make it comfortable for you, buddy," said the cattleman, gently. "It ain't fine inside; but it's the outdoors, anyway, that'll do you the most good. This'll be your room, in here. Anything we got, you ask for it."

He led McGuire into the east room. The floor was bare and clean. White curtains waved in the gulf breeze through the open windows. A big willow rocker, two straight chairs, a long table covered with newspapers, pipes, tobacco, spurs, and cartridges stood in the centre. Some well-mounted heads of deer and one of an enormous black javeli projected from the walls. A wide, cool cot-bed stood in a corner. Nueces County people regarded this guest chamber as fit for a prince. McGuire showed his eye teeth at it. He took out his nickel and spun it up to the ceiling.

"T'ought I was lyin' about the money, did ye? Well, you can frisk me if you wanter. Dat's the last simoleon in the treasury. Who's goin' to pay?"

The cattleman's clear gray eyes looked steadily from under his grizzly brows into the huckleberry optics of his guest. After a little he said simply, and not ungraciously, "I'll be much obliged to you, son, if you won't mention money any more. Once was quite a plenty. Folks I ask to my ranch don't have to pay anything, and they very scarcely ever offers it. Supper'll be ready in half an hour. There's water in the pitcher, and some cooler to drink, in that red jar hanging on the gallery."

"Where's the bell?" asked McGuire, looking about.

"Bell for what?"

"Bell to ring for things. I can't—see here," he exploded in a sudden weak fury, "I never asked you to bring me here. I never held you up for a cent. I never gave you a hard-luck story till you asked me. Here I am fifty mile from a bellboy or a cocktail. I'm sick. I can't hustle. Gee! but I'm up against it!" McGuire fell upon the cot and sobbed shiveringly.

Raidler went to the door and called. A slender, bright-complexioned Mexican youth about twenty came quickly. Raidler spoke to him in Spanish.

"Ylario, it is in my mind that I promised you the position of *vaquero* on the San Carlos range at the fall *rodeo*."

"*Si señor*, such was your goodness."

"Listen. This *señorito* is my friend. He is very sick. Place yourself at his side. Attend to his wants at all times. Have much patience and care with him. And when he is well, or—and when he is well, instead of *vaquero* I will make you *mayordomo* of the Rancho de las Piedras. *Está bueno?*"

"*Si, si—mil gracias, señor*." Ylario tried to kneel upon the floor in his gratitude, but the cattleman kicked at him benevolently, growling, "None of your opery-house antics, now."

Ten minutes later Ylario came from McGuire's room and stood before Raidler.

"The little *señor*," he announced, "presents his compliments" (Raidler credited Ylario with the preliminary) "and desires some pounded ice, one hot bath, one gin feez-z, that the windows be all closed, toast, one shave, one Newyorkheral', cigarettes, and to send one telegram."

Raidler took a quart bottle of whisky from his medicine cabinet. "Here, take him this," he said.

Thus was instituted the reign of terror at the Solito Ranch. For a few weeks McGuire blustered and boasted and swaggered before the cowpunchers who rode in for miles around to see this latest importation of Raidler's. He was an absolutely new experience to them. He explained to them all the intricate points of sparring and the tricks of training and defence. He opened to their minds' view all the indecorous life of a tagger after professional sports. His jargon of slang was a continuous joy and surprise to them. His gestures, his strange poses, his frank ribaldry of tongue and principle fascinated them. He was like a being from a new world.

Strange to say, this new world he had entered did not exist to him. He was an utter egoist of bricks and mortar. He had dropped out, he felt, into open space for a time, and all it contained was an audience for his reminiscences. Neither the limitless freedom of the prairie days nor the grand hush of the close-drawn, spangled nights touched him. All the hues of Aurora could not win him from the pink pages of a sporting journal. "Get something for nothing," was his mission in life; "T'irty-seventh" Street was his goal.

Nearly two months after his arrival he began to complain that he felt worse. It was then that he became e

ranch's incubus, its harpy, its Old Man of the Sea. He
shut himself in his room like some venomous kobold
or flibbertigibbet, whining, complaining, cursing, accusing. The keynote of his plaint was that he had been inveigled into a gehenna against his will; that he was
dying of neglect and lack of comforts. With all his dire
protestations of increasing illness, to the eye of others
he remained unchanged. His currant-like eyes were as
bright and diabolic as ever; his voice was as rasping;
his callous face, with the skin drawn tense as a drum-
head, had no flesh to lose. A flush on his prominent cheek
bones each afternoon hinted that a clinical thermometer
might have revealed a symptom, and percussion might
have established the fact that McGuire was breathing
with only one lung, but his appearance remained the
same.

In constant attendance upon him was Ylario, whom
the coming reward of the *mayordomoship* must have
greatly stimulated, for McGuire chained him to a bitter
existence. The air—the man's only chance for life—he
commanded to be kept out by closed windows and drawn
curtains. The room was always blue and foul with
cigarette smoke; whosoever entered it must sit, suffo-
cating, and listen to the imp's interminable gasconade
concerning his scandalous career.

The oddest thing of all was the relation existing
between McGuire and his benefactor. The attitude of
the invalid toward the cattleman was something like

that of a peevish, perverse child toward an indulgent parent. When Raidler would leave the ranch McGuire would fall into a fit of malevolent, silent sullenness. When he returned, he would be met by a string of violent and stinging reproaches. Raidler's attitude toward his charge was quite inexplicable in its way. The cattle-man seemed actually to assume and feel the character assigned him by McGuire's intemperate accusations— the character of tyrant and guilty oppressor. He seemed to have adopted the responsibility of the fellow's condition, and he always met his tirades with a pacific, patient, and even remorseful kindness that never altered.

One day Raidler said to him, "Try more air, son. You can have the buckboard and a driver every day if you'll go. Try a week or two in one of the cow camps. I'll fix you up plum comfortable. The ground, and the air next to it—them's the things to cure you. I knowed a man from Philadelphy, sicker than you are, got lost on the Guadalupe, and slept on the bare grass in sheep camps for two weeks. Well, sir, it started him getting well, which he done. Close to the ground—that's where the medicine in the air stays. Try a little hossback riding now. There's a gentle pony——"

"What've I done to yer?" screamed McGuire. "Did I ever double-cross yer? Did I ask you to bring me here? Drive me out to your camps if you wanter; or stick a knife in me and save trouble. Ride! I can't lift my feet. I couldn't sidestep a jar from a five-year-old kid. That's

what your d—d ranch has done for me. There's nothing
to eat, nothing to see, and nobody to talk to but a lot
of Reubens who don't know a punching bag from a
lobster salad."

"It's a lonesome place, for certain," apologized Raidler
abashedly. "We got plenty, but it's rough enough. Anything you think of you want, the boys'll ride up and
fetch it down for you."

It was Chad Murchison, a cowpuncher from the Circle
Bar outfit, who first suggested that McGuire's illness
was fraudulent. Chad had brought a basket of grapes for
him thirty miles, and four out of his way, tied to his
saddle-horn. After remaining in the smoke-tainted room
for a while, he emerged and bluntly confided his sus-
picions to Raidler.

"His arm," said Chad, "is harder'n a diamond. He
interduced me to what he called a shore-perplexus punch,
and 'twas like being kicked twice by a mustang. He's
playin' it low down on you, Curt. He ain't no sicker'n
I am. I hate to say it, but the runt's workin' you for range
and shelter."

The cattleman's ingenuous mind refused to entertain
Chad's view of the case, and when, later, he came to
apply the test, doubt entered not into his motives.

One day, about noon, two men drove up to the ranch,
alighted, hitched, and came in to dinner; standing and
general invitations being the custom of the country. One
of them was a great San Antonio doctor, whose costly

services had been engaged by a wealthy cowman who
had been laid low by an accidental bullet. He was now
being driven to the station to take the train back to
town. After dinner Raidler took him aside, pushed a
twenty-dollar bill against his hand, and said:

"Doc, there's a young chap in that room I guess has
got a bad case of consumption. I'd like for you to look
him over and see just how bad he is, and if we can do
anything for him."

"How much was that dinner I just ate, Mr. Raidler?"
said the doctor bluffly, looking over his spectacles. Raidler returned the money to his pocket. The doctor immediately entered McGuire's room, and the cattleman
seated himself upon a heap of saddles on the gallery,
ready to reproach himself in the event the verdict should
be unfavorable.

In ten minutes the doctor came briskly out. "Your
man," he said promptly, "is as sound as a new dollar.
His lungs are better than mine. Respiration, temperature,
and pulse normal. Chest expansion four inches. Not a
sign of weakness anywhere. Of course I didn't examine
for the bacillus, but it isn't there. You can put my name
to the diagnosis. Even cigarettes and a vilely close room
haven't hurt him. Coughs, does he? Well, you tell him
it isn't necessary. You asked if there is anything we
could do for him. Well, I advise you to set him digging
post-holes or breaking mustangs. There's our team ready.
Good day, sir." And like a puff of wholesome, blustery

wind the doctor was off.

Raidler reached out and plucked a leaf from a mesquite bush by the railing, and began chewing it thoughtfully.

The branding season was at hand, and the next morning Ross Hargis, foreman of the outfit, was mustering his force of some twenty-five men at the ranch, ready to start for the San Carlos range, where the work was to begin. By six o'clock the horses were all saddled, the grub wagon ready, and the cowpunchers were swinging themselves upon their mounts, when Raidler bade them wait. A boy was bringing up an extra pony, bridled and saddled, to the gate. Raidler walked to McGuire's room and threw open the door. McGuire was lying on his cot, not yet dressed, smoking.

"Get up," said the cattleman, and his voice was clear and brassy, like a bugle.

"How's that?" asked McGuire, a little startled.

"Get up and dress. I can stand a rattlesnake, but I hate a liar. Do I have to tell you again?" He caught McGuire by the neck and stood him on the floor.

"Say, friend," cried McGuire wildly, "are you bughouse? I'm sick—see? I'll croak if I got to hustle. What've I done to yer?"—he began his chronic whine—"I never asked yer to——"

"Put on your clothes," called Raidler, in a rising tone.

Swearing, stumbling, shivering, keeping his amazed, shiny eyes upon the now menacing form of the aroused cattleman, McGuire managed to tumble into his clothes. Then Raidler took him by the collar and shoved him out and across the yard to the extra pony hitched at the gate. The cowpunchers lolled in their saddles, open-mouthed.

"Take this man," said Raidler to Ross Hargis, "and put him to work. Make him work hard, sleep hard, and eat hard. You boys know I done what I could for him, and he was welcome. Yesterday the best doctor in San Antone examined him, and says he's got the lungs of a burro and the constitution of a steer. You know what to do with him, Ross."

Ross Hargis only smiled grimly.

"Aw," said McGuire, looking intently at Raidler, with a peculiar expression upon his face, "the croaker said I was all right, did he? Said I was fakin', did he? You put him onto me. You t'ought I wasn't sick. You said I was a liar. Say, friend, I talked rough, I know, but I didn't mean most of it. If you felt like I did—aw! I forgot— I ain't sick, the croaker says. Well, friend, now I'll go work for yer. Here's where you play even."

He sprang into the saddle easily as a bird, got the quirt from the horn, and gave his pony a slash with it. "Cricket," who once brought in Good Boy by a neck at Hawthorne—and a 10 to 1 shot—had his foot in the stirrups again.

McGuire led the cavalcade as they dashed away from San Carlos, and the cowpunchers gave a yell of applause as they closed in behind his dust.

But in less than a mile he had lagged to the rear, and was last man when they struck the patch of high chaparral below the horse pens. Behind a clump of this he drew rein, and held a handkerchief to his mouth. He took it away drenched with bright, arterial blood, and threw it carefully into a clump of prickly pear. Then he slashed with his quirt again, gasped "G'wan" to his astonished pony, and galloped after the gang.

The night Raidler received a message from his old home in Alabama. There had been a death in the family; an estate was to divide, and they called for him to come. Daylight found him in the buckboard, skimming the prairies for the station. It was two months before he returned. When he arrived at the ranch house he found it well-nigh deserted save for Ylario, who acted as a kind of steward during his absence. Little by little the youth made him acquainted with the work done while he was away. The branding camp, he was informed, was still doing business. On account of many severe storms the cattle had been badly scattered, and the branding had been accomplished but slowly. The camp was now in the valley of the Guadalupe, twenty miles away.

"By the way," said Raidler, suddenly remembering, "that fellow I sent along with them—McGuire—is he working yet?"

"I do not know," said Ylario. "Man's from the camp come verree few times to the ranch. So plentee work

with the leetle calves. They no say. Oh, I think that
fellow McGuire he dead much time ago."

"Dead!" said Raidler. "What you talking about?"

"Verree sick fellow, McGuire," replied Ylario, with a
shrug of his shoulder. "I theenk he no live one, two month
when he go away."

"Shucks!" said Raidler. "He humbugged you, too, did
he? The doctor examined him and said he was sound as
a mesquite knot."

"That doctor," said Ylario, smiling, "he tell you so?
That doctor no see McGuire."

"Talk up," ordered Raidler. "What the devil do you
mean?"

"McGuire," continued the boy tranquilly, "he getting
drink water outside when that doctor come in room.
That doctor take me and pound me all over here with
his fingers"—putting his hand to his chest—"I not know
for what. He put his ear here and here and here, and
listen—I not know for what. He put his little glass stick
in my mouth. He feel my arm here. He make me count
like whisper—so—twenty, *treinta, cuarenta*. Who knows,"
concluded Ylario, with a deprecating spread of his hands,
"for what that doctor do those verree droll and suchlike
things?"

"What horses are up?" asked Raidler, shortly.

"Paisano is grazing out behind the little corral, *señor*."

"Saddle him for me at once."

Within a very few minutes the cattleman was mounted

and away. Paisano, well named after that ungainly but swift-running bird, struck into his long lope that ate up the road like a strip of macaroni. In two hours and a quarter Raidler, from a gentle swell, saw the branding camp by a water hole in the Guadalupe. Sick with expectancy of the news he feared, he rode up, dismounted, and dropped Paisano's reins. So gentle was his heart that at that moment he would have pleaded guilty to the murder of McGuire.

The only being in the camp was the cook, who was just arranging the hunks of barbecued beef, and distributing the tin coffee cups for supper. Raidler evaded a direct question concerning the one subject in his mind.

"Everything all right in camp, Pete?" he managed to inquire.

"So, so," said Pete, conservatively. "Grub give out twice. Wind scattered the cattle, and we've had to rake the brush for forty mile. I need a new coffeepot. And the mosquitoes is some more hellish than common."

"The boys—all well?"

Pete was no optimist. Besides, inquiries concerning the health of cowpunchers were not only superfluous, but bordered on flaccidity. It was not like the boss to make them.

"What's left of 'em don't miss no calls to grub," the cook conceded.

"What's left of 'em?" repeated Raidler in a husky voice.

Mechanically he began to look around for McGuire's grave. He had in his mind a white slab such as he had seen in the Alabama churchyard. But immediately he knew that was foolish.

"Sure," said Pete; "what's left. Cow camps change in two months. Some's gone."

Raidler nerved himself.

"That—chap—I sent along—McGuire—did—he——"

"Say," interrupted Pete, rising with a chunk of corn bread in each hand, "that was a dirty shame, sending that poor, sick kid to a cow camp. A doctor that couldn't tell he was graveyard meat ought to be skinned with a cinch buckle. Game as he was, too—it's a scandal among snakes—lemme tell you what he done. First night in camp the boys started to initiate him in the leather breeches degree. Ross Hargis busted him one swipe with his chaparreras, and what do you reckon the poor child did? Got up, the little skeeter, and licked Ross. Licked Ross Hargis. Licked him good. Hit him plenty and everywhere and hard. Ross'd just get up and pick out a fresh place to lay down on agin.

"Then that McGuire goes off there and lays down with his head in the grass and bleeds. A hem'ridge they calls it. He lays there eighteen hours by the watch, and they can't budge him. Then Ross Hargis, who loves any man who can lick him, goes to work and damns the doctors from Greenland to Poland Chiny; and him and Green Branch Johnson they gets McGuire in a tent, and spells each other feedin' him chopped raw meat and whisky.

"But it looks like the kid ain't got no appetite to git well, for they misses him from the tent in the night and finds him rootin' in the grass, and likewise a drizzle fallin'. 'Gwan,' he says, 'lemme go and die like I wanter. He said I was a liar and a fake and I was playin' sick. Lemme alone.'

"Two weeks," went on the cook, "he laid around, not noticin' nobody, and then——"

A sudden thunder filled the air, and a score of galloping centaurs crashed through the brush into camp.

"Illustrious rattlesnakes!" exclaimed Pete, springing all ways at once: "here's the boys come, and I'm an assassinated man if supper ain't ready in three minutes."

But Raidler saw only one thing. A little brown-faced, grinning chap, springing from his saddle in the full light of the fire. McGuire was not like that, and yet——

In another instant the cattleman was holding him by the hand and shoulder.

"Son, son, how goes it?" was all he found to say.

"Close to the ground, says you," shouted McGuire, crunching Raidler's fingers in grip of steel; "and dat's where I found it—healt' and strengt', and tumbled to what a cheap skate I been actin'. T'anks fer kickin' me out, old man. And—say! de joke's on dat croaker, ain't it? I looked t'rough the window and see him playin' tag on dat kid's solar plexus."

"You son of a tinker," growled the cattleman, "whyn't you talk up and say the doctor never examined you?"

"Aw—g'wan!" said McGuire, with a flash of his old asperity, "nobody can't bluff me. You never ast me. You made your spiel, and you t'rowed me out, and I let it go at dat. And, say, friend, dis chasin' cows is outer sight. Dis is de whitest bunch of sports I ever travelled with. You'll let me stay, won't yer, old man?"

Raidler looked wonderingly toward Ross Hargis.

"That cussed little runt," remarked Ross tenderly, "is the Jo-dartin'est hustler—and the hardest hitter in any-body's cow camp."

HEARTS AND HANDS

AT DENVER, THERE WAS AN INFLUX OF passengers into the coaches on the eastbound B. & M. express. In one coach there sat a very pretty young woman dressed in elegant taste and surrounded by all the luxurious comforts of an experienced traveler. Among the newcomers were two young men, one of handsome presence with a bold, frank countenance and manner; the other a ruffled, glum-faced person, heavily built and roughly dressed. The two were handcuffed together.

As they passed down the aisle of the coach the only vacant seat offered was a reversed one facing the attractive young woman. Here the linked couple seated themselves. The young woman's glance fell upon them with a distant, swift disinterest; then with a lovely smile brightening her countenance and a tender pink tingeing her rounded cheeks, she held out a little gray-gloved hand. When she spoke her voice, full, sweet, and deliberate, proclaimed that its owner was accustomed to speak and be heard.

"Well, Mr. Easton, if you *will* make me speak first, I suppose I must. Don't you ever recognize old friends when you meet them in the West?"

The younger man roused himself sharply at the sound of her voice, seemed to struggle with a slight embarrassment which he threw off instantly, and then clasped her fingers with his left hand.

"It's Miss Fairchild," he said, with a smile. "I'll ask you to excuse the other hand; it's otherwise engaged just at present."

He slightly raised his right hand, bound at the wrist by the shining "bracelet" to the left one of his companion. The glad look in the girl's eyes slowly changed to a bewildered horror. The glow faded from her cheeks. Her lips parted in a vague, relaxing distress. Easton, with a little laugh, as if amused, was about to speak again when the other forestalled him. The glum-faced man had been watching the girl's countenance with veiled glances from his keen, shrewd eyes.

"You'll excuse me for speaking, miss, but, I see you're acquainted with the marshal here. If you'll ask him to speak a word for me when we get to the pen he'll do it, and it'll make things easier for me there. He's taking me to Leavenworth prison. It's seven years for counterfeiting."

"Oh!" said the girl, with a deep breath and returning color. "So that is what you are doing out here? A marshal!"

"My dear Miss Fairchild," said Easton, calmly, "I had to do something. Money has a way of taking wings unto itself, and you know it takes money to keep step with our crowd in Washington. I saw this opening in the West, and—well, a marshalship isn't quite as high a position as that of ambassador, but——"

"The ambassador," said the girl, warmly, "doesn't call any more. He needn't ever have done so. You ought to know that. And so now you are one of these dashing western heroes, and you ride and shoot and go into all kinds of dangers. That's different from the Washington life. You have been missed from the old crowd."

The girl's eyes, fascinated, went back, widening a little, to rest upon the glittering handcuffs.

"Don't you worry about them, miss," said the other man. "All marshals handcuff themselves to their prisoners to keep them from getting away. Mr. Easton knows his business."

"Will we see you again soon in Washington?" asked the girl.

"Not soon, I think," said Easton. "My butterfly days are over, I fear."

"I love the West," said the girl, irrelevantly. Her eyes were shining softly. She looked away out the car window. She began to speak truly and simply, without the gloss of style and manner: "Mamma and I spent the summer in Denver. She went home a week ago because father was slightly ill. I could live and be happy in the West. I think the air here agrees with me. Money isn't everything. But people always misunderstand things and remain stupid——"

"Say, Mr. Marshal," growled the glum-faced man. "This isn't quite fair. I'm needin' a drink, and haven't had a smoke all day. Haven't you talked long enough? Take me to the smoker now, won't you? I'm half dead for a pipe."

The bound travelers rose to their feet, Easton with the same slow smile on his face.

"I can't deny a petition for tobacco," he said, lightly. "It's the one friend of the unfortunate. Good-bye, Miss Fairchild. Duty calls, you know." He held out his hand for a farewell.

"It's too bad you are not going East," she said, reclothing herself with manner and style. "But you must go on to Leavenworth, I suppose?"

"Yes," said Easton, "I must go on to Leavenworth."

The two men sidled down the aisle into the smoker.

The two passengers in a seat near by had heard most
of the conversation. Said one of them: "That marshal's
a good sort of chap. Some of these Western fellows are
all right."

"Pretty young to hold an office like that, isn't he?"
asked the other.

"Young!" exclaimed the first speaker, "why—— Oh!
didn't you catch on? Say—did you ever know an officer
to handcuff a prisoner to his *right* hand?"

A BLACKJACK
BARGAINER

THE MOST DISREPUTABLE THING IN Yancey Goree's law office was Goree himself, sprawled in his creaky old armchair. The rickety little office, built of red brick, was set flush with the street—the main street of the town of Bethel.

Bethel rested upon the foothills of the Blue Ridge. Above it the mountains were piled to the sky. Far below it the turbid Catawba gleamed yellow along its disconsolate valley.

The June day was at its sultriest hour. Bethel dozed in the tepid shade. Trade was not. It was so still that Goree, reclining in his chair, distinctly heard the clicking of the chips in the grand jury room, where the "courthouse gang" was playing poker. From the open back door of the office a well-worn path meandered across the grassy lot to the the courthouse. The treading out of that path had cost

Goree all he ever had—first inheritance of a few thousand dollars, next the old family home, and, latterly, the last shreds of his self-respect and manhood. The "gang" had cleaned him out. The broken gambler had turned drunkard and parasite; he had lived to see this day come when the men who had stripped him denied him a seat at the game. His word was no longer to be taken. The daily bout at cards had arranged itself accordingly, and to him was assigned the ignoble part of the onlooker. The sheriff, the county clerk, a sportive deputy, a gay attorney, and a chalk-faced man hailing "from the valley," sat at table, and the sheared one was thus tacitly advised to go and grow more wool.

Soon wearying of his ostracism, Goree had departed for his office, muttering to himself as he unsteadily traversed the unlucky pathway. After a drink of corn whiskey from a demijohn under the table, he had flung himself into the chair, staring, in a sort of maudlin apathy, out at the mountains immersed in the summer haze. The little white patch he saw away up on the side of Blackjack was Laurel, the village near which he had been born and bred. There, also, was the birthplace of the feud between the Gorees and the Coltranes. Now no direct heir of the Gorees survived except this plucked and singed bird of misfortune. To the Coltranes, also, but one male supporter was left—Colonel Abner Coltrane, a man of substance and standing, a member of the State Legislature, and a contemporary with Goree's father. The feud had been a typical one of the region; it had left a red record of hate, wrong, and slaughter.

But Yancey Goree was not thinking of feuds. His befuddled brain was hopelessly attacking the problem of the future maintenance of himself and his favorite follies. Of late, old friends of the family had seen to it that he had whereof to eat and a place to sleep, but whiskey they would not buy for him, and he must have whiskey. His law business was extinct; no case had been intrusted to him in two years. He had been a borrower and a sponge, and it seemed that if he fell no lower it would be from lack of opportunity. One more chance—he was saying to himself—if he had one more stake at the game, he thought he could win; but he had nothing left to sell, and his credit was more than exhausted.

He could not help smiling, even in his misery, as he thought of the man to whom, six months before, he had sold the old Goree homestead. There had come from "back yan'" in the mountains two of the strangest creatures, a man named Pike Garvey and his wife. "Back yan'," with a wave of the hand toward the hills, was understood among the mountaineers to designate the remotest fastnesses, the unplumbed gorges, the haunts of lawbreakers, the wolf's den, and the boudoir of the bear. In the cabin far up on Blackjack's shoulder, in the wildest part of these retreats, this odd couple had lived for twenty years. They had neither dog nor children to mitigate the heavy silence of the hills. Pike Garvey was little known in the settlements, but all who had dealt with him pronounced him "crazy as a loon." He acknowledged no occupation save that of a squirrel hunter, but he "moonshined" occasionally by way of diversion. Once the "revenues" had dragged him from his lair, fighting silently and desperately like a terrier, and he had been sent to state's prison for two years. Released, he popped back into his hole like an angry weasel.

Fortune, passing over many anxious wooers, made a freakish flight into Blackjack's bosky pockets to smile upon Pike and his faithful partner.

One day a party of spectacled, knickerbockered, and altogether absurd prospectors invaded the vicinity of the Garveys' cabin. Pike lifted his squirrel rifle off the hook and took a shot at them at long range on the chance of their being revenues. Happily he missed, and the unconscious agents of good luck drew nearer, disclosing their innocence of anything resembling law or justice. Later on, they offered the Garveys an enormous quantity of ready, green, crisp money for their thirty-acre patch of cleared land, mentioning, as an excuse for such a mad action, some irrelevant and inadequate nonsense about a bed of mica underlying the said property.

When the Garveys became possessed of so many dollars that they faltered in computing them, the deficiencies of life on Blackjack began to grow prominent. Pike began to talk of new shoes, a hogshead of tobacco to set in the corner, a new lock to his rifle; and, leading

Martella to a certain spot on the mountainside, he pointed out to her how a small cannon—doubtless a thing not beyond the scope of their fortune in price— might be planted so as to command and defend the sole accessible trail to the cabin, to the confusion of revenues and meddling strangers forever.

But Adam reckoned without his Eve. These things represented to him the applied power of wealth, but there slumbered in his dingy cabin an ambition that soared far above his primitive wants. Somewhere in Mrs. Garvey's bosom still survived a spot of femininity unstarved by twenty years of Blackjack. For so long a time the sounds in her ears had been the scaly-barks dropping in the woods at noon, and the wolves singing among the rocks at night, and it was enough to have purged her vanities. She had grown fat and sad and yellow and dull. But when the means came, she felt a rekindled desire to assume the perquisites of her sex— to sit at tea tables; to buy inutile things; to whitewash the hideous veracity of life with a little form and cere- mony. So she coldly vetoed Pike's proposed system of fortifications, and announced that they would descend upon the world, and gyrate socially.

And thus, at length, it was decided, and the thing done. The village of Laurel was their compromise be- tween Mrs. Garvey's preference for one of the large towns and Pike's hankering for primeval solitudes. Laurel yielded a halting round of feeble social distractions com-

portable with Martella's ambitions, and was not entirely
without recommendation to Pike, its contiguity to the
mountains presenting advantages for sudden retreat in
case fashionable society should make it advisable.

Their descent upon Laurel had been coincident with
Yancey Goree's feverish desire to convert property into
cash, and they bought the old Goree homestead, paying
four thousand dollars of ready money into the spendthrift's shaking hand.

Thus it happened that while the disreputable last
of the Gorees sprawled in his disreputable office, at the
end of his row, spurned by the cronies whom he had
gorged, strangers dwelt in the halls of his fathers.

A cloud of dust was rolling slowly up the parched
street, with something traveling in the midst of it. A
little breeze wafted the cloud to one side, and a new,
brightly painted carryall, drawn by a slothful gray horse,
became visible. The vehicle deflected from the middle
of the street as it neared Goree's office, and stopped in
the gutter directly in front of his door.

On the front seat sat a gaunt, tall man, dressed in
black broadcloth, his rigid hands incarcerated in yellow
kid gloves. On the back seat was a lady who triumphed
over the June heat. Her stout form was armored in a
skin-tight silk dress of the description known as "change-
able," being a gorgeous combination of shifting hues.
She sat erect, waving a much-ornamented fan, with her
eyes fixed stonily far down the street. However Martella

Garvey's heart might be rejoicing at the pleasures of her new life, Blackjack had done his work with her exterior. He had carved her countenance to the image of emptiness and inanity; had imbued her with the stolidity of his crags and the reserve of his hushed interiors. She always seemed to hear, whatever her surroundings were, the scaly-barks falling and pattering down the mountainside. She could always hear the awful silence of Blackjack sounding through the stillest of nights.

Goree watched this solemn equipage, as it drove to his door, with only faint interest but when the lank driver wrapped the reins about his whip, and awkwardly descended, and stepped into the office, he rose unsteadily to receive him, recognizing Pike Garvey, the new, the transformed, the recently civilized.

The mountaineer took the chair Goree offered him. They who cast doubts upon Garvey's soundness of mind had a strong witness in the man's countenance. His face was too long, a dull saffron in hue, and immobile as a statue's. Pale blue, unwinking round eyes without lashes added to the singularity of his gruesome visage. Goree was at a loss to account for the visit.

"Everything all right at Laurel, Mr. Garvey?" he inquired.

"Everything all right, sir, and mighty pleased is Missis Garvey and me with the property. Missis Garvey likes yo' old place, and she likes the neighborhood. Society is what she 'lows she wants, and she is gettin' of it. The

Rogerses, the Hapgoods, the Pratts, and the Troys hev
been to see Missis Garvey, and she hev et meals to
most of thar houses. The best folks hev axed her to
differ'nt of doin's. I cyan't say, Mr. Goree, that sech
things suits me—fur me, give me them thar." Garvey's
huge yellow-gloved hand flourished in the direction of
the mountains. "That's whar I b'long, 'mongst the wild
honey bees and the b'ars. But that ain't what I come
fur to say, Mr. Goree. Thar's somethin' you got what
me and Missis Garvey wants to buy."

"Buy!" echoed Goree. "From me?" Then he laughed
harshly. "I reckon you are mistaken about that. I sold
out to you, as you yourself expressed it, 'lock, stock, and
barrel.' There isn't even a ramrod left to sell."

"You've got it; and we 'uns want it. 'Take the money,'
says Missis Garvey, 'and buy it fa'r and squar'.' "

Goree shook his head. "The cupboard's bare," he said.

"We've riz," pursued the mountaineer, undeflected
from his object, "a heap. We was pore as possums, and
now we could hev folks to dinner every day. We been
reco'nized, Missis Garvey says, by the best society. But
there's somethin' we need we ain't got. She says it ought
to been put in the 'ventory ov the sale, but it 'tain't thar.
'Take the money, then,' she says, 'and buy it fa'r and
squar'.' "

"Out with it," said Goree. His racked nerves were
growing impatient.

Garvey threw his slouch hat upon the table, and

leaned forward, fixing his unblinking eyes upon Goree's.

"There's a old feud," he said, distinctly and slowly, "'tween you 'uns and the Coltranes."

Goree frowned ominously. To speak of his feud to a feudist is a serious breach of the mountain etiquette. The man from "back yan'" knew it as well as the lawyer did.

"Na offense," he went on, "but purely in the way of business. Missis Garvey hev studied all about feuds. Most of the quality folks in the mountains hev 'em. The Settles and the Goforths, the Rankins and the Boyds, the Silers and the Galloways, hev all been cyarin' on feuds f'om twenty to a hundred year. The last man to drap was when yo' uncle, Jedge Paisley Goree, 'journed co't and shot Len Coltrane f'om the bench. Missis Garvey and me, we come f'om the po' white trash. Nobody wouldn't pick a feud with we'uns, no mo'n with a fam'ly of treetoads. Quality people everywhar, says Missis Garvey, has feuds. We 'uns ain't quality, but we're buyin' into it as fur as we can. 'Take the money, then,' says Missis Garvey, 'and buy Mr. Goree's feud, fa'r and squar'.'"

The squirrel hunter straightened a leg half across the room, drew a roll of bills from his pocket, and threw them on the table.

"Thar's two hundred dollars, Mr. Goree, what you would call a fa'r price for a feud that's been 'lowed to run down like yourn hev. Thar's only you left to cyar' on yo' side of it, and you'd make mighty po' killin'. I'll take it off yo' hands, and it'll set me and Missis Garvey up among the quality. Thar's the money."

The little roll of currency on the table slowly untwisted itself, writhing and jumping as its folds relaxed. In the silence that followed Garvey's last speech the rattling of the poker chips in the courthouse could be plainly heard. Goree knew that the sheriff had just won a pot, for the subdued whoop with which he always greeted a victory floated across the square upon the crinkly heat waves. Beads of moisture stood on Goree's brow. Stooping, he drew the wicker-covered demijohn from under the table, and filled a tumbler from it.

"A little corn liquor, Mr. Garvey? Of course you are joking about—what you spoke of? Opens quite a new market, doesn't it? Feuds, prime, two-fifty to three. Feuds, slightly damaged—two hundred, I believe you said, Mr. Garvey?"

Goree laughed self-consciously.

The mountaineer took the glass Goree handed him, and drank the whiskey without a tremor of the lids of his staring eyes. The lawyer applauded the feat by a look of envious admiration. He poured his own drink, and took it like a drunkard, by gulps, and with shudders at the smell and taste.

"Two hundred," repeated Garvey. "Thar's the money."

A sudden passion flared up in Goree's brain. He struck the table with his fist. One of the bills flipped over and touched his hand. He flinched as if something had stung him.

"Do you come to me," he shouted, "seriously with such a ridiculous, insulting, darn fool proposition?"

"It's fa'r and squar'," said the squirrel hunter, but he reached out his hand as if to take back the money; and then Goree knew that his own flurry of rage had not been from pride or resentment, but from anger at himself, knowing that he would set foot in the deeper depths that were being opened to him. He turned in an instant from an outraged gentleman to an anxious chafferer recommending his goods.

"Don't be in a hurry, Garvey," he said, his face crimson and his speech thick. "I accept your p-p-proposition, though it's dirt cheap at two hundred. A t-trade's all right when both p-purchaser and b-buyer are s-satisfied. Shall I w-wrap it up for you, Mr. Garvey?"

Garvey rose, and shook out his broadcloth. "Missis Garvey will be pleased. You are out of it, and it stands Coltrane and Garvey. Just a scrap ov writin', Mr. Goree, you bein' a lawyer, to show we traded."

Goree seized a sheet of paper and a pen. The money was clutched in his moist hand. Everything else suddenly seemed to grow trivial and light.

"Bill of sale, by all means. 'Right, title, and interest in and to' . . . 'forever warrant and——' No, Garvey, we'll have to leave out that 'defend,'" said Goree with a loud laugh. "You'll have to defend this title yourself."

The mountaineer received the amazing screed that the lawyer handed him, folded it with immense labor, and placed it carefully in his pocket.

Goree was standing near the window. "Step here," he said, raising his finger, "and I'll show you your recently purchased enemy. There he goes, down the other side of the street."

The mountaineer crooked his long frame to look through the window in the direction indicated by the other. Colonel Abner Coltrane, an erect, portly gentleman of about fifty wearing the inevitable long, double-breasted frock coat of the southern lawmaker, and an old high silk hat, was passing on the opposite sidewalk. As Garvey looked, Goree glanced at his face. If there be such a thing as a yellow wolf, here was its counterpart. Garvey snarled as his unhuman eyes followed the moving figure, disclosing long amber-colored fangs.

"Is that him? Why, that's the man who sent me to the pen'tentiary once!"

"He used to be district attorney," said Goree, carelessly. "And, by the way, he's a first-class shot."

"I kin hit a squirrel's eye at a hundred yard," said Garvey. "So that thar's Coltrane! I made a better trade than I was thinkin'. I'll take keer of this feud, Mr. Goree, better'n you ever did!"

He moved toward the door, but lingered there, betraying a slight perplexity.

"Anything else today?" inquired Goree with frothy

sarcasm. "Any family traditions, ancestral ghosts, or skeletons in the closet? Prices as low as the lowest."

"Thar was another thing," replied the unmoved squirrel hunter, "that Missis Garvey was thinkin' of. 'Tain't so much in my line as t'other, but she wanted partic'lar that I should inquire, and ef you was willin', 'pay fur it,' she says, 'fa'r and squar'.' Thar's a buryin' groun', as you know, Mr. Goree, in the yard of yo' old place, under the cedars. Them that lies thar is yo' folks what was killed by the Coltranes. The monyments has the names on 'em. Missis Garvey says a fam'ly buryin' groun' is a sho' sign of quality. She says ef we git the feud, thar's somethin' else ought to go with it. The names on them monyments is 'Goree,' but they can be changed to ourn by——"

"Go! Go!" screamed Goree, his face turning purple. He stretched out both hands toward the mountaineer, his fingers hooked and shaking. "Go, you ghoul! Even a Ch-Chinaman protects the g-graves of his ancestors— go!"

The squirrel hunter slouched out of the door to his carryall. While he was climbing over the wheel Goree was collecting, with feverish celerity, the money that had fallen from his hand to the floor. As the vehicle slowly turned about, the sheep with a coat of newly grown wool was hurrying, in indecent haste, along the path to the courthouse.

At three o'clock in the morning they brought him back to his office, shorn and unconscious. The sheriff, the sportive deputy, the county clerk, and the gay attorney carried him, the chalk-faced man "from the valley" acting as escort.

"On the table," said one of them, and they deposited him among the litter of his unprofitable books and papers.

"Yance thinks a lot of a pair of deuces when he's liquored up," sighed the sheriff, reflectively.

"Too much," said the gay attorney. "A man has no business to play poker who drinks as much as he does. I wonder how much he dropped tonight."

"Close to two hundred. What I wonder is whar he got it. Yance ain't had a cent fur over a month, I know."

"Struck a client, maybe. Well, let's get home before daylight. He'll be all right when he wakes up, except for a sort of beehive about the cranium."

The gang slipped away through the early morning twilight. The next eye to gaze upon the miserable Goree was the orb of day. He peered through the uncurtained window, first deluging the sleeper in a flood of faint gold, but soon pouring upon the mottled red of his flesh a searching, white, summer heat. Goree stirred, half-unconsciously, among the table's débris, and turned his face from the window. His movement dislodged a heavy law book, which crashed upon the floor. Opening his eyes, he saw, bending over him, a man in a black frock coat. Looking higher, he discovered a well-worn silk hat, and beneath it the kindly face of Colonel Abner Coltrane.

A little uncertain of the outcome, the colonel waited

for the other to make some sign of recognition. Not in twenty years had male members of these two families faced each other in peace. Goree's eyelids puckered as he strained his blurred sight toward this visitor, and then he smiled serenely.

"Have you brought Stella and Lucy over to play?" he said, calmly.

"Do you know me, Yancey?" asked Coltrane.

"Of course I do. You brought me a whip with a whistle in the end."

So he had—twenty-four years ago; when Yancey's father was his best friend.

Goree's eyes wandered about the room. The colonel understood. "Lie still, and I'll bring you some," said he. There was a pump in the yard at the rear, and Goree closed his eyes, listening with rapture to the click of its handle and the bubbling of the falling stream. Coltrane brought a pitcher of the cool water, and held it for him to drink. Presently Goree sat up—a most forlorn object, his summer suit of flax soiled and crumpled, his discreditable head tousled and unsteady. He tried to wave one of his hands toward the colonel.

"Ex-excuse—everything, will you?" he said. "I must have drunk too much whiskey last night, and gone to bed on the table." His brows knitted into a puzzled frown.

"Out with the boys a while?" asked Coltrane, kindly.

"No, I went nowhere. I haven't had a dollar to spend in the last two months. Struck the demijohn too often, I reckon, as usual."

Colonel Coltrane touched him on the shoulder.

"A little while ago, Yancey," he began, "you asked me if I had brought Stella and Lucy over to play. You weren't quite awake then, and must have been dreaming you were a boy again. You are awake now, and I want you to listen to me. I have come from Stella and Lucy to their old playmate, and my old friend's son. They know that I am going to bring you home with me, and you will find them as ready with a welcome as they were in the old days. I want you to come to my house and stay until you are yourself again, and as much longer as you will. We heard of your being down in the world, and in the midst of temptation, and we agreed that you should come over and play at our house once more. Will you come, my boy? Will you drop our old family trouble and come with me?"

"Trouble!" said Goree, opening his eyes wide. "There was never any trouble between us that I know of. I'm sure we've always been the best of friends. But, good Lord, Colonel, how could I go over to your home as I am —a drunken wretch, a miserable, degraded spendthrift and gambler——"

He lurched from the table to his armchair, and began to weep maudlin tears, mingled with genuine drops of remorse and shame. Coltrane talked to him persistently and reasonably, reminding him of the simple mountain pleasures of which he had once been so fond, and insisting upon the genuineness of the invitation.

Finally he landed Goree by telling him he was counting upon his help in the engineering and transportation of a large amount of felled timber from a high mountainside to a waterway. He knew that Goree had once invented a device for this purpose—a series of slides and chutes—upon which he had justly prided himself. In an instant the poor fellow, delighted at the idea of his being of use to anyone, had paper spread upon the table, and was drawing rapid but pitifully shaky lines in demonstration of what he could and would do.

The man was sickened of the husks; his prodigal heart was turning again toward the mountains. His mind was yet strangely clogged, and his thoughts and memories were returning to his brain one by one, like carrier pigeons over a stormy sea. But Coltrane was satisfied with the progress he had made.

Bethel received the surprise of its existence that afternoon when a Coltrane and a Goree rode amicably together through the town. Side by side they rode, out from the dusty streets and gaping townspeople, down across the creek bridge, and up toward the mountain. The prodigal had brushed and washed and combed himself to a more decent figure, but he was unsteady in the saddle, and he seemed to be deep in the contemplation of some vexing problem. Coltrane left him in his mood, relying upon the influence of changed surroundings to restore his equilibrium.

Once Goree was seized with a shaking fit, and almost

came to a collapse. He had to dismount and rest at the side of the road. The colonel, foreseeing such a condition, had provided a small flask of whiskey for the journey but when it was offered to him Goree refused it almost with violence, declaring he would never touch it again. By and by he was recovered, and went quietly enough for a mile or two. Then he pulled up his horse suddenly, and said:

"I lost two hundred dollars last night, playing poker. Now, where did I get that money?"

"Take it easy, Yancey. The mountain air will soon clear it up. We'll go fishing, first thing, at the Pinnacle Falls. The trout are jumping there like bullfrogs. We'll take Stella and Lucy along, and have a picnic on Eagle Rock. Have you forgotten how a hickory-cured ham sandwich tastes, Yancey, to a hungry fisherman?"

Evidently the colonel did not believe the story of his lost wealth; so Goree retired again into brooding silence.

By late afternoon they had traveled ten of the twelve miles between Bethel and Laurel. Half a mile this side of Laurel lay the old Goree place; a mile or two beyond the village lived the Coltranes. The road was now steep and laborious, but the compensations were many. The tilted aisles of the forest were opulent with leaf and bird and bloom. The tonic air put to shame the pharmacopœia. The glades were dark with mossy shade, and bright with shy rivulets winking from the ferns and laurels. On the lower side they viewed, framed in the near foliage, exquisite sketches of the far valley swooning in its opal haze.

Coltrane was pleased to see that his companion was yielding to the spell of the hills and woods. For now they had but to skirt the base of Painter's Cliff, to cross Elder Branch and mount the hill beyond, and Goree would have to face the squandered home of his fathers. Every rock he passed, every tree, every foot of the roadway, was familiar to him. Though he had forgotten the woods, they thrilled him like the music of *Home, Sweet Home.*

They rounded the cliff, descended into Elder Branch, and paused there to let the horses drink and splash in the swift water. On the right was a rail fence that cornered there, and followed the road and stream. Inclosed by it was the old apple orchard of the home place; the house was yet concealed by the brow of the steep hill. Inside and along the fence, pokeberries, elders, sassafras, and sumac grew high and dense. At a rustle of their branches, both Goree and Coltrane glanced up, and saw a long, yellow, wolfish face above the fence, staring at them with pale, unwinking eyes. The head quickly disappeared; there was a violent swaying of the bushes, and an ungainly figure ran up through the apple orchard in the direction of the house zigzagging among the trees.

"That's Garvey," said Coltrane; "the man you sold out to. There's no doubt but he's considerably cracked. I had to send him up for moonshining once, several years ago, in spite of the fact that I believed him irresponsible.

Why, what's the matter, Yancey?"

Goree was wiping his forehead, and his face had lost
its color. "Do I look queer, too?" he asked, trying to
smile. "I'm just remembering a few more things." Some
of the alcohol had evaporated from his brain. "I recollect
now where I got that two hundred dollars."

"Don't think of it," said Coltrane, cheerfully. "Later on
we'll figure it all out together."

They rode out of the branch, and when they reached
the foot of the hill Goree stopped again.

"Did you ever suspect I was a very vain kind of fellow,
Colonel?" he asked. "Sort of foolish proud about appearances?"

The colonel's eyes refused to wander to the soiled, sag-
ging suit of flax and the faded slouch hat.

"It seems to me," he replied, mystified, but humoring
him, "I remember a young buck about twenty, with the
tightest coat, the sleekest hair, and the most prancing of
saddle horses in the Blue Ridge."

"Right you are," said Goree, eagerly. "And it's in me
yet, though it don't show. Oh, I'm as vain as a turkey
gobbler, and as proud as Lucifer. I'm going to ask you to
indulge this weakness of mine in a little matter."

"Speak out, Yancey. We'll create you Duke of Laurel
and Baron of Blue Ridge, if you choose; and you shall
have a feather out of Stella's peacock's tail to wear in
your hat."

"I'm in earnest. In a few minutes we'll pass the house

up there on the hill where I was born, and where my people have lived for nearly a century. Strangers live there now—and look at me! I am about to show myself to them ragged and poverty-stricken, a wastrel and a beggar. Colonel Coltrane, I'm ashamed to do it. I want you to let me wear your coat and hat until we are out of sight beyond. I know you think it a foolish pride, but I want to make as good a showing as I can when I pass the old place."

"Now, what does this mean?" said Coltrane to himself, as he compared his companion's sane looks and quiet demeanor with his strange request. But he was already unbuttoning the coat, assenting readily, as if the fancy were in no wise to be considered strange.

The coat and hat fitted Goree well. He buttoned the former about him with a look of satisfaction and dignity. He and Coltrane were nearly the same size—rather tall, portly, and erect. Twenty-five years were between them, but in appearance they might have been brothers. Goree looked older than his age; his face was puffy and lined; the colonel had the smooth, fresh complexion of a temperate liver. He put on Goree's disreputable old flax coat and faded slouch hat.

"Now," said Goree, taking up the reins, "I'm all right. I want you to ride about ten feet in the rear as we go by, Colonel, so that they can get a good look at me. They'll see I'm no back number yet, by any means. I'll show up pretty well to them once more, anyhow. Let's ride on."

He set out up the hill at a smart trot, the colonel following, as he had been requested.

Goree sat straight in the saddle, with head erect, but his eyes were turned to the right, sharply scanning every shrub and fence and hiding-place in the old homestead yard. Once he muttered to himself, "Will the crazy fool try it, or did I dream half of it?"

It was when he came opposite the little family burying ground that he saw what he had been looking for—a puff of white smoke, coming from the thick cedars in one corner. He toppled so slowly to the left that Coltrane had time to urge his horse to that side, and catch him with one arm.

The squirrel hunter had not overpraised his aim. He had sent the bullet where he intended, and where Goree had expected that it would pass—through the breast of Colonel Coltrane's black frock coat.

Goree leaned heavily against Coltrane, but he did not fall. The horses kept pace, side by side, and the colonel's arm kept him steady. The little white houses of Laurel shone through the trees, half a mile away. Goree reached out one hand and groped until it rested upon Coltrane's fingers, which held his bridle.

"Good friend," he said, and that was all.

Thus did Yancey Goree, as he rode past his old home, make, considering all things, the best showing that was in his power.

✦✦

A CHAPARRAL
CHRISTMAS GIFT

T HE ORIGINAL CAUSE OF THE TROUBLE
was about twenty years in growing.

At the end of that time it was worth it.

Had you lived anywhere within fifty miles of Sundown
Ranch you would have heard of it. It possessed a quantity of jet-black hair, a pair of extremely frank, deep
brown eyes, and a laugh that rippled across the prairie
like the sound of a hidden brook. The name of it was
Rosita McMullen; and she was the daughter of old man
McMullen of the Sundown Sheep Ranch.

There came riding on red roan steeds—or, to be more
explicit, on a paint and flea-bitten sorrel—two wooers.

One was Madison Lane, and the other was the Frio Kid. But at that time they did not call him the Frio Kid, for he had not earned the honors of special nomenclature. His name was simply Johnny McRoy.

It must not be supposed that these two were the sum of the agreeable Rosita's admirers. The bronchos of a dozen champed their bits at the long hitching rack of the Sundown Ranch. Many were the sheep's eyes that were cast in those savannas that did not belong to the flocks of Dan McMullen. But of all the cavaliers, Madison Lane and Johnny McRoy galloped far ahead, wherefore they are to be chronicled.

Madison Lane, a young cattleman from the Nueces country, won the race. He and Rosita were married one Christmas day. Armed, hilarious, vociferous, magnanimous, the cowmen and the sheepmen, laying aside their hereditary hatred, joined forces to celebrate the occasion.

Sundown Ranch was sonorous with the cracking of jokes and sixshooters, the shine of buckles and bright eyes, the outspoken congratulations of the herders of kine.

But while the wedding feast was at its liveliest there descended upon it Johnny McRoy, bitten by jealousy, like one possessed.

"I'll give you a Christmas present," he yelled, shrilly, at the door, with his .45 in his hand. Even then he had some reputation as an offhand shot.

His first bullet cut a neat underbit in Madison Lane's

right ear. The barrel of his gun moved an inch. The next shot would have been the bride's had not Carson, a sheepman, possessed a mind with triggers somewhat well oiled and in repair. The guns of the wedding party had been hung, in their belts, upon nails in the wall when they sat at table, as a concession to good taste. But Carson, with great promptness, hurled his plate of roast venison and frijoles at McRoy, spoiling his aim. The second bullet then, only shattered the white petals of a Spanish dagger flower suspended two feet above Rosita's head.

The guests spurned their chairs and jumped for their weapons. It was considered an improper act to shoot the bride and groom at a wedding. In about six seconds there were twenty or so bullets due to be whizzing in the direction of Mr. McRoy.

"I'll shoot better next time," yelled Johnny; "and there'll be a next time." He backed rapidly out of the door.

Carson, the sheepman, spurred on to attempt further exploits by the success of his plate throwing, was first to reach the door. McRoy's bullet from the darkness laid him low.

The cattlemen then swept out upon him, calling for vengeance, for, while the slaughter of a sheepman has not always lacked condonement, it was a decided misdemeanor in this instance. Carson was innocent; he was no accomplice at the matrimonial proceedings; nor had anyone heard him quote the line "Christmas comes but once a year" to the guests.

But the sortie failed in its vengeance. McRoy was on his horse and away, shouting back curses and threats as he galloped into the concealing chaparral.

That night was the birthnight of the Frio Kid. He became the "bad man" of that portion of the State. The rejection of his suit by Miss McMullen turned him to a dangerous man. When officers went after him for the shooting of Carson, he killed two of them, and entered upon the life of an outlaw. He became a marvellous shot with either hand. He would turn up in towns and settlements, raise a quarrel at the slightest opportunity, pick off his man, and laugh at the officers of the law. He was so cool, so deadly, so rapid, so inhumanly bloodthirsty that none but faint attempts were ever made to capture him. When he was at last shot and killed by a little one-armed Mexican who was nearly dead himself from fright, the Frio Kid had the deaths of eighteen men on his head. About half of these were killed in fair duels depending upon the quickness of the draw. The other half were men whom he assassinated from absolute wantonness and cruelty.

Many tales are told along the border of his impudent courage and daring. But he was not one of the breed of desperados who have seasons of generosity and even of softness. They say he never had mercy on the object of his anger. Yet at this and every Christmastide it is well to give each one credit, if it can be done, for whatever speck of good he may have possessed. If the Frio Kid ever did a kindly act or felt a throb of generosity in his heart it was once at such a time and season, and this is the way it happened.

One who has been crossed in love should never breathe the odor of the blossoms of the ratama tree. It stirs the memory to a dangerous degree.

One December in the Frio country there was a ratama tree in full bloom, for the winter had been as warm as springtime. That way rode the Frio Kid and his satellite and co-murderer, Mexican Frank. The Kid reined in his mustang, and sat in his saddle, thoughtful and grim, with dangerously narrowing eyes. The rich, sweet scent touched him somewhere beneath his ice and iron.

"I don't know what I've been thinking about, Mex," he remarked in his usual mild draw, "to have forgot all about a Christmas present I got to give. I'm going to ride over tomorrow night and shoot Madison Lane in his own house. He got my girl—Rosita would have had me if he hadn't cut into the game. I wonder why I happened to overlook it up to now?"

"Ah, shucks, Kid," said Mexican, "don't talk foolishness. You know you can't get within a mile of Mad Lane's house tomorrow night. I see old man Allen day before yesterday, and he says Mad is going to have Christmas doings at his house. You remember how you shot up the

festivities when Mad was married, and about the threats
you made? Don't you suppose Mad Lane'll kind of keep
his eye open for a certain Mr. Kid? You plumb make me
tired, Kid, with such remarks."

"I'm going," repeated the Frio Kid, without heat, "to
go to Madison Lane's Christmas doings, and kill him.
I ought to have done it a long time ago. Why, Mex, just
two weeks ago I dreamed me and Rosita was married
instead of her and him and we was living in a house, and
I could see her smiling at me, and—oh! h—l, Mex, he
got her; and I'll get him—yes, sir, on Christmas Eve he
got her, and then's when I'll get him."

"There's other ways of committing suicide," advised
Mexican. "Why don't you go and surrender to the
sheriff?"

"I'll get him," said the Kid.

Christmas Eve fell as balmy as April. Perhaps there
was a hint of far-away frostiness in the air, but it tingled
like seltzer, perfumed faintly with late prairie blossoms
and the mesquite grass.

When night came the five or six rooms of the ranch
house were brightly lit. In one room was a Christmas
tree, for the Lanes had a boy of three, and a dozen or
more guests were expected from the nearer ranches.

At nightfall Madison Lane called aside Jim Belcher
and three other cowboys employed on his ranch.

"Now, boys," said Lane, "keep your eyes open. Walk
around the house and watch the road well. All of you

know the 'Frio Kid,' as they call him now, and if you see him, open fire on him without asking any questions. I'm not afraid of his coming around, but Rosita is. She's been afraid he'd come in on us every Christmas since we were married."

The guests had arrived in buckboards and on horseback, and were making themselves comfortable inside.

The evening went along pleasantly. The guests enjoyed and praised Rosita's excellent supper, and afterward the men scattered in groups about the rooms or on the broad "gallery," smoking and chatting.

The Christmas tree, of course, delighted the youngsters, and above all were they pleased when Santa Claus himself in magnificent white beard and furs appeared and began to distribute the toys.

"It's my papa," announced Billy Sampson, aged six. "I've seen him wear 'em before."

Berkly, a sheepman, an old friend of Lane, stopped Rosita as she was passing by him on the gallery, where he was sitting smoking.

"Well, Mrs. Lane," said he, "I suppose by this Christmas you've gotten over being afraid of that fellow McRoy, haven't you? Madison and I have talked about it, you know."

"Very nearly," said Rosita, smiling, "but I am still nervous sometimes. I shall never forget that awful time when he came so near to killing us."

"He's the most cold-hearted villain in the world," said

Berkly. "The citizens all along the border ought to turn
out and hunt him down like a wolf."

"He has committed awful crimes," said Rosita, "but—I
—don't—know. I think there is a spot of good somewhere
in everybody. He was not always bad—that I know."

Rosita turned into the hallway between the rooms.
Santa Claus, in muffling whiskers and furs, was just coming through.

"I heard what you said through the window, Mrs.
Lane," he said. "I was just going down in my pocket for
a Christmas present for your husband. But I've left one
for you, instead. It's in the room to your right."

"Oh, thank you, kind Santa Claus," said Rosita,
brightly.

Rosita went into the room, while Santa Claus stepped
into the cooler air of the yard.

She found no one in the room but Madison.

"Where is my present that Santa said he left for me in
here?" she asked.

"Haven't seen anything in the way of a present," said
her husband, laughing, "unless he could have meant me."

The next day Gabriel Radd, the foreman of the XO
Ranch, dropped into the post office at Loma Alta.

"Well, the Frio Kid's got his dose of lead at last," he
remarked to the postmaster.

"That's so? How'd it happen?"

"One of old Sanchez s Mexican sheep herders did it—

think of it! the Frio Kid killed by a sheep herder! The Mexican saw him riding along past his camp about twelve o'clock last night, and was so skeered that he up with a Winchester and let him have it. Funniest part of it was that the Kid was dressed all up with white Angora-skin whiskers and a regular Santy Claus rig-out from head to foot. Think of the Frio Kid playing Santy!"

TWO
THANKSGIVING DAY
GENTLEMEN

THERE IS ONE DAY THAT IS OURS. THERE is one day when all we Americans who are not self-made go back to the old home to eat saleratus biscuits and marvel how much nearer to the porch the old pump looks than it used to. Bless the day. President Roosevelt gives it to us. We hear some talk of the Puritans, but don't just remember who they were. Bet we can lick 'em, anyhow, if they try to land again. Plymouth Rocks? Well, that sounds more familiar. Lots of us have had to come down to hens since the Turkey Trust got its work in. But somebody in Washington is leaking out advance information to 'em about all these Thanksgiving Day proclamations.

The big city east of the cranberry bogs has made Thanksgiving Day an institution. The last Thursday in November is the only day in the year on which it recognizes the part of America lying across the ferries. It is the one day that is purely American. Yes, a day of celebration, exclusively American.

And now for the story which is to prove to you that we have traditions on this side of the ocean that are becoming older at a much more rapid rate than those of England are—thanks to our git-up and enterprise.

Stuffy Pete took his seat on the third bench to the right as you enter Union Square from the east, at the walk opposite the fountain. Every Thanksgiving Day for nine years he had taken his seat there promptly at one o'clock. For every time he had done so things had happened to him—Charles Dickensy things that swelled his waistcoat above his heart, and equally on the other side.

But today Stuffy Pete's appearance at the annual trysting place seemed to have been rather the result of habit than of the yearly hunger which, as the philanthropists seem to think, afflicts the poor at such extended intervals.

Certainly Pete was not hungry. He had just come from a feast that had left him of his powers barely those of respiration and locomotion. His eyes were like two pale gooseberries firmly imbedded in a swollen and gravy-smeared mask of putty. His breath came in short wheezes; a senatorial roll of adipose tissue denied a

fashionable set to his upturned coat collar. Buttons that
had been sewed upon his clothes by kind Salvation
fingers a week before flew like popcorn, strewing the
earth around him. Ragged he was, with a split shirt
front open to the wishbone; but the November breeze,
carrying fine snowflakes, brought him only a grateful
coolness. For Stuffy Pete was overcharged with the
caloric produced by a super-bountiful dinner, beginning
with oysters and ending with plum pudding, and in-
cluding (it seemed to him) all the roast turkey and baked
potatoes and chicken salad and squash pie and ice cream
in the world. Wherefore he sat, gorged, and gazed upon
the world with after-dinner contempt.

The meal had been an unexpected one. He was passing
a red brick mansion near the beginning of Fifth Avenue,
in which live two old ladies of ancient family and a
reverence for traditions. They even denied the existence
of New York, and believed that Thanksgiving Day was
declared solely for Washington Square. One of their
traditional habits was to station a servant at the postern
gate with orders to admit the first hungry wayfarer that
came along after the hour of noon had struck, and
banquet him to a finish. Stuffy Pete happened to pass
by on his way to the park, and the seneschals gathered
him in and upheld the custom of the castle.

After Stuffy Pete had gazed straight before him for
ten minutes he was conscious of a desire for a more
varied field of vision. With a tremendous effort he moved

his head slowly to the left. And then his eyes bulged out fearfully, and his breath ceased, and the roughshod ends of his short legs wriggled and rustled on the gravel.

For the Old Gentleman was coming across Fourth Avenue toward his bench.

Every Thanksgiving Day for nine years the Old Gentleman had come there and found Stuffy Pete on his bench. That was a thing that the Old Gentleman was trying to make a tradition of. Every Thanksgiving Day for nine years he had found Stuffy there, and led him to a restaurant and watched him eat a big dinner. They do those things in England unconsciously. But this is a young country, and nine years is not so bad. The Old Gentleman was a stanch American patriot, and considered himself a pioneer in American tradition. In order to become picturesque we must keep on doing one thing for a long time without ever letting it get away from us. Something like collecting the weekly dimes in industrial insurance. Or cleaning the streets.

The Old Gentleman moved, straight and stately, toward the Institution that he was rearing. Truly, the annual feeding of Stuffy Pete was nothing national in its character, such as the Magna Charta or jam for breakfast was in England. But it was a step. It was almost feudal. It showed, at least, that a Custom was not impossible to New Y—ahem!—America.

The Old Gentleman was thin and tall and sixty. He was dressed all in black, and wore the old-fashioned kind

of glasses that won't stay on your nose. His hair was
whiter and thinner than it had been last year, and he
seemed to make more use of his big, knobby cane with
the crooked handle.

As his established benefactor came up Stuffy wheezed
and shuddered like some woman's over-fat pug when
a street dog bristles up at him. He would have flown, but
all the skill of Santos-Dumont[1] could not have separated
him from his bench. Well had the myrmidons of the two
old ladies done their work.

"Good morning," said the Old Gentleman. "I am glad
to perceive that the vicissitudes of another year have
spared you to move in health about the beautiful world.
For that blessing alone this day of thanksgiving is well
proclaimed to each of us. If you will come with me, my
man, I will provide you with a dinner that should make
your physical being accord with the mental."

That is what the Old Gentleman said every time.
Every Thanksgiving Day for nine years. The words themselves almost formed an Institution. Nothing could be
compared with them except the Declaration of Independence. Always before they had been music in Stuffy's
ears. But now he looked up at the Old Gentleman's face
with tearful agony in his own. The fine snow almost
sizzled when it fell upon his perspiring brow. But the
Old Gentleman shivered a little and turned his back to
the wind.

Stuffy had always wondered why the Old Gentleman

---

[1] a famous aeronaut.

spoke his speech rather sadly. He did not know that it was because he was wishing every time that he had a son to succeed him. A son who would come there after he was gone—a son who would stand proud and strong before some subsequent Stuffy, and say: "In memory of my father." Then it would be an Institution.

But the Old Gentleman had no relatives. He lived in rented rooms in one of the decayed old family brownstone mansions in one of the quiet streets east of the park. In the winter he raised fuchsias in a little conservatory the size of a steamer trunk. In the spring he walked in the Easter parade. In the summer he lived at a farmhouse in the New Jersey hills, and sat in a wicker armchair, speaking of a butterfly, the *ornithoptera amphrisius,* that he hoped to find some day. In the autumn he fed Stuffy a dinner. These were the Old Gentleman's occupations.

Stuffy Pete looked up at him for half a minute, stewing and helpless in his own self-pity. The Old Gentleman's eyes were bright with the giving-pleasure. His face was getting more lined each year, but his little black necktie was in as jaunty a bow as ever, and his linen was beautiful and white, and his gray mustache was curled gracefully at the ends. And then Stuffy made a noise that sounded like peas bubbling in a pot. Speech was intended; and as the Old Gentleman had heard the sounds nine times before, he rightly construed them into Stuffy's old formula of acceptance.

"Thankee, sir. I'll go with ye, and much obliged. I'm very hungry, sir."

The coma of repletion had not prevented from entering Stuffy's mind the conviction that he was the basis of an Institution. His Thanksgiving appetite was not his own; it belonged by all the sacred rights of established custom, if not by the actual Statute of Limitations, to this kind old gentleman who had preempted it. True, America is free; but in order to establish tradition some one must be a repetend—a repeating decimal. The heroes are not all heroes of steel and gold. See one here that wielded only weapons of iron, badly silvered, and tin.

The Old Gentleman led his annual protégé southward to the restaurant, and to the table where the feast had always occurred. They were recognized.

"Here comes de old guy," said a waiter, "dat blows dat same bum to a meal every Thanksgiving."

The Old Gentleman sat across the table glowing like a smoked pearl at his cornerstone of future ancient Tradition. The waiters heaped the table with holiday food —and Stuffy, with a sigh that was mistaken for hunger's expression, raised knife and fork and carved for himself a crown of imperishable bay.

No more valiant hero ever fought his way through the ranks of an enemy. Turkey, chops, soups, vegetables, pies, disappeared before him as fast as they could be served. Gorged nearly to the uttermost when he entered the restaurant, the smell of food had almost caused him to lose his honor as a gentleman, but he rallied like a true knight. He saw the look of beneficent happiness on the Old Gentleman's face—a happier look than even the fuchsias and the *ornithoptera amphrisius* had ever brought to it—and he had not the heart to see it wane.

In an hour Stuffy leaned back with a battle won.

"Thankee kindly, sir," he puffed like a leaky steam pipe; "thankee kindly for a hearty meal."

Then he arose heavily with glazed eyes and started toward the kitchen. A waiter turned him about like a top, and pointed him toward the door. The Old Gentleman carefully counted out $1.30 in silver change, leaving three nickels for the waiter.

They parted as they did each year at the door, the Old Gentleman going south, Stuffy north.

Around the first corner Stuffy turned, and stood for one minute. Then he seemed to puff out his rags as an owl puffs out his feathers, and fell to the sidewalk like a sunstricken horse.

When the ambulance came the young surgeon and the driver cursed softly at his weight. There was no smell of whiskey to justify a transfer to the patrol wagon, so Stuffy and his two dinners went to the hospital.

There they stretched him on a bed and began to test him for strange diseases, with the hope of getting a chance at some problem with the bare steel.

And lo! an hour later another ambulance brought the

Old Gentleman. And they laid him on another bed and
spoke of appendicitis, for he looked good for the bill.

But pretty soon one of the young doctors met one of
the young nurses whose eyes he liked, and stopped to
chat with her about the cases.

"That nice old gentleman over there, now," he said,
"you wouldn't think that was a case of almost starvation.
Proud old family, I guess. He told me he hadn't eaten
a thing for three days."

THE REFORMATION
OF CALLIOPE

C<small>ALLIOPE CATESBY WAS IN HIS HUMORS</small>
again. Ennui was upon him. This goodly promontory,
the earth—particularly that portion of it known as Quicksand—was to him no more than a pestilent congregation
of vapors. Overtaken by the megrims, the philosopher
may seek relief in soliloquy; my lady find solace in
tears; the flaccid Easterner scold at the millinery bills of
his women folk. Such recourse was insufficient to the
denizens of Quicksand. Calliope, especially, was wont
to express his ennui according to his lights.

Overnight Calliope had hung out signals of approaching low spirits. He had kicked his own dog on the porch

of the Occidental Hotel, and refused to apologize. He
had become capricious and fault-finding in conversation.
While strolling about he reached often for twigs of
mesquite and chewed the leaves fiercely. That was always
an ominous act. Another symptom alarming to those
who were familiar with the different stages of his dol-
drums was his increasing politeness and a tendency to
use formal phrases. A husky softness succeeded the
usual penetrating drawl in his tones. A dangerous courtesy marked his manners. Later, his smile became
crooked, the left side of his mouth slanting upward,
and Quicksand got ready to stand from under.

At this stage Calliope generally began to drink. Finally, about midnight, he was seen going homeward,
saluting those whom he met with exaggerated but in-
offensive courtesy. Not yet was Calliope's melancholy
at the danger point. He would seat himself at the window of the room he occupied over Silvester's tonsorial
parlors and there chant lugubrious and tuneless ballads
until morning, accompanying the noises by appropriate
maltreatment of a jingling guitar. More magnanimous
than Nero, he would thus give musical warning of the
forthcoming municipal upheaval that Quicksand was
scheduled to endure.

A quiet, amiable man was Calliope Catesby at other
times—quiet to indolence, and amiable to worthlessness.
At best he was a loafer and a nuisance; at worst he was
the Terror of Quicksand. His ostensible occupation was

something subordinate in the real estate line; he drove
the beguiled Easterner around in a buckboard to look
over lots and ranch property. Originally he came from
one of the Gulf States, his lank six feet, slurring rhythm
of speech, and sectional idioms giving evidence of his
birthplace.

And yet, after taking on Western adjustments, this
languid pine-box whittler, cracker-barrel hugger, shady
corner lounger of the cotton fields and sumac hills of
the South became famed as a bad man among men who
had made a lifelong study of the art of truculence.

At nine the next morning Calliope was fit. Inspired by
his own barbarous melodies and the contents of his jug,
he was ready-primed to gather fresh laurels from the
diffident brow of Quicksand. Encircled and criss-crossed
with cartridge belts, abundantly garnished with revolvers, and copiously drunk, he poured forth into Quicksand's main street. Too chivalrous to surprise and capture a town by silent sortie, he paused at the nearest
corner and emitted his slogan—that fearful, brassy yell,
so reminiscent of the steam piano, that had gained for
him the classic appellation that had superseded his own
baptismal name. Following close upon his vociferation
came three shots from his forty-five by way of limbering
up the guns and testing his aim. A yellow dog, the personal property of Colonel Swazey, the proprietor of the
Occidental, fell feet upward in the dust with one farewell yelp. A Mexican who was crossing the street from

the Blue Front Grocery, carrying in his hand a bottle
of kerosene, was stimulated to a sudden and admirable
burst of speed, still grasping the neck of the shattered
bottle. The new gilt weathercock on Judge Riley's lemon
and ultra-marine two-story residence shivered, flapped,
and hung by a splinter, the sport of the wanton breezes.

The artillery was in trim. Calliope's hand was steady.
The high, calm ecstasy of habitual battle was upon him,
though slightly embittered by the sadness of Alexander
in that his conquests were limited to the small world
of Quicksand.

Down the street went Calliope, shooting right and
left. Glass fell like hail; dogs vamoosed; chickens flew,
squawking; feminine voices shrieked concernedly to
youngsters at large. The din was perforated at intervals
by the *staccato* of the Terror's guns, and was drowned
periodically by the brazen screech that Quicksand knew
so well. The occasions of Calliope's low spirits were legal
holidays in Quicksand. All along the main street in advance of his coming clerks were putting up shutters and
closing doors. Business would languish for a space. The
right of way was Calliope's, and as he advanced, observing the dearth of opposition and the few opportunities for distraction, his ennui perceptibly increased.

But some four squares farther down lively preparations were being made to minister to Mr. Catesby's love
for interchange of compliments and repartee. On the
previous night numerous messengers had hastened to

advise Buck Patterson, the city marshal, of Calliope's
impending eruption. The patience of that official, often
strained in extending lenience toward the disturber's
misdeeds, had been overtaxed. In Quicksand some in-
dulgence was accorded the natural ebullition of human
nature. Providing that the lives of the more useful citizens were not recklessly squandered, or too much property needlessly laid waste, the community sentiment was
against a too strict enforcement of the law. But Calliope
had raised the limit. His outbursts had been too frequent
and too violent to come within the classification of a
normal and sanitary relaxation of spirit.

Buck Patterson had been expecting and awaiting in
his little ten-by-twelve frame office that preliminary
yell announcing that Calliope was feeling blue. When
the signal came the City Marshal rose to his feet and
buckled on his guns. Two deputy sheriffs and three
citizens who had proven the edible qualities of fire also
stood up, ready to bandy with Calliope's leaden
jocularities.

"Gather that fellow in," said Buck Patterson, setting
for the lines of the campaign. "Don't have no talk, but
shoot as soon as you can get a show. Keep behind cover
and bring him down. He's a nogood 'un. It's up to Calliope to turn up his toes this time, I reckon. Go to him all
spraddled out, boys. And don't git too reckless, for what
Calliope shoots at he hits."

Buck Patterson, tall, muscular, and solemn-faced, with

his bright "City Marshal" badge shining on the breast of
his blue flannel shirt, gave his posse directions for the
onslaught upon Calliope. The plan was to accomplish
the downfall of the Quicksand Terror without loss to the
attacking party, if possible.

The splenetic Calliope, unconscious of retributive
plots, was steaming down the channel, cannonading on
either side, when he suddenly became aware of breakers
ahead. The City Marshal and one of the deputies rose
up behind some dry-goods boxes half a square to the
front and opened fire. At the same time the rest of the
posse, divided, shelled him from two side streets up
which they were cautiously manœuvring from a well-
executed detour.

The first volley broke the lock of one of Calliope's
guns, cut a neat underbit in his right ear, and exploded
a cartridge in his crossbelt, scorching his ribs as it burst.
Feeling braced up by this unexpected tonic to his spirit-
ual depression, Calliope executed a fortissimo note from
his upper registers, and returned the fire like an echo.
The upholders of the law dodged at his flash, but a trifle
too late to save one of the deputies a bullet just above
the elbow, and the marshal a bleeding cheek from a
splinter that a ball tore from a box he had ducked behind.

And now Calliope met the enemy's tactics in kind.
Choosing with a rapid eye the street from which the
weakest and least accurate fire had come, he invaded it
double-quick, abandoning the unprotected middle of

the street. With rare cunning the opposing force in that direction—one of the deputies and two of the valorous volunteers—waited, concealed by beer barrels, until Calliope had passed their retreat, and then peppered him from the rear. In another moment they were reinforced by the marshal and his other men, and then Calliope felt that in order to successfully prolong the delights of the controversy he must find some means of reducing the great odds against him. His eye fell upon a structure that seemed to hold out this promise, providing he could reach it.

Not far away was the little railroad station, its building a strong box house, ten by twenty feet, resting upon a platform four feet above ground. Windows were in each of its walls. Something like a fort it might become to a man thus sorely pressed by superior numbers.

Calliope made a bold and rapid spurt for it, the marshal's crowd "smoking" him as he ran. He reached the haven in safety, the station agent leaving the building by a window as the garrison entered the door.

Patterson and his supporters halted under protection of a pile of lumber and held consultations. In the station was an unterrified desperado who was an excellent shot and carried an abundance of ammunition. For thirty yards on each side of the besieged was a stretch of bare, open ground. It was a sure thing that the man who attempted to enter that unprotected area would be stopped by one of Calliope's bullets.

The City Marshal was resolved. He had decided that Calliope Catesby should no more wake the echoes of Quicksand with his strident whoop. He had so announced. Officially and personally he felt imperatively bound to put the soft pedal on that instrument of discord. It played bad tunes.

Standing near was a hand truck used in the manipulation of small freight. It stood by a shed full of sacked wool, a consignment from one of the sheep ranches. On this truck the marshal and his men piled three heavy sacks of wool. Stooping low, Buck Patterson started for Calliope's fort, slowly pushing this loaded truck before him for protection. The posse, scattering broadly, stood ready to nip the besieged in case he should show himself in an effort to repel the juggernaut of justice that was creeping upon him. Only once did Calliope make demonstration. He fired from a window and some tufts of wool spurted from the marshal's trustworthy bulwark. The return shots from the posse pattered against the window frame of the fort. No loss resulted on either side.

The marshal was too deeply engrossed in steering his protected battleship to be aware of the approach of the morning train until he was within a few feet of the platform. The train was coming up on the other side of it. It stopped only one minute at Quicksand. What an opportunity it would offer to Calliope! He had only to step out the other door, mount the train, and away.

Abandoning his breastworks, Buck, with his gun ready, dashed up the steps and into the room, driving open the closed door with one heave of his weighty shoulder. The members of the posse heard one shot fired inside, and then there was silence.

At length the wounded man opened his eyes. After a blank space he again could see and hear and feel and think. Turning his eyes about, he found himself lying on a wooden bench. A tall man with a perplexed countenance, wearing a big badge with "City Marshal" engraved upon it, stood over him. A little old woman in black, with a wrinkled face and sparkling black eyes was holding a wet handkerchief against one of his temples. He was trying to get these facts fixed in his mind and connected with past events, when the old woman began to talk.

"There now, great, big, strong man! That bullet never tetched ye! Jest skeeted along the side of your head and sort of paralyzed ye for a spell. I've heerd of sech things afor! con-cussion is what they names it. Abel Wadkins used to kill squirrels that way—barkin' em, Abe called it. You jest been barked, sir, and you'll be all right in a little bit. Feel lots better already, don't ye! You just lay still a while longer and let me bathe your head. You don't know me, I reckon, and 'tain't surprisin' that you shouldn't. I come in on that train from Alabama to see my son. Big son, ain't he? Lands! you wouldn't hardly think he'd ever been a baby, would ye? This big strong man is my son, sir."

Half turning, the old woman looked up at the standing man, her worn face lighting with a proud and wonderful smile. She reached out one veined and calloused hand and took one of her son's. Then smiling cheerily down at the prostrate man, she continued to dip the handkerchief in the waiting-room tin washbasin and gently apply it to his temple. She had the benevolent garrulity of old age.

"I ain't seen my son before," she continued, "in eight years. One of my nephews, Elkanah Price, he's a conductor on one of them railroads, and he got me a pass to come out here. I can stay a whole week on it, and then it'll take me back again. Jest think, now, that little boy of mine has got to be a officer—a city marshal of a whole town! That's something like a constable, ain't it? I never knowed he was a officer; he didn't say nothin' about it in his letters. I reckon he thought his old mother'd be skeered about the danger he was in. But, laws! I never was much of a hand to git skeered. 'Tain't no use. I heard them guns a-shootin' while I was gittin' off them cars, and I see smoke a-comin' out of the depot, but I jest walked right along. Then I see son's face lookin' out through the window. I knowed him at oncet. He met me at the door, and squeezed me 'most to death. And there you was, sir, a-lyin' there jest like you was dead, and I 'lowed we'd see what might be done to help sot you up."

"I think I'll sit up now," said the concussion patient. "I'm feeling pretty fair by this time."

He sat, somewhat weakly yet, leaning against the wall. He was a rugged man, big-boned and straight. His eyes, steady and keen, seemed to linger upon the face of the man standing so still above him. His look wandered often from the face he studied to the marshal's badge upon the other's breast.

"Yes, yes, you'll be all right," said the old woman, patting his arm, "if you don't get to cuttin' up agin, and havin' folks shootin' at you. Son told me about you, sir, while you was layin' senseless on the floor. Don't you take it as meddlesome fer an old woman with a son as big as you to talk about it. And you mustn't hold no grudge ag'in my son for havin' to shoot at ye. A officer has got to take up for the law—it's his duty—and them that acts bad and lives wrong has to suffer. Don't blame my son any, sir—'tain't his fault. He's always been a good boy—good when he was growin' up, and kind and 'bedient and well-behaved. Won't you let me advise you, sir, not to do so no more? Be a good man, and leave liquor alone and live peaceably and godly. Keep away from bad company and work honest and sleep sweet."

The black-mittened hand of the old pleader gently touched the breast of the man she addressed. Very earnest and candid her old, worn face looked. In her rusty black dress and antique bonnet she sat, near the close of a long life, and epitomized the experience of the world.

Still the man to whom she spoke gazed above her head, contemplating the silent son of the old mother.

"What does the marshal say?" he asked. "Does he believe the advice is good? Suppose the marshal speaks up and says if the talk's all right?"

The tall man moved uneasily. He fingered the badge on his breast for a moment, and then he put an arm around the old woman and drew her close to him. She smiled the unchanging mother smile of three-score years, and patted his big brown hand with her crooked, mittened fingers while son spake.

"I say this," he said, looking squarely into the eyes of the other man, "that if I was in your place I'd follow it. If I was a drunken, desp'rate character, without shame or hope, I'd follow it. If I was in your place and you was in mine I'd say: 'Marshal, I'm willin' to swear if you'll give me the chance I'll quit the racket. I'll drop the tanglefoot and the gun play, and won't play hoss no more. I'll be a good citizen and go to work and quit my foolishness. So help me God!' That's what I'd say to you if you was marshal and I was in your place."

"Hear my son talkin'," said the old woman, softly. "Hear him, sir. You promise to be good and he won't do you no harm. Forty-one year ago his heart first beat ag'in mine, and it's beat true ever since."

The other man rose to his feet, trying his limbs and stretching his muscles.

"Then," said he, "if you was in my place and said that,

and I was marshal, I'd say: 'Go free, and do your best to keep your promise'."

"Lawsy!" exclaimed the old woman, in a sudden flutter, "ef I didn't clear forget that trunk of mine! I see a man settin' it on the platform jest as I seen son's face in the window, and it went plum out of my head. There's eight jars of homemade quince jam in that trunk that I made myself. I wouldn't have nothin' happen to them jars for a red apple."

Away to the door she trotted, spry and anxious, and then Calliope Catesby spoke out to Buck Patterson:

"I just couldn't help it, Buck. I seen her through the window a-comin' in. She had never heard a word 'bout my tough ways. I didn't have the nerve to let her know I was a worthless cuss bein' hunted down by the community. There you was lyin' where my shot laid you, like you was dead. The idea struck me sudden, and I just took your badge off and fastened it onto myself, and I fastened my reputation onto you. I told her I was the marshal and you was a holy terror. You can take your badge back now, Buck."

With shaking fingers Calliope began to unfasten the disc of metal from his shirt.

"Easy there!" said Buck Patterson. "You keep that badge right where it is, Calliope Catesby. Don't you dare to take it off till the day your mother leaves this town. You'll be city marshal of Quicksand as long as she's here to know it. After I stir around town a bit and put 'em on I'll guarantee that nobody won't give the thing away to her. And say, you leather-headed, rip-roarin', lowdown son of a locoed cyclone, you follow that advice she gave me! I'm goin' to take some of it myself, too."

"Buck," said Calliope, feelingly, "ef I don't I hope I may——"

"Shut up," said Buck. "She's a-comin' back."

✦

OUT OF NAZARETH

OKOCHEE, IN GEORGIA, HAD A BOOM, and J. Pinkney Bloom came out of it with a "wad." Okochee came out of it with a half-million-dollar debt, a two and a half per cent city property tax, and a city council that showed a propensity for traveling the back streets of the town. These things came about through a fatal resemblance of the river Cooloosa to the Hudson, as set forth and expounded by a Northern tourist. Okochee felt that New York should not be allowed to consider itself the only alligator in the swamp, so to speak. And then that harmless, but persistent, individual so numerous in the South—the man who is always clamoring for more cotton mills, and is ready to take a dollar's worth of stock, provided he can borrow the dollar—that man added his

221

deadly work to a tourist's innocent praise; Okochee fell.

The Cooloosa River winds through a range of small mountains, passes Okochee, and then blends its waters trippingly, as fall the mellifluous Indian syllables, with the Chattahoochee.

Okochee rose, as it were, from its sunny seat on the post-office stoop, hitched up its suspender, and threw a granite dam two hundred and forty feet long and sixty feet high across the Cooloosa one mile above the town. Thereupon, a dimpling, sparkling lake backed up twenty miles among the little mountains. Thus in the great game of municipal rivalry did Okochee match that famous drawing card, the Hudson. It was conceded that nowhere could the Palisades be judged superior in the way of scenery and grandeur. Following the picture card was played the ace of commercial importance. Fourteen thousand horsepower would this dam furnish. Cotton mills, factories, and manufacturing plants would rise up as the green corn after a shower. The spindle and the flywheel and turbine would sing the shrewd glory of Okochee. Along the picturesque heights above the lake would rise in beauty the costly villas and the splendid summer residences of capital. The naphtha launch of the millionaire would spit among the romantic coves; the verdured hills would take formal shapes of terrace, lawn, and park. Money would be spent like water in Okochee, and water would be turned into money.

The fate of the good town is quickly told. Capital de-

cided not to invest. Of all the great things promised, the
scenery alone came to fulfilment. The wooded peaks, the
impressive promontories of solemn granite, the beautiful
green slants of bank and ravine did all they could to
reconcile Okochee to the delinquency of miserly gold.
The sunsets gilded the dreamy draws and coves with a
minting that should charm away heartburning. Okochee,
true to the instinct of its blood and clime, was lulled by
the spell. It climbed out of the arena, loosed its suspender, sat down again on the post-office stoop, and took
a chew. It consoled itself by drawling sarcasms at the city
council which was not to blame, causing the fathers, as
has been said, to seek back streets and figure perspiringly
on the sinking fund and appropriations for interest due.

The youth of Okochee—they who were to carry into
the rosy future the burden of the debt—accepted failure
with youth's uncalculating joy. For, here was sport,
aquatic and nautical, added to the meagre round of life's
pleasures. In yachting caps and flowing neckties they
pervaded the lake to its limits. Girls wore silk waists
embroidered with anchors in blue and pink. The trousers
of the young men widened at the bottom, and their hands
were proudly calloused by the oft-plied oar. Fishermen
were under the spell of a deep and tolerant joy. Sailboats
and rowboats furrowed the lenient waves, popcorn and
ice-cream booths sprang up about the little wooden pier.
Two small excursion steamboats were built, and plied the
delectable waters. Okochee philosophically gave up the

hope of eating turtle soup with a gold spoon, and settled back, not ill content, to its regular diet of lotus and fried hominy. And out of this slow wreck of great expectations rose up J. Pinkney Bloom with his "wad" and his prosperous, cheery smile.

Needless to say J. Pinkney was no product of Georgia soil. He came out of that flushed and capable region known as the "North." He called himself a "promoter"; his enemies had spoken of him as a "grafter"; Okochee took a middle course, and held him to be no better and no worse than a "Yank."

Far up the lake—eighteen miles above the town—the eye of this cheerful camp-follower of booms had spied out a graft. He purchased there a precipitous tract of five hundred acres at forty-five cents per acre; and this he laid out and subdivided as the city of Skyland—the Queen City of the Switzerland of the South. Streets and avenues were surveyed; parks designed; corners of central squares reserved for the "proposed" opera house, board of trade, lyceum, market, public schools, and "Exposition Hall." The price of lots ranged from five to five hundred dollars. Positively, no lot would be priced higher than five hundred dollars.

While the boom was growing in Okochee, J. Pinkney's circulars, maps, and prospectuses were flying through the mails to every part of the country. Investors sent in their money by post, and the Skyland Real Estate Company (J. Pinkney Bloom) returned to each a deed, duly placed

on record, to the best lot, at the price, on hand that day.
All this time the catamount screeched upon the reserved
lot of the Skyland Board of Trade, the opossum swung
by his tail over the site of the exposition hall, and the owl
hooted a melancholy recitative to his audience of young
squirrels in opera house square. Later, when the money
was coming in fast, J. Pinkney caused to be erected in the
coming city half a dozen cheap box houses, and persuaded a contingent of indigent natives to occupy them,
thereby assuming the role of "population" in subsequent
prospectuses, which became, accordingly, more seductive
and remunerative.

So, when the dream faded and Okochee dropped back
to digging bait and nursing its two and a half per cent tax,
J. Pinkney Bloom (unloving of checks and drafts and the
cold interrogatories of bankers) strapped about his fifty-
two-inch waist a soft leather belt containing eight thousand dollars in big bills, and said that all was very good.

One last trip he was making to Skyland before departing to other salad fields. Skyland was a regular post office,
and the steamboat, *Dixie Belle,* under contract, delivered
the mail bag (generally empty) twice a week. There was
a little business there to be settled—the postmaster was
to be paid off for his light but lonely services, and the
"inhabitants" had to be furnished with another month's
homely rations, as per agreement. And then Skyland
would know J. Pinkney Bloom no more. The owners of
these precipitous, barren, useless lots might come and

view the scene of their invested credulity, or they might leave them to their fit tenants, the wild hog and the browsing deer. The work of the Skyland Real Estate Company was finished.

The little steamboat *Dixie Belle* was about to shove off on her regular up-the-lake trip, when a rickety hired carriage rattled up to the pier, and a tall, elderly gentleman in black stepped out, signaling courteously but vivaciously for the boat to wait. Time was of the least importance in the schedule of the *Dixie Belle;* Captain MacFarland gave the order, and the boat received its ultimate two passengers. For, upon the arm of the tall, elderly gentleman, as he crossed the gangway, was a little elderly lady, with a gray curl depending quaintly forward of her left ear.

Captain MacFarland was at the wheel; therefore it seemed to J. Pinkney Bloom, who was the only other passenger, that it should be his to play the part of host to the boat's new guests, who were, doubtless, on a scenery-viewing expedition. He stepped forward, with that translucent, child-candid smile upon his fresh, pink countenance, with that air of unaffected sincerity that was redeemed from bluffness only by its exquisite calculation, with that promptitude and masterly decision of manner that so well suited his calling—with all his stock in trade well to the front, he stepped forward to receive Colonel and Mrs. Peyton Blaylock. With the grace of a grand marshal or a wedding usher, he escorted the two pas-

sengers to the side of the upper deck, from which the
scenery was supposed to present itself to the observer in
increased quantity and quality. There, in comfortable
steamer chairs, they sat and began to piece together the
random lines that were to form an intelligent paragraph
in the big history of little events.

"Our home, sir," said Colonel Blaylock, removing his
wide-brimmed, rather shapeless black felt hat, "is in
Holly Springs—Holly Springs, Georgia. I am very proud
to make your acquaintance, Mr. Bloom. Mrs. Blaylock
and myself have just arrived in Okochee this morning,
sir, on business—business of importance in connection
with the recent rapid march of progress in this section of
our state."

The Colonel smoothed back, with a sweeping gesture,
his long, smooth, gray locks. His dark eyes, still fiery
under the heavy black brows, seemed inappropriate to
the face of a business man. He looked rather to be an old
courtier handed down from the reign of Charles, and re-
attired in a modern suit of fine, but raveling and seam-
worn, broadcloth.

"Yes, sir," said Mr. Bloom, in his heartiest prospectus
voice, "things have been whizzing around Okochee. Big-
gest industrial revival and waking up to natural resources
Georgia ever had. Did you happen to squeeze in on the
ground floor in any of the gilt-edged grafts, Colonel?"

"Well, sir," said the Colonel, hesitating in courteous
doubt, "if I understand your question, I may say that I

took the opportunity to make an investment that I believe will prove quite advantageous—yes, sir, I believe it will result in both pecuniary profit and agreeable occupation."

"Colonel Blaylock," said the little elderly lady, shaking her gray curl and smiling indulgent explanation at J. Pinkney Bloom, "is so devoted to business. He has such a talent for financiering and markets and investments and those kind of things. I think myself extremely fortunate in having secured him for a partner on life's journey—I am so unversed in those formidable but very useful branches of learning."

Colonel Blaylock rose and made a bow—a bow that belonged with silk stockings and lace ruffles and velvet.

"Practical affairs," he said, with a wave of his hand toward the promoter, "are, if I may use the comparison, the garden walks upon which we tread through life, viewing upon either side of us the flowers which brighten that journey. It is my pleasure to be able to lay out a walk or two. Mrs. Blaylock, sir, is one of those fortunate higher spirits whose mission it is to make the flowers grow. Perhaps, Mr. Bloom, you have perused the lines of Lorella, the Southern poetess. That is the name above which Mrs. Blaylock has contributed to the press of the South for many years."

"Unfortunately," said Mr. Bloom, with a sense of the loss clearly written upon his frank face, "I'm like the Colonel—in the walk-making business myself—and I haven't had time to even take a sniff at the flowers. Poetry is a line I never dealt in. It must be nice, though—quite nice."

"It is the region," smiled Mrs. Blaylock, "in which my soul dwells. My shawl, Peyton, if you please—the breeze comes a little chilly from yon verdured hills."

The Colonel drew from the tail pocket of his coat a small shawl of knitted silk and laid it solicitously about the shoulders of the lady. Mrs. Blaylock sighed contentedly, and turned her expressive eyes—still as clear and unworldly as a child's—upon the steep slopes that were slowly slipping past. Very fair and stately they looked in the clear morning air. They seemed to speak in familiar terms to the responsive spirit of Lorella. "My native hills!" she murmured, dreamily. "See how the foliage drinks the sunlight from the hollows and dells."

"Mrs. Blaylock's maiden days," said the Colonel, interpreting her mood to J. Pinkney Bloom, "were spent among the mountains of northern Georgia. Mountain air and mountain scenery recall to her those days. Holly Springs, where we have lived for twenty years, is low and flat. I fear that she may have suffered in health and spirits by so long a residence there. That is one potent reason for the change we are making. My dear, can you not recall those lines you wrote—entitled, I think, 'The Georgia Hills'—the poem that was so extensively copied by the Southern press and praised so highly by the Atlanta critics?"

Mrs. Blaylock turned a glance of speaking tenderness

upon the Colonel, fingered for a moment the silvery curl
that drooped upon her bosom, then looked again toward
the mountains. Without preliminary or affectation or de-
murral she began, in rather thrilling and more deeply
pitched tones, to recite these lines:

> "The Georgia hills, the Georgia hills!—
>   Oh, heart, why dost thou pine?
> Are not these sheltered lowlands fair
>   With mead and bloom and vine?
> Ah! as the slow-paced river here
>   Broods on its natal rills
> My spirit drifts, in longing sweet,
>   Back to the Georgia hills.
>
> "And through the close-drawn, curtained night
>   I steal on sleep's slow wings
> Back to the heart's ease—slopes of pine—
>   Where end my wanderings.
> Oh, heaven seems nearer from their tops—
>   And farther earthly ills—
> Even in dreams, if I may but
>   Dream of my Georgia hills.
>
> "The grass upon their orchard sides
>   Is a fine couch to me;
> The common note of each small bird
>   Passes all minstrelsy.
> It would not seem so dread a thing
>   If, when the Reaper wills,
> He might come there and take my hand
>   Up in the Georgia hills."

"That's great stuff, ma'am," said J. Pinkney Bloom, enthusiastically, when the poetess had concluded. "I wish I had looked up poetry more than I have. I was raised in the pine hills myself."

"The mountains ever call to their children," murmured Mrs. Blaylock. "I feel that life will take on the rosy hue of hope again in among these beautiful hills. Peyton—a little taste of the currant wine, if you will be so good. The journey, though delightful in the extreme, slightly fatigues me."

Colonel Blaylock again visited the depths of his prolific coat, and produced a tightly corked, rough, black bottle. Mr. Bloom was on his feet in an instant. "Let me bring a glass, ma'am. You come along, Colonel—there's a little table we can bring, too. Maybe we can scare up some fruit or a cup of tea on board. I'll ask Mac."

Mrs. Blaylock reclined at ease. Few royal ladies have held their royal prerogative with the serene grace of the petted Southern woman. The Colonel, with an air as gallant and assiduous as in the days of his courtship, and J. Pinkney Bloom, with a ponderous agility half professional and half directed by some resurrected, unnamed, long-forgotten sentiment, formed a diversified but attentive court. The currant wine—wine home made from the Holly Springs fruit—went round; and then J. Pinkney began to hear something of Holly Springs life.

It seemed (from the conversation of the Blaylocks) that the Springs was decadent. A third of the population had moved away. Business—and the Colonel was an authority on business—had dwindled to nothing. After carefully studying the field of opportunities open to capital he had sold his little property there for eight hundred dollars and invested it in one of the enterprises opened up by the book in Okochee.

"Might I inquire, sir," and Mr. Bloom, "in what particular line of business you inserted your coin? I know that town as well as I know the regulations for illegal use of the mails. I might give you a hunch as to whether you can make the game go or not."

J. Pinkney, somehow, had a kindly feeling toward these unsophisticated representatives of bygone days. They were so simple, impractical, and unsuspecting. He was glad that he happened not to have a gold brick or a block of that western Bad Boy Silver Mine stock along with him. He would have disliked to unload on people he liked so well as he did these; but there are some temptations too enticing to be resisted.

"No, sir," said Colonel Blaylock, pausing to arrange the queen's wrap. "I did not invest in Okochee. I have made an exhaustive study of business conditions, and I regard old settled towns as unfavorable fields in which to place capital that is limited in amount. Some months ago, through the kindness of a friend, there came into my hands a map and description of this new town of Skyland that has been built upon the lake. The description was so pleasing, the future of the town set forth in such convincing arguments, and its increasing prosperity portrayed in such an attractive style that I decided to take advantage of the opportunity it offered. I carefully selected a lot in the centre of the business district, although its price was the highest in the schedule—five hundred dollars—and made the purchase at once."

"Are you the man—I mean, did you pay five hundred dollars for a lot in Skyland?" asked J. Pinkney Bloom.

"I did, sir," answered the Colonel, with the air of a modest millionaire explaining his success; "a lot most excellently situated on the same square with the opera house, and only two squares from the board of trade. I consider the purchase a most fortuitous one. It is my intention to erect a small building upon it at once, and open a modest book and stationery store. During past years I have met with many pecuniary reverses, and I now find it necessary to engage in some commercial occupation that will furnish me with a livelihood. The book and stationery business, though an humble one, seems to me not inapt nor altogether uncongenial. I am a graduate of the University of Virginia; and Mrs. Blaylock's really wonderful acquaintance with belles-lettres and poetic literature should go far toward insuring success. Of course, Mrs. Blaylock would not personally serve behind the counter. With the nearly three hundred dollars I have remaining I can manage the building of a house, by giving a lien on the lot. I have an old friend in Atlanta who is a partner in a large bookstore, and he has agreed to furnish me with a stock of goods on credit, on extremely easy terms. I am pleased to hope, sir, that Mrs. Blaylock's health and happiness will be increased by the change of locality. Already I fancy I can perceive the return of those roses that were once the hope and despair of Georgia cavaliers."

Again followed that wonderful bow, as the Colonel lightly touched the pale cheek of the poetess. Mrs. Blaylock, blushing like a girl, shook her curl and gave the Colonel an arch, reproving tap. Secret eternal youth— where are thou? Every second the answer comes—"Here, here, here." Listen to thine own heartbeats, O weary seeker after external miracles.

"Those years," said Mrs. Blaylock, "in Holly Springs were long, long, long. But now is the promised land in sight. Skyland!—a lovely name."

"Doubtless," said the Colonel, "we shall be able to secure comfortable accommodations at some modest hotel at reasonable rates. Our trunks are in Okochee, to be forwarded when we shall have made permanent arrangements."

J. Pinkney Bloom excused himself, went forward, and stood by the captain at the wheel.

"Mac," said he, "do you remember my telling you once that I sold one of those five-hundred-dollar lots in Skyland?"

"Seems I do," grinned Captain MacFarland.

"I'm not a coward, as a general rule," went on the promoter, "but I always said that if I ever met the sucker that bought that lot I'd run like a turkey. Now, you see that old babe-in-the-wood over there? Well, he's the boy that drew the prize. That was the only five-hundred-dollar lot that went. The rest ranged from ten dollars to two hundred. His wife writes poetry. She's invented one about the high grounds of Georgia, that's way up in G. They're going to Skyland to open a bookstore."

"Well," said MacFarland, with another grin, "it's a good thing you are along, J. P.; you can show 'em around town until they begin to feel at home."

"He's got three hundred dollars left to build a house and store with," went on J. Pinkney, as if he were talking to himself. "And he thinks there's an opera house up there."

Captain MacFarland released the wheel long enough to give his leg a roguish slap.

"You old fat rascal!" he chuckled, with a wink.

"Mac, you're a fool," said J. Pinkney Bloom, coldly. He went back and joined the Blaylocks, where he sat, less talkative, with that straight furrow between his brows that always stood as a signal of schemes being shaped within.

"There's a good many swindles connected with these booms," he said presently. "What if this Skyland should turn out to be one—that is, suppose business should be sort of dull there, and no special sale for books?"

"My dear sir," said Colonel Blaylock, resting his hand

upon the back of his wife's chair, "three times I have been reduced to almost penury by the duplicity of others, but I have not yet lost faith in humanity. If I have been deceived again, still we may glean health and content, if not worldly profit. I am aware that there are dishonest schemers in the world who set traps for the unwary, but even they are not altogether bad. My dear, can you recall those verses entitled, 'He Giveth the Increase,' that you composed for the choir of our church in Holly Springs?"

"That was four years ago," said Mrs. Blaylock; "perhaps I can repeat a verse or two:

> "The lily springs from the rotting mould;
>   Pearls from the deep sea slime;
>   Good will come out of Nazareth
>   All in God's own time.

> "To the hardest heart the softening grace
>   Cometh, at last, to bless;
>   Guiding it right to help and cheer
>   And succor in distress.

"I cannot remember the rest. The lines were not ambitious. They were written to the music composed by a dear friend."

"It's a fine rhyme, just the same," declared Mr. Bloom. "It seems to ring the bell, all right. I guess I gather the sense of it. It means that the rankest kind of a phony will give you the best end of it once in a while."

Mr. Bloom strayed thoughtfully back to the captain, and stood meditating.

"Ought to be in sight of the spires and gilded domes of Skyland now in a few minutes," chirruped MacFarland, shaking with enjoyment.

"Go to the devil," said Mr. Bloom, still pensive.

And now, upon the left bank, they caught a glimpse of a white village, high up on the hills, smothered among green trees. That was Cold Branch—no boom town, but the slow growth of many years. Cold Branch lay on the edge of the grape and corn lands. The big country road ran just back of the heights. Cold Branch had nothing in common with the frisky ambition of Okochee with its impertinent lake.

"Mac," said J. Pinkney suddenly, "I want you to stop at Cold Branch. There's a landing there that they made to use sometimes when the river was up."

"Can't," said the captain, grinning more broadly. "I've got the United States mails on board. Right today this boat's in the government service. Do you want to have the poor old captain keelhauled by Uncle Sam? And the great city of Skyland all disconsolate, waiting for its mail? I'm ashamed of your extravagance, J. P."

"Mac," almost whispered J. Pinkney, in his danger-line voice, "I looked into the engine room of the *Dixie Belle* a while ago. Don't you know of somebody that needs a new boiler? Cement and black japan can't hide flaws from me. And then, those shares of building and loan that you traded for repairs—they were all yours, of course. I hate to mention these things, but——"

"Oh, come now, J. P.," said the captain. "You know I was fooling. I'll put you off at Cold Branch, if you say so."

"The other passengers get off there, too," said Mr. Bloom.

Further conversation was held, and in ten minutes the *Dixie Belle* turned her nose toward a little, cranky wooden pier on the left bank, and the captain, relinquishing the wheel to a roustabout, came to the passenger deck and made the remarkable announcement: "All out for Skyland."

The Blaylocks and J. Pinkney Bloom disembarked, and the *Dixie Belle* proceeded on her way up the lake. Guided by the indefatigable promoter, they slowly climbed the steep hillside, pausing often to rest and admire the view. Finally they entered the village of Cold Branch. Warmly both the Colonel and his wife praised it for its homelike and peaceful beauty. Mr. Bloom conducted them to a two-story building on a shady street that bore the legend, "Pinetop Inn." Here he took his leave, receiving the cordial thanks of the two for his attentions, the Colonel remarking that he thought they would spend the remainder of the day in rest, and take a look at his purchase on the morrow.

J. Pinkney Bloom walked down Cold Branch's main street. He did not know this town, but he knew towns, and his feet did not falter. Presently he saw a sign over a door: "Frank E. Cooly, Attorney-at-Law and Notary

Public." A young man was Mr. Cooly, awaiting business.

"Get your hat, son," said Mr. Bloom, in his breezy way, "and a blank deed, and come along. It's a job for you."

"Now," he continued, when Mr. Cooly had responded with alacrity, "is there a bookstore in town?"

"One," said the lawyer. "Henry Williams's."

"Get there," said Mr. Bloom. "We're going to buy it."

Henry Williams was behind his counter. His store was a small one, containing a mixture of books, stationery, and fancy rubbish. Adjoining it was Henry's home—a decent cottage, vine-embroidered and cosy. Henry was lank and soporific, and not inclined to rush his business.

"I want to buy your house and store," said Mr. Bloom. "I haven't got time to dicker—name your price."

"It's worth eight hundred," said Henry, too much dazed to ask more than its value.

"Shut that door," said Mr. Bloom to the lawyer. Then he tore off his coat and vest, and began to unbutton his shirt.

"Wanter fight about it, do yer?" said Henry Williams, jumping up and cracking his heels together twice. "All right, hunky—sail in and cut yer capers."

"Keep your clothes on," said Mr. Bloom. "I'm only going down to the bank."

He drew eight one-hundred-dollar bills from his money belt and planked them down on the counter. Mr. Cooly showed signs of future promise, for he already had the

deed spread out, and was reaching across the counter for
the ink bottle. Never before or since was such quick
action had in Cold Branch.

"Your name, please?" asked the lawyer.

"Make it out to Peyton Blaylock," said Mr. Bloom.
"God knows how to spell it."

Within thirty minutes Henry Williams was out of business, and Mr. Bloom stood on the brick sidewalk with Mr.
Cooly, who held in his hand the signed and attested deed.

"You'll find the party at the Pinetop Inn," said J. Pinkney Bloom. "Get it recorded, and take it down and give it
to him. He'll ask you a hell's mint of questions; so here's
ten dollars for the trouble you'll have in not being able to
answer 'em. Never run much to poetry, did you, young
man?"

"Well," said the really talented Cooly, who even yet
retained his right mind, "now and then."

"Dig into it," said Mr. Bloom, "it'll pay you. Never
heard a poem, now, that run something like this, did
you:

> "A good thing out of Nazareth
>   Comes up sometimes, I guess,
> On hand, all right, to help and cheer
>   A sucker in distress."

"I believe not," said Mr. Cooly.

"It's a hymn," said J. Pinkney Bloom. "Now, show me
the way to a livery stable, son, for I'm going to hit the dirt
road back to Okochee."

‡

A CALL LOAN

IN THOSE DAYS THE CATTLEMEN WERE
the anointed. They were the grandees of the grass, kings
of the kine, lords of the lea, barons of beef and bone.
They might have ridden in golden chariots had their
tastes so inclined. The cattleman was caught in a stampede of dollars. It seemed to him that he had more money
than was decent. But when he had bought a watch with
precious stones set in the case so large that they hurt his
ribs, and a California saddle with silver nails and Angora-
skin *suaderos,* and ordered everybody up to the bar for
whisky—what else was there for him to spend money for?

Not so circumscribed in expedient for the reduction of
surplus wealth were those lairds of the lariat who had
womenfolk to their name. In the breast of the rib-sprung

sex the genius of purse lightening may slumber through
years of inopportunity, but never, my brothers, does it
become extinct.

So, out of the chaparral came Long Bill Longley from
the Bar Circle Branch on the Frio—a wife-driven man—
to taste the urban joys of success. Something like half a
million dollars he had, with an income steadily increasing.

Long Bill was a graduate of the camp and trail. Luck
and thrift, a cool head, and a telescopic eye for mavericks
had raised him from cowboy to be a cowman. Then came
the boom in cattle, and Fortune, stepping gingerly among
the cactus thorns, came and emptied her cornucopia at
the doorstep of the ranch.

In the little frontier city of Chaparosa, Longley built a
costly residence. Here he became a captive, bound to the
chariot of social existence. He was doomed to become a
leading citizen. He struggled for a time like a mustang in
his first corral, and then he hung up his quirt and spurs.
Time hung heavily on his hands. He organized the First
National Bank of Chaparosa, and was elected its president.

One day a dyspeptic man, wearing double-magnifying
glasses, inserted an official-looking card between the bars
of the cashier's window of the First National Bank. Five
minutes later the bank force was dancing at the beck and
call of a national bank examiner.

This examiner, Mr. J. Edgar Todd, proved to be a
thorough one.

At the end of it all the examiner put on his hat, and called the president, Mr. William R. Longley, into the private office.

"Well, how do you find things?" asked Longley, in his slow, deep tones. "Any brands in the roundup you didn't like the looks of?"

"The bank checks up all right, Mr. Longley," said Todd; "and I find your loans in very good shape—with one exception. You are carrying one very bad bit of paper— one that is so bad that I have been thinking that you surely do not realize the serious position it places you in. I refer to a call loan of $10,000 made to Thomas Merwin. Not only is the amount in excess of the maximum sum the bank can loan any individual legally, but it is absolutely without endorsement or security. Thus you have doubly violated the national banking laws, and have laid yourself open to criminal prosecution by the Government. A report of the matter to the Comptroller of the Currency— which I am bound to make—would, I am sure, result in the matter being turned over to the Department of Justice for action. You see what a serious thing it is."

Bill Longley was leaning his lengthy, slowly moving frame back in his swivel chair. His hands were clasped behind his head, and he turned a little to look the examiner in the face. The examiner was surprised to see a smile creep about the rugged mouth of the banker, and a kindly twinkle in his light-blue eyes. If he saw the seriousness of the affair, he did not show it.

"Of course, you don't know Tom Merwin," said Longley, almost genially. "Yes, I know about that loan. It
hasn't any security except Tom Merwin's word. Somehow,
I've always found that when a man's word is good, it's
the best security there is. Oh, yes, I know the Government doesn't think so. I guess I'll see Tom about that
note."

Mr. Todd's dyspepsia seemed to grow suddenly worse.
He looked at the chaparral banker through his double-
magnifying glasses in amazement.

"You see," said Longley, easily explaining the thing
away, "Tom heard of 2000 head of two-year-olds down
near Rocky Ford on the Rio Grande that could be had for
$8 a head. I reckon 'twas one of old Laendro Garcia's out-
fits that he had smuggled over, and he wanted to make a
quick turn on 'em. Those cattle are worth $15 on the hoof
in Kansas City. Tom knew it and I knew it. He had $6,000,
and I let him have the $10,000 to make the deal with. His
brother Ed took 'em on to market three weeks ago. He
ought to be back 'most any day now with the money.
When he comes Tom'll pay that note."

The bank examiner was shocked. It was, perhaps, his
duty to step out to the telegraph office and wire the
situation to the Comptroller. But he did not. He talked
pointedly and effectively to Longley for three minutes.
He succeeded in making the banker understand that he
stood upon the border of a catastrophe. And then he
offered a tiny loophole of escape.

"I am going to Hilldale tonight," he told Longley, "to examine a bank there. I will pass through Chaparosa on my way back. At twelve tomorrow I shall call at this bank. If this loan has been cleared out of the way by that time it will not be mentioned in my report. If not—I will have to do my duty."

With that the examiner bowed and departed.

The President of the First National lounged in his chair half an hour longer, and then he lit a mild cigar, and went over to Tom Merwin's house. Merwin, a ranchman in brown duck, with a contemplative eye, sat with his feet upon a table, plaiting a rawhide quirt.

"Tom," said Longley, leaning against the table, "you heard anything from Ed yet?"

"Not yet," said Merwin, continuing his plaiting. "I guess Ed'll be along back now in a few days."

"There was a bank examiner," said Longley, "nosing around our place today, and he bucked a sight about that note of yours. You know I know it's all right, but the thing *is* against the banking laws. I was pretty sure you'd have paid it off before the bank was examined again, but the son-of-a-gun slipped in on us, Tom. Now, I'm short of cash myself just now, or I'd let you have the money to take it up with. I've got till twelve o'clock tomorrow, and then I've got to show the cash in place of that note or——"

"Or what, Bill?" asked Merwin, as Longley hesitated.

"Well, I suppose it means be jumped on with both of

Uncle Sam's feet."

"I'll try to raise the money for you on time," said Merwin, interested in his plaiting.

"All right, Tom," concluded Longley, as he turned toward the door. "I knew you would if you could."

Merwin threw down his whip and went to the only other bank in town, a private one, run by Cooper & Craig.

"Cooper," he said, to the partner by that name, "I've got to have $10,000 today or tomorrow. I've got a house and lot here that's worth about $6,000 and that's all the actual collateral. But I've got a cattle deal on that's sure to bring me in more than that much profit within a few days."

Cooper began to cough.

"Now, for God's sake don't say no," said Merwin. "I owe that much money on a call loan. It's been called, and the man that called it is a man I've laid on the same blanket with in cow camps and ranger camps for ten years. He can call anything I've got. He can call the blood out of my veins and it'll come. He's got to have the money. He's in a devil of a—— Well, he needs the money, and I've got to get it for him. You know my word's good, Cooper."

"No doubt of it," assented Cooper, urbanely, "but I've a partner, you know. I'm not free in making loans. And even if you had the best security in your hands, Merwin, we couldn't accommodate you in less than a week. We're just making a shipment of $15,000 to Myer Brothers in

Rockdell, to buy cotton with. It goes down on the narrow gauge tonight. That leaves our cash quite short at present. Sorry we can't arrange it for you."

Merwin went back to his little bar office and plaited at his quirt again. About four o'clock in the afternoon he went to the First National and leaned over the railing of Longley's desk.

"I'll try to get that money for you tonight—I mean tomorrow, Bill."

"All right, Tom," said Longley, quietly.

At nine o'clock that night Tom Merwin stepped cautiously out of the small frame house in which he lived. It was near the edge of the little town, and few citizens were in the neighborhood at that hour. Merwin wore two six-shooters in a belt and a slouch hat. He moved swiftly down a lonely street, and then followed the sandy road that ran parallel to the narrow-gauge track until he reached the water tank, two miles below the town. There Tom Merwin stopped, tied a black silk handkerchief about the lower part of his face, and pulled his hat down low.

In ten minutes the night train for Rockdell pulled up at the tank, having come from Chaparosa.

With a gun in each hand Merwin raised himself from behind a clump of chaparral and started for the engine. But before he had taken three steps, two long, strong arms clasped him from behind, and he was lifted from his feet and thrown, face downward, upon the grass. There was a heavy knee pressing against his back, and an iron hand grasping each of his wrists. He was held thus, like a child, until the engine had taken water, and until the train had moved, with accelerating speed, out of sight. Then he was released, and rose to his feet to face Bill Longley.

"The case never needed to be fixed up this way, Tom," said Longley. "I saw Cooper this evening, and he told me what you and him talked about. Then I went down to your house tonight and saw you come out with your guns on, and I followed you. Let's go back, Tom."

They walked away together, side by side.

" 'Twas the only chance I saw," said Merwin, presently. "You called your loan, and I tried to answer you. Now, what'll you do, Bill, if they sock it to you?"

"What would you have done if they'd socked it to you?" was the answer Longley made.

"I never thought I'd lay in a bush to stick up a train," remarked Merwin; "but a call loan's different. A call's a call with me. We've got twelve hours yet, Bill, before this spy jumps onto you. We've got to raise them spondulicks somehow. Maybe we can—Great Sam Houston! do you hear that?"

Merwin broke into a run, and Longley kept with him, hearing only a rather pleasing whistle somewhere in the night rendering the lugubrious air of "The Cowboy's Lament."

"It's the only tune he knows," shouted Merwin, as he ran. "I'll bet——"

They were at the door of Merwin's house. He kicked it open and fell over an old valise lying in the middle of the floor. A sunburned, firm-jawed youth, stained by travel, lay upon the bed puffing at a brown cigarette.

"What's the word, Ed?" gasped Merwin.

"So, so," drawled that capable youngster. "Just got in on the 9:30. Sold the bunch for fifteen, straight. Now, buddy, you want to quit kickin' a valise around that's got $29,000 in greenbacks in its in'ards."

THE GREEN DOOR

SUPPOSE YOU SHOULD BE WALKING down Broadway after dinner, with ten minutes allotted to the consummation of your cigar while you are choosing between a diverting tragedy and something serious in the way of vaudeville. Suddenly a hand is laid upon your arm. You turn to look into the thrilling eyes of a beautiful woman, wonderful in diamonds and Russian sables. She thrusts hurriedly into your hand an extremely hot buttered roll, flashes out a tiny pair of scissors, snips off the second button of your overcoat, meaningly ejaculates the one word, "parallelogram!" and swiftly flies down a cross street, looking back fearfully over her shoulder.

That would be pure adventure. Would you accept it?

Not you. You would flush with embarrassment; you would sheepishly drop the roll and continue down Broadway, fumbling feebly for the missing button. This you would do unless you are one of the blessed few in whom the pure spirit of adventure is not dead.

True adventurers have never been plentiful. They who are set down in print as such have been mostly business men with newly invented methods. They have been out after the things they wanted—golden fleeces, holy grails, lady loves, treasure, crowns and fame. The true adventurer goes forth aimless and uncalculating to meet and greet unknown fate. A fine example was the Prodigal Son—when he started back home.

Half-adventurers—brave and splendid figures—have been numerous. From the Crusades to the Palisades they have enriched the arts of history and fiction and the trade of historical fiction. But each of them had a prize to win, a goal to kick, an axe to grind, a race to run, a new thrust in tierce to deliver, a name to carve, a crow to pick—so they were not followers of true adventure.

In the big city the twin spirits Romance and Adventure are always abroad seeking worthy wooers. As we roam the streets they slyly peep at us and challenge us in twenty different guises. Without knowing why, we look up suddenly to see in a window a face that seems to belong to our gallery of intimate portraits; in a sleeping thoroughfare we hear a cry of agony and fear coming from an empty and shuttered house; instead of at our

familiar curb a cab driver deposits us before a strange
door, which one, with a smile, opens for us and bids us
enter; a slip of paper, written upon, flutters down to our
feet from the high lattices of Chance; we exchange
glances of instantaneous hate, affection, and fear with
hurrying strangers in the passing crowds; a sudden souse
of rain—and our umbrella may be sheltering the daughter of the Full Moon and first cousin of the Sidereal System; at every corner handkerchiefs drop, fingers beckon,
eyes besiege, and the lost, the lonely, the rapturous, the
mysterious, the perilous changing clues of adventure are
slipped into our fingers. But few of us are willing to hold
and follow them. We are grown stiff with the ramrod of
convention down our backs. We pass on; and some day
we come, at the end of a very dull life, to reflect that our
romance has been a pallid thing of a marriage or two, a
satin rosette kept in a safe-deposit drawer, and a lifelong
feud with a steam radiator.

Rudolf Steiner was a true adventurer. Few were the
evenings on which he did not go forth from his hall bedchamber in search of the unexpected and the egregious.
The most interesting thing in life seemed to him to be
what might lie just around the next corner. Sometimes his
willingness to tempt fate led him into strange paths.
Twice he had spent the night in a station house; again
and again he had found himself the dupe of ingenious
and mercenary tricksters; his watch and money had been
the price of one flattering allurement. But with undimin-

ished ardor he picked up every glove cast before him into the merry lists of adventure.

One evening Rudolf was strolling along a crosstown street in the older central part of the city. Two streams of people filled the sidewalks—the home-hurrying, and that restless contingent that abandons home for the specious welcome of the thousand-candle-power *table d'hôte.*

The young adventurer was of pleasing presence, and moved serenely and watchfully. By daylight he was a salesman in a piano store. He wore his tie drawn through a topaz ring instead of fastened with a stickpin; and once he had written to the editor of a magazine that *Junie's Love Test,* by Miss Libbey, had been the book that had most influenced his life.

During his walk a violent chattering of teeth in a glass case on the sidewalk seemed at first to draw his attention (with a qualm) to a restaurant before which it was set; but a second glance revealed the electric letters of a dentist's sign high above the next door. A giant negro, fantastically dressed in a red embroidered coat, yellow trousers and a military cap, discreetly distributed cards to those of the passing crowd who consented to take them.

This mode of dentistic advertising was a common sight to Rudolf. Usually he passed the dispenser of the dentist's cards without reducing his store; but tonight the African slipped one into his hand so deftly that he retained it there smiling a little at the successful feat.

When he had traveled a few yards further he glanced
at the card indifferently. Surprised, he turned it over and
looked again with interest. One side of the card was
blank; on the other was written in ink three words, "The
Green Door." And then Rudolf saw, three steps in front
of him, a man throw down the card the negro had given
him as he passed. Rudolph picked it up. It was printed
with the dentist's name and address and the usual schedule of "plate work" and "bridgework" and "crowns," and
specious promises of "painless" operations.

The adventurous piano salesman halted at the corner
and considered. Then he crossed the street, walked down
a block, recrossed and joined the upward current of
people again. Without seeming to notice the negro as he
passed the second time, he carelessly took the card that
was handed him. Ten steps away he inspected it. In the
same handwriting that appeared on the first card "The
Green Door" was inscribed upon it. Three or four cards
were tossed to the pavement by pedestrians both following and leading him. These fell blank side up. Rudolph
turned them over. Every one bore the printed legend of
the dental "parlors."

Rarely did the arch sprite Adventure need to beckon
twice to Rudolf Steiner, his true follower. But twice it
had been done, and the quest was on.

Rudolf walked slowly back to where the giant negro
stood by the case of rattling teeth. This time as he passed

he received no card. In spite of his gaudy and ridiculous garb, the Ethiopian displayed a natural barbaric dignity as he stood, offering the cards suavely to some, allowing others to pass unmolested. Every half minute he chanted a harsh, unintelligible phrase akin to the jabber of car conductors and grand opera. And not only did he withhold a card this time but it seemed to Rudolf that he received from the shining and massive black countenance a look of cold, almost contemptuous disdain.

The look stung the adventurer. He read in it a silent accusation that he had been found wanting. Whatever the mysterious written words on the cards might mean, the black had selected him twice from the throng for their recipient; and now seemed to have condemned him as deficient in the wit and spirit to engage the enigma.

Standing aside from the rush, the young man made a rapid estimate of the building in which he conceived that his adventure must lie. Five stories high it rose. A small restaurant occupied the basement.

The first floor, now closed, seemed to house millinery or furs. The second floor, by the winking electric letters, was the dentist's. Above this a polyglot babel of signs struggled to indicate the abodes of palmists, dressmakers, musicians, and doctors. Still higher up draped curtains and milk bottles white on the window sills proclaimed the regions of domesticity.

After concluding his survey Rudolf walked briskly up the high flight of stone steps into the house. Up two flights of the carpeted stairway he continued; and at its top paused. The hallway there was dimly lighted by two pale jets of gas—one far to his right, the other nearer, to his left. He looked toward the nearer light and saw, within its wan halo, a green door. For one moment he hesitated; then he seemed to see the contumelious sneer of the African juggler of cards; and then he walked straight to the green door and knocked against it.

Moments like those that passed before his knock was answered measure the quick breath of true adventure. What might not be behind those green panels! Gamesters at play; cunning rogues baiting their traps with subtle skill; beauty in love with courage, and thus planning to be sought by it; danger, death, love, disappointment, ridicule—any of these might respond to that temerarious rap.

A faint rustle was heard inside, and the door slowly opened. A girl not yet twenty stood there white-faced and tottering. She loosed the knob and swayed weakly, groping with one hand. Rudolf caught her and laid her on a faded couch that stood against the wall. He closed the door and took a swift glance around the room by the light of a flickering gas jet. Neat, but extreme poverty was the story that he read.

The girl lay still, as if in a faint. Rudolf looked around the room excitedly for a barrel. People must be rolled upon a barrel who—no, no; that was for drowned persons. He began to fan her with his hat. That was successful, for he struck her nose with the brim of his derby and she opened her eyes. And then the young man saw that hers, indeed, was the one missing face from his heart's gallery of intimate portraits. The frank, gray eyes, the little nose, turning pertly outward; the chestnut hair, curling like the tendrils of a pea vine, seemed the right end and reward of all his wonderful adventures. But the face was woefully thin and pale.

The girl looked at him calmly, and then smiled.

"Fainted, didn't I?" she asked, weakly. "Well, who wouldn't? You try going without anything to eat for three days and see!"

"Himmel!" exclaimed Rudolf, jumping up. "Wait till I come back."

He dashed out the green door and down the stairs. In twenty minutes he was back again kicking at the door with his toe for her to open it. With both arms he hugged an array of wares from the grocery and the restaurant. On the table he laid them—bread and butter, cold meats, cakes, pies, pickles, oysters, a roasted chicken, a bottle of milk and one of red-hot tea.

"This is ridiculous," said Rudolf, blusteringly, "to go without eating. You must quit making election bets of this kind. Supper is ready." He helped her to a chair at the table and asked: "Is there a cup for the tea?" "On the shelf by the window," she answered. When he turned again with the cup he saw her, with eyes shining rapturously, beginning upon a huge dill pickle that she had rooted out from the paper bags with a woman's unerring instinct. He took it from her, laughingly, and poured the cup full of milk. "Drink that first," he ordered, "and then you shall have some tea and then a chicken wing. If you are very good you shall have a pickle tomorrow. And now, if you'll allow me to be your guest we'll have supper."

He drew up the other chair. The tea brightened the girl's eyes and brought back some of her color. She began to eat with a sort of dainty ferocity like some starved wild animal. She seemed to regard the young man's presence and the aid he had rendered her as a natural thing —not as though she undervalued the conventions; but as one whose great stress gave her the right to put aside the artificial for the human. But gradually, with the return of strength and comfort, came also a sense of the little conventions that belong; and she began to tell him her little story. It was one of a thousand such as the city yawns at every day—the shopgirl's story of insufficient wages, further reduced by "fines" that go to swell the store's profits; of time lost through illness; and then of lost positions, lost hope, and—the knock of the adventurer upon the green door.

But to Rudolf the history sounded as big as the *Iliad* or the crisis in *Junie's Love Test*.

"To think of you going through all that," he exclaimed.

"It was something fierce," said the girl, solemnly.

"And you have no relatives or friends in the city?"

"None whatever."

"I am all alone in the world, too," said Rudolf, after a pause.

"I am glad of that," said the girl, promptly; and somehow it pleased the young man to hear that she approved of his bereft condition.

Very suddenly her eyelids dropped and she sighed deeply.

"I'm awfully sleepy," she said, "and I feel so good."

Rudolf rose and took his hat.

"Then I'll say good night. A long night's sleep will be fine for you."

He held out his hand, and she took it and said "good night." But her eyes asked a question so eloquently, so frankly and pathetically that he answered it with words.

"Oh, I'm coming back tomorrow to see how you are getting along. You can't get rid of me so easily."

Then, at the door, as though the way of his coming had been so much less important than the fact that he had come, she asked: "How did you come to knock at my door?"

He looked at her for a moment, remembering the cards, and felt a sudden jealous pain. What if they had fallen into other hands as adventurous as his? Quickly he decided that she must never know the truth. He would never let her know he was aware of the strange expedient to which she had been driven by her great distress.

"One of our piano tuners lives in this house," he said.
"I knocked at your door by mistake."

The last thing he saw in the room before the green
door closed was her smile.

At the head of the stairway he paused and looked
curiously about him. And then he went along the hallway to its other end; and, coming back, ascended to the
floor above and continued his puzzled explorations.
Every door that he found in the house was painted green.

Wondering, he descended to the sidewalk. The fantastic African was still there. Rudolf confronted him with
his two cards in his hand.

"Will you tell me why you gave me these cards and
what they mean?" he asked.

In a broad, good-natured grin the negro exhibited a
splendid advertisement of his master's profession.

"There it is, sah," he said, pointing down the street.
"But I 'spect you are a little late for the first act."

Looking the way he pointed Rudolf saw above the entrance to a theatre the blazing electric sign of its new
play, "The Green Door."

"I'm informed that it's a first-rate show, sah," said the
negro. "The agent what represents it presented me with a
dollah, sah, to distribute a few of his cards along with the
doctor's. May I offer you one of the doctor's cards, sah?"

At the corner of the block in which he lived Rudolf
stopped for a glass of beer and a cigar. When he had

come out with his lighted weed he buttoned his coat, pushed back his hat and said, stoutly, to the lamppost on the corner:

"All the same, I believe it was the hand of Fate that doped out the way for me to find her."

Which conclusion, under the circumstances, certainly admits Rudolf Steiner to the ranks of the true followers of Romance and Adventure.

HEARTS AND
CROSSES

BALDY WOODS REACHED FOR THE
bottle, and got it. Whenever Baldy went for anything
he usually—but this is not Baldy's story. He poured out
a third drink that was larger by a finger than the first
and second. Baldy was in consultation; and the con-
sultee is worthy of his hire.

"I'd be king if I was you," said Baldy, so positively
that his holster creaked and his spurs rattled.

Webb Yeager pushed back his flat-brimmed Stetson,
and made further disorder in his straw-colored hair. The
tonsorial recourse being without avail, he followed the
liquid example of the more resourceful Baldy.

"If a man marries a queen, it oughtn't to make him a two-spot," declared Webb, epitomizing his grievances.

"Sure not," said Baldy, sympathetic, still thirsty, and genuinely solicitous concerning the relative value of the cards. "By rights you're a king. If I was you, I'd call for a new deal. The cards have been stacked on you—I'll tell you what you are, Webb Yeager."

"What?" asked Webb, with a hopeful look in his pale blue eyes.

"You're a prince consort."

"Go easy," said Webb. "I never blackguarded you none."

"It's a title," explained Baldy, "up among the picture cards; but it don't take no tricks. I'll tell you, Webb. It's a brand they've got for certain animals in Europe. Say that you or me or one of them Dutch dukes marries in a royal family. Well, by and by our wife gets to be queen. Are we king? Not in a million years. At the coronation ceremonies we march between little casino and the Ninth Grand Custodian of the Royal Hall Bedchamber. The only use we are is to appear in photographs, and accept the responsibility for the heir apparent. That ain't any square deal. Yes, sir, Webb, you're a prince consort; and if I was you, I'd start a interregnum or a habeas corpus or somethin'; and I'd be king if I had to turn from the bottom of the deck."

Baldy emptied his glass to the ratification of his Warwick pose.

"Baldy," said Webb, solemnly, "me and you punched cows in the same outfit for years. We been runnin' on the same range, and ridin' the same trails since we was boys. I wouldn't talk about my family affairs to nobody but you. You was line-rider on the Nopalito Ranch when I married Santa McAllister. I was foreman then; but what am I now? I don't amount to a knot in a stake rope."

"When old McAllister was the cattle king of West Texas," continued Baldy with Satanic sweetness, "you was some tallow. You had as much to say on the ranch as he did."

"I did," admitted Webb, "up to the time he found out I was tryin' to get my rope over Santa's head. Then he kept me out on the range as far from the ranch house as he could. When the old man died they commenced to call Santa the 'cattle queen.' I'm boss of the cattle— that's all. She 'tends to all the business; she handles all the money; I can't sell even a beef steer to a party of campers, myself. Santa's the 'queen'; and I'm Mr. Nobody."

"I'd be a king if I was you," repeated Baldy Woods, the royalist. "When a man marries a queen he ought to grade up with her—on the hoof—dressed—dried— corned—any old way from the chaparral to the packing-house. Lots of folks thinks it's funny, Webb, that you don't have the say-so on the Nopalito. I ain't reflectin' none on Miz Yeager—she's the finest little lady between

the Rio Grande and next Christmas—but a man ought
to be boss of his own camp."

The smooth, brown face of Yeager lengthened to a
mask of wounded melancholy. With that expression,
and his rumpled yellow hair and guileless blue eyes, he
might have been likened to a schoolboy whose leadership had been usurped by a youngster of superior
strength. But his active and sinewy seventy-two inches
and his girded revolvers forbade the comparison.

"What was that you called me, Baldy?" he asked.
"What kind of a concert was it?"

"A 'consort,'" corrected Baldy—"'a prince consort.'
It's a kind of short-card pseudonym. You come in sort
of between Jack-high and a four-card flush."

Webb Yeager sighed, and gathered the strap of his
Winchester scabbard from the floor.

"I'm ridin' back to the ranch today," he said, half-
heartedly. "I've got to start a bunch of beeves for San
Antone in the morning."

"I'm your company as far as Dry Lake," announced
Baldy. "I've got a roundup camp on the San Marcos
cuttin' out two-year-olds."

The two *compañeros* mounted their ponies and trotted
away from the little railroad settlement, where they
had foregathered in the thirsty morning.

At Dry Lake, where their routes diverged, they
reined up for a party cigarette. For miles they had ridden
in silence save for the soft drum of the ponies' hoofs on

the matted mesquite grass, and the rattle of the chaparral
against their wooden stirrups. But in Texas discourse
is seldom continuous. You may fill in a mile, a meal, and
a murder between your paragraphs without detriment
to your thesis. So, without apology, Webb offered an ad-
dendum to the conversation that had begun ten miles
away.

"You remember, yourself, Baldy, that there was a
time when Santa wasn't quite so independent. You remember the days when Old McAllister was keepin' us
apart, and how she used to send me the sign that she
wanted to see me? Old man Mac promised to make
me look like a colander if I ever come in gunshot of
the ranch. You remember the sign she used to send,
Baldy—the heart with a cross inside of it?"

"Me?" cried Baldy, with intoxicated archness.

"You old sugar-stealing coyote! Don't I remember!
Why, you dad-blamed old long-horned turtledove, the
boys in camp was all cognoscious about them hiero-
glyphs. The 'gizzard-and-crossbones' we used to call it.
We used to see 'em on truck that was sent out from the
ranch. They was marked in charcoal on the sacks of
flour and in lead pencil on the newspapers. I see one of
'em once chalked on the back of a new cook that old
man McAllister sent out from the ranch—danged if I
didn't."

"Santa's father," exclaimed Webb gently, "got her to
promise that she wouldn't write to me or send me any

word. That heart-and-cross sign was her scheme. Whenever she wanted to see me in particular she managed to put that mark on somethin' at the ranch that she knew I'd see. And I never laid eyes on it but what I burnt the wind for the ranch the same night. I used to see her in that coma mott back of the little horse corral."

"We knowed it," chanted Baldy; "but we never let on. We was all for you. We knowed why you always kept that fast paint in camp. And when we see that gizzard-and-crossbones figured out on the truck from the ranch we knowed old Pinto was goin' to eat up miles that night instead of grass. You remember Scurry —that educated horse-wrangler we had—the college fellow that tangle-foot drove to the range? Whenever Scurry saw that come-meet-your-honey brand on anything from the ranch, he'd wave his hand like that, and say, 'Our friend Lee Andrews will again swim the Hell's point tonight.'"

"The last time Santa sent me the sign," said Webb, "was once when she was sick. I noticed it as soon as I hit camp, and I galloped Pinto forty mile that night. She wasn't at the coma mott. I went to the house; and old McAllister met me at the door. 'Did you come here to get killed?' says he; 'I'll disoblige you for once. I just started a Mexican to bring you. Santa wants you. Go in that room and see her. And then come out here and see me.'

"Santa was lyin' in bed pretty sick. But she gives out

a kind of a smile, and her hand and mine lock horns, and I sets down by the bed—mud and spurs and chaps and all. 'I've heard you ridin' across the grass for hours, Webb,' she says. 'I was sure you'd come. You saw the sign?' she whispers. 'The minute I hit camp,' says I. ' 'Twas marked on the bag of potatoes and onions.' 'They're always together,' says she, softlike—'always together in life.' 'They go well together,' I says, 'in a stew.' 'I mean hearts and crosses,' says Santa. 'Our sign—to love and to suffer—that's what they mean.'

"And there was old Doc Musgrove amusin' himself with whisky and a palm-leaf fan. And by and by Santa goes to sleep; and Doc feels her forehead; and he says to me: 'You're not such a bad febrifuge. But you'd better slide out now, for the diagnosis don't call for you in regular doses. The little lady'll be all right when she wakes up.'

"I seen old McAllister outside. 'She's asleep,' says I. 'And now you can start in with your colander-work. Take your time; for I left my gun on my saddle-horn.'

"Old Mac laughs, and he says to me: 'Pumpin' lead into the best ranch boss in West Texas don't seem to me good business policy. I don't know where I could get as good a one. It's the son-in-law idea, Webb, that makes me admire for to use you as a target. You ain't my idea for a member of the family. But I can use you on the Nopalito if you'll keep outside of a radius with the ranch house in the middle of it. You go upstairs and lay down on a cot, and when you get some sleep we'll talk it over.' "

Baldy Woods pulled down his hat, and uncurled his leg from his saddle-horn. Webb shortened his rein, and his pony danced, anxious to be off. The two men shook hands with Western ceremony.

"*Adios*, Baldy," said Webb. "I'm glad I seen you and had this talk."

With a pounding rush that sounded like the rise of a covey of quail, the riders sped away toward different points of the compass. A hundred yards on his route Baldy reined in on the top of a bare knoll and emitted a yell. He swayed on his horse; had he been on foot, the earth would have risen and conquered him; but in the saddle he was a master of equilibrium, and laughed at whisky, and despised the centre of gravity.

Webb turned in his saddle at the signal.

"If I was you," came Baldy's strident and perverting tones, "I'd be king!"

At eight o'clock on the following morning Bud Turner rolled from his saddle in front of the Nopalito ranch house, and stumbled with whizzing rowels toward the gallery. Bud was in charge of the bunch of beef cattle that was to strike the trail that morning for San Antonio. Mrs. Yeager was on the gallery watering a cluster of hyacinths growing in a red earthenware jar.

"King" McAllister had bequeathed to his daughter many of his strong characteristics—his resolution, his

gay courage, his contumacious self-reliance, his pride
as a reigning monarch of hoofs and horns. *Allegro* and
fortissimo had been McAllister's tempo and tone. In
Santa they survived, transposed to the feminine key.
Substantially, she preserved the image of the mother
who had been summoned to wander in other and less
finite green pastures long before the waxing herds of
kine had conferred royalty upon the house. She had
her mother's slim, strong figure and grave, soft prettiness
that relieved in her the severity of the imperious Mc-
Allister eye and the McAllister air of royal independence.

Webb stood on one end of the gallery giving orders
to two or three sub-bosses of various camps and outfits
who had ridden in for instructions.

"'Morning," said Bud, briefly. "Where do you want
them beeves to go in town—to Barber's, as usual?"

Now, to answer that had been the prerogative of the
queen. All the reins of business—buying, selling, and
banking—had been held by her capable fingers. The
handling of the cattle had been entrusted fully to her
husband. In the days of "King" McAllister, Santa had
been his secretary and helper; and she had continued
her work with wisdom and profit. But before she could
reply, the prince consort spake up with calm decision:

"You drive that bunch to Zimmerman and Nesbit's
pens. I spoke to Zimmerman about it some time ago."

Bud turned on his high boot-heels.

"Wait!" called Santa quickly. She looked at her husband with surprise in her steady gray eyes.

"Why, what do you mean, Webb?" she asked, with a small wrinkle gathering between her brows. "I never deal with Zimmerman and Nesbit. Barber has handled every head of stock from this ranch in that market for five years. I'm not going to take the business out of his hands." She faced Bud Turner. "Deliver those cattle to Barber," she concluded positively.

Bud gazed impartially at the water-jar hanging on the gallery, stood on his other leg, and chewed a mesquite leaf.

"I want this bunch of beeves to go to Zimmerman and Nesbit," said Webb, with a frosty light in his blue eyes.

"Nonsense," said Santa impatiently. "You'd better start on, Bud, so as to noon at the Little Elm waterhole. Tell Barber we'll have another lot of culls ready in about a month."

Bud allowed a hesitating eye to steal upward and meet Webb's. Webb saw apology in his look, and fancied he saw commiseration.

"You deliver them cattle," he said grimly, "to——"

"Barber," finished Santa sharply. "Let that settle it. Is there anything else you are waiting for, Bud?"

"No, m'm," said Bud. But before going he lingered while a cow's tail could have switched thrice; for a man is man's ally; and even the Philistines must have blushed when they took Samson in the way they did.

"You hear your boss!" cried Webb, sardonically. He took off his hat, and bowed until it touched the floor before his wife.

"Webb," said Santa rebukingly, "you're acting mighty foolish today."

"Court fool, your Majesty," said Webb, in his slow tones, which had changed their quality. "What else can you expect? Let me tell you. I was a man before I married a cattle queen. What am I now? The laughing-stock of the camps. I'll be a man again."

Santa looked at him closely.

"Don't be unreasonable, Webb," she said calmly. "You haven't been slighted in any way. Do I ever interfere in your management of the cattle? I know the business side of the ranch much better than you do. I learned it from Dad. Be sensible."

"Kingdoms and queendoms," said Webb, "don't suit me unless I am in the pictures, too. I punch the cattle and you wear the crown. All right. I'd rather be High Chancellor of a cow camp than the eight-spot in a queen-high flush. It's your ranch; and Barber gets the beeves."

Webb's horse was tied to the rack. He walked into the house and brought out his roll of blankets that he never took with him except on long rides, and his "slicker," and his longest stake-rope of plaited rawhide. These he began to tie deliberately upon his saddle. Santa, a little pale, followed him.

Webb swung up into the saddle. His serious, smooth

face was without expression except for a stubborn light that smouldered in his eyes.

"There's a herd of cows and calves," said he, "near the Hondo waterhole on the Frio that ought to be moved away from timber. Lobos have killed three of the calves. I forgot to leave orders. You'd better tell Simms to attend to it."

Santa laid a hand on the horse's bridle, and looked her husband in the eye.

"Are you going to leave me, Webb?" she asked quietly.

"I am going to be a man again," he answered.

"I wish you success in a praiseworthy attempt," she said, with a sudden coldness. She turned and walked directly into the house.

Webb Yeager rode to the southeast as straight as the topography of West Texas permitted. And when he reached the horizon he might have ridden on into blue space as far as knowledge of him on the Nopalito went. And the days, with Sundays at their head, formed into hebdomadal squads; and the weeks, captained by the full moon, closed ranks into menstrual companies carrying *Tempus Fugit* on their banners; and the months marched on toward the vast camp-ground of the years; but Webb Yeager came no more to the dominions of his queen.

One day a being named Bartholomew, a sheepman—and therefore of little account—from the lower Rio Grande country, rode in sight of the Nopalito ranch

house, and felt hunger assail him. *Ex consuetudine* he
was soon seated at the midday dining table of that hospitable kingdom. Talk like water gushed from him: he
might have been smitten with Aaron's rod—that is your
gentle shepherd when an audience is vouchsafed him
whose ears are not overgrown with wool.

"Missis Yeager," he babbled, "I see a man the other
day on the Rancho Seco down in Hidalgo County by
your name—Webb Yeager was his. He'd just been
engaged as manager. He was a tall, light-haired man,
not saying much. Maybe he was some kin of yours, do
you think?"

"A husband," said Santa cordially. "The Seco has
done well. Mr. Yeager is one of the best stockmen in
the West."

The dropping out of a prince consort rarely dis-
organizes a monarchy. Queen Santa had appointed as
mayordomo of the ranch, a trusty subject, named Ram-
say, who had been one of her father's faithful vassals.
And there was scarcely a ripple on the Nopalito ranch
save when the gulf breeze created undulations in the
grass of its wide acres.

For several years the Nopalito had been making experiments with an English breed of cattle that looked
down with aristocratic contempt upon the Texas longhorns. The experiments were found satisfactory; and a
pasture had been set apart for the bluebloods. The fame
of them had gone forth into the chaparral and pear as

far as men ride in saddles. Other ranches woke up, rubbed their eyes, and looked with new dissatisfaction upon the longhorns.

As a consequence, one day a sunburned, capable, silk-kerchiefed nonchalant youth, garnished with revolvers, and attended by three Mexican *vaqueros*, alighted at the Nopalito ranch and presented the following businesslike epistle to the queen thereof.

Mrs. Yeager—The Napolito Ranch:
Dear Madam:

I am instructed by the owners of the Rancho Seco to purchase 100 head of two and three-year-old cows of the Sussex breed owned by you. If you can fill the order please deliver the cattle to the bearer; and a check will be forwarded to you at once.

Respectfully,
Webster Yeager,
Manager of the Rancho Seco.

Business is business, even—very scantily did it escape being written "especially"—in a kingdom.

That night the 100 head of cattle were driven up from the pasture and penned in a corral near the ranch house for delivery in the morning.

When night closed down and the house was still, did Santa Yeager throw herself down, clasping that formal note to her bosom, weeping, and calling out a name that pride (either in one or the other) had kept from

her lips many a day? Or did she file the letter, in her
business way, retaining her royal balance and strength?

Wonder, if you will; but royalty is sacred, and there
is a veil. But this much you shall learn.

At midnight Santa slipped softly out of the ranch
house, clothed in something dark and plain. She paused
for a moment under the live oak trees. The prairies were
somewhat dim, and the moonlight was pale orange, di-
luted with particles of an impalpable, flying mist. But
the mockingbird whistled on every bough of vantage;
leagues of flowers scented the air; and a kindergarten of
little shadowy rabbits leaped and played in an open
space near by. Santa turned her face to the southeast
and threw kisses thitherward; for there was none to see.

Then she sped silently to the blacksmith shop, fifty
yards away; and what she did there can only be sur-
mised. But the forge glowed red; and there was a faint
hammering such as Cupid might make when he sharpens
his arrow points.

Later she came forth with a queer-shaped, handled
thing in one hand, and a portable furnace, such as are
seen in branding-camps, in the other. To the corral
where the Sussex cattle were penned she sped with these
things swiftly in the moonlight.

She opened the gate and slipped inside the corral. The
Sussex cattle were mostly a dark red. But among this
bunch was one that was milky white—notable among
the others.

And now Santa shook from her shoulder something that we had not seen before—a rope lasso. She freed the loop of it, coiling the length in her left hand, and plunged into the thick of the cattle.

The white cow was her object. She swung the lasso, which caught one horn and slipped off. The next throw encircled the forefeet and the animal fell heavily. Santa made for it like a panther; but it scrambled up and dashed against her, knocking her over like a blade of grass.

Again she made the cast, while the aroused cattle milled round the four sides of the corral in a plunging mass. This throw was fair; the white cow came to earth again; and before it could rise Santa had made the lasso fast around a post of the corral with a swift and simple knot, and had leaped upon the cow again with the rawhide hobbles.

In one minute the feet of the animal were tied (no record-breaking deed) and Santa leaned against the corral for the same space of time, panting and lax.

And then she ran swiftly to her furnace at the gate and brought the branding-iron, queerly shaped and white-hot.

The bellow of the outraged white cow, as the iron was applied, should have stirred the slumbering auricular nerves and consciences of the nearby subjects of the Nopalito, but it did not. And it was amid the deepest nocturnal silence that Santa ran like a lapwing back to

the ranch house and there fell upon a cot and sobbed—
sobbed as though queens had hearts as simple ranch-
men's wives have, and as though she would gladly make
kings of prince consorts, should they ride back again
from over the hills and far away.

In the morning the capable, revolvered youth and his
vaqueros set forth, driving the bunch of Sussex cattle
across the prairies to the Rancho Seco. Ninety miles it
was, a six days' journey, grazing and watering the animals on the way.

The beasts arrived at Rancho Seco one evening at
dusk; and were received and counted by the foreman
of the ranch.

The next morning at eight o'clock a horseman loped
out of the brush to the Nopalito ranch house. He dismounted stiffly, and strode, with whizzing spurs, to the
house. His horse gave a great sigh and swayed foam-
streaked, with down-drooping head and closed eyes.

But waste not your pity upon Belshazzar, the flea-
bitten sorrel. Today, in the Nopalito horse pasture he
survives, pampered, beloved, unridden, cherished record-
holder of long-distance rides.

The horseman stumbled into the house. Two arms fell
around his neck and someone cried out in the voice
of woman and queen alike: "Webb—oh, Webb!"

"I was a skunk," said Webb Yeager.

"Hush," said Santa, "did you see it?"

"I saw it," said Webb.

What they meant God knows; and you shall know, if you rightly read the primer of events.

"Be the cattle queen," said Webb; "and overlook it if you can. I was a mangy, sheep-stealing coyote."

"Hush!" said Santa again, laying her fingers upon his mouth. "There's no queen here. Do you know who I am? I am Santa Yeager, First Lady of the Bedchamber. Come here."

She dragged him from the gallery into the room to the right. There stood a cradle with an infant in it—a red, ribald, unintelligible, babbling, beautiful infant, sputtering at life in an unseemly manner.

"There's no queen on this ranch," said Santa again. "Look at the king. He's got your eyes, Webb. Down on your knees and look at his Highness."

But jingling rowels sounded on the gallery, and Bud Turner stumbled there again with the same query that he had brought, lacking a few days, a year ago.

"'Morning. Them beeves is just turned out on the trail. Shall I drive 'em to Barber's, or——"

He saw Webb and stopped, open-mouthed.

"Ba-ba-ba-ba-ba-ba!" shrieked the king in his cradle, beating the air with his fists.

"You hear your boss, Bud," said Webb Yeager, with a broad grin—just as he had said a year ago.

And that is all, except that when old man Quinn, owner of the Rancho Seco, went out to look over the herd of Sussex cattle that he had bought from the

Nopalito ranch, he asked his new manager:

"What's the Nopalito ranch brand, Wilson?"

"X Bar Y," said Wilson.

"I thought so," said Quinn. "But look at that white heifer there; she's got another brand—a heart with a cross inside of it. What brand is that?"

THE ADVENTURES OF
SHAMROCK JOLNES

I AM SO FORTUNATE AS TO COUNT
Shamrock Jolnes, the great New York detective, among
my muster of friends. Jolnes is what is called the "inside
man" of the city detective force. He is an expert in the
use of the typewriter, and it is his duty, whenever there
is a "murder mystery" to be solved, to sit at a desk telephone at headquarters and take down the messages of
"cranks" who phone in their confessions to having committed the crime.

But on certain "off" days when confessions are coming
in slowly and three or four newspapers have run to earth
as many different guilty persons, Jolnes will knock about
the town with me, exhibiting, to my great delight and

instruction, his marvellous powers of observation and deduction.

The other day I dropped in at headquarters and found the great detective gazing thoughtfully at a string that was tied tightly around his little finger.

"Good morning, Whatsup," he said, without turning his head. "I'm glad to notice that you've had your house fitted up with electric lights at last."

"Will you please tell me," I said, in surprise, "how you knew that? I am sure that I never mentioned the fact to anyone, and the wiring was a rush order not completed until this morning."

"Nothing easier," said Jolnes, genially. "As you came in I caught the odor of the cigar you are smoking. I know an expensive cigar; and I know that not more than three men in New York can afford to smoke cigars and pay gas bills too at the present time. That was an easy one. But I am working just now on a little problem of my own."

"Why have you that string on your finger?" I asked.

"That's the problem," said Jolnes. "My wife tied that on this morning to remind me of something I was to send up to the house. Sit down, Whatsup, and excuse me for a few moments."

The distinguished detective went to a wall telephone, and stood with the receiver to his ear for probably ten minutes.

"Were you listening to a confession?" I asked, when he had returned to his chair.

"Perhaps," said Jolnes, with a smile, "it might be called something of the sort. To be frank with you, Whatsup, I've cut out the dope. I've been increasing the quantity for so long that morphine doesn't have much effect on me anymore. I've got to have something more powerful. That telephone I just went to is connected with a room in the Waldorf where there's an author's reading in progress. Now, to get at the solution of this string."

After five minutes of silent pondering, Jolnes looked at me, with a smile, and nodded his head.

"Wonderful man!" I exclaimed; "already?"

"It is quite simple," he said, holding up his finger. "You see that knot? That is to prevent my forgetting. It is, therefore, a forget-me-knot. A forget-me-not is a flower. It was a sack of flour that I was to send home!"

"Beautiful!" I could not help crying out in admiration.

"Suppose we go out for a ramble," suggested Jolnes.

"There is only one case of importance on hand now. Old man McCarty, one hundred and four years old, died from eating too many bananas. The evidence points so strongly to the Mafia that the police have surrounded the Second Avenue Katzenjammer Gambrinus Club No. 2, and the capture of the assassin is only the matter of a few hours. The detective force has not yet been called on for assistance."

Jolnes and I went out and up the street toward the corner, where we were to catch a surface car.

Halfway up the block we met Rheingelder, an acquaintance of ours, who held a City Hall position.

"Good morning, Rheingelder," said Jolnes, halting. "Nice breakfast that was you had this morning."

Always on the lookout for the detective's remarkable feats of deduction, I saw Jolnes's eye flash for an instant upon a long yellow splash on the shirt bosom and a smaller one upon the chin of Rheingelder—both undoubtedly made by the yolk of an egg.

"Oh, dot is some of your detectiveness," said Rheingelder, shaking all over with a smile. "Vell, I bet you trinks and cigars all around dot you cannot tell vot I haf eaten for breakfast."

"Done," said Jolnes. "Sausage, pumpernickel, coffee."

Rheingelder admitted the correctness of the surmise and paid the bet. When we had proceeded on our way I said to Jolnes:

"I thought you looked at the egg spilled on his chin and shirt front."

"I did," said Jolnes. "That is where I began my deduction. Rheingelder is a very economical, saving man. Yesterday eggs dropped in the market to twenty-eight cents per dozen. Today they are quoted at forty-two. Rheingelder ate eggs yesterday, and today he went back to his usual fare. A little thing like this isn't anything, Whatsup; it belongs to the primary arithmetic class."

When we boarded the streetcar we found the seats all occupied—principally by ladies. Jolnes and I stood on the rear platform.

About the middle of the car there sat an elderly man with a short, gray beard, who looked to be the typical, well-dressed New Yorker. At successive corners other ladies climbed aboard, and soon three or four of them were standing over the man, clinging to straps and glaring meaningly at the man who occupied the coveted seat. But he resolutely retained his place.

"We New Yorkers," I remarked to Jolnes, "have about lost our manners, as far as the exercise of them in public goes."

"Perhaps so," said Jolnes, lightly; "but the man you evidently refer to happens to be a very chivalrous and courteous gentleman from Old Virginia. He is spending a few days in New York with his wife and two daughters, and he leaves for the South tonight."

"You know him, then?" I said, in amazement.

"I never saw him before we stepped on the car," declared the detective, smilingly.

"By the gold tooth of the Witch of Endor!" I cried, "if you can construe all that from his appearance you are dealing in nothing else than black art."

"The habit of observation—nothing more," said Jolnes. "If the old gentleman gets off the car before we do, I can demonstrate to you the accuracy of my deduction."

Three blocks farther along the gentleman rose to leave the car. Jolnes addressed him at the door:

"Pardon me, sir, but are you not Colonel Hunter, of Norfolk, Virginia?"

"No, suh," was the extremely courteous answer. "My name, suh, is Ellison—Major Winfield R. Ellison, from Fairfax County, in the same state. I know a good many people, suh, in Norfolk—the Goodriches, the Tollivers, and the Crabtrees, suh, but I never had the pleasure of meeting yo' friend, Colonel Hunter. I am happy to say, suh, that I am going back to Virginia tonight, after having spent a week in yo' city with my wife and three daughters. I shall be in Norfolk in about ten days, and if you will give me yo' name, suh, I will take pleasure in looking up Colonel Hunter and telling him that you inquired after him, suh."

"Thank you," said Jolnes; "tell him that Reynolds sent his regards, if you will be so kind."

I glanced at the great New York detective and saw that a look of intense chagrin had come upon his clear-cut features. Failure in the slightest point always galled Shamrock Jolnes.

"Did you say your *three* daughters?" he asked of the Virginia gentleman.

"Yes, suh, my three daughters, all as fine girls as there are in Fairfax County," was the answer.

With that Major Ellison stopped the car and began to decend the step.

Shamrock Jolnes clutched his arm.

"One moment, sir," he begged, in an urbane voice in which I alone detected the anxiety—"am I not right in believing that one of the young ladies is an *adopted* daughter?"

"You are, suh," admitted the major, from the ground, "but how the devil you knew it, suh, is mo' than I can tell."

"And more than I can tell, too," I said, as the car went on.

Jolnes was restored to his calm, observant serenity by having wrested victory from his apparent failure; so after we got off the car he invited me in to a café promising to reveal the process of his latest wonderful feat.

"In the first place," he began after we were comfortably seated, "I knew the gentleman was no New Yorker because he was flushed and uneasy and restless on account of the ladies that were standing, although he did not rise and give them his seat. I decided from his appearance that he was a Southerner rather than a Westerner.

"Next I began to figure out his reason for not relinquishing his seat to a lady when he evidently felt strongly, but not overpoweringly, impelled to do so. I very quickly decided upon that. I noticed that one of his eyes had received a severe jab in one corner, which was red and inflamed, and that all over his face were tiny round marks about the size of the end of an uncut lead pencil. Also upon both of his patent-leather shoes were a number of deep imprints shaped like ovals cut off square at one end.

"Now, there is only one district in New York City where

a man is bound to receive scars and wounds and indentations of that sort—and that is along the sidewalks of Twenty-third Street and a portion of Sixth Avenue south of there. I knew from the imprints of trampling French heels on his feet and the marks of countless jabs in the face from umbrellas and parasols carried by women in the shopping district that he had been in conflict with the Amazonian troops. And as he was a man of intelligent appearance, I knew he would not have braved such dangers unless he had been dragged thither by his own women folk. Therefore, when he got on the car his anger at the treatment he had received was sufficient to make him keep his seat in spite of his traditions of Southern chivalry."

"That is all very well," I said, "but why did you insist upon daughters—and especially two daughters? Why couldn't a wife alone have taken him shopping?"

"There had to be daughters," said Jolnes, calmly. "If he had only a wife, and she near his own age, he could have bluffed her into going alone. If he had a young wife she would prefer to go alone. So there you are."

"I'll admit that," I said; "but, now, why two daughters? And how, in the name of all the prophets, did you guess that one was adopted when he told you he had three?"

"Don't say 'guess'," said Jolnes, with a touch of pride in his air. "There is no such word in the lexicon of ratiocination. In Major Ellison's buttonhole there was a carnation and a rosebud backed by a geranium leaf. No woman ever combined a carnation and a rosebud into a boutonnière. Close your eyes, Whatsup, and give the logic of your imagination a chance. Cannot you see the lovely Adele fastening the carnation to the lapel so that papa may be gay upon the street? And then the romping Edith May dancing up with sisterly jealousy to add her rosebud to the adornment?"

"And then," I cried, beginning to feel enthusiasm, "when he declared that he had three daughters——"

"I could see," said Jolnes, "one in the background who added no flower; and I knew that she must be——"

"Adopted!" I broke in. "I give you every credit; but how did you know he was leaving for the South tonight?"

"In his breast pocket," said the great detective, "something large and oval made a protuberance. Good liquor is scarce on trains, and it is a long journey from New York to Fairfax County."

"Again, I must bow to you," I said. "And tell me this, so that my last shred of doubt will be cleared away; why did you decide that he was from Virginia?"

"It was very faint, I admit," answered Shamrock Jolnes, "but no trained observer could have failed to detect the odor of mint in the car."

THE PASSING OF
BLACK EAGLE

FOR SOME MONTHS OF A CERTAIN YEAR
a grim bandit infested the Texas border along the Rio
Grande. Peculiarly striking to the optic nerve was this
notorious marauder. His personality secured him the
title of "Black Eagle, the Terror of the Border." Many
fearsome tales are on record concerning the doings of
him and his followers. Suddenly, in the space of a single
minute, Black Eagle vanished from earth. He was never
heard of again. His own band never even guessed the
mystery of his disappearance. The border ranches and
settlements feared he would come again to ride and

ravage the mesquite flats. He never will. It is to disclose
the fate of Black Eagle that this narrative is written.

The initial movement of the story is furnished by the
foot of a bartender in St. Louis. His discerning eye fell
upon the form of Chicken Ruggles as he pecked with
avidity at the free lunch. Chicken was a "hobo." He had
a long nose like the bill of a fowl, an inordinate appetite
for poultry, and a habit of gratifying it without expense,
which accounts for the name given him by his fellow
vagrants.

Physicians agree that the partaking of liquids at meal-
times is not a healthy practice. The hygiene of the saloon
promulgates the opposite. Chicken had neglected to
purchase a drink to accompany his meal. The bartender
rounded the counter, caught the injudicious diner by the
ear with a lemon squeezer, led him to the door and kicked
him into the street.

Thus the mind of Chicken was brought to realize the
signs of coming winter. The night was cold; the stars
shone with unkindly brilliancy; people were hurrying
along the streets in two egotistic, jostling streams. Men
had donned their overcoats, and Chicken knew to an ex-
act percentage the increased difficulty of coaxing dimes
from those buttoned-in vest pockets. The time had come
for his annual exodus to the South.

A little boy, five or six years old, stood looking with
covetous eyes in a confectioner's window. In one small
hand he held an empty two-ounce vial; in the other he

grasped tightly something flat and round, with a shining milled edge. The scene presented a field of operations commensurate to Chicken's talents and daring. After sweeping the horizon to make sure that no official tug was cruising near, he insidiously accosted his prey. The boy, having been early taught by his household to regard altruistic advances with extreme suspicion, received the overtures coldly.

Then Chicken knew that he must make one of those desperate, nerve-shattering plunges into speculation that fortune sometimes requires of those who would win her favor. Five cents was his capital, and this he must risk against the chance of winning what lay within the close grasp of the youngster's chubby hand. It was a fearful lottery, Chicken knew. But he must accomplish his end by strategy, since he had a wholesome terror of plundering infants by force. Once, in a park, driven by hunger, he had committed an onslaught upon a bottle of peptonized infant's food in the possession of an occupant of a baby carriage. The outraged infant had so promptly opened its mouth and pressed the button that communicated with the welkin, that help arrived, and Chicken did his thirty days in a snug coop. Wherefore he was, as he said, "leary of kids."

Beginning artfully to question the boy concerning his choice of sweets, he gradually drew out the information he wanted. Mamma said he was to ask the drugstore man for ten cents' worth of paregoric in the bottle; he was to keep his hand shut tight over the dollar; he must not stop to talk to anyone in the street; he must ask the drugstore man to wrap up the change and put it in the pocket of his trousers. Indeed, they had pockets—two of them! And he liked chocolate creams best.

Chicken went into the store and turned plunger. He invested his entire capital in C. A. N. D. Y. stocks, simply to pave the way to the greater risk following.

He gave the sweets to the youngster, and had the satisfaction of perceiving that confidence was established. After that it was easy to obtain leadership of the expedition, to take the investment by the hand and lead it to a nice drugstore he knew of in the same block. There Chicken, with a parental air, passed over the dollar and called for the medicine, while the boy crunched his candy, glad to be relieved of the responsibility of the purchase. And then the successful investor searching his pockets, found an overcoat button—the extent of his winter trousseau—and, wrapping it carefully, placed the ostensible change in the pocket of confiding juvenility. Setting the youngster's face homeward, and patting him benevolently on the back—for Chicken's heart was as soft as those of his feathered namesakes—the speculator quit the market with a profit of 1,700 per cent, on his invested capital.

Two hours later an Iron Mountain freight engine pulled out of the railroad yards, Texas bound, with a string of empties. In one of the cattle cars, half buried

in excelsior, Chicken lay at ease. Beside him in his nest
was a quart bottle of very poor whiskey and a paper bag
of bread and cheese. Mr. Ruggles, in his private car, was
on his trip south for the winter season.

For a week that car was trundled southward, shifted,
laid over, and manipulated after the manner of rolling
stock, but Chicken stuck to it, leaving it only at necessary times to satisfy his hunger and thirst. He knew it
must go down to the cattle country, and San Antonio, in
the heart of it, was his goal. There the air was salubrious
and mild; the people indulgent and long-suffering. The
bartenders there would not kick him. If he should eat
too long or too often at one place they would swear at
him as if by rote and without heat. They swore so drawl-
ingly, and they rarely paused short of their full vocabulary, which was copious, so that Chicken had often
gulped a good meal during the process of the vitupera-
tive prohibition. The season there was always springlike;
the plazas were pleasant at night, with music and
gayety; except during the slight and infrequent cold
snaps one could sleep comfortably out of doors in case
the interiors should develop inhospitality.

At Texarkana his car was switched to the I. and G. N.
Then still southward it trailed until, at length, it crawled
across the Colorado bridge at Austin, and lined out,
straight as an arrow, for the run to San Antonio.

When the freight halted at that town Chicken was fast
asleep. In ten minutes the train was off again for Laredo,

the end of the road. Those empty cattle cars were for
distribution along the line at points from which the
ranches shipped their stock.

When Chicken awoke his car was stationary. Looking
out between the slats he saw it was a bright, moonlit
night. Scrambling out, he saw his car with three others
abandoned on a little siding in a wild and lonesome
country. A cattle pen and chute stood on one side of the
track. The railroad bisected a vast, dim ocean of prairie,
in the midst of which Chicken, with his futile rolling
stock, was as completely stranded as was Robinson with
his land-locked boat.

A white post stood near the rails. Going up to it,
Chicken read the letters at the top, S. A. 90. Laredo was
nearly as far to the south. He was almost a hundred miles
from any town. Coyotes began to yelp in the mysterious
sea around him. Chicken felt lonesome. He had lived in
Boston without an education, in Chicago without nerve,
in Philadelphia without a sleeping place, in New York
without a pull, and in Pittsburgh sober, and yet he had
never felt so lonely as now.

Suddenly through the intense silence, he heard the
whicker of a horse. The sound came from the side of the
track toward the east, and Chicken began to explore
timorously in that direction. He stepped high along the
mat of curly mesquite grass, for he was afraid of everything there might be in this wilderness—snakes, rats,
brigands, centipedes, mirages, cowboys, fandangoes,

tarantulas, tamales—he had read of them in the story
papers. Rounding a clump of prickly pear that reared
high its fantastic and menacing array of rounded heads,
he was struck to shivering terror by a snort and a thunderous plunge, as the horse, himself startled, bounded
away some fifty yards, and then resumed his grazing. But
here was the one thing in the desert that Chicken did not
fear. He had been reared on a farm; he had handled
horses, understood them, and could ride.

Approaching slowly and speaking soothingly, he followed the animal, which, after its first flight, seemed
gentle enough, and secured the end of the twenty-foot
lariat that dragged after him in the grass. It required
him but a few moments to contrive the rope into an ingenious nose-bridle, after the style of the Mexican *borsal*.
In another he was upon the horse's back and off at a
splendid lope, giving the animal free choice of direction.
"He will take me somewhere," said Chicken to himself.

It would have been a thing of joy, that untrammelled
gallop over the moonlit prairie, even to Chicken, who
loathed exertion, but that his mood was not for it. His
head ached; a growing thirst was upon him; the "somewhere" whither his lucky mount might convey him was
full of dismal peradventure.

And now he noted that the horse moved to a definite
goal. Where the prairie lay smooth he kept his course
straight as an arrow's toward the east. Deflected by hill
or arroyo or impracticable spinous brakes, he quickly

flowed again into the current, charted by his unerring
instinct. At last, upon the side of a gentle rise, he suddenly subsided to a complacent walk. A stone's cast away
stood a little mott of coma trees; beneath it a jacal such
as the Mexicans erect—a one-room house of upright
poles daubed with clay and roofed with grass or tule
reeds. An experienced eye would have estimated the spot
as the headquarters of a small sheep ranch. In the moonlight the ground in the nearby corral showed pulverized
to a level smoothness by the hoofs of the sheep. Everywhere was carelessly distributed the paraphernalia of the
place—ropes, bridles, saddles, sheep pelts, wool sacks,
feed troughs, and camp litter. The barrel of drinking
water stood in the end of the two-horse wagon near the
door. The harness was piled, promiscuous, upon the
wagon tongue, soaking up the dew.

Chicken slipped to earth, and tied the horse to a tree.
He halloed again and again, but the house remained
quiet. The door stood open, and he entered cautiously.
The light was sufficient for him to see that no one was at
home. He struck a match and lighted a lamp that stood
on a table. The room was that of a bachelor ranchman
who was content with the necessaries of life. Chicken
rummaged intelligently until he found what he had
hardly hoped for—a small brown jug that still contained
something near a quart of his desire.

Half an hour later, Chicken—now a gamecock of
hostile aspect—emerged from the house with unsteady

steps. He had drawn upon the absent ranchman's equipment to replace his own ragged attire. He wore a suit of coarse brown ducking, the coat being a sort of rakish bolero, jaunty to a degree. Boots he had donned, and spurs that whirred with every lurching step. Buckled around him was a belt full of cartridges with a big six-shooter in each of its two holsters.

Prowling about, he found blankets, a saddle and bridle with which he caparisoned his steed. Again mounting, he rode swiftly away, singing a loud and tuneless song.

Bud King's band of desperadoes, outlaws and horse and cattle thieves were in camp at a secluded spot on the bank of the Frio. Their depredations in the Rio Grande country, while no bolder than usual, had been advertised more extensively, and Captain Kinney's company of rangers had been ordered down to look after them. Consequently, Bud King, who was a wise general, instead of cutting out a hot trail for the upholders of the law, as his men wished to do, retired for the time to the prickly fastnesses of the Frio valley.

Though the move was a prudent one, and not incompatible with Bud's well-known courage, it raised dissension among the members of the band. In fact, while they thus lay ingloriously *perdu* in the brush, the question of Bud King's fitness for the leadership was argued, with closed doors, as it were, by his followers. Never before had Bull's skill or efficiency been brought to criticism;

but his glory was waning (and such is glory's fate) in the light of a newer star. The sentiment of the band was crystallizing into the opinion that Black Eagle could lead them with more luster, profit, and distinction.

This Black Eagle—subtitled the "Terror of the Border" —had been a member of the gang about three months.

One night while they were in camp on the San Miguel waterhole a solitary horseman on the regulation fiery steed dashed in among them. The newcomer was of portentous and devastating aspect. A beaklike nose with a predatory curve projected above a mass of bristling, blue-black whiskers. His eye was cavernous and fierce. He was spurred, sombreroed, booted, garnished with revolvers, abundantly drunk, and very much unafraid. Few people in the country drained by the Rio Bravo would have cared thus to invade alone the camp of Bud King. But this fell bird swooped fearlessly upon them and demanded to be fed.

Hospitality in the prairie country is not limited. Even if your enemy pass your way you must feed him before you shoot him. You must empty your larder into him before you empty your lead. So the stranger of undeclared intentions was set down to a mighty feast.

A talkative bird he was, full of most marvellous loud tales and exploits, and speaking a language at times obscure but never colorless. He was a new sensation to Bud King's men, who rarely encountered new types. They hung, delighted, upon his vainglorious boasting, the spicy strangeness of his lingo, his contemptuous familiarity with life, the world, and remote places, and the extravagant frankness with which he conveyed his sentiments.

To their guest the band of outlaws seemed to be nothing more than a congregation of country bumpkins whom he was "stringing for grub" just as he would have told his stories at the back door of a farmhouse to wheedle a meal. And, indeed, his ignorance was not without excuse, for the "bad man" of the Southwest does not run to extremes. Those brigands might justly have been taken for a little party of peaceable rustics assembled for a fishfry or pecan gathering. Gentle of manner, slouching of gait, soft-voiced, unpicturesquely clothed; not one of them presented to the eye any witness of the desperate records they had earned.

For two days the glittering stranger within the camp was feasted. Then, by common consent, he was invited to become a member of the band. He consented, presenting for enrollment the prodigious name of "Captain Montressor." This was immediately overruled by the band, and "Piggy" substituted as a compliment to the awful and insatiate appetite of its owner.

Thus did the Texas border receive the most spectacular brigand that ever rode its chaparral.

For the next three months Bud King conducted business as usual, escaping encounters with law officers and being content with reasonable profits. The band ran off some very good companies of horses from the ranges, and a few bunches of fine cattle which they got safely across the Rio Grande and disposed of to fair advantage. Often the band would ride into the little villages and Mexican settlements, terrorizing the inhabitants and plundering for the provisions and ammunition they needed. It was during these bloodless raids that Piggy's ferocious aspect and frightful voice gained him a renown more widespread and glorious than those other gentle-voiced and sad-faced desperadoes could have acquired in a lifetime.

The Mexicans, most apt in nomenclature, first called him the Black Eagle, and used to frighten the babes by threatening them with tales of the dreadful robber who carried off little children in his great beak. Soon the name extended, and Black Eagle, the Terror of the Border, became a recognized factor in exaggerated newspaper reports and ranch gossip.

The country from the Nueces to the Rio Grande was a wild but fertile stretch, given over to the sheep and cattle ranches. Range was free; the inhabitants were few; the law was mainly a letter, and the pirates met with little opposition until the flaunting and garish Piggy gave the band undue advertisement. Then Kinney's ranger company headed for those precincts, and Bud King knew that it meant grim and sudden war or else temporary retirement. Regarding the risk to be unnecessary, he drew off his band to an almost inaccessible spot on the bank of the Frio. Wherefore, as has been said, dissatisfaction arose among the members, and impeachment proceedings against Bud were premeditated, with Black Eagle in high favor for the succession. Bud King was not unaware of the sentiment, and he called aside Cactus Taylor, his trusted lieutenant, to discuss it.

"If the boys," said Bud, "ain't satisfied with me, I'm willin' to step out. They're buckin' against my way of handlin' 'em. And 'specially because I concludes to hit the brush while Sam Kinney is ridin' the line. I saves 'em from bein' shot or sent up on a state contract, and they up and says I'm no good."

"It ain't so much that," explained Cactus, "as it is they're plum locoed about Piggy. They want them whiskers and that nose of his to split the wind at the head of the column."

"There's somethin' mighty seldom about Piggy," declared Bud, musingly. "I never yet see anything on the hoof that he exactly grades up with. He can shore holler a plenty, and he straddles a hoss from where you laid the chunk. But he ain't never been smoked yet. You know, Cactus, we ain't had a row since he's been with us. Piggy's all right for skearin' the Mexican kids and layin' waste a crossroads store. I reckon he's the finest canned oyster buccaneer and cheese pirate that ever was, but how's his appetite for fightin'? I've knowed some citizens you'd think was starvin' for trouble get a bad case of dyspepsy the first dose of lead they had to take."

"He talks all spraddled out," said Cactus, " 'bout the

rookuses he's been in. He claims to have saw the elephant and hearn the owl."

"I know," replied Bud, using the cowpuncher's expressive phrase of skepticism, "but it sounds to me!"

This conversation was held one night in camp while the other members of the band—eight in number—were sprawling around the fire, lingering over their supper. When Bud and Cactus ceased talking they heard Piggy's formidable voice holding forth to the others as usual while he was engaged in checking, though never satisfying, his ravening appetite.

"What's de use," he was saying, "of chasin' little red cowses and hosses 'round for t'ousands of miles? Dere ain't nuttin' in it. Gallopin' t'rough dese bushes and briers, and gettin' a t'irst dat a brewery couldn't put out, and missin' meals! Say! You know what I'd do if I was main finger of dis bunch? I'd stick up a train. I'd blow de express car and make hard dollars where you guys get wind. Youse makes me tired. Dis sook-cow kind of cheap sport gives me a pain."

Later on, a deputation waited on Bud. They stood on one leg, chewed mesquite twigs and circumlocuted, for they hated to hurt his feelings. Bud foresaw their business, and made it easy for them. Bigger risks and larger profits were what they wanted.

The suggestion of Piggy's about holding up a train had fired their imagination and increased their admiration for the dash and boldness of the instigator. They were such simple, artless, and custom-bound bushrangers that they had never before thought of extending their habits beyond the running off of livestock and the shooting of such of their acquaintances as ventured to interfere.

Bud acted "on the level," agreeing to take a subordinate place in the gang until Black Eagle should have been given a trial as leader.

After a great deal of consultation, studying of time-tables and discussion of the country's topography, the time and place for carrying out their new enterprise was decided upon. At that time there was a feedstuff famine in Mexico and a cattle famine in certain parts of the United States, and there was a brisk international trade. Much money was being shipped along the railroads that connected the two republics. It was agreed that the most promising place for the contemplated robbery was at Espina, a little station on the I. and G. N., about forty miles north of Laredo. The train stopped there one minute; the country around was wild and unsettled; the station consisted of but one house in which the agent lived.

Black Eagle's band set out, riding by night. Arriving in the vicinity of Espina they rested their horses all day in a thicket a few miles distant.

The train was due at Espina at 10:30 P.M. They could rob the train and be well over the Mexican border with their booty by daylight the next morning.

To do Black Eagle justice, he exhibited no signs of flinching from the responsible honors that had been conferred upon him.

He assigned his men to their respective posts with discretion, and coached them carefully as to their duties. On each side of the track four of the band were to lie concealed in the chaparral. Gotch-Ear Rodgers was to stick up the station agent. Bronco Charlie was to remain with the horses, holding them in readiness. At a spot where it was calculated the engine would be when the train stopped, Bud King was to lie hidden on one side, and Black Eagle himself on the other. The two would get the drop on the engineer and fireman, force them to descend and proceed to the rear. Then the express car would be looted, and the escape made. No one was to move until Black Eagle gave the signal by firing his revolver. The plan was perfect.

At ten minutes to train time every man was at his post, effectually concealed by the thick chaparral that grew almost to the rails. The night was dark and lowering, with a fine drizzle falling from the flying gulf clouds. Black Eagle crouched behind a bush within five yards of the track. Two six-shooters were belted around him. Occasionally he drew a large black bottle from his pocket and raised it to his mouth.

A star appeared far down the track which soon waxed into the headlight of the approaching train. It came on with an increasing roar; the engine bore down upon the

ambushing desperadoes with a glare and a shriek like
some avenging monster come to deliver them to justice.
Black Eagle flattened himself upon the ground. The engine, contrary to their calculations, instead of stopping
between him and Bud King's place of concealment,
passed fully forty yards farther before it came to a stand.

The bandit leader rose to his feet and peered around
the bush. His men all lay quiet, awaiting the signal. Immediately opposite Black Eagle was a thing that drew his
attention. Instead of being a regular passenger train it
was a mixed one. Before him stood a boxcar, the door of
which, by some means, had been left slightly open. Black
Eagle went up to it and pushed the door farther open.
An odor came forth—a damp, rancid, familiar, musty,
intoxicating, beloved odor stirring strongly at old memories of happy days and travels. Black Eagle sniffed at
the witching smell as the returned wanderer smells of
the rose that twines his boyhood's cottage home. Nostal-
gia seized him. He put his hand inside. Excelsior—dry,
springy, curly, soft, enticing—covered the floor. Outside
the drizzle had turned to a chilling rain.

The train bell clanged. The bandit chief unbuckled his
belt and cast it, with its revolvers, upon the ground. His
spurs followed quickly, and his broad sombrero. Black
Eagle was moulting. The train started with a rattling
jerk. The ex-Terror of the Border scrambled into the
boxcar and closed the door. Stretched luxuriously upon
the excelsior, with the black bottle clasped closely to his

breast, his eyes closed, and a foolish, happy smile upon his terrible features Chicken Ruggles started upon his return trip.

Undisturbed, with the band of desperate bandits lying motionless, awaiting the signal to attack, the train pulled out from Espina. As its speed increased, and the black masses of chaparral went whizzing past on either side, the express messenger, lighting his pipe, looked through his window and remarked, feelingly:

"What a jim-dandy place for a holdup!"

THE CALIPH AND
THE CAD

SURELY THERE IS NO PASTIME MORE
diverting than that of mingling, incognito, with persons
of wealth and station. Where else but in those circles can
one see life in its primitive, crude state unhampered by
the conventions that bind the dwellers in a lower sphere?

There was a certain Caliph of Bagdad who was accustomed to go down among the poor and lowly for the
solace obtained from the relation of their tales and his-
tories. Is it not strange that the humble and poverty-
stricken have not availed themselves of the pleasure they
might glean by donning diamonds and silks and playing

Caliph among the haunts of the upper world?

There was one who saw the possibilities of thus turning the tables on Haroun al Raschid. His name was Corny Brannigan, and he was a truck driver for a Canal Street importing firm. And if you read further you will learn how he turned upper Broadway into Bagdad and learned something about himself that he did not know before.

Many people would have called Corny a snob—preferably by means of a telephone. His chief interest in life, his chosen amusement, and his sole diversion after working hours, was to place himself in juxtaposition—since he could not hope to mingle—with people of fashion and means.

Every evening after Corny had put up his team and dined at a lunch counter that made immediateness a specialty, he would clothe himself in evening raiment as correct as any you will see in the palm rooms. Then he would betake himself to that ravishing, radiant roadway devoted to Thespis, Thais, and Bacchus.

For a time he would stroll about the lobbies of the best hotels, his soul steeped in blissful content. Beautiful women, cooing like doves, but feathered like birds of Paradise, flicked him with their robes as they passed. Courtly gentlemen attended them, gallant and assiduous. And Corny's heart within him swelled like Sir Lancelot's, for the mirror spoke to him as he passed and said: "Corny, lad, there's not a guy among 'em that looks a bit the sweller than yerself. And you drivin' of a truck and them swearin' off their taxes and playin' the red in art galleries with the best in the land!"

And the mirrors spake the truth. Mr. Corny Brannigan had acquired the outward polish, if nothing more. Long and keen observation of polite society had gained for him its manner, its genteel air, and—most difficult of acquirement—its repose and ease.

Now and then in the hotels Corny had managed conversation and temporary acquaintance with substantial, if not distinguished, guests. With many of these he had exchanged cards, and the ones he received he carefully treasured for his own use later. Leaving the hotel lobbies, Corny would stroll leisurely about, lingering at the theatre entrance, dropping into the fashionable restaurants as if seeking some friend. He rarely patronized any of these places; he was no bee come to suck honey, but a butterfly flashing his wings among the flowers whose calyces held no sweets for him. His wages were not large enough to furnish him with more than the outside garb of the gentleman. To have been one of the beings he so cunningly imitated, Corny Brannigan would have given his right hand.

One night Corny had an adventure. After absorbing the delights of an hour's lounging in the principal hotels along Broadway, he passed up into the stronghold of Thespis. Cab drivers hailed him as a likely fare, to his prideful content. Languishing eyes were turned upon him as a hopeful source of lobsters and the delectable,

ascendant globules of effervescence. These overtures and
unconscious compliments Corny swallowed as manna,
and hoped Bill, the off horse, would be less lame in the
left forefoot in the morning.

Beneath a cluster of milky globes of electric light
Corny paused to admire the sheen of his low-cut patent
leather shoes. The building occupying the angle was a
pretentious café. Out of this came a couple, a lady in a
white, cobwebby evening gown, with a lace wrap like a
wreath of mist thrown over it, and a man, tall, faultless,
assured—too assured. They moved to the edge of the
sidewalk and halted. Corny's eye, ever alert for "pointers"
in "swell" behavior, took them in with a sidelong glance.

"The carriage is not here," said the lady. "You ordered
it to wait?"

"I ordered it for nine-thirty," said the man. "It should
be here now."

A familiar note in the lady's voice drew a more especial
attention from Corny. It was pitched in a key well known
to him. The soft electric shone upon her face. Sisters of
sorrow have no quarters fixed for them. In the index to
the book of breaking hearts you will find that Broadway
follows very soon after the Bowery. This lady's face was
sad, and her voice was attuned with it. They waited, as
if for the carriage. Corny waited too, for it was out of
doors, and he was never tired of accumulating and profit-
ing by knowledge of gentlemanly conduct.

"Jack," said the lady, "don't be angry. I've done every-

thing I could to please you this evening. Why do you act
so?"

"Oh, you're an angel," said the man. "Depend upon
woman to throw the blame upon a man."

"I'm not blaming you. I'm only trying to make you
happy."

"You go about it in a very peculiar way."

"You have been cross with me all the evening without
any cause."

"Oh, there isn't any cause except—you make me tired."

Corny took out his card case and looked over his collection. He selected one that read: "Mr. R. Lionel Whyte-
Melville, Bloomsbury Square, London." This card he had
inveigled from a tourist at the King Edward Hotel. Corny
stepped up to the man and presented it with a correctly
formal air.

"May I ask why I am selected for the honor?" asked the
lady's escort.

Now, Mr. Corny Brannigan had a very wise habit of
saying little during his imitations of the Caliph of Bagdad. The advice of Lord Chesterfield: "Wear a black
coat and hold your tongue," he believed in without having heard. But now speech was demanded and required
of him.

"No gent," said Corny, "would talk to a lady like you
done. Fie upon you, Willie! Even if she happens to be
your wife you ought to have more respect for your

clothes than to chin her back that way. Maybe it ain't my butt-in, but it goes, anyhow—you strike me as bein' a whole lot to the wrong."

The lady's escort indulged in more elegantly expressed but fetching repartee. Corny, eschewing his truck driver's vocabulary, retorted as nearly as he could in polite phrases. Then diplomatic relations were severed; there was a brief but lively set-to with other than oral weapons, from which Corny came forth easily victor.

A carriage dashed up, driven by a tardy and solicitous coachman.

"Will you kindly open the door for me?" asked the lady. Corny assisted her to enter, and took off his hat. The escort was beginning to scramble up from the sidewalk.

"I beg your pardon, ma'am," said Corny, "if he's your man."

"He's no man of mine," said the lady. "Perhaps he— but there's no chance of his being now. Drive home, Michael. If you care to take this—with my thanks."

Three red roses were thrust out through the carriage window into Corny's hand. He took them, and the hand for an instant; and then the carriage sped away.

Corny gathered his foe's hat and began to brush the dust from his clothes.

"Come along," said Corny, taking the other man by the arm.

His late opponent was yet a little dazed by the hard knocks he had received. Corny led him carefully into a saloon three doors away.

"Drinks for us," said Corny, "me and my friend."

"You're a queer feller," said the lady's late escort, "lick a man and then want to set 'em up."

"You're my best friend," said Corny, exultantly. "You don't understand? Well, listen. You just put me wise to somethin'. I been playin' gent a long time, thinkin' it was just the glad rags I had and nothin' else. Say—you're a swell, ain't you? Well, you trot in that class, I guess. I don't; but I found out one thing—I'm a gentleman, by —— and I know it now. What'll you have to drink?"

FRIENDS IN
SAN ROSARIO

THE WESTBOUND STOPPED AT SAN Rosario on time at 8:20 A.M. A man with a thick black leather wallet under his arm left the train and walked rapidly up the main street of the town. There were other passengers who also got off at San Rosario, but they either slouched limberly over to the railroad eating house or the Silver Dollar Saloon, or joined the groups of idlers about the station.

Indecision had no part in the movements of the man with the wallet. He was short in stature, but strongly built, with very light, closely trimmed hair, smooth, determined face, and aggressive, gold-rimmed nose glasses. He was well dressed in the prevailing eastern style. His air denoted a quiet but conscious reserve force, if not actual authority.

315

After walking a distance of three squares he came to
the center of the town's business area. Here another
street of importance crossed the main one, forming the
hub of San Rosario's life and commerce. Upon one corner
stood the post office. Upon another stood the Clothing
Emporium. The other two diagonally opposing corners
were occupied by the town's two banks, the First National and the Stockmen's National. Into the First
National Bank of San Rosario the newcomer walked,
never slowing his brisk step until he stood at the cashier's
window. The bank opened for business at nine, and the
working force was already assembled, each member preparing his department for the day's business. The cashier
was examining the mail when he noticed the stranger
standing at his window.

"Bank doesn't open 'til nine," he remarked, curtly, but
without feeling. He had had to make that statement
so often to early birds since San Rosario adopted city
banking hours.

"I am well aware of that," said the other man, in cool,
brittle tones. "Will you kindly receive my card?"

The cashier drew the small, spotless parallelogram
inside the bars of his wicket, and read:

J. F. C. NETTLEWICK

NATIONAL BANK EXAMINER

"Oh—er—will you walk around inside, Mr.—er— Nettlewick. Your first visit—didn't know your business, of course. Walk right around, please."

The examiner was quickly inside the sacred precincts of the bank, where he was ponderously introduced to each employee in turn by Mr. Edlinger, the cashier—a middle-aged gentleman of deliberation, discretion, and method.

"I was kind of expecting Sam Turner round again, pretty soon," said Mr. Edlinger. "Sam's been examining us now for about four years. I guess you'll find us all right, though considering the tightness in business. Not overly much money on hand, but able to stand the storms, sir, stand the storms."

"Mr. Turner and I have been ordered by the Comptroller to exchange districts," said the examiner, in his decisive, formal tones. "He is covering my old territory in southern Illinois and Indiana. I will take the cash first, please."

Perry Dorsey, the teller, was already arranging his cash on the counter for the examiner's inspection. He knew it was right to a cent, and he had nothing to fear, but he was nervous and flustered. So was every man in the bank. There was something so icy and swift, so impersonal and uncompromising about this man that his very presence seemed an accusation. He looked to be a man who would never make nor overlook an error.

Mr. Nettlewick first seized the currency, and with a

rapid, almost juggling motion, counted it by packages. Then he spun the sponge cup toward him and verified the count by bills. His thin, white fingers flew like some expert musician's upon the keys of a piano. He dumped the gold upon the counter with a crash, and the coins whined and sang as they skimmed across the marble slab from the tips of his nimble digits. The air was full of fractional currency when he came to the halves and quarters. He counted the last nickel and dime. He had the scales brought, and he weighed every sack of silver in the vault. He questioned Dorsey concerning each of the cash memoranda—certain checks, charge slips, etc., carried over from the previous day's work—with unimpeachable courtesy, yet with something so mysteriously momentous in his frigid manner, that the teller was reduced to pink cheeks and a stammering tongue.

The newly imported examiner was so different from Sam Turner. It had been Sam's way to enter the bank with a shout, pass the cigars, and tell the latest stories he had picked up on his rounds. His customary greeting to Dorsey had been, "Hello, Perry! Haven't skipped out with the boodle yet, I see." Turner's way of counting the cash had been different too. He would finger the packages of bills in a tired kind of way, and then go into the vault and kick over a few sacks of silver, and the thing was done. Halves and quarters and dimes? Not for Sam Turner. "No chicken feed for me," he would say when they were set before him. "I'm not in the agricultural department." But, then, Turner was a Texan, an old friend of the bank's president, and had known Dorsey since he was a baby.

While the examiner was counting the cash, Major Thomas B. Kingman—known to every one as "Major Tom"—the president of the First National, drove up to the side door with his old dun horse and buggy, and came inside. He saw the examiner busy with the money, and, going into the little 'pony corral," as he called it, in which his desk was railed off, he began to look over his letters.

Earlier, a little incident had occurred that even the sharp eyes of the examiner had failed to notice. When he had begun his work at the cash counter, Mr. Edlinger had winked significantly at Roy Wilson, the youthful bank messenger, and nodded his head slightly toward the front door. Roy understood, got his hat and walked leisurely out, with his collector's book under his arm. Once outside, he made a beeline for the Stockmen's National. That bank was also getting ready to open. No customers had, as yet, presented themselves.

"Say, you people!" cried Roy, with the familiarity of youth and long acquaintance, "you want to get a move on you. There's a new bank examiner over at the First, and he's a stem-winder. He's counting nickels on Perry, and he's got the whole outfit bluffed. Mr. Edlinger gave me the tip to let you know."

Mr. Buckley, president of the Stockmen's National—

a stout, elderly man, looking like a farmer dressed for
Sunday—heard Roy from his private office at the rear
and called him.

"Has Major Kingman come down to the bank yet?"
he asked of the boy.

"Yes, sir, he was just driving up as I left," said Roy.

"I want you to take him a note. Put it into his own
hands as soon as you get back."

Mr. Buckley sat down and began to write.

Roy returned and handed to Major Kingman the envelope containing the note. The major read it, folded it,
and slipped it into his vest pocket. He leaned back in his
chair for a few moments as if he were meditating deeply,
and then rose and went into the vault. He came out with
the bulky, old-fashioned leather note case stamped on
the back in gilt letters, "Bills Discounted." In this were
the notes due the bank with their attached securities,
and the major, in his rough way, dumped the lot upon
his desk and began to sort them over.

By this time Nettlewick had finished his count of the
cash. His pencil fluttered like a swallow over the sheet
of paper on which he had set his figures. He opened his
black wallet, which seemed to be also a kind of secret
memorandum book, made a few rapid figures in it,
wheeled and transfixed Dorsey with the glare of his spectacles. That look seemed to say: "You're safe this time,
but——"

"Cash all correct," snapped the examiner. He made a

dash for the individual bookkeeper, and, for a few minutes there was a fluttering of ledger leaves and a sailing of balance sheets through the air.

"How often do you balance your passbooks?" he demanded, suddenly.

"Er—once a month," faltered the individual bookkeeper, wondering how many years they would give him.

"All right," said the examiner, turning and charging upon the general bookkeeper, who had the statements of his foreign banks and their reconcilement memoranda ready. Everything there was found to be all right. Then the stub book of the certificates of deposit. Flutter—flutter—zip—zip—check! All right, list of overdrafts, please. Thanks. H'm-m. Unsigned bills of the bank next. All right.

Then came the cashier's turn, and easygoing Mr. Edlinger rubbed his nose and polished his glasses nervously under the quick fire of questions concerning the circulation, undivided profits, bank real estate, and stock ownership.

Presently Nettlewick was aware of a big man towering above him at his elbow—a man sixty years of age, rugged and hale, with a rough, grizzled beard, a mass of gray hair, and a pair of penetrating blue eyes that confronted the formidable glasses of the examiner without a flicker.

"Er—Major Kingman, our president—er—Mr. Nettlewick," said the cashier.

Two men of very different types shook hands. One was a finished product of the world of straight lines, conventional methods, and formal affairs. The other was something freer, wider, and nearer to nature. Tom Kingman had not been cut to any pattern. He had been mule-driver, cowboy, ranger, soldier, sheriff, prospector and cattleman. Now, when he was bank president, his old comrades from the prairies, of the saddle, tent, and trail, found no change in him. He had made his fortune when Texas cattle were at the high tide of value, and had organized the First National Bank of San Rosario. In spite of his largeness of heart and sometimes unwise generosity toward his old friends, the bank had prospered, for Major Tom Kingman knew men as well as he knew cattle. Of late years the cattle business had known a depression, and the major's bank was one of the few whose losses had not been great.

"And now," said the examiner, briskly, pulling out his watch, "the last thing is the loans. We will take them up now, if you please."

He had gone through the First National at almost record-breaking speed—but thoroughly, as he did everything. The running order of the bank was smooth and clean, and that had facilitated his work. There was but one other bank in the town. He received from the Government a fee of twenty-five dollars for each bank that he examined. He should be able to go over those loans and discounts in half an hour. If so, he could examine the other bank immediately afterward, and catch the 11:45, the only other train that day in the direction he was working. Otherwise, he would have to spend the night and Sunday in this uninteresting Western town. That was why Mr. Nettlewick was rushing matters.

"Come with me, sir," said Major Kingman, in his deep voice, that united the Southern drawl with the rhythmic twang of the West. "We will go over them together. Nobody in the bank knows those notes as I do. Some of 'em are a little wobbly on their legs, and some are mavericks without extra many brands on their backs, but they'll most all pay out at the roundup."

The two sat down at the president's desk. First, the examiner went through the notes at lightning speed, and added up their total, finding it to agree with the amount of loans carried on the book of daily balances. Next, he took up the larger loans, inquiring scrupulously into the condition of their endorsers or securities. The new examiner's mind seemed to course and turn and make unexpected dashes hither and thither like a bloodhound seeking a trail. Finally he pushed aside all the notes except a few, which he arranged in a neat pile before him, and began a dry, formal little speech.

"I find, sir, the condition of your bank to be very good, considering the poor crops and the depression in the cattle interests of your state. The clerical work seems to be done accurately and punctually. Your past-due paper is moderate in amount, and promises only a small loss. I would recommend the calling in of your large loans, and the making of only sixty and ninety day or call loans until general business revives. And now, there is one thing more, and I will have finished with the bank. Here are six notes aggregating something like $40,000. They are secured, according to their faces, by various stocks, bonds, shares, etc., to the value of $70,000. Those securities are missing from the notes to which they should be attached. I suppose you have them in the safe or vault. You will permit me to examine them."

Major Tom's light-blue eyes turned unflinchingly toward the examiner.

"No, sir," he said, in a low but steady tone; "those securities are neither in the safe nor the vault. I have taken them. You may hold me personally responsible for their absence."

Nettlewick felt a slight thrill. He had not expected this. He had struck a momentous trail when the hunt was drawing to a close.

"Ah!" said the examiner. He waited a moment, and then continued: "May I ask you to explain more definitely?"

"The securities were taken by me," repeated the major. "It was not for my own use, but to save an old friend in trouble. Come in here, sir, and we'll talk it over."

He led the examiner into the bank's private office at the rear, and closed the door. There was a desk, and a table, and half a dozen leather-covered chairs. On the wall was the mounted head of a Texas steer with horns five feet from tip to tip. Opposite hung the major's old cavalry saber that he had carried at Shiloh and Fort Pillow.

Placing a chair for Nettlewick, the major seated himself by the window, from which he could see the post office and the carved limestone front of the Stockmen's National. He did not speak at once, and Nettlewick felt, perhaps that the ice should be broken by something so near its own temperature as the voice of official warning.

"Your statement," he began, "since you have failed to modify it, amounts, as you must know, to a very serious thing. You are aware, also, of what my duty must compel me to do, I shall have to go before the United States Commissioner and make——"

"I know, I know," said Major Tom, with a wave of his hand. "You don't suppose I'd run a bank without being posted on national banking laws and the revised statutes! Do your duty. I'm not asking any favors. But I spoke of my friend. I did want you to hear me tell about Bob."

Nettlewick settled himself in his chair. There would be no leaving San Rosario for him that day. He would have to telegraph to the Comptroller of the Currency;

he would have to swear out a warrant before the
United States Commissioner for the arrest of Major
Kingman; perhaps he would be ordered to close the
bank on account of the loss of the securities. It was
not the first crime the examiner had unearthed. Once
or twice the terrible upheaval of human emotions that
his investigations had loosed had almost caused a ripple
in his official calm. He had seen bank men kneel and
plead and cry like women for a chance—an hour's time
—the overlooking of a single error. One cashier had
shot himself at his desk before him. None of them had
taken it with the dignity and coolness of this stern old
Westerner. Nettlewick felt that he owed it to him at
least to listen if he wished to talk. With his elbow on
the arm of his chair, and his square chin resting upon
the fingers of his right hand, the bank examiner waited
to hear the confession of the president of the First
National Bank of San Rosario.

"When a man's your friend," began Major Tom, somewhat didactically, "for forty years, and tried by water,
fire, earth, and cyclones, when you can do him a little
favor you feel like doing it."

("Embezzle for him $70,000 worth of securities,"
thought the examiner.)

"We were cowboys together, Bob and I," continued
the major, speaking slowly, and deliberately, and musingly, as if his thoughts were rather with the past than
the critical present, "and we prospected together for

gold and silver over Arizona, New Mexico, and a good part of California. We were both in the war of sixty-one, but in different commands. We've fought Indians and horse thieves side by side; we've starved for weeks in a cabin in the Arizona mountains, buried twenty feet in snow; we're ridden herd together when the wind blew so hard the lightning couldn't strike—well, Bob and I have been through some rough spells since the first time we met in the branding camp of the old Anchor-Bar ranch. And during that time we've found it necessary more than once to help each other out of tight places. In those days it was expected of a man to stick to his friend, and he didn't ask any credit for it. Probably next day you'd need him to get at your back and help stand off a band of Apaches, or put a tourniquet on your leg above a rattlesnake bite and ride for whisky. So, after all, it was give and take, and if you didn't stand square with your pardner, why, you might be shy one when you needed him. But Bob was a man who was willing to go further than that. He never played a limit.

"Twenty years ago I was sheriff of this county and I made Bob my chief deputy. That was before the boom in cattle when we both made our stake. I was sheriff and collector, and it was a big thing for me then. I was married, and we had a boy and a girl—a four and a six-year-old. There was a comfortable house next to the courthouse, furnished by the county, rent free, and

I was saving some money. Bob did most of the office
work. Both of us had seen rough times and plenty of
rustling and danger, and I tell you it was great to hear
the rain and the sleet dashing against the windows of
nights, and be warm and safe and comfortable, and
know you could get up in the morning and be shaved
and have folks call you 'mister.' And then, I had the
finest wife and kids that ever struck the range, and my
old friend with me enjoying the first fruits of prosperity
and white shirts, and I guess I was happy. Yes, I was
happy about that time."

The major sighed and glanced casually out of the
window. The bank examiner changed his position, and
leaned his chin upon his other hand.

"One winter," continued the major, "the money for the
county taxes came pouring in so fast that I didn't have
time to take the stuff to the bank for a week. I just
shoved the checks into a cigar box and the money into
a sack, and I locked them in the big safe that belonged
in the sheriff's office.

"I had been overworked that week, and was about
sick, anyway. My nerves were out of order, and my
sleep at night didn't seem to rest me. The doctor had
some scientific name for it, and I was taking medicine.
And so, added to the rest, I went to bed at night with
that money on my mind. Not that there was much need
of being worried, for the safe was a good one, and
nobody but Bob and I knew the combination. On Friday

night there was about $6,500 in cash in the bag. On Saturday morning I went to the office as usual. The safe was locked, and Bob was writing at his desk. I opened the safe, and the money was gone. I called Bob, and roused everybody in the courthouse to announce the robbery. It struck me that Bob took it pretty quiet, considering how much it reflected upon both him and me.

"Two days went by and we never got a clue. It couldn't have been burglars, for the safe had been opened by the combination in the proper way. People must have begun to talk, for one afternoon in comes Alice—that's my wife—and the boy and girl, and Alice stamps her foot, and her eyes flash, and she cries out, 'The lying wretches—Tom, Tom!' and I catch her in a faint, and bring her 'round little by little, and she lays her head down and cries and cries for the first time since she took Tom Kingman's name and fortunes. And Jack and Zilla—the youngsters—they were always wild as tigers cubs to rush at Bob and climb all over him whenever they were allowed to come to the courthouse— they stood and kicked their little shoes, and herded together like scared partridges. They were having their first trip down into the shadows of life. Bob was working at his desk, and he got up and went out without a word. The grand jury was in session then, and the next morning Bob went before them and confessed that he stole the money. He said he lost it in a poker game.

In fifteen minutes they had found a true bill and sent
me the warrant to arrest the man with whom I'd been
closer than a thousand brothers for many a year.

"I did it, and then I said to Bob, pointing: 'There's
my house, and here's my office, and up there's Maine,
and out that way is California, and over there is Florida
—and that's your range 'til court meets. You're in my
charge, and I take the responsibility. You be here when
you're wanted.'

" 'Thanks, Tom,' he said, kind of carelessly; 'I was
sort of hoping you wouldn't lock me up. Court meets
next Monday, so, if you don't object I'll just loaf around
the office until then. I've got one favor to ask, if it isn't
too much. If you'd let the kids come out in the yard
once in a while and have a romp I'd like it.'

" 'Why not?' I answered him. 'They're welcome, and
so are you. And come to my house the same as ever.'
You see, Mr. Nettlewick, you can't make a friend of a
thief, but neither can you make a thief of a friend, all
at once."

The examiner made no answer. At that moment was
heard the shrill whistle of a locomotive pulling into the
depot. That was the train on the little, narrow-gauge
road that struck into San Rosario from the south. The
major cocked his ear and listened for a moment, and
looked at his watch. The narrow-gauge was in on time
—10:35. The major continued.

"So Bob hung around the office, reading the papers

and smoking. I put another deputy to work in his place, and, after a while, the excitement of the case wore off.

"One day when we were alone in the office Bob came over to where I was sitting. He was looking sort of grim and blue—the same look he used to get when he'd been up watching for Indians all night or herd-riding.

" 'Tom,' says he, 'it's harder than standing off redskins; it's harder than lying in the lava desert forty miles from water; but I'm going to stick it out to the end. You know that's been my style. But if you'd tip me the smallest kind of a sign—if you'd just say, "Bob I understand," why, it would make it lots easier.'

"I was surprised. 'I don't know what you mean, Bob,' I said. 'Of course, you know that I'd do anything under the sun to help you that I could. But you've got me guessing.'

" 'All right, Tom,' was all he said, and he went back to his newspaper and lit another cigar.

"It was the night before the court met when I found out what he meant. I went to bed that night with the same old, light-headed, nervous feeling come back upon me. I dropped off to sleep about midnight. When I woke I was standing half dressed in one of the courthouse corridors. Bob was holding one of my arms, our family doctor the other and Alice was shaking me and half crying. She had sent for the doctor without my knowing it, and when he came they had found me out of bed and missing, and had begun a search.

" 'Sleep-walking,' said the doctor.

"All of us went back to the house, and the doctor told us some remarkable stories about the strange things people had done while in that condition. I was feeling rather chilly after my trip out, and, as my wife was out of the room at the time, I pulled open the door of an old wardrobe that stood in the room and dragged out a big quilt I had seen in there. With it tumbled out the bag of money for stealing which Bob was to be tried —and convicted—in the morning.

" 'How the jumping rattlesnakes did that get there?' I yelled, and all hands must have seen how surprised I was. Bob knew in a flash.

" 'You darned old snoozer,' he said, with the old-time look on his face, 'I saw you put it there. I watched you open the safe and take it out, and I followed you. I looked through the window and saw you hide it in that wardrobe.'

" 'Then, you blankety-blank, flop-eared, sheep-headed coyote, what did you say you took it for?'

" 'Because,' said Bob, simply, 'I didn't know you were asleep.'

"I saw him glance toward the door of the room where Jack and Zilla were, and I knew then what it meant to be a man's friend from Bob's point of view."

Major Tom paused, and again directed his glance out of the window. He saw someone in the Stockmen's National Bank reach and draw a yellow shade down the whole length of its plate-glass, big front window, although the position of the sun did not seem to warrant such a defensive movement against its rays.

Nettlewick sat up straight in his chair. He had listened patiently, but without consuming interest, to the major's story. It had impressed him as irrelevant to the situation, and it could certainly have no effect upon the consequences. Those Western people, he thought, had an exaggerated sentimentality. They were not businesslike. They needed to be protected from their friends. Evidently the major had concluded. And what he had said amounted to nothing.

"May I ask," said the examiner, "if you have anything further to say that bears directly upon the question of those abstracted securities?"

"Abstracted securities, sir!" Major Tom turned suddenly in his chair, his blue eyes flashing upon the examiner. "What do you mean, sir?"

He drew from his coat pocket a batch of folded papers held together by a rubber band, tossed them into Nettlewick's hands, and rose to his feet.

"You'll find those securities there, sir, every stock, bond, and share of 'em. I took them from the notes while you were counting the cash. Examine and compare them for yourself."

The major led the way back into the banking-room. The examiner, astounded, perplexed, nettled, at sea, followed. He felt that he had been made the victim of something that was not exactly a hoax, but that left him in the shoes of one who had been played upon, used, and then discarded, without even an inkling of the game. Perhaps, also, his official position had been irreverently juggled with. But there was nothing he could take hold of. An official report of the matter would be an absurdity. And, somehow, he felt that he would never know anything more about the matter than he did then.

Frigidly, mechanically, Nettlewick examined the securities, found them to tally with the notes, gathered his black wallet, and rose to depart.

"I will say," he protested, turning the indignant glare of his glasses upon Major Kingman, "that your statements—your misleading statements, which you have not condescended to explain—do not appear to be quite the thing, regarded either as business or humor. I do not understand such motives or actions."

Major Tom looked down at him serenely and not unkindly.

"Son," he said, "there are plenty of things in the chaparral, and on the prairies, and up the cañons that you don't understand. But I want to thank you for listening to a garrulous old man's prosy story. We old Texans love to talk about our adventures and our old comrades, and the home folks have long ago learned to run when we begin with 'Once upon a time,' so we have to spin our yarns to the stranger within our gates."

The major smiled, but the examiner only bowed

coldly, and abruptly quitted the bank. They saw him travel diagonally across the street in a straight line and enter the Stockmen's National Bank.

Major Tom sat down at his desk and drew from his vest pocket the note Roy had given him. He had read it once, but hurriedly, and now, with something like a twinkle in his eyes, he read it again. These were the words he read:

Dear Tom:

I hear there's one of Uncle Sam's greyhounds going through you, and that means that we'll catch him inside of a couple of hours, maybe. Now, I want you to do something for me. We've got just $2,200 in the bank, and the law requires that we have $20,000. I let Ross and Fisher have $18,000 late yesterday afternoon to buy up that Gibson bunch of cattle. They'll realize $40,000 in less than thirty days on the transaction, but that won't make my cash on hand look any prettier to that bank examiner. Now, I can't show him those notes, for they're just plain notes of hand without any security in sight, but you know very well that Pink Ross and Jim Fisher are two of the finest white men God ever made, and they'll do the square thing. You remember Jim Fisher—he was the one who shot that faro dealer in El Paso. I wired Sam Bradshaw's bank to send me $20,000, and it will get in on the narrow-gauge at 10:35. You can't let a bank examiner in to count $2,200 and close your doors. Tom, you hold that examiner. Hold him. Hold him if you have to rope him and sit on his head. Watch our front window after the narrow-gauge gets in, and when we've got the cash inside we'll pull down the shade for a signal. Don't turn him loose till then, I'm counting on you, Tom.

Your Old Pard,
Bob Buckley,
Prest. Stockmen's National

The major began to tear the note into small pieces and throw them into his wastebasket. He gave a satisfied little chuckle as he did so.

"Confounded old reckless cowpuncher!" he growled, contentedly, "that pays him some on account for what he tried to do for me in the sheriff's office twenty years ago."

THE WHIRLIGIG

OF LIFE

JUSTICE OF THE PEACE BENAJA WIDDUP
sat in the door of his office smoking his elder-stem pipe.
Halfway to the zenith the Cumberland range rose blue-
gray in the afternoon haze. A speckled hen swaggered
down the quiet main street of the tiny "settlement,"
cackling foolishly.

Up the road came a sound of creaking axles, and then
a slow cloud of dust, and then a bull-cart bearing Ransie
Bilbro and his wife. The cart stopped at the Justice's
door, and the two climbed down. Ransie was a narrow

six feet of sallow brown skin and yellow hair. The imperturbability of the mountains hung upon him like a suit of armor. The woman was calicoed, angled, snuff-brushed, and weary with unknown desires. Through it all gleamed a faint protest of cheated youth unconscious of its loss.

The Justice of the Peace slipped his feet into his shoes, for the sake of dignity, and moved to let them enter.

"We-all," said the woman, in a voice like the wind blowing through pine boughs, "wants a divo'ce." She looked at Ransie to see if he noted any flaw or ambiguity or evasion or partiality of self-partisanship in her statement of their business.

"A divo'ce," repeated Ransie, with a solemn nod. "We-all can't git along together nohow. It's lonesome enough fur to live in the mount'ins when a man and a woman keers fur one another. But when she's a-spittin' like a wildcat or a-sullenin' like a hoot owl in the cabin, a man ain't got no call to live with her."

"When he's a no-'count varmint," said the woman, without any especial warmth, "a-traipsin' along of scalawags and moonshiners and a-layin' on his back pizen 'ith co'n whiskey, and a-pesterin' folks with a pack o' hungry, triflin' houn's to feed!"

"When she keeps a-throwin skillet lids," came Ransie's antiphony, "and slings b'ilin' water on the best coon dog in the Cumberlands, and sets herself again' cookin' a man's victuals, and keeps him awake o' nights accusin' him of a sight of doin's!"

"When he's al'ays a-fightin' the revenues, and gits a hard name in the mount'ins fur a mean man, who's gwine to be able fur to sleep o' nights?"

The Justice of the Peace stirred deliberately to his duties. He placed his one chair and a wooden stool for his petitioners. He opened his book of statutes on the table and scanned the index. Presently he wiped his spectacles and shifted his inkstand.

"The law and the statutes," said he, "air silent on the subjeck of divo'ce as fur as the jurisdiction of this co't air concerned. But, accordin' to equity and the Constitution and the golden rule, it's a bad barg'in that can't run both ways. If a justice of the peace can marry a couple, it's plain that he is bound to be able to divo'ce 'em. This here office will issue a decree of divo'ce and abide by the decision of the Supreme Co't to hold it good."

Ransie Bilbro drew a small tobacco bag from his trousers pocket. Out of this he shook upon the table a five-dollar note. "Sold a b'arskin and two foxes fur that," he remarked. "It's all the money we got."

"The regular price of a divo'ce in this co't," said the Justice, "air five dollars." He stuffed the bill into the pocket of his homespun vest with a deceptive air of indifference. With much bodily toil and mental travail he wrote the decree upon half a sheet of foolscap, and then copied it upon the other. Ransie Bilbro and his wife listened to his reading of the document that was to give them freedom:

"Know all men by these presents that Ransie Bilbro and his wife, Ariela Bilbro, this day personally appeared before me and promises that hereinafter they will neither love, honor, nor obey each other, neither for better nor worse, being of sound mind and body, and accept summons for divorce according to the peace and dignity of the State. Herein fail not, so help you God. Benaja Widdup, Justice of the Peace in and for the county of Piedmont, State of Tennessee."

The Justice was about to hand one of the documents to Ransie. The voice of Ariela delayed the transfer. Both men looked at her. Their dull masculinity was confronted by something sudden and unexpected in the woman.

"Judge, don't you give him that air paper yit. 'Tain't all settled, nohow. I got to have my rights first. I got to have my ali-money. 'Tain't no kind of a way to do fur a man to divo'ce his wife 'thout her havin' a cent fur to do with. I'm a-layin' off to be a-goin' up to brother Ed's up on Hogback Mount'in. I'm bound fur to hev a pa'r of shoes and some snuff and things besides. Ef Rance kin affo'd a divo'ce, let him pay me ali-money."

Ransie Bilbro was stricken to dumb perplexity. There had been no previous hint of alimony. Women were always bringing up startling and unlooked-for issues.

Justice Benaja Widdup felt that the point demanded

judicial decision. The authorities were also silent on the subject of alimony. But the woman's feet were bare. The trail to Hogback Mountain was steep and flinty.

"Ariela Bilbro," he asked, in official tones, "how much did you 'low would be good and sufficient ali-money in the case befo' the co't?"

"I 'lowed," she answered, "fur the shoes and all, to say five dollars. That ain't much fur ali-money, but I reckon that'll git me up to brother Ed's."

"The amount," said the Justice, "air not onreasonable. Ransie Bilbro, you air ordered by the co't to pay the plaintiff the sum of five dollars befo' the decree of divo'ce air issued."

"I hain't no mo' money,' breathed Ransie, heavily. "I done paid you all I had."

"Otherwise," said the Justice, looking severely over his spectacles, "you air in contempt of co't."

"I reckon if you gimme till tomorrow," pleaded the husband, "I mout be able to rake or scrape it up somewhars. I never looked for to be a-payin' no ali-money."

"The case air adjourned," said Benaja Widdup, "till tomorrow, when you-all will present yo'selves and obey the order of the co't. Followin' of which the decrees of divo'ce will be delivered." He sat down in the door and began to loosen a shoestring.

"We mout as well go down to Uncle Ziah's," decided Ransie, "and spend the night." He climbed into the cart on one side, and Ariela climbed in on the other. Obeying the flat of his rope, the little red bull slowly came around on a tack, and the cart crawled away in the nimbus arising from its wheels.

Justice of the Peace Benaja Widdup smoked his elderstem pipe. Late in the afternoon he got his weekly paper, and read it until the twilight dimmed its lines. Then he lit the tallow candle on his table, and read until the moon rose, marking the time for supper. He lived in the double log cabin on the slope near the girdled poplar. Going home to supper he crossed a little branch darkened by a laurel thicket. The dark figure of a man stepped from the laurels and pointed a rifle at his breast. His hat was pulled down low, and something covered most of his face.

"I want yo' money," said the figure, "'thout any talk. I'm gettin' nervous, and my finger's a-wabblin' on this here trigger."

"I've only got f-f-five dollars," said the Justice, producing it from his vest pocket.

"Roll it up," came the order, "and stick it in the end of this here gun-bar'l."

The bill was crisp and new. Even fingers that were clumsy and trembling found little difficulty in making a spill of it and inserting it (this with less ease) into the muzzle of the rifle.

"Now I reckon you kin be goin' along," said the robber. The Justice lingered not on his way.

The next day came the little red bull, drawing the cart to the office door. Justice Benaja Widdup had his shoes on, for he was expecting the visit. In his presence Ransie Bilbro handed to his wife a five-dollar bill. The official's eye sharply viewed it. It seemed to curl up as though it had been rolled and inserted into the end of a gun-barrel. But the Justice refrained from comment. It is true that other bills might be inclined to curl. He handed each one a decree of divorce. Each stood awkwardly silent, slowly folding the guarantee of freedom. The woman cast a shy glance full of constraint at Ransie.

"I reckon you'll be goin' back up to the cabin," she said, "along 'ith the bull-cart. There's bread in the tin box settin' on the shelf. I put the bacon in the bilin'-pot to keep the hounds from gettin' it. Don't forget to wind the clock tonight."

"You air a-goin' to your brother Ed's?" asked Ransie, with fine unconcern.

"I was 'lowin' to get along up thar afore night. I ain't sayin' as they'll pester theyselves any to make me welcome, but I hain't nowhar else fur to go. It's a right smart ways, and I reckon I better be goin'. I'll be a-sayin' goodbye, Ranse—that is, if you keer fur to say so."

"I don't know as anybody's a hound dog," said Ransie, in a martyr's voice, "fur to not want to say goodbye—'less you air so anxious to git away that you don't want me to say it."

Ariela was silent. She folded the five-dollar bill and her

decree carefully, and placed them in the bosom of her dress. Benaja Widdup watched the money disappear with mournful eyes behind his spectacles.

And then with his next words he achieved rank (as his thoughts ran) with either the great crowd of the world's sympathizers or the little crowd of its great financiers.

"Be kind o' lonesome in the old cabin tonight, Ransie," he said.

Ransie Bilbro stared out at the Cumberlands, clear blue now in the sunlight. He did not look at Ariela.

"I 'low it might be lonesome," he said; "but when folks gits mad and wants a divo'ce, you can't make folks stay."

"Ther's others wanted a divo'ce," said Ariela, speaking to the wooden stool. "Besides, nobody don't want nobody to stay."

"Nobody never said they didn't."

"Nobody never said they did. I reckon I better start on now to brother Ed's."

"Nobody can't wind that old clock."

"Want me to go along 'ith you in the cart and wind it fur you, Ranse?"

The mountaineer's countenance was proof against emotion. But he reached out a big hand and enclosed Ariela's thin brown one. Her soul peeped out once through her impassive face, hallowing it.

"Them hounds sha'n't pester you no more," said Ransie. "I reckon I been mean and low down. You wind that clock, Ariela."

"My heart hit's in that cabin, Ranse," she whispered, "along 'ith you. I ain't a-goin' to git mad no more. Let's be startin', Ranse, so's we kin git home by sundown."

Justice of the Peace Benaja Widdup interposed as they started for the door, forgetting his presence.

"In the name of the State of Tennessee," he said, "I forbid you-all to be a-defyin' of its laws and statutes. This co't is mo' than willin' and full of joy to see the clouds of discord and misunderstandin' rollin' away from two lovin' hearts, but it air the duty of the co't to p'eserve the morals and integrity of the State. The co't reminds you that you air no longer man and wife, but air divo'ced by regular decree, and as such air not entitled to the benefits and 'purtenances of the mattermonal estate."

Ariela caught Ransie's arm. Did those words mean that she must lose him now when they had just learned the lesson of life?

"But the co't air prepared," went on the Justice, "fur to remove the disabilities set up by the decree of divo'ce. The co't air on hand to perform the solemn ceremony of marri'ge, thus fixin' things up and enablin' the parties in the case to resume the honor'ble and elevatin' state of matter-mony which they desires. The fee fur performin' said ceremony will be, in this case, to wit, five dollars."

Ariela caught the gleam of promise in his words. Swiftly her hand went to her bosom. Freely as an alighting dove the bill fluttered to the Justice's table. Her sallow cheek colored as she stood hand in hand with Ransie and listened to the reuniting words.

Ransie helped her into the cart, and climbed in beside her. The little red bull turned once more, and they set out, hand-clasped, for the mountains.

Justice of the Peace Benaja Widdup sat in his door and took off his shoes. Once again he fingered the bill tucked down in his vest pocket. Once again he smoked his elder-stem pipe. Once again the speckled hen swaggered down the main street of the "settlement," cackling foolishly.

WHISTLING DICK'S
CHRISTMAS
STOCKING

I**T WAS WITH MUCH CAUTION THAT**
Whistling Dick slid back the door of the boxcar, for
Article 5716, City Ordinances, authorized (perhaps un-
constitutionally) arrest on suspicion, and he was familiar
of old with this ordinance. So, before climbing out, he
surveyed the field with all the care of a good general.

He saw no change since his last visit to this big, alms-
giving, long-suffering city of the South, the cold weather
paradise of the tramps. The levee where his freight car
stood was pimpled with dark bulks of merchandise. The
breeze reeked with the well-remembered, sickening
smell of the old tarpaulins that covered bales and barrels. The dun river slipped along among the shipping

with an oily gurgle. Far down toward Chalmette he could see the great bend in the stream, outlined by the row of electric lights. Across the river Algiers lay, a long, irregular blot, made darker by the dawn which lightened the sky beyond. An industrious tug or two, coming for some early sailing ship, gave a few appalling toots, that seemed to be the signal for breaking day. The Italian luggers were creeping nearer their landing, laden with early vegetables and shellfish. A vague roar, subterranean in quality, from dray wheels and streetcars, began to make itself heard and felt; and the ferryboats, the Mary Anns of water craft, stirred sullenly to their menial morning tasks.

Whistling Dick's red head popped suddenly back into the car. A sight too imposing and magnificent for his gaze had been added to the scene. A vast, incomparable policeman rounded a pile of rice sacks and stood within twenty yards of the car. The daily miracle of the dawn, now being performed above Algiers, received the flattering attention of this specimen of municipal official splendor. He gazed with unbiased dignity at the faintly glowing colors until, at last, he turned to them his broad back, as if convinced that legal interference was not needed, and the sunrise might proceed unchecked. So he turned his face to the rice bags, and, drawing a flat flask from an inside pocket, he placed it to his lips and regarded the firmament.

Whistling Dick, professional tramp, possessed a half-friendly acquaintance with this officer. They had met several times before on the levee at night, for the officer, himself a lover of music, had been attracted by the exquisite whistling of the shiftless vagabond. Still, he did not care, under the present circumstances, to renew the acquaintance. There is a difference between meeting a policeman upon a lonely wharf and whistling a few operatic airs with him, and being caught by him crawling out of a freight car. So Dick waited, as even a New Orleans policeman must move on sometime—perhaps it is a retributive law of nature—and before long "Big Fritz" majestically disappeared between the trains of cars.

Whistling Dick waited as long as his judgment advised, and then slid swiftly to the ground. Assuming as far as possible the air of an honest laborer who seeks his daily toil, he moved across the network of railway lines, with the intention of making his way by quiet Girod Street to a certain bench in Lafayette Square, where, according to appointment, he hoped to rejoin a pal known as "Slick," this adventurous pilgrim having preceded him by one day in a cattle car into which a loose slat had enticed him.

As Whistling Dick picked his way where night still lingered among the big, reeking, musty warehouses, he gave way to the habit that had won for him his title. Subdued, yet clear, with each note as true and liquid as a bobolink's, his whistle tinkled about the dim, cold

mountains of brick like drops of rain falling into a
hidden pool. He followed an air, but it swam mistily
into a swirling current of improvisation. You could cull
out the trill of mountain brooks, the staccato of green
rushes shivering above the chilly lagoons, the pipe of
sleepy birds.

Rounding a corner, the whistler collided with a
mountain of blue and brass.

"So," observed the mountain calmly, "you are already
pack. Und dere vill not pe frost before two veeks yet!
Und you haf forgotten how to vistle. Dere was a valse
note in dot last bar."

"Watcher know about it?" said Whistling Dick, with
tentative familiarity; "you wit yer little Gherman-band
nixcumrous chunes. Watcher know about music? Pick
yer ears, and listen agin. Here's de way I whistled it
—see?"

He puckered his lips, but the big policeman held up
his hand.

"Shtop," he said, "und learn der right way. Und learn
also dot a rolling shtone can't vistle for a cent."

Big Fritz's heavy moustache rounded into a circle,
and from its depths came a sound deep and mellow as
that from a flute. He repeated a few bars of the air the
tramp had been whistling. The rendition was cold, but
correct, and he emphasized the note that he had taken
exception to.

"Dot p is p natural, and not p vlat. Py der vay, you petter pe glad I meet you. Von hour later, und I vould haf to put you in a gage to vistle mit der chail pirds. Der orders are to bull all der pums after sunrise."

"To which?"

"To bull der pums—eferybody mitout fisible means. Dirty days is der price, or fifteen tollars."

"Is dat straight, or a game you givin' me?"

"It's der pest tip you efer had. I gif it to you pecause I pelief you are not so bad as der rest. Und pecause you can vistle 'Der Freischütz' bezzer dan I myself gan. Don't run against any more bolicemans aroundt der corners, but go away from town a few tays. Goot-pye."

So Madame Orleans had at last grown weary of the strange and ruffled brood that came yearly to nestle beneath her charitable pinions.

After the big policeman had departed, Whistling Dick stood for an irresolute minute, feeling all the outraged indignation of a delinquent tenant who is ordered to vacate his premises. He had pictured to himself a day of dreamful ease when he should have joined his pal; a day of lounging on the wharf, munching the bananas and cocoanuts scattered in unloading the fruit steamers; and then a feast along the free lunch counters from which the easygoing owners were too good-natured or too generous to drive him away, and afterward a pipe in one of the little flowery parks and a snooze in some

shady corner of the wharf. But here was a stern order
to exile, and one that he knew must be obeyed. So, with
a wary eye open for the gleam of brass buttons, he began
his retreat toward a rural refuge. A few days in the
country need not necessarily prove disastrous. Beyond
the possibility of a slight nip of frost, there was no
formidable evil to be looked for.

However, it was with a depressed spirit that Whistling
Dick passed the old French market on his chosen route
down the river. For safety's sake he still presented to
the world his portrayal of the part of the worthy artisan
on his way to labor. A stall-keeper in the market, un-
deceived, hailed him by the generic name of his ilk,
and "Jack" halted, taken by surprise. The vendor, melted
by this proof of his own acuteness, bestowed a foot of
Frankfurter and half a loaf, and thus the problem of
breakfast was solved.

When the streets, from topographical reasons, began
to shun the riverbank the exile mounted to the top of
the levee, and on its well-trodden path pursued his way.
The suburban eye regarded him with cold suspicion,
individuals reflected the stern spirit of the city's heartless edict. He missed the seclusion of the crowded town
and the safety he could always find in the multitude.

At Chalmette, six miles upon his desultory way, there
suddenly menaced him a vast and bewildering industry.
A new port was being established; the dock was being
built, compresses were going up; picks and shovels and

barrows struck at him like serpents from every side. An arrogant foreman bore down upon him, estimating his muscles with the eye of a recruiting sergeant. Brown men and black men all about him were toiling away. He fled in terror.

By noon he had reached the country of the plantations, the great, sad, silent levels bordering the mighty river. He overlooked fields of sugar cane so vast that their farthest limits melted into the sky. The sugar-making season was well advanced, and the cutters were at work; the wagons creaked drearily after them; the Negro teamsters inspired the mules to greater speed with mellow and sonorous imprecations. Dark-green groves, blurred by the blue of distance, showed where the plantation houses stood. The tall chimneys of the sugar mills caught the eye miles distant, like lighthouses at sea.

At a certain point Whistling Dick's unerring nose caught the scent of frying fish. Like a pointer to a quail, he made his way down the levee side straight to the camp of a credulous and ancient fisherman, whom he charmed with song and story, so that he dined like an admiral, and then like a philosopher annihilated the worst three hours of the day by a nap under the trees.

When he awoke and again continued his hegira, a frosty sparkle in the air succeeded the drowsy warmth of the day, and as this portent of a chilly night translated itself to the brain of Sir Peregrine, he lengthened his stride and bethought him of shelter. He traveled a

road that faithfully followed the convolutions of the
levee, running along its base, but whither he knew not.
Bushes and rank grass crowded it to the wheel ruts,
and out of this ambuscade the pests of the lowlands
swarmed after him, humming a keen vicious soprano.
And as the night grew nearer, although colder, the whine
of the mosquitoes became a greedy, petulant snarl that
shut out all other sounds. To his right, against the
heavens, he saw a green light moving, and, accompanying it, the masts and funnels of a big incoming steamer,
moving as upon a screen at a magic-lantern show. And
there were mysterious marshes at his left, out of which
came queer gurgling cries and a choked croaking. The
whistling vagrant struck up a merry warble to offset
these melancholy influences, and it is likely that never
before, since Pan himself jiggered it on his reeds, had
such sounds been heard in those depressing solitudes.

A distant clatter in the rear quickly developed into
the swift beat of horses' hoofs, and Whistling Dick
stepped aside into the dew-wet grass to clear the track.
Turning his head, he saw approaching a fine team of
stylish grays drawing a double surrey. A stout man with
a white moustache occupied the front seat, giving all
his attention to the rigid lines in his hands. Behind him
sat a placid, middle-aged lady and a brilliant-looking girl
hardly arrived at young ladyhood. The lap robe had
slipped partly from the knees of the gentleman driving,
and Whistling Dick saw two stout canvas bags between

his feet—bags such as, while loafing in cities, he had seen warily transferred between express wagons and bank doors. The remaining space in the vehicle was filled with parcels of various sizes and shapes.

As the surrey swept even with the sidetracked tramp, the bright-eyed girl, seized by some merry, madcap impulse, leaned out toward him with a sweet, dazzling smile, and cried, "Mer-ry Christ-mas!" in a shrill, plaintive treble.

Such a thing had not often happened to Whistling Dick, and he felt handicapped in devising the correct response. But lacking time for reflection, he let his instinct decide, and snatching off his battered derby, he rapidly extended it at arm's length, and drew it back with a continuous motion, and shouted a loud, but ceremonious, "Ah, there!" after the flying surrey.

The sudden movement of the girl had caused one of the parcels to become unwrapped, and something limp and black fell from it into the road. The tramp picked it up and found it to be a new black silk stocking, long and fine and slender. It crunched crisply, and yet with a luxurious softness, between his fingers.

"Ther bloomin' little skeezicks!" said Whistling Dick, with a broad grin bisecting his freckled face. "Wot d'yer think of dat, now! 'Mer-ry Chris-mus!' Sounded like a cuckoo clock, dat's what she did. Dem guys is swells, too, bet yer life, an' der old 'un stacks dem sacks of dough down under his trotters like dey was common

as dried apples. Been shoppin' for Chrismus, and de
kid's lost one of her new socks w'ot she was goin' to
hold up Santy wid. De bloomin' little skeezicks! Wit'
her 'Mer-ry Chris-mus!' W'ot 'd yer t'ink! Same as to
say, 'Hello, Jack, how goes it?' and as swell as Fift'
Av'noo, and as easy as a blowout in Cincinnat'."

Whistling Dick folded the stocking carefully and
stuffed it into his pocket.

It was nearly two hours later when he came upon
signs of habitation. The buildings of an extensive plantation were brought into view by a turn in the road. He
easily selected the planter's residence in a large square
building with two wings, with numerous good-sized,
well-lighted windows, and broad verandas running
around its full extent. It was set upon a smooth lawn,
which was faintly lit by the far-reaching rays of the
lamps within. A noble grove surrounded it, and old-
fashioned shrubbery grew thickly about the walls and
fences. The quarters of the hands and the mill buildings
were situated at a distance in the rear.

The road was now enclosed on each side by a fence,
and presently, as Whistling Dick drew nearer the houses,
he suddenly stopped and sniffed the air.

"If dere ain't a hobo stew cookin' somewhere in dis
immediate precinct," he said to himself, "me nose has
quit tellin' de trut'."

Without hesitation he climbed the fence to windward.
He found himself in an apparently disused lot, where

piles of old bricks were stacked, and rejected, decaying lumber. In a corner he saw the faint glow of a fire that had become little more than a bed of living coals, and he thought he could see some dim human forms sitting or lying about it. He drew nearer, and by the light of a little blaze that suddenly flared up he saw plainly the fat figure of a ragged man in an old brown sweater and cap.

"Dat man," said Whistling Dick to himself softly, "is a dead ringer for Boston Harry. I'll try him wit' de high sign."

He whistled one or two bars of a ragtime melody, and the air was immediately taken up, and then quickly ended with a peculiar run. The first whistler walked confidently up to the fire. The fat man looked up and spake in a loud, asthmatic wheeze:

"Gents, the unexpected but welcome addition to our circle is Mr. Whistling Dick, an old friend of mine for whom I fully vouches. The waiter will lay another cover at once. Mr. W. D. will join us at supper, during which function he will enlighten us in regard to the circumstances that give us the pleasure of his company."

"Chewin' de stuffin' out'n de dictionary, as usual, Boston," said Whistling Dick; "but t'anks all de same for de invitashun. I guess I finds meeself here about de same way as yous guys. A cop gimme de tip dis mornin'. Yous workin' on dis farm?"

"A guest," said Boston sternly, "shouldn't never insult

his entertainers until he's filled up wid grub. 'Tain't good business sense. Workin'!—but I will restrain myself. We five—me, Deaf Pete, Blinky, Goggles, and Indiana Tom —got put on to this scheme of Noo Orleans to work visiting gentlemen upon her dirty streets, and we hit the road last evening just as the tender hues of twilight had flopped down upon the daisies and things. Blinky, pass the empty oyster-can at your left to the empty gentleman at your right."

For the next ten minutes the gang of roadsters paid their undivided attention to the supper. In an old five-gallon kerosene can they had cooked a stew of potatoes, meat, and onions which they partook of from smaller cans they had found scattered about the vacant lot.

Whistling Dick had known Boston Harry of old, and knew him to be one of the shrewdest and most success-ful of his brotherhood. He looked like a prosperous stock drover or a solid merchant from some country village. He was stout and hale, with a ruddy, always smoothly shaven face. His clothes were strong and neat, and he gave special attention to his decent-appearing shoes. During the past ten years he had acquired a reputation for working a larger number of successfully managed confidence games than any of his acquaintances, and he had not a day's work to be counted against him. It was rumored among his associates that he had saved a considerable amount of money. The four other men were fair specimens of the slinking, ill-clad, noisome

genus who carried their labels of "suspicious" in plain
view.

After the bottom of the large can had been scraped,
and pipes lit at the coals, two of the men called Boston
aside and spake with him slowly and mysteriously. He
nodded decisively, and then said aloud to Whistling Dick:

"Listen, sonny, to some plain talky-talk. We five are
on a lay. I've guaranteed you to be square, and you're
to come in on the profits equal with the boys, and you've
got to help. Two hundred hands on this plantation are
expecting to be paid a week's wages tomorrow morning.
Tomorrow's Christmas, and they want to lay off. Says
the boss: 'Work from five to nine in the morning to get
a trainload of sugar off, and I'll pay every man cash
down for the week and a day extra.' They say: 'Hooray
for the boss! It goes.' He drives to Noo Orleans today,
and fetches back the cold dollars. Two thousand and
seventy-four fifty is the amount. I got the figures from
a man who talks too much, who got 'em from the bookkeeper. The boss of this plantation thinks he's going to
pay this wealth to the hands. He's got it down wrong;
he's going to pay it to us. It's going to stay in the leisure
class, where it belongs. Now, half of this haul goes to
me, and the other half the rest of you may divide. Why
the difference? I represent the brains. It's my scheme.
Here's the way we're going to get it. There's some company at supper in the house, but they'll leave about
nine. They've just happened in for an hour or so. If they

don't go pretty soon, we'll work the scheme anyhow.
We want all night to get away good with the dollars.
They're heavy. About nine o'clock Deaf Pete and
Blinky'll go down the road about a quarter beyond the
house, and set fire to a big cane field there that the
cutters haven't touched yet. The wind's just right to have
it roaring in two minutes. The alarm'll be given, and
every man Jack about the place will be down there
in ten minutes, fighting fire. That'll leave the money
sacks and the women alone in the house for us to handle.
You've heard cane burn? Well, there's mighty few women
can screech loud enough to be heard above its crackling.
The thing's dead safe. The only danger is in being
caught before we can get far enough away with the
money. Now, if you——"

"Boston," interrupted Whistling Dick, rising to his
feet, "t'anks for de grub yous fellers has given me, but
I'll be movin' on now."

"What do you mean?" asked Boston, also rising.

"W'y, you can count me outer dis deal. You oughter
know that. I'm on de bum all right enough, but dat
other t'ing don't go wit' me. Burglary is no good. I'll
say good night and many t'anks fer——"

Whistling Dick had moved away a few steps as he
spoke, but he stopped very suddenly. Boston had covered him with a short revolver of roomy calibre.

"Take your seat," said the tramp leader. "I'd feel
mighty proud of myself if I let you go and spoil the

game. You'll stick right in this camp until we finish the job. The end of that brick pile is your limit. You go two inches beyond that, and I'll have to shoot. Better take it easy, now."

"It's my way of doin'," said Whistling Dick. "Easy goes. You can depress de muzzle of dat twelve-incher, and run 'em back on de trucks. I remains, as de newspapers says, 'in yer midst.'"

"All right," said Boston, lowering his piece, as the other returned and took his seat again on a projecting plank in a pile of timber. "Don't try to leave; that's all. I wouldn't miss this chance even if I had to shoot an old acquaintance to make it go. I don't want to hurt anybody specially, but this thousand dollars I'm going to get will fix me for fair. I'm going to drop the road, and start a saloon in a little town I know about. I'm tired of being kicked around."

Boston Harry took from his pocket a cheap silver watch and held it near the fire.

"It's a quarter to nine," he said. "Pete, you and Blinky start. Go down the road past the house and fire the cane in a dozen places. Then strike for the levee, and come back on it, instead of the road, so you won't meet anybody. By the time you get back the men will all be striking out for the fire, and we'll break for the house and collar the dollars. Everybody cough up what matches he's got."

The two surly tramps made a collection of all the

matches in the party, Whistling Dick contributing his quota with propitiatory alacrity, and then they departed in the dim starlight in the direction of the road.

Of the three remaining vagrants, two, Goggles and Indiana Tom, reclined lazily upon convenient lumber and regarded Whistling Dick with undisguised disfavor. Boston, observing that the dissenting recruit was disposed to remain peaceably, relaxed a little of his vigilance. Whistling Dick arose presently and strolled leisurely up and down keeping carefully within the territory assigned him.

"Dis planter chap," he said, pausing before Boston Harry, "w'ot makes yer t'ink he's got de tin in de house wit' 'im?"

"I'm advised of the facts in the case," said Boston. "He drove to Noo Orleans and got it, I say, today. Want to change your mind now and come in?"

"Naw, I was just askin'. Wot kind o' team did de boss drive?"

"Pair of grays."

"Double surrey?"

"Yep."

"Women folks along?"

"Wife and kid. Say, what morning paper are you trying to pump news for?"

"I was just conversin' to pass de time away. I guess dat team passed me in de road dis evenin'. Dat's all."

As Whistling Dick put his hands into his pockets and

continued his curtailed beat up and down by the fire, he felt the silk stocking he had picked up in the road.

"Ther bloomin' little skeezicks," he muttered, with a grin.

As he walked up and down he could see, through a sort of natural opening or lane among the trees, the planter's residence some seventy-five yards distant. The side of the house toward him exhibited spacious, well-lighted windows through which a soft radiance streamed, illuminating the broad veranda and some extent of the lawn beneath.

"What's that you said?" asked Boston, sharply.

"Oh, nuttin' 't all," said Whistling Dick, lounging carelessly, and kicking meditatively at a little stone on the ground.

"Just as easy," continued the warbling vagrant softly to himself, "an' sociable an' swell, an' sassy, wit' her 'Mer-ry Chris-mus.' Wot d'yer t'ink, now!"

Dinner, two hours late, was being served in the Belle-meade plantation dining room.

The dining room and all its appurtenances spoke of an old regime that was here continued rather than suggested to the memory. The plate was rich to the extent that its age and quaintness alone saved it from being showy; there were interesting names signed in the corners of the pictures on the walls; the viands were of the kind that bring a shine into the eyes of gourmets.

The service was swift, silent, lavish, as in the days when
the waiters were assets like the plate. The names by
which the planter's family and their visitors addressed
one another were historic in the annals of two nations.
Their manners and conversation had that most difficult
kind of ease—the kind that still preserves punctilio. The
planter himself seemed to be the dynamo that generated
the larger portion of the gaiety and wit. The younger
ones at the board found it more than difficult to turn
back on him his guns of raillery and banter. It is true,
the young men attempted to storm his works repeatedly,
incited by the hope of gaining the approbation of their
fair companions; but even when they sped a well-aimed
shaft, the planter forced them to feel defeat by the
tremendous discomfiting thunder of the laughter with
which he accompanied his retorts. At the head of the
table, serene, matronly, benevolent, reigned the mistress
of the house, placing here and there the right smile, the
right word, the encouraging glance.

The talk of the party was too desultory, too evanescent
to follow, but at last they came to the subject of the
tramp nuisance, one that had of late vexed the plantations for many miles around. The planter seized the
occasion to direct his good-natured fire of raillery at
the mistress, accusing her of encouraging the plague.
"They swarm up and down the river every winter," he
said. "They overrun New Orleans, and we catch the
surplus, which is generally the worst part. And, a day

or two ago, Madame New Orleans, suddenly discovering that she can't go shopping without brushing her skirts against great rows of the vagabonds sunning themselves on the banquettes, says to the police: 'Catch 'em all,' and the police catch a dozen or two, and the remaining three or four thousand overflow up and down the levees, and madame there"—pointing tragically with the carving-knife at her—"feeds them. They won't work, they defy my overseers, and they make friends with my dogs; and you, madame, feed them before my eyes, and intimidate me when I would interfere. Tell us, please, how many today did you thus incite to future laziness and depredation?"

"Six, I think," said madame, with a reflective smile; "but you know two of them offered to work, for you heard them yourself."

The planter's disconcerting laugh rang out again.

"Yes, at their own trades. And one was an artificial-flower maker, and the other a glass blower. Oh, they were looking for work! Not a hand would they consent to lift to labor of any other kind."

"And another one," continued the soft-hearted mistress, "used quite good language. It was really extraordinary for one of his class. And he carried a watch. And had lived in Boston. I don't believe they are all bad. They have always seemed to me to rather lack development. I always look upon them as children with whom wisdom has remained at a standstill while whiskers

have continued to grow. We passed one this evening
as we were driving home who had a face as good as
it was incompetent. He was whistling the intermezzo
from 'Cavalleria' and blowing the spirit of Mascagni
himself into it."

A bright-eyed young girl who sat at the left of the
mistress leaned over and said in a confidential under-
tone:

"I wonder, Mamma, if that tramp we passed on the
road found my stocking, and do you think he will hang
it up tonight? Now I can hang up but one. Do you know
why I wanted a new pair of silk stockings when I have
plenty? Well, old Aunt Judy says, if you hang up two
that have never been worn, Santa Claus will fill one
with good things, and Monsieur Pambe will place in
the other payment for all the words you have spoken—
good or bad—on the day before Christmas. That's why
I've been unusually nice and polite to everyone today.
Monsieur Pambe, you know, is a witch gentleman!
he——"

The words of the young girl were interrupted by a
startling thing.

Like the wraith of some burned-out shooting star,
a black streak came crashing through the windowpane
and upon the table, where it shivered into fragments
nearly a dozen pieces of crystal and chinaware, then
glanced between the heads of the guests to the wall,
imprinting therein a deep, round indentation, at which,

today, the visitor to Bellemeade marvels as he gazes upon it and listens to this tale as it is told.

The women screamed in many keys, and the men sprang to their feet, and would have laid their hands upon their swords had not the verities of chronology forbidden.

The planter was the first to act; he sprang to the intruding missile and held it up to view.

"By Jupiter!" he cried. "A meteoric shower of hosiery! Has communication at last been established with Mars?"

"I should say—ahem!—Venus," ventured a young gentleman visitor, looking hopefully for approbation toward the unresponsive young-lady visitors.

The planter held at arm's length the unceremonious visitor—a long dangling black stocking. "It's loaded," he announced.

As he spoke he reversed the stocking, holding it by the toe, and down from it dropped a roundish stone, wrapped about by a piece of yellowish paper. "Now for the first interstellar message of the century!" he cried; and nodding to the company, who had crowded about him, he adjusted his glasses with provoking deliberation, and examined it closely. When he finished he had changed from the jolly host to the practical, decisive man of business. He immediately struck a bell, and said to the silent-footed mulatto man who responded: "Go and tell Mr. Wesley to get Reeves and Maurice and about ten stout hands they can rely upon, and come to

the hall door at once. Tell him to have the men arm
themselves, and bring plenty of ropes and plough lines.
Tell him to hurry." And then he read aloud from the
paper these words:

> To the Gent of de Hous:
> Dere is five tuff hoboes xcept meself in the vaken
> lot near de road war de old brick piles is. Dey got me
> stuck up wid a gun see and I taken dis means of
> comunikaten. 2 of der lads is gone down to set fire to
> de cain field below de hous and when yous fellers goes
> to turn on de hoes on it de hole gang is goin to rob de
> house of de money yoo gotto pay off wit say git a move
> on ye say de kid dropt dis sock in der rode tel her mery
> crismus de same as she told me. Ketch de bums down
> de rode first and den sen a relefe core to get me out of
> soke youres truly,
>
> > Whistlen Dick

There was quiet but rapid maneuvering at Belle-
meade during the ensuing half hour, which ended in
five disgusted and sullen tramps being captured and
locked securely in an outhouse pending the coming
of the morning and retribution. For another result, the
visiting young gentlemen had secured the unqualified
worship of the visiting young ladies by their distinguished and heroic conduct. For still another, behold
Whistling Dick, the hero, seated at the planter's table,
feasting upon viands his experience had never before

included, and waited upon by admiring femininity in shapes of such beauty and "swellness" that even his ever-full mouth could scarcely prevent him from whistling. He was made to disclose in detail his adventure with the evil gang of Boston Harry, and how he cunningly wrote the note and wrapped it around the stone and placed it in the toe of the stocking, and, watching his chance, sent it silently, with a wonderful centrifugal momentum, like a comet, at one of the big lighted windows of the dining room.

The planter vowed that the wanderer should wander no more; that his was a goodness and an honesty that should be rewarded, and that a debt of gratitude had been made that must be paid; for had he not saved them from a doubtless imminent loss, and maybe a greater calamity? He assured Whistling Dick that he might consider himself a charge upon the honor of Bellemeade; that a position suited to his powers would be found for him at once, and hinted that the way would be heartily smoothed for him to rise to as high places of emolument and trust as the plantation afforded.

But now, they said, he must be weary, and the immediate thing to consider was rest and sleep. So the mistress spoke to a servant, and Whistling Dick was conducted to a room in the wing of the house occupied by the servants. To this room, in a few minutes, was brought a portable tin bathtub filled with water, which was placed on a piece of oiled cloth upon the floor.

There the vagrant was left to pass the night.

By the light of the candle he examined the room. A bed, with the covers neatly turned back, revealed snowy pillows and sheets. A worn, but clean, red carpet covered the floor. There was a dresser with a beveled mirror, a washstand with a flowered bowl and pitcher; the two or three chairs were softly upholstered. A little table held books, papers, and a day-old cluster of roses in a jar. There were towels on a rack and soap in a white dish.

Whistling Dick set his candle on a chair and placed his hat carefully under the table. After satisfying what we must suppose to have been his curiosity by a sober scrutiny, he removed his coat, folded it, and laid it upon the floor, near the wall, as far as possible from the unused bathtub. Taking his coat for a pillow, he stretched himself luxuriously upon the carpet.

When on Christmas morning the first red streaks of dawn broke above the marshes, Whistling Dick awoke and reached instinctively for his hat. Then he remembered that the skirts of Fortune had swept him into their folds on the night previous, and he went to the window and raised it, to let the fresh breath of the morning cool his brow and fix the yet dreamlike memory of his good luck within his brain.

As he stood there, certain dread and ominous sounds pierced the fearful hollow of his ear.

The force of plantation workers, eager to complete the

shortened task alloted to them, were all astir. The mighty din of the ogre Labor shook the earth, and the poor tattered and forever disguised Prince in search of his fortune held tight to the window sill even in the enchanted castle, and trembled.

Already from the bosom of the mill came the thunder of rolling barrels of sugar, and (prisonlike sounds) there was a great rattling of chains as the mules were harried with stimulant imprecations to their places by the wagontongues. A little vicious "dummy" engine, with a train of flatcars in tow, stewed and fumed on the plantation tap of the narrow-gauge railroad, and a toiling, hurrying, hallooing stream of workers were dimly seen in the half darkness loading the train with the weekly output of sugar. Here was a poem, an epic—nay, a tragedy—with work, the curse of the world, for its theme.

The December air was frosty, but the sweat broke out upon Whistling Dick's face. He thrust his head out of the window and looked down. Fifteen feet below him, against the wall of the house, he could make out that a border of flowers grew, and by that token he overhung a bed of soft earth.

Softly as a burglar goes, he clambered out upon the sill, lowered himself until he hung by his hands alone, and then dropped safely. No one seemed to be about upon this side of the house. He dodged low and skimmed swiftly across the yard to the low fence. It was an easy matter to vault this, for a terror urged him such as lifts the gazelle over the thorn bush when the lion pursues. A crash through the dew-drenched weeds on the roadside, a clutching, slippery rush up the grassy side of the levee to the footpath at the summit, and—he was free!

The east was blushing and brightening. The wind, himself a vagrant rover, saluted his brother upon the cheek. Some wild geese, high above, gave cry. A rabbit skipped along the path before him, free to turn to the right or to the left as his mood should send him. The river slid past, and certainly no one could tell the ultimate abiding place of its waters.

A small, ruffled, brown-breasted bird, sitting upon a dogwood sapling, began a soft, throaty, tender little piping in praise of the dew which entices foolish worms from their holes; but suddenly he stopped, and sat with his head turned sidewise, listening.

From the path along the levee there burst forth a jubilant, stirring, buoyant, thrilling whistle, loud and keen and clear as the cleanest notes of the piccolo. The soaring sound rippled and trilled and arpeggioed as the songs of wild birds do not; but it had a wild free grace that, in a way, reminded the small brown bird of something familiar, but exactly what he could not tell. There was in it the birdcall, or reveille, that all birds know; but a great waste of lavish, unmeaning things that art had added and arranged, besides, and that were quite puzzling and strange; and the little brown bird sat with his head on one side until the sound had died away in the distance.

The little bird did not know that the part of that strange warbling that he understood was just what kept the warbler without his breakfast; but he knew very well that the part he did not understand did not concern him, so he gave a little flutter of his wings and swooped down like a brown bullet upon a big fat worm that was wriggling along the levee path.

‡

MAMMON AND THE
ARCHER

Old anthony rockwall, retired manufacturer and proprietor of Rockwall's Eureka Soap, looked out the library window of his Fifth Avenue mansion and grinned. His neighbour to the right—the aristocratic clubman, G. Van Schuylight Suffolk-Jones— came out to his waiting motorcar, wrinkling a contume- lious nostril, as usual, at the Italian renaissance sculpture of the soap palace's front elevation.

"Stuck-up old statuette of nothing doing!" commented the ex-Soap King. "The Eden Musée'll get that old frozen Nesselrode yet if he don't watch out. I'll have this house painted red, white, and blue next summer and see if that'll make his Dutch nose turn up any higher."

And then Anthony Rockwall, who never cared for bells,

went to the door of his library and shouted "Mike!" in the same voice that had once chipped off pieces of the welkin on the Kansas prairies.

"Tell my son," said Anthony to the answering menial, "to come in here before he leaves the house."

When young Rockwall entered the library the old man laid aside his newspaper, looked at him with a kindly grimness on his big, smooth, ruddy countenance, rumpled his mop of white hair with one hand and rattled the keys in his pocket with the other.

"Richard," said Anthony Rockwall, "what do you pay for the soap that you use?"

Richard, only six months home from college, was startled a little. He had not yet taken the measure of this sire of his, who was as full of unexpectedness as a girl at her first party.

"Six dollars a dozen, I think, dad."

"And your clothes?"

"I suppose about sixty dollars, as a rule."

"You're a gentleman," said Anthony, decidedly. "I've heard of these young bloods spending $24 a dozen for soap, and going over the hundred mark for clothes. You've got as much money to waste as any of 'em, and yet you stick to what's decent and moderate. Now I use the old Eureka—not only for sentiment, but it's the purest soap made. Whenever you pay more than 10 cents a cake for soap you buy bad perfumes and labels. But 50 cents is doing very well for a young man in your genera-

tion, position and condition. As I said, you're a gentleman. They say it takes three generations to make one.
They're off. Money'll do it as slick as soap grease. It's
made you one. By hokey! it's almost made one of me.
I'm nearly as impolite and disagreeable and ill-mannered
as those two old knickerbocker gents on each side of me
that can't sleep of nights because I bought in between
'em."

"There are some things that money can't accomplish,"
remarked young Rockwall, rather gloomily.

"Now, don't say that," said old Anthony, shocked. "I
bet my money on money every time. I've been through
the encylopedia down to Y looking for something you
can't buy with it; and I expect to have to take up the
appendix next week. I'm for money against the field. Tell
me something money won't buy."

"For one thing," answered Richard, rankling a little,
"it won't buy one into the exclusive circles of society."

"Oho! won't it?" thundered the champion of the root
of evil. "You tell me where your exclusive circles would
be if the first Astor hadn't had the money to pay for his
steerage passage over?"

Richard sighed.

"And that's what I was coming to," said the old man,
less boisterously. "That's why I asked you to come in.
There's something going wrong with you, boy. I've been
noticing it for two weeks. Out with it. I guess I could lay
my hands on eleven millions within twenty-four hours,

besides the real estate. If it's your liver, there's the *Rambler* down in the bay, coaled, and ready to steam down to the Bahamas in two days."

"Not a bad guess, dad; you haven't missed it far."

"Ah," said Anthony, keenly; "what's her name?"

Richard began to walk up and down the library floor. There was enough comradeship and sympathy in this crude old father of his to draw his confidence.

"Why don't you ask her?" demanded old Anthony. "She'll jump at you. You've got the money and the looks, and you're a decent boy. Your hands are clean. You've got no Eureka soap on 'em. You've been to college, but she'll overlook that."

"I haven't had a chance," said Richard.

"Make one," said Anthony. "Take her for a walk in the park, or a straw ride, or walk home with her from church. Chance! Pshaw!"

"You don't know the social mill, dad. She's part of the stream that turns it. Every hour and minute of her time is arranged for days in advance. I must have that girl, dad, or this town is a blackjack swamp forevermore. And I can't write it—I can't do that."

"Tut!" said the old man. "Do you mean to tell me that with all the money I've got you can't get an hour or two of a girl's time for yourself?"

"I've put it off too late. She's going to sail for Europe at noon day after tomorrow for a two years' stay. I'm to see her alone tomorrow evening for a few minutes. She's

at Larchmont now at her aunt's. I can't go there. But
I'm allowed to meet her with a cab at the Grand Central
Station tomorrow evening at the 8:30 train. We drive
down to Wallack's at a gallop, where her mother and a
box party will be waiting for us in the lobby. Do you
think she would listen to a declaration from me during
that six or eight minutes under those circumstances? No.
And what chance would I have in the theatre or afterward? None. No, dad, this is one tangle that your money
can't unravel. We can't buy one minute of time with
cash; if we could, rich people would live longer. There's
no hope of getting a talk with Miss Lantry before she
sails."

"All right, Richard, my boy," said old Anthony, cheerfully. "You may run along down to your club now. I'm
glad it ain't your liver. But don't forget to burn a few
punk sticks in the joss house to the great god Mazuma
from time to time. You say money won't buy time? Well,
of course, you can't order eternity wrapped up and delivered at your residence for a price, but I've seen Father
Time get pretty bad stone bruises on his heels when he
walked through the gold diggings."

That night came Aunt Ellen, gentle, sentimental,
wrinkled, sighing, oppressed by wealth, in to Brother
Anthony at his evening paper, and began discourse on
the subject of lovers' woes.

"He told me all about it," said Brother Anthony, yawn-
ing. "I told him my bank account was at his service. And

then he began to knock money. Said money couldn't help. Said the rules of society couldn't be bucked for a yard by a team of ten millionaires."

"Oh, Anthony," sighed Aunt Ellen, "I wish you would not think so much of money. Wealth is nothing where a true affection is concerned. Love is all-powerful. If he only had spoken earlier! She could not have refused our Richard. But now I fear it is too late. He will have no opportunity to address her. All your gold cannot bring happiness to your son."

At eight o'clock the next evening Aunt Ellen took a quaint old gold ring from a moth-eaten case and gave it to Richard.

"Wear it tonight, nephew," she begged. "Your mother gave to it me. Good luck in love she said it brought. She asked me to give it to you when you had found the one you loved."

Young Rockwall took the ring reverently and tried it on his smallest finger. It slipped as far as the second joint and stopped. He took it off and stuffed it into his vest pocket, after the manner of man. And then he phoned for his cab.

At the station he captured Miss Lantry out of the gabbing mob at eight thirty-two.

"We mustn't keep mamma and the others waiting," said she.

"To Wallack's Theatre as fast as you can drive!" said Richard, loyally.

They whirled up Forty-second to Broadway, and then down the white-starred lane that leads from the soft meadows of sunset to the rocky hills of morning.

At Thirty-fourth Street young Richard quickly thrust up the trap and ordered the cabman to stop.

"I've dropped a ring," he apologized, as he climbed out. "It was my mother's, and I'd hate to lose it. I won't detain you a minute—I saw where it fell."

In less than a minute he was back in the cab with the ring.

But within that minute a crosstown car had stopped directly in front of the cab. The cabman tried to pass to the left, but a heavy express wagon cut him off. He tried the right and had to back away from a furniture van that had no business to be there. He tried to back out, but dropped his reins and swore dutifully. He was blockaded in a tangled mess of vehicles and horses.

One of those street blockades had occurred that sometimes tie up commerce and movement quite suddenly in the big city.

"Why don't you drive on?" said Miss Lantry impatiently. "We'll be late."

Richard stood up in the cab and looked around. He saw a congested flood of wagons, trucks, cabs, vans and streetcars filling the vast space where Broadway, Sixth Avenue, and Thirty-fourth Street cross one another as a twenty-six inch maiden fills her twenty-two inch girdle. And still from all the cross streets they were hurrying and rattling toward the converging point at full speed, and hurling themselves into the straggling mass, locking wheels and adding their drivers' imprecations to the clamor. The entire traffic of Manhattan seemed to have jammed itself around them. The oldest New Yorker among the thousands of spectators that lined the sidewalks had not witnessed a street blockade of the proportions of this one.

"I'm very sorry," said Richard, as he resumed his seat, "but it looks as if we are stuck. They won't get this jumble loosened up in an hour. It was my fault. If I hadn't dropped the ring we——"

"Let me see the ring," said Miss Lantry. "Now that it can't be helped, I don't care. I think theatres are stupid, anyway."

At eleven o'clock that night somebody tapped lightly on Anthony Rockwall's door.

"Come in," shouted Anthony, who was in a red dressing-gown, reading a book of piratical adventures.

Somebody was Aunt Ellen, looking like a gray-haired angel that had been left on earth by mistake.

"They're engaged, Anthony," she said, softly. "She has promised to marry our Richard. On their way to the theatre there was a street blockade, and it was two hours before their cab could get out of it.

"And oh, Brother Anthony, don't ever boast of the power of money again. A little emblem of true love—a little ring that symbolized unending and unmercenary affection—was the cause of our Richard finding his happiness. He dropped it in the street, and got out to recover it. And before they could continue the blockade occurred. He spoke to his love and won her there while the cab was hemmed in. Money is dross compared with true love, Anthony."

"All right," said Anthony. "I'm glad the boy has got what he wanted. I told him I wouldn't spare any expense in the matter if——"

"But, Brother Anthony, what good could your money have done?"

"Sister," said Anthony Rockwall. "I've got my pirate in a devil of a scrape. His ship has just been scuttled, and he's too good a judge of the value of money to let drown. I wish you would let me go on with this chapter."

The story should end here. I wish it would as heartily as you who read it wish it did. But we must go to the bottom of the well for truth.

The next day a person with red hands and a blue polka dot necktie, who called himself Kelly, called at Anthony Rockwall's house, and was at once received in the library.

"Well," said Anthony, reaching for his checkbook, "it was a good bilin' of soap. Let's see—you had $5,000 in cash."

"I paid out $300 more of my own," said Kelly. "I had to go a little above the estimate. I got the express wagons and cabs mostly for $5; but the trucks and two-horse teams mostly raised me to $10. The motormen wanted $10, and some of the loaded teams $20. The cops struck me hardest—$50 I paid two, and the rest $20 and $25. But didn't it work beautiful, Mr. Rockwall? I'm glad William A. Brady wasn't onto that little outdoor vehicle mob scene. I wouldn't want William to break his heart with jealousy. And never a rehearsal, either! The boys was on time to the fraction of a second. It was two hours before a snake could get below Greeley's statue."

"Thirteen hundred—there you are, Kelly," said Anthony, tearing off a check. "Your thousand, and the $300 you were out. You don't despise money, do you Kelly?"

"Me?" said Kelly. "I can lick the man that invented poverty."

Anthony called Kelly when he was at the door.

"You didn't notice," said he, "anywhere in the tie-up, a kind of a fat boy without any clothes on shooting arrows around with a bow, did you?"

"Why, no," said Kelly, mystified. "I didn't. If he was like you say, maybe the cops pinched him before I got there."

"I thought the little rascal wouldn't be on hand," chuckled Anthony. "Good-bye, Kelly."

THE PIMIENTA
PANCAKES

WHILE WE WERE ROUNDING UP A bunch of the Triangle-O cattle in the Frio bottoms, a projecting branch of a dead mesquite caught my wooden stirrup and gave my ankle a wrench that laid me up in camp for a week.

On the third day of my compulsory idleness I crawled out near the grub wagon, and reclined helpless under the conversational fire of Judson Odom, the camp cook. Jud was a monologist by nature, whom Destiny, with customary blundering, had set in a profession wherein he was bereaved, for the greater portion of his time, of an audience.

Therefore I was manna in the desert of Jud Odom's obmutescence.

Betimes I was stirred by invalid longings for something to eat that did not come under the caption of "grub." I had visions of the maternal pantry "deep as first love, and wild with all regret," and then I asked:

"Jud, can you make pancakes?"

Jud laid down his sixshooter, with which he was preparing to pound an antelope steak, and stood over me in what I felt to be a menacing attitude. He further indorsed my impression that his pose was resentful by fixing upon me with his light blue eyes a look of cold suspicion.

"Say, you," he said, with candid, though not excessive, choler, "did you mean that straight, or was you trying to throw the gaff into me? Some of the boys been telling you about me and that pancake racket?"

"No, Jud," I said, sincerely, "I meant it. It seems to me I'd swap my pony and saddle for a stack of buttered brown pancakes with some first crop, open kettle, New Orleans sweetening. Was there a story about pancakes?"

Jud was mollified at once when he saw that I had not been dealing in allusions. He brought some mysterious bags and tin boxes from the grub wagon and set them in the shade of the hackberry where I lay reclined. I watched him as he began to arrange them leisurely and untie their many strings.

"No, not a story," said Jud, as he worked, "but just the logical disclosures in the case of me and that pink-eyed snoozer from Mired Mule Cañada and Miss Willella

Learight. I don't mind telling you.

"I was punching then for old Bill Toomey, on the San Miguel. One day I gets all ensnared up in aspirations for to eat some canned grub that hasn't ever mooed or baaed or grunted or been in peck measures. So, I gets on my bronc and pushes the wind for Uncle Emsley Telfair's store at the Pimienta Crossing on the Nueces.

"About three in the afternoon I throwed my bridle over a mesquite limb and walked the last twenty yards into Uncle Emsley's store. I got up on the counter and told Uncle Emsley that the signs pointed to the devastation of the fruit crop of the world. In a minute I had a bag of crackers and a long-handled spoon, with an open can each of apricots and pineapples and cherries and greengages beside of me with Uncle Emsley busy chopping away with the hatchet at the yellow clings. I was feeling like Adam before the apple stampede, and was digging my spurs into the side of the counter and working with my twenty-four-inch spoon when I happened to look out of the window into the yard of Uncle Emsley's house, which was next to the store.

"There was a girl standing there—an imported girl with fixings on—philandering with a croquet maul and amusing herself by watching my style of encouraging the fruit canning industry.

"I slid off the counter and delivered up my shovel to Uncle Emsley.

" 'That's my niece,' says he; 'Miss Willella Learight, down from Palestine on a visit. Do you want that I should make you acquainted?'

" 'The Holy Land,' I says to myself, my thoughts milling some as I tried to run 'em into the corral. 'Why not? There was sure angels in Pales—— why yes, Uncle Emsley,' I says out loud, 'I'd be awful edified to meet Miss Learight.'

"So Uncle Emsley took me out in the yard and gave us each other's entitlements.

"I never was shy about women. I never could understand why some men who can break a mustang before breakfast and shave in the dark, get all left-handed and full of perspiration and excuses when they see a bolt of calico draped around what belongs in it. Inside of eight minutes me and Miss Willella was aggravating the croquet balls around as amiable as second cousins. She gave me a dig about the quantity of canned fruit I had eaten, and I got back at her, flat-footed, about how a certain lady named Eve started the fruit trouble in the first free-grass pasture—'Over in Palestine, wasn't it?' says I, as easy and pat as roping a one-year-old.

"That was how I acquired cordiality for the proximities of Miss Willella Learight; and the disposition grew larger as time passed. She was stopping at Pimienta Crossing for her health, which was very good, and for the climate, which was forty per cent hotter than Palestine.

I rode over to see her once every week for a while; and then I figured it out that if I doubled the number of trips I would see her twice as often.

"One week I slipped in a third trip; and that's where the pancakes and the pink-eyed snoozer busted into the game.

"That evening, while I set on the counter with a peach and two damsons in my mouth, I asked Uncle Emsley how Miss Willella was.

"'Why,' says Uncle Emsley, 'she's gone riding with Jackson Bird, the sheep man from over at Mired Mule Cañada.'

"I swallowed the peach seed and the two damson seeds. I guess somebody held the counter by the bridle while I got off; and then I walked out straight ahead till I butted against the mesquite where my roan was tied.

"'She's gone riding,' I whispered in my bronc's ear, 'with Birdstone Jack, the hired mule from Sheep Man's Cañada. Did you get that, old Leather-and-Gallops?'

"That bronc of mine wept, in his way. He'd been raised a cow pony and he didn't care for snoozers.

"I went back and said to Uncle Emsley: 'Did you say a sheep man?'

"'I said a sheep man,' says Uncle again. 'You must have heard tell of Jackson Bird. He's got eight sections of grazing and four thousand head of the finest Merinos south of the Arctic Circle.'

"I went out and sat on the ground in the shade of the

store and leaned against a prickly pear. I sifted sand into
my boots with unthinking hands while I soliloquized a
quantity about this bird with the Jackson plumage to his
name.

"I never had believed in harming sheep men. I see one,
one day, reading a Latin grammar on hossback, and I
never touched him! They never irritated me like they
do most cowmen. You wouldn't go to work now, and
impair and disfigure snoozers, would you, that eat on
tables and wear little shoes and speak to you on subjects?
I had always let 'em pass, just as you would a jack rabbit;
with a polite word and a guess about the weather, but
no stopping to swap canteens. I never thought it was
worthwhile to be hostile with a snoozer. And because
I'd been lenient, and let 'em live, here was one going
around riding with Miss Willella Learight!

"An hour by sun they come loping back, and stopped
at Uncle Emsley's gate. The sheep person helped her
off; and they stood throwing each other sentences all
sprightful and sagacious for a while. And then this
feathered Jackson flies up in his saddle and raises his
little stewpot of a hat, and trots off in the direction of
his mutton ranch. By this time I had turned the sand out
of my boots and unpinned myself from the prickly pear;
and by the time he gets half a mile out of Pimienta, I
singlefoots up beside him on my bronc.

"I said that snoozer was pink-eyed, but he wasn't. His
seeing arrangement was gray enough, but his eyelashes

was pink and his hair was sandy, and that gave you the idea. Sheep man—he wasn't more than a lamb man, anyhow—a little thing with his neck involved in a yellow silk handkerchief, and shoes tied up in bowknots.

" 'Afternoon!' says I to him. 'You now ride with a equestrian who is commonly called Dead-Moral-Certainty Judson, on account of the way I shoot. When I want a stranger to know me I always introduce myself before the draw, for I never did like to shake hands with ghosts.'

" 'Ah,' says he, just like that—'ah, I'm glad to know you, Mr. Judson. I'm Jackson Bird, from over at Mired Mule Ranch.'

"Just then one of my eyes saw a roadrunner skipping down the hill with a young tarantula in his bill, and the other eye noticed a rabbit hawk sitting on a dead limb in a water elm. I popped over one after the other with my forty-five, just to show him. 'Two out of three,' says I. 'Birds just naturally seem to draw my fire wherever I go.'

" 'Nice shooting,' says the sheep man, without a flutter. 'But don't you sometimes ever miss the third shot? Elegant fine rain that was last week for the young grass, Mr. Judson,' says he.

" 'Willie,' says I, riding over close to his palfrey, 'your infatuated parents may have denounced you by the name of Jackson, but you sure moulted into a twittering Willie —let us slough off this here analysis of rain and the elements, and get down to talk that is outside the vocabulary of parrots. That is a bad habit you have got of riding with young ladies over at Pimienta. I've known birds,' says I, 'to be served on toast for less than that. Miss Willella,' says I, 'don't ever want any nest made out of sheep's wool by a tomtit of the Jacksonian branch of ornithology. Now, are you going to quit, or do you wish for to gallop up against this Dead-Moral-Certainty attachment to my name, which is good for two hyphens and at least one set of funeral obsequies?'

"Jackson Bird flushed up some, and then he laughed.

" 'Why, Mr. Judson,' says he, 'you've got the wrong idea. I've called on Miss Learight a few times; but not for the purpose you imagine. My object is purely a gastronomical one.'

"I reached for my gun.

" 'Any coyote,' says I, 'that would boast of dishonorable——'

" 'Wait a minute,' says this Bird, 'till I explain. What would I do with a wife? If you ever saw that ranch of mine! I do my own cooking and mending. Eating—that's all the pleasure I get out of sheep raising. Mr. Judson, did you ever taste the pancakes that Miss Learight makes?'

" 'Me? No,' I told him. 'I never was advised that she was up to any culinary maneuvers.'

" 'They're golden sunshine,' says he, 'honey-browned by the ambrosial fires of Epicurus. I'd give two years of

my life to get the recipe for making them pancakes.
That's what I went to see Miss Learight for,' says Jackson
Bird, 'but I haven't been able to get it from her. It's an
old recipe that's been in the family for seventy-five years.
They hand it down from one generation to another, but
they don't give it away to outsiders. If I could get that
recipe, so I could make them pancakes for myself on my
ranch, I'd be a happy man,' says Bird.

"'Are you sure,' I says to him, 'that it ain't the hand
that mixes the pancakes that you're after?'

"'Sure,' says Jackson. 'Miss Learight is a mighty nice
girl, but I can assure you my intentions go no further
than the gastro—' but he seen my hand going down to
my holster and he changed his similitude—'than the desire to procure a copy of the pancake recipe,' he finishes.

"'You ain't such a bad little man,' says I, trying to be
fair. 'I was thinking some of making orphans of your
sheep, but I'll let you fly away this time. But you stick to
pancakes,' says I, 'as close as the middle one of a stack;
and don't go and mistake sentiments for syrup, or there'll
be singing at your ranch, and you won't hear it.'

"'To convince you that I am sincere,' says the sheep
man, 'I'll ask you to help me. Miss Learight and you being closer friends, maybe she would do for you what she
wouldn't do for me. If you will get me a copy of that
pancake recipe, I give you my word that I'll never call
upon her again.'

"'That's fair,' I says, and I shook hands with Jackson

Bird. 'I'll get it for you if I can, and glad to oblige.' And he turned off down the big pear flat on the Piedra, in the direction of Mired Mule; and I steered northwest for old Bill Toomey's ranch.

"It was five days afterward when I got another chance to ride over to Pimienta. Miss Willella and me passed a gratifying evening at Uncle Emsley's. She sang some, and exasperated the piano quite a lot with quotations from the operas. I gave imitations of a rattlesnake, and told her about Snaky McFee's new way of skinning cows, and described the trip I made to Saint Louis once. We was getting along in one another's estimations fine. Thinks I, if Jackson can now be persuaded to migrate, I win. I recollect his promise about the pancake receipt, and I thinks I will persuade it from Miss Willella and give it to him; and then if I catches Birdie off of Mired Mule again, I'll make him hop the twig.

"So, along about ten o'clock, I put on a wheedling smile and says to Miss Willella: 'Now if there's anything I do like better than the sight of a red steer on green grass it's the taste of a nice hot pancake smothered in sugarhouse molasses.'

"Miss Willella gives a little jump on the piano stool, and looked at me curious.

" 'Yes,' says she, 'they're real nice. What did you say was the name of that street in Saint Louis, Mr. Odom, where you lost your hat?'

" 'Pancake Avenue,' says I, with a wink, to show her

that I was on about the family receipt, and couldn't be side-corralled off of the subject. 'Come, now, Miss Will-ella,' I says, 'let's hear how you make 'em. Pancakes is just whirling in my head like wagon wheels. Start her off, now—pound of flour, eight dozen eggs, and so on. How does the catalogue of constituents run?'

" 'Excuse me for a moment, please,' says Miss Willella, and she gives me a quick kind of sideways look, and slides off the stool. She ambled out into the other room, and directly Uncle Emsley comes in in his shirt sleeves, with a pitcher of water. He turns around to get a glass on the table, and I see a forty-five in his hip pocket. 'Great post-holes!' thinks I, 'but here's a family thinks a heap of cooking receipts, protecting it with firearms. I've known outfits that wouldn't do that much by a family feud.'

" 'Drink this here down,' says Uncle Emsley, handing me the glass of water. 'You've rid too far today, Jud, and got yourself over-excited. Try to think about something else now.'

" 'Do you know how to make them pancakes, Uncle Emsley?' I asked.

" 'Well, I'm not as apprised in the anatomy of them as some,' says Uncle Emsley, 'but I reckon you take a sifter of plaster of paris and a little dough and saleratus and corn meal, and mix 'em with eggs and buttermilk as usual. Is old Bill going to ship beeves to Kansas City again this spring, Jud?'

"That was all the pancake specifications I could get that night. I didn't wonder that Jackson Bird found it uphill work. So I dropped the subject and talked with Uncle Emsley a while about hollow-horn and cyclones. And then Miss Willella came and said 'Good-night,' and I hit the breeze for the ranch.

"About a week afterward I met Jackson Bird riding out of Pimienta as I rode in, and we stopped in the road for a few frivolous remarks.

"'Got the bill of particulars for them flapjacks yet?' I asked him.

"'Well, no,' says Jackson. 'I don't seem to have any success in getting hold of it. Did you try?'

"'I did,' says I, 'and 'twas like trying to dig a prairie dog out of his hole with a peanut hull. That pancake receipt must be a jooka-lorum, the way they hold on to it.'

"'I'm 'most ready to give it up,' says Jackson, so discouraged in his pronunciations that I felt sorry for him; 'but I did want to know how to make them pancakes to eat on my lonely ranch,' says he. 'I lie awake at nights thinking how good they are.'

"'You keep on trying for it,' I tells him, 'and I'll do the same. One of us is bound to get a rope over its horns before long. Well, so long, Jacksy.'

"You see, by this time we was on the peacefullest of terms. When I saw that he wasn't after Miss Willella I had more endurable contemplations of that sandy-haired snoozer. In order to help out the ambitions of his appetite I kept on trying to get that receipt from Miss Willella. But every time I would say 'pancakes' she would get sort of remote and fidgety about the eye, and try to change the subject. If I held her to it she would slide out and round up Uncle Emsley with his pitcher of water and hip-pocket howitzer.

"One day I galloped over to the store with a fine bunch of blue verbenas that I cut out of a herd of wild flowers over on Poisoned Dog Prairie. Uncle Emsley looked at 'em with one eye shut and says:

" 'Haven't ye heard the news?'

" 'Cattle up?' I asks.

" 'Willella and Jackson Bird was married in Palestine yesterday,' says he. 'Just got a letter this morning.'

"I dropped them flowers in a cracker barrel, and let the news trickle in my ears and down toward my upper left-hand shirt pocket until it got to my feet.

" 'Would you mind saying that over again once more, Uncle Emsley?' says I. 'Maybe my hearing has got wrong, and you only said that prime heifers was 4.80 on the hoof, or something like that.'

" 'Married yesterday,' says Uncle Emsley, 'and gone to Waco and Niagara Falls on a wedding tour. Why, didn't you see none of the signs all along? Jackson Bird has been courting Willella ever since that day he took her out riding.'

" 'Then,' says I, in a kind of yell, 'what was all this

zizzaparoola he gives me about pancakes? Tell me *that*.'

"When I said 'pancakes' Uncle Emsley sort of dodged and stepped back.

" 'Somebody's been dealing me pancakes from the bottom of the deck.' I says, 'and I'll find out. I believe you know. Talk up,' says I, 'or we'll mix a panful of batter right here.'

"I slid over the counter after Uncle Emsley. He grabbed at his gun, but it was in a drawer, and he missed it by two inches. I got him by the front of his shirt and shoved him in a corner.

" 'Talk pancakes,' says I, 'or be made into one. Does Miss Willella make 'em?'

" 'She never made one in her life and I never saw one,' says Uncle Emsley, soothing. 'Calm down now, Jud— calm down. You've got excited, and that wound in your head is contaminating your sense of intelligence. Try not to think about pancakes.'

" 'Uncle Emsley,' says I, 'I'm not wounded in the head except so far as my natural cogitative instincts run to runts. Jackson Bird told me he was calling on Miss Willella for the purpose of finding out her system of producing pancakes, and he asked me to help him get the bill of lading of the ingredients. I done so, with the results as you see. Have I been sodded down with Johnson grass by a pink-eyed snoozer, or what?'

" 'Slack up your grip on my dress shirt,' says Uncle

Emsley, and I'll tell you. Yes, it looks like Jackson Bird has gone and humbugged you some. The day after he went riding with Willella, he came back and told her to watch out for you whenever you got to talking about pancakes. He said you was in camp once where they was cooking flapjacks, and one of the fellows cut you over the head with a frying pan. Jackson said that whenever you got over-hot or excited that wound hurt you and made you kind of crazy, and you went raving about pancakes. He told us to just get you worked off of the subject and soothed down, and you wouldn't be dangerous. So, me and Willella done the best by you we knew how. Well, well,' says Uncle Emsley, 'that Jackson Bird is sure a seldom kind of a snoozer.'"

During the progress of Jud's story he had been slowly but deftly combining certain portions of the contents of his sacks and cans. Toward the close of it he set before me the finished product—a pair of red-hot, rich-hued pancakes on a tin plate. From some secret hoarding place he also brought a lump of excellent butter and a bottle of golden syrup.

"How long ago did these things happen?" I asked him.

"Three years," said Jud. "They're living on the Mired Mule Ranch now. But I haven't seen either of 'em since. They say Jackson Bird was fixing his ranch up fine with rocking chairs and window curtains all the time he was putting me up the pancake tree. Oh, I got over it after a while. But the boys kept the racket up."

"Did you make these cakes by the famous recipe?" I asked.

"Didn't I tell you there wasn't no receipt?" said Jud. "The boys hollered pancakes till they got pancake hungry, and I cut this receipt out of a newspaper. How does the truck taste?"

"They're delicious," I answered. "Why don't you have some, too, Jud?"

I was sure I heard a sigh.

"Me?" said Jud. "I don't never eat 'em."

THE LAST LEAF

In A LITTLE DISTRICT WEST OF Washington Square the streets have run crazy and broken themselves into small strips called "places." These "places" make strange angles and curves. One street crosses itself a time or two. An artist once discovered a valuable possibility in this street. Suppose a collector with a bill for paints, paper and canvas should, in traversing this route, suddenly meet himself coming back, without a cent having been paid on account!

So to quaint old Greenwich Village the art people soon came prowling, hunting for north windows and eighteenth-century gables and Dutch attics and low rents. Then they imported some pewter mugs and a chafing dish or two from Sixth Avenue, and became a "colony."

At the top of a squatty, three-story brick Sue and Johnsy had their studio. "Johnsy" was familiar for Joanna. One was from Maine, the other from California. They had met at the *table d'hôte* of an Eighth Street "Delmonico's," and found their tastes in art, chicory salad and bishop sleeves so congenial that the joint studio resulted.

That was in May. In November a cold unseen stranger, whom the doctors called Pneumonia, stalked about the colony touching one here and there with his icy fingers. Over on the east side this ravager strode boldly, smiting his victims by scores, but his feet trod slowly through the maze of the narrow and moss-grown "places."

Mr. Pneumonia was not what you would call a chivalric old gentleman. A mite of a little woman with blood thinned by California zephyrs was hardly fair game for the red-fisted, short-breathed old duffer. But Johnsy he smote; and she lay scarcely moving on her painted iron bedstead, looking through the small Dutch windowpanes at the blank side of the next brick house.

One morning the busy doctor invited Sue into the hallway with a shaggy, gray eyebrow.

"She has one chance in—let us say, ten," he said as he shook down the mercury in his clinical thermometer. "And that chance is for her to want to live. This way people have of lining up on the side of the undertaker makes the entire pharmacopœia look silly. Your little lady has made up her mind that she's not going to get well. Has she anything on her mind?"

"She—she wanted to paint the Bay of Naples some-day," said Sue.

"Paint?—bosh! Has she anything on her mind worth thinking about twice—a man, for instance?"

"A man?" said Sue, with a jew's-harp twang in her voice. "Is a man worth—but, no, doctor; there is nothing of the kind."

"Well, it is the weakness, then," said the doctor. "I will do all that science, so far as it may filter through my efforts, can accomplish. But whenever my patient begins to count the carriages in her funeral procession I subtract 50 per cent from the curative power of medicines. If you will get her to ask one question about the new winter styles in cloak sleeves I will promise you a one-in-five chance for her, instead of one in ten."

After the doctor had gone Sue went into the workroom and cried a Japanese napkin to a pulp. Then she swaggered into Johnsy's room with her drawing board, whistling ragtime.

Johnsy lay scarcely making a ripple under the bed-clothes, with her face toward the window. Sue stopped whistling, thinking she was asleep.

She arranged her board and began a pen-and-ink drawing to illustrate a magazine story. Young artists must pave their way to Art by drawing pictures for magazine stories that young authors write to pave their way to Literature.

As Sue was sketching a pair of elegant horseshow riding trousers and a monocle on the figure of the hero, an Idaho cowboy, she heard a low sound, several times repeated. She went quickly to the bedside.

Johnsy's eyes were open wide. She was looking out the window and counting—counting backward.

"Twelve," she said, and a little later "eleven"; and then "ten," and "nine"; and then "eight" and "seven," almost together.

Sue looked solicitously out of the window. What was there to count? There was only a bare dreary yard to be seen, and the blank side of the brick house twenty feet away. An old, old ivy vine, gnarled and decayed at the roots, climbed halfway up the brick wall. The cold breath of autumn had stricken the leaves from the vine until its skeleton branches clung, almost bare, to the crumbling bricks.

"What is it, dear?" asked Sue.

"Six," said Johnsy, in almost a whisper. "They're falling faster now. Three days ago there were almost a hundred. It made my head ache to count them. But now it's easy. There goes another one. There are only five left now."

"Five what, dear? Tell your Sudie."

"Leaves. On the ivy vine. When the last one falls I must go, too. I've known that for three days. Didn't the doctor tell you?"

"Oh, I never heard of such nonsense," complained Sue, with magnificent scorn. "What have old ivy leaves to do with your getting well? And you used to love that vine so, you naughty girl. Don't be a goosey. Why, the doctor told me this morning that your chances for getting well real soon were—let's see exactly what he said—he said the chances were ten to one! Why, that's almost as good a chance as we have in New York when we ride on the streetcars or walk past a new building. Try to take some broth now, and let Sudie go back to her drawing, so she can sell the editor man with it, and buy port wine for her sick child, and pork chops for her greedy self."

"You needn't get any more wine," said Johnsy, keeping her eyes fixed out the window. "There goes another. No, I don't want any broth. That leaves just four. I want to see the last one fall before it gets dark. Then I'll go, too."

"Johnsy, dear," said Sue, bending over her, "will you promise me to keep your eyes closed, and not look out the window until I am done working? I must hand those drawings in by tomorrow. I need the light, or I would draw the shade down."

"Couldn't you draw in the other room?" asked Johnsy, coldly.

"I'd rather be here by you," said Sue. "Besides, I don't want you to keep looking at those silly ivy leaves."

"Tell me as soon as you have finished," said Johnsy, closing her eyes, and lying white and still as a fallen statue, "because I want to see the last one fall. I'm tired of waiting. I'm tired of thinking. I want to turn loose my hold on everything, and go sailing down, down, just like one of those poor tired leaves."

"Try to sleep," said Sue. "I must call Behrman up to be

my model for the old hermit miner. I'll not be gone a minute. Don't try to move 'til I come back."

Old Behrman was a painter who lived on the ground floor beneath them. He was past sixty and had a Michelangelo's Moses beard curling down from the head of a satyr along the body of an imp. Behrman was a failure in art. Forty years he had wielded the brush without getting near enough to touch the hem of his mistress's robe. He had been always about to paint a masterpiece, but had never yet begun it. For several years he had painted nothing except now and then a daub in the line of commerce or advertising. He earned a little by serving as a model to those young artists in the colony who could not pay the price of a professional. He drank gin to excess, and still talked of his coming masterpiece. For the rest he was a fierce little old man, who scoffed terribly at softness in anyone, and who regarded himself as a special mastiff-in-waiting to protect the two young artists in the studio above.

Sue found Behrman smelling strongly of juniper berries in his dimly lighted den below. In one corner was a blank canvas on an easel that had been waiting there for twenty-five years to receive the first line of the masterpiece. She told him of Johnsy's fancy, and how she feared she would indeed, light and fragile as a leaf herself, float away when her slight hold upon the world grew weaker.

Old Behrman, with his red eyes plainly streaming, shouted his derision for such idiotic imaginings.

"Vass!" he cried. "Is dere people in de world mit der foolishness to die because leafs dey drop off from a confounded vine? I haf not heard of such a thing. No, I will not bose as a model for your fool hermit-dunderhead. Vy do you allow dot silly pusiness to come in der brain of her? Ach, dot poor leetle Miss Yohnsy."

"She is very ill and weak," said Sue, "and the fever has left her mind morbid and full of strange fancies. Very well, Mr. Behrman, if you do not care to pose for me, you needn't. But I think you are a horrid old—old flibberti-gibbet."

"You are just like a woman!" yelled Behrman. "Who said I will not bose? Go on. I come mit you. For half an hour I haf peen trying to say dot I am ready to bose. Gott! dis is not any blace in which one so goot as Miss Yohnsy shall lie sick. Some day I vill baint a masterpiece, and ve shall all go away. Gott! yes."

Johnsy was sleeping when they went upstairs. Sue pulled the shade down to the window sill, and motioned Behrman into the other room. In there they peered out the window fearfully at the ivy vine. Then they looked at each other for a moment without speaking. A persistent, cold rain was falling, mingled with snow. Behrman, in his old blue shirt, took his seat as the hermit miner on an upturned kettle for a rock.

When Sue awoke from an hour's sleep the next morning she found Johnsy with dull, wide-open eyes staring at the drawn green shade.

"Pull it up; I want to see," she ordered in a whisper.

Wearily Sue obeyed.

But, lo! after the beating rain and fierce gusts of wind that had endured through the livelong night, there yet stood out against the brick wall one ivy leaf. It was the last on the vine. Still dark green near its stem, but with its serrated edges tinted with the yellow of dissolution and decay, it hung bravely from a branch some twenty feet above the ground.

"It is the last one," said Johnsy. "I thought it would surely fall during the night. I heard the wind. It will fall today, and I shall die at the same time."

"Dear, dear!" said Sue, leaning her worn face down to the pillow. "Think of me, if you won't think of yourself. What would I do?"

But Johnsy did not answer. The lonesomest thing in all the world is a soul when it is making ready to go on its mysterious far journey. The fancy seemed to possess her more strongly as one by one the ties that bound her to friendship and to earth were loosed.

The day wore away, and even through the twilight they could see the lone ivy leaf clinging to its stem against the wall. And then with the coming of the night the north wind was again loosed, while the rain still beat against the windows and pattered down from the low Dutch eaves.

When it was light enough Johnsy, the merciless, commanded that the shade be raised.

The ivy leaf was still there.

Johnsy lay for a long time looking at it. And then she called to Sue, who was stirring her chicken broth over the gas stove.

"I've been a bad girl, Sudie," said Johnsy. "Something has made that last leaf stay there to show me how wicked I was. It is a sin to want to die. You may bring me a little broth now, and some milk with a little port in it, and— no; bring me a hand mirror first, and then pack some pillows about me, and I will sit up and watch you cook."

An hour later she said:

"Sudie, some day I hope to paint the Bay of Naples."

The doctor came in the afternoon, and Sue had an excuse to go into the hallway as he left.

"Even chances," said the doctor, taking Sue's thin, shaking hand in his. "With good nursing you'll win. And now I must see another case I have downstairs. Behrman, his name is—some kind of an artist, I believe. Pneumonia, too. He is an old, weak man, and the attack is acute. There is no hope for him; but he goes to the hospital today to be made more comfortable."

The next day the doctor said to Sue, "She's out of danger. You've won. Nutrition and care now—that's all."

And that afternoon Sue came to the bed where Johnsy lay, contentedly knitting a very blue and very useless woollen shoulder scarf, and put one arm around her, pillows and all.

"I have something to tell you, white mouse," she said.

"Mr. Behrman died of pneumonia today in the hospital. He was ill only two days. The janitor found him on the morning of the first day in his room downstairs helpless with pain. His shoes and clothing were wet through and icy cold. They couldn't imagine where he had been on such a dreadful night. And then they found a lantern, still lighted, and a ladder that had been dragged from its place, and some scattered brushes, and a palette with green and yellow colors mixed on it, and—look out the window, dear, at the last ivy leaf on the wall. Didn't you wonder why it never fluttered or moved when the wind blew? Ah, darling, it's Behrman's masterpiece—he painted it there the night that the last leaf fell."

✢
✢

A DEPARTMENTAL

CASE

IN TEXAS YOU MAY TRAVEL A THOUsand miles in a straight line. If your course is a crooked
one, it is likely that both the distance and your rate of
speed may be vastly increased. Clouds there sail serenely
against the wind. The whippoorwill delivers its disconsolate cry with the notes exactly reversed from those of
the Northern brother. Given a drought and a subsequently lively rain, and lo! from a glazed and stony soil
will spring in a single night blossomed lilies, miraculously fair. Tom Green County was once the standard of
measurement. I have forgotten how many New Jerseys
and Rhode Islands it was that could have been stowed
away and lost in its chaparral. But the legislative axe has
slashed Tom Green into a handful of counties hardly

larger than European kingdoms. The legislature con-
venes at Austin, near the centre of the state; and, while
the representative from Rio Grande country is gathering
his palm-leaf fan and his linen duster to set out for the
capital, the Panhandle solon winds his muffler above his
well-buttoned overcoat and kicks the snow from his well-
greased boots ready for the same journey. All this merely
to hint that the big ex-republic of the Southwest forms a
sizable star on the flag, and to prepare for the corollary
that things sometimes happen there uncut to pattern and
unfettered by metes and bounds.

The Commissioner of Insurance, Statistics, and History
of the State of Texas was an official of no very great or
very small importance. The past tense is used, for now
he is Commissioner of Insurance alone. Statistics and
history are no longer proper nouns in the government
records.

In the year 188–, the governor appointed Luke Coonrod Standifer to be the head of this department. Standifer
was then fifty-five years of age, and a Texan to the core.
His father had been one of the state's earliest settlers
and pioneers. Standifer himself had served the commonwealth as Indian fighter, soldier, ranger, and legislator.
Much learning he did not claim, but he had drunk pretty
deep of the spring of experience.

If other grounds were less abundant, Texas should be
well up in the lists of glory as the grateful republic. For
both as republic and state, it has busily heaped honors

and solid rewards upon its sons who rescued it from the wilderness.

Wherefore and therefore, Luke Coonrod Standifer, son of Ezra Standifer, ex-Terry ranger, simon-pure democrat, and lucky dweller in an unrepresented portion of the politico-geographical map, was appointed Commissioner of Insurance, Statistics, and History.

Standifer accepted the honor with some doubt as to the nature of the office he was to fill and his capacity for filling it—but he accepted, and by wire. He immediately set out from the little country town where he maintained (and was scarcely maintained by) a somnolent and unfruitful office of surveying and map-drawing. Before departing, he had looked up under the I's, S's, and H's in the "Encyclopedia Britannica" to see what information and preparation toward his official duties those weighty volumes afforded.

A few weeks of incumbency diminished the new commissioner's awe of the great and important office he had been called upon to conduct. An increasing familiarity with its workings soon restored him to his accustomed placid course of life. In his office was an old spectacled clerk—a consecrated, informed, able machine, who held his desk regardless of changes of administrative heads. Old Kauffman instructed his new chief gradually in the knowledge of the department without seeming to do so, and kept the wheels revolving without the slip of a cog.

Indeed, the Department of Insurance, Statistics, and
History carried no great heft of the burden of state.
Its main work was the regulating of the business done
in the state by foreign insurance companies, and the
letter of the law was its guide. As for statistics—well,
you wrote letters to county officers, and scissored other
people's reports, and each year you got out a report of
your own about the corn crop and the cotton crop and
pecans and pigs and black and white population, and a
great many columns of figures headed "bushels" and
"acres" and "square miles," etc.—and there you were.
History? The branch was purely a receptive one. Old
ladies interested in the science bothered you some with
long reports of proceedings of their historical societies.
Some twenty or thirty people would write you each year
that they had secured Sam Houston's pocketknife or
Santa Ana's whisky flask or Davy Crockett's rifle—all
absolutely authenticated—and demanded legislative appropriation to purchase. Most of the work in the history
branch went into pigeonholes.

One sizzling August afternoon the commissioner reclined in his office chair, with his feet upon the long,
official table covered with green billiard cloth. The commissioner was smoking a cigar, and dreamily regarding
the quivering landscape framed by the window that
looked upon the treeless capitol grounds. Perhaps he
was thinking of the rough and ready life he had led, of
the old days of breathless adventure and movement, of

the comrades who now trod other paths or had ceased
to tread any, of the changes civilization and peace had
brought, and, maybe, complacently, of the snug and
comfortable camp pitched for him under the dome of
the capitol of the state that had not forgotten his services.

The business of the department was lax. Insurance
was easy. Statistics were not in demand. History was
dead. Old Kauffman, the efficient and perpetual clerk,
had requested an infrequent half-holiday, incited to the
unusual dissipation by the joy of having successfully
twisted the tail of a Connecticut insurance company
that was trying to do business contrary to the edicts of
the great Lone Star State.

The office was very still. A few subdued noises trickled
in through the open door from the other departments
—a dull tinkling crash from the treasurer's office adjoining, as a clerk tossed a bag of silver to the floor of
the vault—the vague, intermittent clatter of a dilatory
typewriter—a dull tapping from the state geologist's
quarters as if some woodpecker had flown in to bore
for his prey in the cool of the massive building—and
then a faint rustle, and the light shuffling of the well-
worn shoes along the hall, the sounds ceasing at the
door toward which the commissioner's lethargic back
was presented. Following this, the sound of a gentle
voice speaking words unintelligible to the commissioner's
somewhat dormant comprehension, but giving evidence
of bewilderment and hesitation.

The voice was feminine; the commissioner was of the race of cavaliers who make salaam before the trail of a skirt without considering the quality of its cloth.

There stood in the door a faded woman, one of the numerous sisterhood of the unhappy. She was dressed all in black—poverty's perpetual mourning for lost joys. Her face had the contours of twenty and the lines of forty. She may have lived that intervening score of years in a twelve-month. There was about her yet an aura of indignant, unappeased, protesting youth that shone faintly through the premature veil of unearned decline.

"I beg your pardon, ma'am," said the commissioner, gaining his feet to the accompaniment of a great creaking and sliding of his chair.

"Are you the governor, sir?" asked the vision of melancholy.

The commissioner hesitated at the end of his best bow, with his hand in the bosom of his double-breasted "frock." Truth at last conquered.

"Well, no, ma'am. I am not the governor. I have the honor to be Commissioner of Insurance, Statistics, and History. Is there anything, ma'am, I can do for you? Won't you have a chair, ma'am?"

The lady subsided into the chair handed her, probably from purely physical reasons. She wielded a cheap fan—last token of gentility to be abandoned. Her clothing seemed to indicate a reduction almost to extreme

poverty. She looked at the man who was not the governor, and saw kindliness and simplicity and a rugged,
unadorned courtliness emanating from a countenance
tanned, and toughened by forty years of outdoor life.
Also, she saw that his eyes were clear and strong and
blue. Just as they had been when he used them to skim
the horizon for raiding Kiowas and Sioux. His mouth
was as set and firm as it had been on that day when
he bearded the old lion Sam Houston himself, and de-
fied him during that season when secession was the
theme. Now, in bearing and dress, Luke Coonrod Standifer endeavored to do credit to the important arts and
sciences of Insurance, Statistics, and History. He had
abandoned the careless dress of his country home. Now,
his broad-brimmed black slouch hat, and his long-tailed
"frock" made him not the least imposing of the official
family, even if his office was reckoned to stand at the
tail of the list.

"You wanted to see the governor, ma'am?" asked the
commissioner, with a deferential manner he always used
toward the fair sex.

"I hardly know," said the lady, hesitatingly. "I suppose
so." And then, suddenly drawn by the sympathetic look
of the other, she poured forth the story of her need.

It was a story so common that the public has come to
look at its monotony instead of its pity. The old tale of
an unhappy married life—made so by a brutal, con-
scienceless husband, a robber, a spendthrift, a moral

coward, and a bully, who failed to provide even the means of the barest existence. Yes, he had come down in the scale so low as to strike her. It happened only the day before—there was the bruise on one temple— she had offended his highness by asking for a little money to live on. And yet she must needs, womanlike, append a plea for her tyrant—he was drinking; he had rarely abused her thus when sober.

"I thought," mourned this pale sister of sorrow, "that maybe the state might be willing to give me some relief. I've heard of such things being done for the families of old settlers. I've heard tell that the state used to give land to the men who fought for it against Mexico, and settled up the country, and helped drive out the Indians. My father did all of that, and he never received anything. He never would take it. I thought the governor would be the one to see, and that's why I came. If Father was entitled to anything, they might let it come to me."

"It's possible, ma'am," said Standifer, "that such might be the case. But 'most all the veterans and settlers got their land certificates issued and located long ago. Still, we can look that up in the land office and be sure. Your father's name, now, was——"

"Amos Colvin, sir."

"Good Lord!" exclaimed Standifer, rising and unbuttoning his tight coat, excitedly. "Are you Amos Colvin's daughter? Why, ma'am, Amos Colvin and me were thicker than two hoss thieves for more than ten years! We fought Kiowas, drove cattle, and rangered side by side nearly all over Texas. I remember seeing you once before, now. You were a kid, about seven, a-riding a little yellow pony up and down. Amos and me stopped at your home for a little grub when we were trailing that band of Mexican cattle thieves down through Karnes and Bee. Great tarantulas! and you're Amos Colvin's little girl! Did you ever hear your father mention Luke Standifer—just kind of casually—as if he'd met me once or twice?"

A little pale smile flitted across the lady's white face.

"It seems to me," she said, "that I don't remember hearing him talk about much else. Every day there was some story he had to tell about what he and you had done. Mighty near the last thing I heard him tell was about the time when the Indians wounded him, and you crawled out to him through the grass, with a canteen of water while they——"

"Yes, yes—well—oh, that wasn't anything," said Standifer, "hemming" loudly and buttoning his coat again briskly. "And now, ma'am, who was the infernal skunk—I beg your pardon, ma'am—who was the gentleman you married?"

"Benton Sharp."

The commissioner plumped down again into his chair with a groan. This gentle, sad little woman in the rusty black gown the daughter of his oldest friend, the wife

of Benton Sharp! Benton Sharp, one of the most noted
"bad" men in that part of the state—a man who had
been a cattle thief, an outlaw, a desperado, and was
now a gambler, a swaggering bully, who plied his trade
in the larger frontier towns, relying upon his record and
the quickness of his gun play to maintain his supremacy.
Seldom did anyone take the risk of going "up against"
Benton Sharp. Even the law officers were content to let
him make his own terms of peace. Sharp was a ready
and an accurate shot, and as lucky as a brand-new penny
at coming clear of scrapes. Standifer wondered how this
pillaging eagle ever came to be mated with Amos Colvin's little dove, and expressed his wonder.

Mrs. Sharp sighed.

"You see, Mr. Standifer, we didn't know anything
about him, and he can be very pleasant and kind when
he wants to. We lived down in the little town of Goliad.
Benton came riding down that way and stopped there
a while. I reckon I was some better looking then than
I am now. He was good to me for a whole year after we
were married. He insured his life for me for five thousand dollars. But for the last six months he has done
everything but kill me. I often wish he had done that,
too. He got out of money for a while, and abused me
shamefully for not having anything he could spend. Then
Father died and left me the little home in Goliad. My
husband made me sell that and turned me out into the
world. I've barely been able to live, for I'm not strong

enough to work. Lately, I heard he was making money in San Antonio, so I went there, and found him, and asked for a little help. This," touching the livid bruise on her temple, "is what he gave me. So I came on to Austin to see the governor. I once heard Father say that there was some land or a pension coming to him from the state that he never would ask for."

Luke Standifer rose to his feet, and pushed his chair back. He looked rather perplexedly around the big office with its handsome furniture.

"It's a long trail to follow," he said, slowly, "trying to get back dues from the government. There's red tape and lawyers and rulings and evidences and courts to keep you waiting. I'm not certain," continued the commissioner, with a profoundly meditative frown, "whether this department that I'm the boss of has any jurisdiction or not. It's only Insurance, Statistics, and History, ma'am, and it don't sound as if it would cover the case. But sometimes a saddle blanket can be made to stretch. You keep your seat, just for a few minutes, ma'am, till I step into the next room and see about it."

The state treasurer was seated within his massive, complicated railings, reading a newspaper. Business for the day was about over. The clerks lolled at their desks, awaiting the closing hour. The Commissioner of Insurance, Statistics, and History entered, and leaned in at the window.

The treasurer, a little, brisk old man, with snow-white

moustache and beard, jumped up youthfully and came forward to greet Standifer. They were friends of old.

"Uncle Frank," said the commissioner, using the familar name by which the historic treasurer was addressed by every Texan, "how much money have you got on hand?"

The treasurer named the sum of the last balance down to the odd cents—something more than a million dollars.

The commissioner whistled lowly, and his eyes grew hopefully bright.

"You know, or else you've heard of, Amos Colvin, Uncle Frank?"

"Knew him well," said the treasurer, promptly. "A good man. A valuable citizen. One of the first settlers in the Southwest."

"His daughter," said Standifer, "is sitting in my office. She's penniless. She's married to Benton Sharp, a coyote and a murderer. He's reduced her to want and broken her heart. Her father helped build up this state, and it's the state's turn to help his child. A couple of thousand dollars will buy back her home and let her live in peace. The State of Texas can't afford to refuse it. Give me the money, Uncle Frank, and I'll give it to her right away. We'll fix up the red-tape business afterward."

The treasurer looked a little bewildered.

"Why, Standifer," he said, "you know I can't pay a cent out of the treasury without a warrant from the

comptroller. I can't disburse a dollar without a voucher
to show for it."

The commissioner betrayed a slight impatience.

"I'll give you a voucher,' he declared. "What's this
job they've given me for? Am I just a knot on a mesquite
stump? Can't my office stand for it? Charge it up to Insurance and the other two sideshows. Don't Statistics
show that Amos Colvin came to this state when it was
in the hands of Mexicans and rattlesnakes and Co-
manches, and fought day and night to make a white
man's country of it? Don't they show that Amos Colvin's
daughter is brought to ruin by a villain who's trying to
pull down what you and I and old Texans shed our blood
to build up? Don't History show that the Lone Star State
never yet failed to grant relief to the suffering and oppressed children of the men who made her the grandest
commonwealth in the Union? If Statistics and History
don't bear out the claim of Amos Colvin's child I'll ask
the next legislature to abolish my office. Come, now,
Uncle Frank, let her have the money. I'll sign the papers
officially, if you say so; and then if the governor or the
comptroller or the janitor or anybody else makes a kick,
by the Lord I'll refer the matter to the people, and see
if they won't indorse the act."

The treasurer looked sympathetic but shocked. The
commissioner's voice had grown louder as he rounded
off the sentences that, however praiseworthy they might
be in sentiment, reflected somewhat upon the capacity

of the head of a more or less important department of state. The clerks were beginning to listen.

"Now, Standifer," said the treasurer, soothingly, "you know I'd like to help in this matter, but stop and think a moment, please. Every cent in the treasury is expended only by appropriation made by the legislature, and drawn out by checks issued by the comptroller. I can't control the use of a cent of it. Neither can you. Your department isn't disbursive—it isn't even administrative —it's purely clerical. The only way for the lady to obtain relief is to petition the legislature, and——"

"To the devil with the legislature," said Standifer, turning away.

The treasurer called him back.

"I'd be glad, Standifer, to contribute a hundred dollars personally toward the immediate expenses of Colvin's daughter." He reached for his pocketbook.

"Never mind, Uncle Frank," said the commissioner, in a softer tone. "There's no need of that. She hasn't asked for anything of that sort yet. Besides, her case is in my hands. I see now what a little rag-tag, bob-tail, gotch-eared department I've been put in charge of. It seems to be about as important as an almanac or a hotel register. But while I'm running it, it won't turn away any daughters of Amos Colvin without stretching its jurisdiction to cover, if possible. You want to keep your eye on the Department of Insurance, Statistics, and History."

The commissioner returned to his office, looking thoughtful. He opened and closed an inkstand on his desk many times with extreme and undue attention before he spoke. "Why don't you get a divorce?" he asked, suddenly.

"I haven't the money to pay for it," answered the lady.

"Just at present," announced the commissioner, in a formal tone, "the powers of my department appear to be considerably stringhalted. Statistics seem to be overdrawn at the bank, and History isn't good for a square meal. But you've come to the right place, ma'am. The department will see you through. Where did you say your husband is, ma'am?"

"He was in San Antonio yesterday. He is living there now."

Suddenly the commissioner abandoned his official air. He took the faded little woman's hands in his, and spoke in the old voice he used on the trail and around campfires.

"Your name's Amanda, isn't it?"

"Yes, sir."

"I thought so. I've heard your dad say it often enough. Well, Amanda, here's your father's best friend, the head of a big office in the state government, that's going to help you out of your troubles. And here's the old bushwhacker and cowpuncher that your father has helped out of scrapes time and time again wants to ask you a question. Amanda, have you got enough money to run you for the next two or three days?"

Mrs. Sharp's white face flushed the least bit.

"Plenty, sir—for a few days."

"All right, then, ma'am. Now you go back where you are stopping here, and you come to the office again the day after tomorrow at four o'clock in the afternoon. Very likely by that time there will be something definite to report to you." The commissioner hesitated, and looked a trifle embarrassed. "You said your husband had insured his life for $5,000. Do you know whether the premiums have been kept paid upon it or not?"

"He paid for a whole year in advance about five months ago," said Mrs. Sharp. "I have the policy and receipts in my trunk."

"Oh, that's all right, then," said Standifer. "It's best to look after things of that sort. Some day they may come in handy."

Mrs. Sharp departed, and soon afterward Luke Standifer went down to the little hotel where he boarded and looked up the railroad timetable in the daily paper. Half an hour later he removed his coat and vest, and strapped a peculiarly constructed pistol holster across his shoulders, leaving the receptacle close under his left armpit. Into the holster he shoved a short-barreled .44-calibre revolver. Putting on his clothes again, he strolled down to the station and caught the five-twenty afternoon train for San Antonio.

The San Antonio *Express* of the following morning contained this sensational piece of news:

BENTON SHARP MEETS HIS MATCH
THE MOST NOTED DESPERADO IN SOUTHWEST TEXAS
SHOT TO DEATH IN THE GOLD FRONT RESTAURANT
PROMINENT STATE OFFICIAL SUCCESSFULLY
DEFENDS HIMSELF AGAINST THE NOTED BULLY
MAGNIFICENT EXHIBITION OF QUICK GUN PLAY.

Last night about eleven o'clock Benton Sharp, with two other men, entered the Gold Front Restaurant and seated themselves at a table. Sharp had been drinking, and was loud and boisterous, as he always was when under the influence of liquor. Five minutes after the party was seated a tall, well-dressed, elderly gentleman entered the restaurant. Few present recognized the Honorable Luke Standifer, the recently appointed Commissioner of Insurance, Statistics, and History.

Going over to the same side where Sharp was, Mr. Standifer prepared to take a seat at the next table. In hanging his hat upon one of the hooks along the wall he let it fall upon Sharp's head. Sharp turned, being in an especially ugly humor, and cursed the other roundly. Mr. Standifer apologized calmly for the accident, but Sharp continued his vituperations. Mr. Standifer was observed to draw near and speak a few sentences to the desperado in so low a tone that no one else caught the words. Sharp sprang up, wild with rage. In the meantime Mr. Standifer had stepped some yards away, and was standing quietly with his arms folded across the breast of his loosely hanging coat.

With that impetuous and deadly rapidity that made

Sharp so dreaded, he reached for the gun he always carried in his hip pocket—a movement that has preceded the death of at least a dozen men at his hands. Quick as the motion was, the bystanders assert that it was met by the most beautiful exhibition of lightning gun-pulling ever witnessed in the Southwest. As Sharp's pistol was being raised—and the act was really quicker than the eye could follow—a glittering .44 appeared as if by some conjuring trick in the right hand of Mr. Standifer, who, without a perceptible movement of his arm, shot Benton Sharp through the heart. It seems that the new Commissioner of Insurance, Statistics, and History has been an old-time Indian fighter and ranger for many years, which accounts for the happy knack he has of handling a .44.

It is not believed that Mr. Standifer will be put to any inconvenience beyond a necessary formal hearing today, as all the witnesses who were present unite in declaring that the deed was done in self-defense.

When Mrs. Sharp appeared at the office of the commissioner, according to appointment, she found that gentleman calmly eating a golden russet apple. He greeted her without embarrassment and without hesitation at approaching the subject that was the topic of the day.

"I had to do it, ma'am," he said, simply, "or get it myself. Mr. Kauffman," he added, turning to the old clerk, "please look up the records of the Security Life Insurance Company and see if they are all right."

"No need to look," grunted Kauffman, who had everything in his head. "It's all O. K. They pay all losses within ten days."

Mrs. Sharp soon rose to depart. She had arranged to remain in town until the policy was paid. The commissioner did not detain her. She was a woman, and he did not know just what to say to her at present. Rest and time would bring her what she needed.

But, as she was leaving, Luke Standifer indulged himself in an official remark:

"The Department of Insurance, Statistics, and History, ma'am, has done the best it could with your case. 'Twas a case hard to cover according to red tape. Statistics failed, and History missed fire, but, if I may be permitted to say it, we came out particularly strong on Insurance."

✦

VANITY AND
SOME SABLES

WHEN "KID" BRADY WAS SENT TO THE
ropes by Molly McKeever's blue-black eyes he withdrew
from the Stovepipe Gang. So much for the power of a
colleen's blanderin' tongue and stubborn truehearted-
ness. If you are a man who read this, may such an influence be sent you before 2 o'clock tomorrow; if you
are a woman, may your Pomeranian greet you this morning with a cold nose—a sign of dog health and your
happiness.

The Stovepipe Gang borrowed its name from a sub-
district of the city called the "Stovepipe," which is a
narrow and natural extension of the familiar district
known as "Hell's Kitchen." The "Stovepipe" strip of town

runs along Eleventh and Twelfth avenues on the river, and bends a hard and sooty elbow around little, lost homeless De Witt Clinton park. Consider that a stovepipe is an important factor in any kitchen and the situation is analyzed. The chefs in "Hell's Kitchen" are many, and the "Stovepipe" gang wears the cordon blue.

The members of this unchartered but widely known brotherhood appeared to pass their time on street corners arrayed like the lilies of the conservatory and busy with nail files and penknives. Thus displayed as a guarantee of good faith, they carried on an innocuous conversation in a 200-word vocabulary, to the casual observer as innocent and immaterial as that heard in the clubs seven blocks to the east.

But off exhibition the "Stovepipes" were not mere street corner ornaments addicted to posing and manicuring. Their serious occupation was the separating of citizens from their coin and valuables. Preferably this was done by weird and singular tricks without noise or bloodshed; but whenever the citizen honored by their attentions refused to impoverish himself gracefully, his objections came to be spread finally upon some police station blotter or hospital register.

The police held the "Stovepipe" gang in perpetual suspicion and respect. As the nightingale's liquid note is heard in the deepest shadows, so along the "Stovepipe's" dark and narrow confines the whistle for reserves punctures the dull ear of night. Whenever there was smoke in the "Stovepipe" the tasselled men in blue knew there was a fire in "Hell's Kitchen."

"Kid" Brady promised Molly to be good. "Kid" was the vainest, the strongest, the wariest, and the most successful plotter in the gang. Therefore, the boys were sorry to give him up.

But they witnessed his fall to a virtuous life without protest. For, in the Kitchen it is considered neither unmanly nor improper for a guy to do as his girl advises.

Black her eyes for love's sake, if you will; but it is all-to-the-good business to do a thing when she wants you to do it.

"Turn off the hydrant," said the Kid, one night when Molly, tearful, besought him to amend his ways. "I'm going to cut out the gang. You for mine, and the simple life on the side. I'll tell you, Moll—I'll get work; and in a year we'll get married. I'll do it for you. We'll get a flat and a flute, and a sewing machine and a rubber plant and live as honest as we can."

"Oh, Kid," sighed Molly, wiping the powder off his shoulder with her handkerchief, "I'd rather hear you say that than to own all of New York. And we can be happy on so little!"

The Kid looked down at his speckless cuffs and shining patent leathers with a suspicion of melancholy.

"It'll hurt hardest in the rags department," said he. "I've kind of always liked to rig out swell when I could. You know how I hate cheap things, Moll. This suit set me back sixty-five. Anything in the wearing apparel line has got to be just so, or it's to the misfit parlors for it, for mine. If I work I won't have so much coin to hand over to the little man with the big shears."

"Never mind, Kid. I'll like you just as much in a blue jumper as I would in a red automobile."

Before the Kid had grown large enough to knock out his father he had been compelled to learn the plumber's art. So now back to this honorable and useful profession he returned. But it was as an assistant that he engaged himself; and it is the master plumber and not the assistant, who wears diamonds as large as hailstones and looks contemptuously upon the marble colonnades of Senator Clark's mansion.

Eight months went by as smoothly and surely as though they had "elapsed" on a theatre program. The Kid worked away at his pipes and solder with no symptoms of backsliding. The Stovepipe gang continued its piracy on the high avenues, cracked policeman's heads, held up late travellers, invented new methods of peaceful plundering, copied Fifth Avenue's cut of clothes and neckwear fancies, and comported itself according to its lawless bylaws. But the Kid stood firm and faithful to his Molly, even though the polish was gone from his fingernails and it took him 15 minutes to tie his purple silk ascot so that the worn places would not show.

One evening he brought a mysterious bundle with him to Molly's house.

"Open that, Moll!" he said in his large, quiet way. "It's for you."

Molly's eager fingers tore off the wrappings. She shrieked aloud, and in rushed a sprinkling of little McKeevers, and Ma McKeever, dishwashy, but an undeniable relative of the late Mrs. Eve.

Again Molly shrieked, and something dark and long and sinuous flew and enveloped her neck like an anaconda.

"Russian sables," said the Kid, pridefully, enjoying the sight of Molly's round cheek against the clinging fur. "The real thing. They don't grow anything in Russia too good for you, Moll!"

Molly plunged her hands into the muff, overturned a row of the family infants, and flew to the mirror. Hint for the beauty column. To make bright eyes, rosy cheeks, and a bewitching smile: recipe—one set Russian sables. Apply.

When they were alone Molly became aware of a small cake of the ice of common sense floating down the full tide of her happiness.

"You're a bird, all right, Kid," she admitted, gratefully. "I never had any furs on before in my life. But ain't Russian sables awful expensive? Seems to me I've heard they were."

"Have I ever chucked any bargain-sale stuff at you, Moll?" asked the Kid, with calm dignity. "Did you ever notice me leaning on the remnant counter or peering in

the window of the five-and-ten? Call that scarf $250 and
the muff $175 and you won't make any mistake about the
price of Russian sables. The swell goods for me. Say,
they look fine on you, Moll."

Molly hugged the sables to her bosom in rapture. And
then her smile went away little by little, and she looked
the Kid straight in the eye sadly and steadily.

He knew what every look of hers meant; and he
laughed with a faint flush upon his face.

"Cut it out," he said with affectionate roughness. "I
told you I was done with that. I bought 'em and paid for
'em, all right, with my own money."

"Out of the money you worked for, Kid? Out of $75 a
month?"

"Sure. I been saving up."

"Let's see—saved $425 in eight months, Kid?"

"Ah, let up," said the Kid, with some heat. "I had some
money when I went to work. Do you think I've been
holding 'em up again? I told you I'd quit. They're paid
for on the square. Put 'em on and come out for a walk."

Molly calmed her doubts. Sables are soothing. Proud
as a queen she went forth in the streets at the Kid's side.
In all that region of low-lying streets Russian sables had
never been seen before. The word sped, and the doors
and windows blossomed with heads eager to see the
swell furs Kid Brady had given his girl. All down the
street there were "Oh's" and "Ah's" and the reported
fabulous sum paid for the sables was passed from lip to

lip, increasing as it went. At her right elbow sauntered the Kid with the air of a prince. Work had not diminished his love of pomp and show and his passion for the costly and genuine. On a corner they saw a group of the Stovepipe Gang loafing, immaculate. They raised their hats to the Kid's girl and went on with their calm, unaccented palaver.

Three blocks behind the admired couple strolled Detective Ransom, of the Central office. Ransom was the only detective on the force who could walk abroad with safety in the Stovepipe district. He was fair dealing and unafraid and went there with the hypothesis that the inhabitants were human. Many liked him, and now and then would tip him off to something that he was looking for.

"What's the excitement down the street?" asked Ransom of a pale youth in a red sweater.

"Dey're out rubberin' at a set of Buffalo robes Kid Brady staked his girl to," answered the youth. "Some say he paid $900 for de skins. Dey're swell all right enough."

"I hear Brady has been working at his old trade for nearly a year," said the detective. "He doesn't travel with the gang any more, does he?"

"He's workin', all right," said the red sweater, "but— say, sport, are you trailin' anything in the fur lines? A job in a plumbin' shop don't match wid dem skins de Kid's girl's got on."

Ransom overtook the strolling couple on an empty
street near the river bank. He touched the Kid's arm from
behind.

"Let me see you a moment, Brady," he said, quietly.
His eye rested for a second on the long fur scarf thrown
stylishly back over Molly's left shoulder. The Kid, with
his old-time police-hating frown on his face, stepped a
yard or two aside with the detective.

"Did you go to Mrs. Hethcote's on West 7—th Street
yesterday to fix a leaky water pipe?" asked Ransom.

"I did," said the Kid. "What of it?"

"The lady's $1,000 set of Russian sables went out of
the house about the same time you did. The description
fits the ones this lady has on."

"To h—Harlem with you," cried the Kid, angrily. "You
know I've cut out that sort of thing, Ransom. I bought
them sables yesterday at——"

The Kid stopped short.

"I know you've been working straight lately," said
Ransom. "I'll give you every chance. I'll go with you
where you say you bought the furs and investigate. The
lady can wear 'em along with us and nobody'll be on.
That's fair, Brady."

"Come on," agreed the Kid, hotly. And then he stopped
suddenly in his tracks and looked with an odd smile at
Molly's distressed and anxious face.

"No use," he said, grimly. "They're the Hethcote sables,
all right. You'll have to turn 'em over, Moll, but they

ain't too good for you if they cost a million."

Molly, with anguish in her face, hung upon the Kid's arm.

"Oh, Kiddy, you've broke my heart," she said. "I was so proud of you—and now they'll do you—and where's our happiness gone?"

"Go home," said the Kid, wildly. "Come on, Ransom— take the furs. Let's get away from here. Wait a minute— I've got a good mind to—— No, I'll be d— if I can do it—run along, Moll—I'm ready, Ransom."

Around the corner of a lumberyard came Policeman Kohen on his way to his beat along the river. The detective signed to him for assistance. Kohen joined the group. Ransom explained.

"Sure," said Kohen. "I hear about those saples dat vas stole. You say you have dem here?"

Policeman Kohen took the end of Molly's late scarf in his hands and looked at it closely.

"Once," he said, "I sold furs in Sixth Avenue. Yes, dese are saples. Dey came from Alaska. Dis scarf is vort $12 and dis muff——"

"Biff!" came the palm of the Kid's powerful hand upon the policeman's mouth. Kohen staggered and rallied. Molly screamed. The detective threw himself upon Brady and with Kohen's aid got the nippers on his wrist.

"The scarf is vort $12 and the muff is vort $9," persisted the policeman. "Vot is dis talk about $1,000 saples?"

The Kid sat upon a pile of lumber and his face turned dark red.

"Correct! You figured it, copper," he sneered. "I paid $21.50 for the set. I'd rather have got six months and not have told it. Me, the swell guy that wouldn't look at anything cheap! I'm a plain bluffer. Moll—my salary couldn't spell sables in Russian."

Molly cast herself upon his neck.

"What do I care for all the sables and money in the world," she cried. "It's my Kiddy I want. Oh, you dear, stuck-up, crazy blockhead!"

"You can take dose nippers off," said Kohen to the detective. "Before I leaf de station de report come in dat de lady vind her saples—hanging in her wardrobe. Young man, I excuse you dat punch in my vace—dis von time."

Ransom handed Molly her furs. Her eyes were smiling upon the Kid. She wound the scarf and threw the end over her left shoulder with a duchess's grace.

"A gouple of young vools," said Policeman Kohen to Ransom; "come on away."

BEXAR SCRIP

NO. 2692

WHENEVER YOU VISIT AUSTIN YOU should by all means go to see the General Land Office.

As you pass up the avenue you turn sharp round the corner of the courthouse, and on a steep hill before you, see a medieval castle.

You think of the Rhine, the "castled crag of Drachenfels," the Lorelei, and the vine-clad slopes of Germany. And German it is in every line of its architecture and design.

The plan was drawn by an old draftsman from the "Vaterland," whose heart still loved the scenes of his native land, and it is said he reproduced the design of a certain castle near his birthplace with remarkable fidelity.

Under the present administration a new coat of paint has vulgarized its ancient and venerable walls. Modern tiles have replaced the limestone slabs of its floors, worn in hollows by the tread of thousands of feet, and smart and gaudy fixtures have usurped the place of the time-worn furniture that has been consecrated by the touch of hands that Texas will never cease to honor.

But even now, when you enter the building, you lower your voice, and time turns backward for you, for the atmosphere which you breathe is cold with the exudations of buried generations.

The building is stone with a coating of concrete; the walls are immensely thick; it is cold in the summer and warm in the winter; it is isolated and sombre; standing apart from the other state buildings, sullen and decaying, brooding on the past.

Twenty years ago it was much the same as now; twenty years from now the garish newness will be worn off and it will return to its appearance of gloomy decadence.

People living in other states can form no conception of the vastness and importance of the work performed and the significance of the millions of records and papers composing the archives of this office.

The title deeds, patents, transfers, and legal documents connected with every foot of land owned in the state of Texas are filed here.

Volumes could be filled with accounts of the knavery, the double-dealing, the cross-purposes, the perjury, the lies, the bribery, the alteration and erasing, the suppressing and destroying of papers, the various schemes and plots that for the sake of the almighty dollar have left their stains upon the record of the General Land Office.

No reference is made to the employees. No more faithful, competent, and efficient force of men exists in the clerical portions of any government, but there is— or was, for their day is now over—a class of land speculators commonly called land sharks, unscrupulous and greedy, who have left their trail in every department of this office, in the shape of titles destroyed, patents cancelled, homes demolished and torn away, forged transfers and lying affidavits.

Before the modern tiles were laid upon the floors, there were deep hollows in the limestone slabs, worn by the countless feet that daily trod uneasily through its echoing corridors, pressing from file room to business room, from commissioner's sanctum to record books and back again.

The honest but ignorant settler, bent on saving the little plot of land he called home, elbowed the wary land shark who was searching the records for evidence to oust him; the lordly cattle baron, relying on his influence and money, stood at the Commissioner's desk side by side with the pre-emptor, whose little potato patch lay like a minute speck of island in the vast, billowy sea of his princely pastures, and played the old game of "freeze-out," which is as old as Cain and Abel.

The trail of the serpent is through it all.

Honest, earnest men have wrought for generations striving to disentangle the shameful coil that certain years of fraud and infamy have wound. Look at the files and see the countless endorsements of those in authority:

"Transfer doubtful—locked up."

"Certificate a forgery—locked up."

"Signature a forgery."

"Patent refused—duplicate patented elsewhere."

"Field notes forged."

"Certificates stolen from office"—and so on, ad infinitum.

The record books, spread upon long tables in the big room upstairs, are open to the examination of all.

Open them, and you will find the dark and greasy fingerprints of half a century's handling. The quick hand of the land grabber has fluttered the leaves a million times; the damp clutch of the perturbed tiller of the soil has left traces of his calling on the ragged leaves.

Interest centers in the file room.

This is a large room, built as a vault, fireproof, and entered by but a single door.

There is "No Admission" on the portal; and the precious files are handed out by a clerk in charge only on presentation of an order signed by the Commissioner or chief clerk.

In years past too much laxity prevailed in its management, and the files were handled by all comers, simply on their request, and returned at their will or not at all.

In those days most of the mischief was done. In the file room, there are about —— files, each in a paper wrapper, and comprising the title papers of a particular tract of land.

You ask the clerk in charge for the papers relating to any survey in Texas. They are arranged simply in districts and numbers.

He disappears from the door, you hear the sliding of a tin box, the lid snaps, and the file is in your hand.

Go up there some day and call for Bexar Scrip No. 2692.

The file clerk stares at you for a second, says shortly: "Out of file."

It has been missing twenty years.

The history of that file has never been written before.

Twenty years ago there was a shrewd land agent living in Austin who devoted his undoubted talents and vast knowledge of land titles, and the laws governing them, to the locating of surveys made by illegal certificates or improperly made, and otherwise of no value through non-compliance with the statutes, or whatever flaws his ingenious and unscrupulous mind could unearth.

He found a fatal defect in the title of the land as on
file in Bexar Scrip No. 2692 and placed a new certificate
upon the survey in his own name.

The certificate by virtue of which the original survey
had been made was missing.

It was not to be found in the file, and there was no
memorandum or date on the wrapper to show that it had
ever been filed.

The law was on his side.

Every sentiment of justice, of right, and humanity was
against him.

Under the law the land was vacant, unappropriated
public domain and open to location.

The land was occupied by a widow and her only son,
and she supposed her title good.

The railroad had surveyed a new line through the
property, and it had doubled in value.

Sharp, the land agent, did not communicate with her
in any way until he had filed his papers, rushed his claim
through the departments and into the patent room for
patenting.

Then he wrote her a letter, offering her the choice of
buying from him or vacating at once.

He received no reply.

One day he was looking through some files and came
across the missing certificate. Someone, probably an
employee of the office, had by mistake, after making
some examination, placed it in the wrong file, and curi-

ously enough another inadvertence, in there being no record of its filing on the wrapper, had completed the appearance of its having never been filed.

Sharp called for the file in which it belonged and scrutinized it carefully, fearing he might have overlooked some endorsement regarding its return to the office.

On the back of the certificate was plainly endorsed the date of filing, according to law, and signed by the chief clerk.

If this certificate should be seen by the examining clerk, his own claim, when it came up for patenting, would not be worth the paper on which it was written.

Sharp glanced furtively around. A young man, or rather a boy about eighteen years of age, stood a few feet away regarding him closely with keen black eyes.

Sharp, a little confused, thrust the certificate into the file where it properly belonged and began gathering up the other papers.

The boy came up and leaned on the desk beside him.

"A right interesting office, sir!" he said. "I have never been in here before. All those papers, now, they are about lands, are they not? The titles and deeds, and such things?"

"Yes," said Sharp. "They are supposed to contain all the title papers."

"This one, now," said the boy, taking up Bexar Scrip No. 2692, "what land does this represent the title of? Ah, I see 'Six hundred and forty acres in B—— county,

Absalom Harris, original grantee.' Please tell me, I am
so ignorant of these things, how can you tell a good
survey from a bad one? I am told that there are a great
many illegal and fraudulent surveys in this office. I suppose this one is all right?"

"No," said Sharp. "The certificate is missing. It is invalid."

"That paper I just saw you place in that file I suppose
is something else—field notes, or a transfer probably?"

"Yes," said Sharp, hurriedly, "corrected field notes.
Excuse me, I am a little pressed for time."

The boy was watching him with bright, alert eyes.

It would never do to leave the certificate in the file;
but he could not take it out with that inquisitive boy
watching him.

He turned to the file room, with a dozen or more files
in his hands, and accidentally dropped part of them on
the floor. As he stooped to pick them up he swiftly thrust
the file of Bexar Scrip No. 2692 into the inside breast
pocket of his coat.

This happened at just half past four, and when the file
clerk took the files he threw them in a pile in his room,
came out and locked the door.

The clerks were moving out of the doors in long,
straggling lines.

It was closing time.

Sharp did not desire to take the file from the Land
Office. The boy might have seen him place the file in his

pocket, and the penalty of the law for such an act was very severe.

Some distance back from the file room was the draftsman's room now entirely vacated by its occupants.

Sharp dropped behind the outgoing stream of men, and slipped slyly into this room.

The clerks trooped noisily down the iron stairway, singing, whistling, and talking.

Below, the night watchman awaited their exit, ready to close and bar the great doors to the south and east.

It is his duty to take careful note each day that no one remains in the building after the hour of closing.

Sharp waited until all sounds had ceased.

It was his intention to linger until everything was quiet, and then to remove the certificate from the file, and throw the latter carelessly on some draftsman's desk, as if it had been left there during the business of the day.

He knew also that he must remove the certificate from the office or destroy it, as the chance finding of it by a clerk would lead to its immediately being restored to its proper place, and the consequent discovery that his location over the old survey was absolutely worthless.

As he moved cautiously along the stone floor the loud barking of the little black dog, kept by the watchman, told that the dog's keen ears had heard his steps.

The great, hollow rooms echoed loudly, move as lightly as he could.

Sharp sat down at a desk and laid the file before him.

In all his queer practices and cunning tricks he had not yet included any act that was downright criminal.

He had always kept on the safe side of the law, but in the deed he was about to commit there was no compromise to be made with what little conscience he had left.

There is no well-defined boundary line between honesty and dishonesty.

The frontiers of one blend with the outside limits of the other, and he who attempts to tread this dangerous ground may be sometimes in the one domain and sometimes in the other; so the only safe road is the broad highway that leads straight through and has been well defined by line and compass.

Sharp was a man of what is called high standing in the community. That is, his word in a trade was as good as any man's; his check was as good as so much cash, and so regarded; he went to church regularly, went in good society and owed no man anything.

He was regarded as a sure winner in any land trade he chose to make, but that was his occupation.

The act he was about to commit now would place him forever in the ranks of those who chose evil for their portion—if it was found out.

More than that, it would rob a widow and her son of property soon to be of great value, which, if not legally theirs, was theirs certainly by every claim of justice.

But he had gone too far to hesitate.

His own survey was in the patent room for patenting. His own title was about to be perfected by the State's own hand.

The certificate must be destroyed.

He leaned his head on his hands for a moment, and as he did so a sound behind him caused his heart to leap with guilty fear, but before he could rise, a hand came over his shoulder and grasped the file.

He rose quickly, as white as paper, rattling his chair loudly on the stone floor.

The boy who had spoken to him earlier stood contemplating him with contemptuous and flashing eyes, and quietly placed the file in the left breast pocket of his coat.

"So, Mr. Sharp, by nature as well as by name," he said, "it seems that I was right in waiting behind the door in order to see you safely out. You will appreciate the pleasure I feel in having done so when I tell you my name is Harris. My mother owns the land on which you have filed, and if there is any justice in Texas she shall hold it. I am not certain, but I think I saw you place a paper in this file this afternoon, and it is barely possible that it may be of value to me. I was also impressed with the idea that you desired to remove it again, but had not the opportunity. Anyway, I shall keep it until tomorrow and let the Commissioner decide."

Far back among Mr. Sharp's ancestors there must have been some of the old berserker blood, for his caution, his presence of mind left him, and left him possessed of a blind, devilish, unreasoning rage that showed itself in a moment in the white glitter of his eye.

"Give me that file, boy," he said, thickly, holding out his hand.

"I am no such fool, Mr. Sharp," said the youth. "This file shall be laid before the Commissioner tomorrow for examination. If he finds—— Help! Help!"

Sharp was upon him like a tiger and bore him to the floor. The boy was strong and vigorous, but the suddenness of the attack gave him no chance to resist. He struggled up again to his feet, but it was an animal, with blazing eyes and cruel-looking teeth, that fought him, instead of a man.

Mr. Sharp, a man of high standing and good report, was battling for his reputation.

Presently there was a dull sound, and another, and still one more, and a blade flashing white and then red, and Edward Harris dropped down like some stuffed effigy of a man, that boys make for sport, with limbs all crumpled and lax on the stone floor of the Land Office.

The old watchman was deaf and heard nothing.

The little dog barked at the foot of the stairs until his master made him come into his room.

Sharp stood there for several minutes holding in his hand his bloody clasp knife, listening to the cooing of the pigeons on the roof, and the loud ticking of the clock above the receiver's desk.

A map rustled on the wall and his blood turned to ice; a rat ran across some strewn papers, and his scalp prickled, and he could scarcely moisten his dry lips with his tongue.

Between the file room and the draftsman's room there is a door that opens on a small dark spiral stairway that winds from the lower floor to the ceiling at the top of the house.

This stairway was not used then, nor is it now.

It is inconvenient, dusty, and dark as night, a blunder of the architect who designed the building.

This stairway ends above at the tent-shaped space between the roof and the joists.

That space is dark and forbidding, and, being useless, is rarely visited.

Sharp opened this door and gazed for a moment up this narrow cobwebbed stairway.

After dark that night, a man opened cautiously one of the lower windows of the Land Office, crept out with great circumspection and disappeared in the shadows.

One afternoon, a week after this time, Sharp lingered behind after the clerks had left and the office closed.

The next morning the first comers noticed a broad mark in the dust on the upstairs floor, and the same mark was observed below stairs near a window.

It appeared as if some heavy and rather bulky object had been dragged along through the limestone dust. A memorandum book with "E. Harris" written on the fly-leaf was picked up on the stairs, but nothing particular was thought of any of these signs.

Circulars and advertisements appeared for a long time in the papers asking for information concerning Edward Harris, who left his mother's home on a certain date and had never been heard of since.

After a while these things were succeeded by affairs of more recent interest, and faded from the public mind.

Sharp died two years ago, respected and regretted. The last two years of his life were clouded with a settled melancholy for which his friends could assign no reason.

The bulk of his comfortable fortune was made from the land he obtained by fraud and crime.

The disappearance of the file was a mystery that created some commotion in the Land Office at the time, but Sharp got his patent.

It is a well-known tradition in Austin and vicinity that there is a buried treasure of great value somewhere on the banks of Shoal Creek, about a mile west of the city.

Three young men living in Austin recently became possessed of what they thought was a clue to the whereabouts of the treasure, and Thursday night they repaired to the place after dark and plied the pickaxe and shovel with great diligence for about three hours.

At the end of that time their efforts were rewarded by

the finding of a box buried about four feet below the surface, which they hastened to open.

The light of a lantern disclosed to their view the flesh-less bones of a human skeleton with clothing still wrapping its uncanny limbs.

They immediately left the scene and notified the proper authorities of their ghastly find.

On closer examination, in the left breast pocket of the skeleton's coat, there was found a flat, oblong packet of papers, cut through and through in three places by a knife blade, and so completely soaked and clotted with blood that it had become an almost indistinguishable mass.

With the aid of a microscope and the exercise of a little imagination this much can be made out of the letters at the top of the papers:

B—x a— ——rip N—2—92.

THE RANSOM
OF MACK

$\bigstar$

ME AND OLD MACK LONSBURY, WE
got out of that Little Hide-and-Seek gold mine affair
with about $40,000 apiece. I say "old" Mack; but he
wasn't old. Forty-one, I should say; but he always seemed
old.

"Andy," he says to me, "I'm tired of hustling. You and
me have been working hard together for three years. Say
we knock off for a while, and spend some of this idle
money we've coaxed our way."

"The proposition hits me just right," says I. "Let's be
nabobs a while and see how it feels. What'll we do—take
in the Niagara Falls, or buck at faro?"

"For a good many years," says Mack, "I've thought that if I ever had extravagant money I'd rent a two-room cabin somewhere, hire a Chinese cook, and sit in my stocking feet, reading Buckle's 'History of Civilization'."

"That sounds self-indulgent and gratifying without vulgar ostentation," says I; "and I don't see how money could be better invested. Give me a cuckoo clock and a Sep Winner's 'Self-Instructor for the Banjo', and I'll join you."

A week afterward me and Mack hits this small town of Piña, about thirty miles out from Denver, and finds an elegant two-room house that just suits us. We deposited half a peck of money in the Piña bank and shook hands with every one of the 340 citizens in the town. We brought along the Chinese cook, the cuckoo clock and Buckle and the "Instructor" with us from Denver; and they made the cabin seem like home at once.

Never believe it when they tell you that riches don't bring happiness. If you could have seen old Mack sitting in his rocking chair with his blue yarn sock feet up in the window and absorbing in that Buckle stuff through his specs you'd have seen a picture of content that would have made Rockefeller jealous. And I was learning to pick out "Old Zip Coon" on the banjo, and the cuckoo was on time with his remarks, and Am Sing was messing up the atmosphere with the handsomest smell of ham and eggs that ever laid the honeysuckle in the shade. When it got too dark to make out Buckle's nonsense and the notes in the "Instructor," me and Mack would light our pipes and talk about science and pearl diving and sciatica and Egypt and spelling and fish and trade winds and leather and gratitude and eagles, and a lot of subjects that we'd never had time to explain our sentiments about before.

One evening Mack spoke up and asked me if I was much apprised in the habits and policies of womenfolks.

"Why, yes," says I, in a tone of voice; "I know 'em from Alfred to Omaha. The feminine nature and similitude," says I, "is as plain to my sight as the Rocky Mountains is to a blue-eyed burro. I'm onto all their little side-steps and punctual discrepancies."

"I tell you, Andy," says Mack, with a kind of sigh. "I never had the least amount of intersection with their predispositions. Maybe I might have had a proneness in respect to their vicinity, but I never took the time. I made my own living since I was fourteen; and I never seemed to get my ratiocinations equipped with the sentiments usually depicted toward the sect. I sometimes wish I had," says old Mack.

"They're an adverse study," says I, "and adapted to points of view. Although they vary in rationale, I have found 'em quite often obviously differing from each other in divergences of contrast."

"It seems to me," goes on Mack, "that a man had better take 'em in and secure his inspirations of the sect when he's young and so preordained. I let my chance go by;

and I guess I'm too old now to go hopping into the cur-
riculum."

"Oh, I don't know," I tells him. "Maybe you better
credit yourself with a barrel of money and a lot of eman-
cipation from a quantity of uncontent. Still, I don't regret
my knowledge of 'em," I says. "It takes a man who under-
stands the symptoms and by-plays of womenfolks to take
care of himself in this world."

We stayed on in Piña because we liked the place.
Some folks might enjoy their money with noise and rapture and locomotion; but me and Mack we had had
plenty of turmoils and hotel towels. The people were
friendly; Ah Sing got the swing of the grub we liked;
Mack and Buckle were as thick as two body snatchers,
and I was hitting out a cordial resemblance to "Buffalo
Gals, Can't You Come Out Tonight," on the banjo.

One day I got a telegram from Speight, the man that
was working a mine I had an interest in out in New
Mexico. I had to go out there; and I was gone two
months. I was anxious to get back to Piña and enjoy life
once more.

When I struck the cabin I nearly fainted. Mack was
standing in the door; and if angels ever wept, I saw no
reason why they should be smiling then.

That man was a spectacle. Yes; he was worse; he was a
spyglass; he was the great telescope in the Lick Observa-
tory. He had on a coat and shiny shoes and a white vest
and a high silk hat; and a geranium as big as an order of

spinach was spiked onto his front. And he was smirking
and warping his face like an infernal storekeeper or a
kid with colic.

"Hello, Andy," says Mack, out of his face. "Glad to see
you back. Things have happened since you went away."

"I know it," says I, "and a sacrilegious sight it is. God
never made you that way, Mack Lonsbury. Why do you
scarify His works with this presumptious kind of ribaldry?"

"Why, Andy," said he, "they've elected me Justice of
the Peace since you left."

I looked at Mack close. He was restless and inspired.
A justice of the peace ought to be disconsolate and as-
suaged.

Just then a young woman passed on the sidewalk; and
I saw Mack kind of half snicker and blush, and then he
raised up his hat and smiled and bowed, and she smiled
and bowed, and went on by.

"No hope for you," says I, "if you've got the Mary Jane
infirmity at your age. I thought it wasn't going to take
on you. And patent leather shoes! All this in two little
short months!"

"I'm going to marry the young lady who just passed
tonight," says Mack, in a kind of flutter.

"I forgot something at the post office," says I, and
walked away quick.

I overtook that young woman a hundred yards away.
I raised my hat and told her my name. She was about

nineteen, and young for her age. She blushed, and then
looked at me cool, like I was the snow scene from the
"Two Orphans."

"I understand you are to be married tonight," I said.

"Correct," says she. "You got any objections?"

"Listen, sissy," I begins.

"My name is Miss Rebosa Reed," says she in a pained
way.

"I know it," says I. "Now, Rebosa, I'm old enough to
have owed money to your father. And that old, specious,
dressed-up, garbled, seasick ptomaine prancing around
avidiously like an irremediable turkey gobbler with
patent leather shoes on is my best friend. Why did you go
and get him invested in this marriage business?"

"Why, he was the only chance there was," answered
Miss Rebosa.

"Nay," says I, giving a sickening look of admiration at
her complexion and style of features; "with your beauty
you might pick any kind of a man. Listen, Rebosa. Old
Mack ain't the man you want. He was twenty-two when
you was *née* Reed, as the papers say. This bursting into
bloom won't last with him. He's all ventilated with old-
ness and rectitude and decay. Old Mack's down with a
case of Indian summer. He overlooked his bet when he
was young; and now he's suing Nature for the interest on
the promissory note he took from Cupid instead of the
cash. Rebosa, are you really bent on having this marriage
occur?"

"Why, sure I am," says she, oscillating the pansies on her hat, "and so is somebody else, I reckon."

"What time is it to take place?" I asks.

"At six o'clock," says she.

I made up my mind right away what to do. I'd save old Mack if I could. To have a good, seasoned, ineligible man like that turn chicken for a girl that hadn't quit eating slate pencils and buttoning in the back was more than I could look on with easiness.

"Rebosa," says I, earnest, drawing upon my display of knowledge concerning the feminine intuitions of reason, "ain't there a young man in Piña—a nice young man— that you think a heap of?"

"Yep," says Rebosa, nodding her pansies. "Sure there is! What do you think! Gracious!"

"Does he like you?" I asks. "How does he stand in the matter?"

"Crazy," says Rebosa. "Ma has to wet down the front steps to keep him from sitting there all the time. But I guess that'll be all over after tonight," she winds up with a sigh.

"Rebosa," says I, "you don't really experience any of this adoration called love for old Mack, do you?"

"Lord! no," says the girl, shaking her head. "I think he's as dry as a lava bed. The idea!"

"Who is this young man that you like, Rebosa?" I inquires of the girl.

"It's Eddie Bayles," says she. "He clerks in Crosby's

grocery. But he don't make but thirty-five a month. Ella Noakes was wild about him once."

"Old Mack tells me," I says, "that he's going to marry you at six o'clock this evening."

"That's the time," says she. "It's to be at our house."

"Rebosa," says I, "listen to me. If Eddie Bayles had a thousand dollars cash—a thousand dollars, mind you, would buy him a store of his own—if you and Eddie had that much to excuse matrimony on, would you consent to marry him this evening at five o'clock?"

The girl looks at me a minute; and I can see these inaudible cogitations going on inside of her, as women will.

"A thousand dollars?" says she. "Of course I would."

"Come on," says I. "We'll go and see Eddie."

We went up to Crosby's store and called Eddie outside. He looked to be estimable and freckled; and he had chills and fever when I made my proposition.

"At five o'clock?" says he, "for a thousand dollars? Please don't wake me up! Well, you *are* the rich uncle retired from the spice business in India. I'll buy out old Crosby and run the store myself."

We went inside and got old man Crosby apart and explained it. I wrote my check for a thousand dollars and handed it to him. If Eddie and Robosa married each other at five he was to turn the money over to them.

And then I gave 'em my blessing, and went to wander in the wildwood for a season. I sat on a log and made cogitation on life and old age and the zodiac and the

ways of women and all the disorder that goes with a
lifetime. I passed myself congratulations that I had
probably saved my old friend Mack from his attack of
Indian summer. I knew when he got well of it and shed
his infatuation and his patent leather shoes, he would
feel grateful. "To keep old Mack disinvolved," thinks I,
"from relapses like this, is worth more than a thousand
dollars." And most of all I was glad that I'd made a study
of women, and wasn't to be deceived any by their means
of conceit and evolution.

It must have been half-past five when I got back home.
I stepped in; and there sat old Mack on the back of his
neck in his old clothes with his blue socks on the window
and the History of Civilization propped up on his knees.

"This don't look like getting ready for a wedding at
six," I says, to seem innocent.

"Oh," says Mack, reaching for his tobacco, "that was
postponed back to five o'clock. They sent me a note
saying the hour had been changed. It's all over now.
What made you stay away so long, Andy?"

"You heard about the wedding?" I asks.

"I operated it," says he. "I told you I was Justice of
the Peace. The preacher is off East to visit his folks, and
I'm the only one in town that can perform the dispen-
sations of marriage. I promised Eddie and Rebosa a
month ago I'd marry 'em. He's a busy lad; and he'll
have a grocery of his own some day."

"He will," says I.

"There was lots of women at the wedding," says Mack, smoking up. "But I didn't seem to get any ideas from 'em. I wish I was informed in the structure of their attainments like you said you was."

"That was two months ago," says I, reaching up for the banjo.

✦

THE CALIPH,
CUPID
AND THE CLOCK

$\mathbf{P}$RINCE MICHAEL, OF THE ELECTORATE OF
Valleluna, sat on his favorite bench in the park. The coolness of the September night quickened the life in him
like a rare, tonic wine. The benches were not filled; for
park loungers, with their stagnant blood, are prompt to
detect and fly home from the crispness of early autumn.
The moon was just clearing the roofs of the range of
dwellings that bounded the quadrangle on the east. Children laughed and played about the fine-sprayed fountain.
In the shadowed spots fauns and hamadryads wooed, unconscious of the gaze of mortal eyes. A hand-organ—
Philomel by the grace of our stage carpenter, Fancy—

464

fluted and droned in a side street. Around the enchanted boundaries of the little park streetcars spat and mewed, and the stilted trains roared like tigers and lions prowling for a place to enter. And above the trees shone the great, round, shining face of an illuminated clock in the tower of an antique public building.

Prince Michael's shoes were wrecked far beyond the skill of the carefullest cobbler. The ragman would have declined any negotiations concerning his clothes. The two weeks' stubble on his face was gray and brown and red and greenish yellow—as if it had been made up from individual contributions from the chorus of a musical comedy. No man existed who had money enough to wear so bad a hat as his.

Prince Michael sat on his favorite bench and smiled. It was a diverting thought to him that he was wealthy enough to buy every one of those close-ranged, bulky, window-lit mansions that faced him, if he chose. He could have matched gold, equipages, jewels, art treasures, estates and acres with any Crœsus in this proud city of Manhattan, and scarcely have entered upon the bulk of his holdings. He could have sat at table with reigning sovereigns. The social world, the world of art, the fellowship of the elect, adulation, imitation, the homage of the fairest, honors from the highest, praise from the wisest, flattery, esteem, credit, pleasure, fame—all the honey of life was waiting in the comb in the hive of the world for Prince Michael, of the Electorate of Valleluna, whenever he might choose to take it. But his choice was to sit in rags and dinginess on a bench in a park. For he had tasted of the fruit of the tree of life, and, finding it bitter in his mouth, had stepped out of Eden for a time to seek distraction close to the unarmored, beating heart of the world.

These thoughts strayed dreamily through the mind of Prince Michael, as he smiled under the stubble of his polychromatic beard. Lounging thus, clad as the poorest of mendicants in the parks, he loved to study humanity. He found in altruism more pleasure than his riches, his station and all the grosser sweets of life had given him. It was his chief solace and satisfaction to alleviate individual distress, to confer favors upon worthy ones who had need of succor, to dazzle unfortunates by unexpected and bewildering gifts of truly royal magnificence, bestowed, however, with wisdom and judiciousness.

And as Prince Michael's eye rested upon the glowing face of the great clock in the tower, his smile, altruistic as it was, became slightly tinged with contempt. Big thoughts were the Prince's; and it was always with a shake of his head that he considered the subjugation of the world to the arbitrary measures of time. The comings and goings of people in hurry and dread, controlled by the little metal moving hands of a clock, always made him sad.

By and by came a young man in evening clothes and sat upon the third bench from the Prince. For half an hour he smoked cigars with nervous haste, and then he fell to watching the face of the illuminated clock above the trees. His perturbation was evident, and the Prince noted in sorrow that its cause was connected in some manner with the slowly moving hands of the timepiece.

His Highness arose and went to the young man's bench.

"I beg your pardon for addressing you," he said, "but I perceive that you are disturbed in mind. If it may serve to mitigate the liberty I have taken I will add that I am Prince Michael, heir to the throne of the Electorate of Valleluna. I appear incognito, of course, as you may gather from my appearance. It is a fancy of mine to render aid to others whom I think worthy of it. Perhaps the matter that seems to distress you is one that would more readily yield to our mutual efforts."

The young man looked up brightly at the Prince. Brightly, but the perpendicular line of perplexity between his brows was not smoothed away. He laughed, and even then it did not. But he accepted the momentary diversion.

"Glad to meet you, Prince," he said, good humoredly. "Yes, I'd say you were incog. all right. Thanks for your offer of assistance—but I don't see where your butting-in would help things any. It's a kind of private affair, you know—but thanks all the same."

Prince Michael sat at the young man's side. He was often rebuffed but never offensively. His courteous manner and words forbade that.

"Clocks," said the Prince, "are shackles on the feet of

mankind. I have observed you looking persistently at that clock. Its face is that of a tyrant, its numbers are false as those on a lottery ticket; its hands are those of a bunco steerer, who makes an appointment with you to your ruin. Let me entreat you to throw off its humiliating bonds and cease to order your affairs by that insensate monitor of brass and steel."

"I don't usually," said the young man. "I carry a watch except when I've got my radiant rags on."

"I know human nature as I do the trees and grass," said the Prince, with earnest dignity. "I am a master of philosophy, a graduate in art, and I hold the purse of a Fortunatus. There are few mortal misfortunes that I cannot alleviate or overcome. I have read your countenance, and found in it honesty and nobility as well as distress. I beg of you to accept my advice or aid. Do not belie the intelligence I see in your face by judging from my appearance of my ability to defeat your troubles."

The young man glanced at the clock again and frowned darkly. When his gaze strayed from the glowing horologue of time it rested intently upon a four-story red brick house in the row of dwellings opposite to where he sat. The shades were drawn, and the lights in many rooms shone dimly through them.

"Ten minutes to nine!" exclaimed the young man, with an impatient gesture of despair. He turned his back upon the house and took a rapid step or two in a contrary direction.

"Remain!" commanded Prince Michael, in so potent a voice that the disturbed one wheeled around with a somewhat chagrined laugh.

"I'll give her the ten minutes and then I'm off," he muttered, and then aloud to the Prince: "I'll join you in confounding all clocks, my friend, and throw in women, too."

"Sit down," said the Prince, calmly. "I do not accept your addition. Women are the natural enemies of clocks, and, therefore, the allies of those who would seek liberation from these monsters that measure our follies and limit our pleasures. If you will so far confide in me I would ask you to relate to me your story."

The young man threw himself upon the bench with a reckless laugh.

"Your Royal Highness, I will," he said, in tones of mock deference. "Do you see yonder house—the one with the three upper windows lighted? Well, at 6 o'clock I stood in that house with the young lady I am—that is, I was— engaged to. I had been doing wrong, my dear Prince—I had been a naughty boy, and she had heard of it. I wanted to be forgiven, of course—we are always wanting women to forgive us, aren't we, Prince?

" 'I want time to think it over,' said she. 'There is one thing certain; I will either fully forgive you, or I will never see your face again. There will be no halfway business. At half-past eight,' she said, 'at exactly half-past eight you may be watching the middle upper window of the top floor. If I decide to forgive I will hang out of that window a white silk scarf. You will know by it that all is as was before, and you may come to me. If you see no scarf you may consider that everything between us is ended forever.' That," concluded the young man, bitterly, "is why I have been watching that clock. The time for the signal to appear has passed twenty-three minutes ago. Do you wonder that I am a little disturbed, my Prince of Rags and Whiskers?"

"Let me repeat to you," said Prince Michael, in his even, well-modulated tones, "that women are the natural enemies of clocks. Clocks are an evil, women a blessing. The signal may yet appear."

"Never, on your principality!" exclaimed the young man hopelessly. "You don't know Marian—of course. She's always on time, to the minute. That was the first thing about her that attracted me. I've got the mitten instead of the scarf. I ought to have known at 8:31 that my goose was cooked. I'll go West on the 11:45 tonight with Jack Milburn. The jig's up. I'll try Jack's ranch awhile and top off with the Klondike and whiskey. Good-night—er—er—Prince."

Prince Michael smiled his enigmatic, gentle, comprehending smile and caught the coat sleeve of the other. The brilliant light in the Prince's eyes was softening to a dreamier, cloudy translucence.

"Wait," he said solemnly, "till the clock strikes. I have wealth and power and knowledge above most men, but when the clock strikes I am afraid. Stay by me until then. This woman shall be yours. You have the word of the hereditary Prince of Valleluna. On the day of your marriage I will give you $100,000 and a palace on the Hudson. But there must be no clocks in that palace— they measure our follies and limit our pleasures. Do you agree to that?"

"Of course," said the young man, cheerfully, "they're a nuisance, anyway—always ticking and striking and getting you late for dinner."

He glanced again at the clock in the tower. The hands stood at three minutes to nine.

"I think," said Prince Michael, "that I will sleep a little. The day has been fatiguing."

He stretched himself upon a bench with the manner of one who had slept thus before.

"You will find me in this park on any evening when the weather is suitable," said the Prince, sleepily. "Come to me when your marriage day is set and I will give you a check for the money."

"Thanks, Your Highness," said the young man, seriously. "It doesn't look as if I would need that palace on the Hudson, but I appreciate your offer, just the same."

Prince Michael sank into deep slumber. His battered hat rolled from the bench to the ground. The young man lifted it, placed it over the frowsy face and moved one of the grotesquely relaxed limbs into a more comfortable position. "Poor devil!" he said, as he drew the tattered clothes closer about the Prince's breast.

Sonorous and startling came the stroke of 9 from the
clock tower. The young man sighed again, turned his face
for one last look at the house of his relinquished hopes—
and cried aloud profane words of holy rapture.

From the middle upper window blossomed in the dusk
a waving, snowy, fluttering, wonderful, divine emblem of
forgiveness and promised joy.

By came a citizen, rotund, comfortable, home-hurrying,
unknowing of the delights of waving silken scarfs on the
borders of dimly-lit parks.

"Will you oblige me with the time, sir?" asked the
young man; and the citizen, shrewdly conjecturing his
watch to be safe, dragged it out and announced:

"Twenty-nine and a half minutes past eight, sir."

And then, from habit, he glanced at the clock in the
tower, and made further oration.

"By George! that clock's half an hour fast! First time in
ten years I've known it to be off. This watch of mine never
varies a——"

But the citizen was talking to vacancy. He turned and
saw his hearer, a fast receding black shadow flying in the
direction of a house with three lighted upper windows.

And in the morning came along two policemen on their
way to the beats they owned. The park was deserted save
for one dilapidated figure that sprawled, asleep, on a
bench. They stopped and gazed upon it.

"It's Dopy Mike," said one. "He hits the pipe every

night. Park bum for twenty years. On his last legs, I guess."

The other policeman stooped and looked at something crumpled and crisp in the hand of the sleeper.

"Gee!" he remarked. "He's doped out a fifty-dollar bill, anyway. Wish I knew the brand of hop that he smokes."

And then "Rap, rap, rap!" went the club of realism against the shoe soles of Prince Michael, of the Electorate of Valleluna.

✦

ABOUT O. HENRY

ABOUT O. HENRY

O. HENRY, the writer who first made New York City a familiar place for millions of people beyond its reach, was born William Sidney Porter in 1862 in Greensboro, North Carolina. There he spent his youth, encouraged to read by a teacher aunt with whom he lived. He worked in his uncle's drugstore after he left school at fifteen. In Greensboro, too, O. Henry came to know the Southern gentlemen and mountain folk who figure in his stories.

As a young man, O. Henry was threatened with tuberculosis, the same illness to which his mother had succumbed. Like the character "Cricket" McGuire in his story, *Hygeia at the Solito,* he went to live on a ranch in Texas for two years to recover his health, later going to work in the General Land Office at Austin. After his marriage he took a job as teller in a bank which, his biographers say, was run with "astonishing laxity."

Shortages were found in O. Henry's accounts. Inevitably he lost his job, and moved on to Houston where he worked on the Houston *Post*. Sometime later, when he was ordered to stand trial, he left via New Orleans for Honduras. There he remained until his wife's illness called him back to Austin, where he had to stand trial. O. Henry made no attempt to defend himself, and his flight was regarded as positive evidence of his guilt.

It was while serving his term in the federal penitentiary at Columbus, Ohio, that O. Henry took his pen name from Orrin Henry, a guard at the prison, and began to write seriously.

On the basis of the stories he had sold to magazines while in prison, O. Henry came to New York in 1902. There he wrote prodigiously for various magazines and the New York *World*, scarcely able to keep up with the demand for his stories. Barely eight years later, O. Henry was the most widely read author in the country.

It was as interpreter of the American dream and the American scene that O. Henry soared to such popular heights. He saw romance and humor, as well as pathos, in the shabby neighborhoods of the city. A clerk, a cashier or a waitress in an O. Henry story could and did marry the millionaire—or find true happiness with her policeman or cabby or struggling young clerk. Out West one could really make a fresh start. Money was not enough to buy happiness in high society. And the meanest outlaw was capable of kindness and decency.

Millions of readers were amused by O. Henry's humor and charmed with his adroit development of coincidence to bring about desired results. An indispensable ingredient of the modern short story in our literature has been added as a result of O. Henry's stunningly effective use of the surprise ending which has, in fact, come to be known as the "O. Henry twist."

Yet in spite of his fabulous success, O. Henry remained a quiet, considerate man whose favorite pastime was roaming the city's streets, gathering with his reporter's keen eye the details of city life that make his stories so much more than delightfully contrived puzzles. Thanks to O. Henry's observations we have a vivid picture of New York, the West and the South as they were at the beginning of this century.

In 1910 the disease which had stalked his life finally caught up with him. He died in New York of tuberculosis at the age of forty-eight. O. Henry's last words were typical: "Pull up the shades so that I can see New York."